I0760876

37 Nights

MONICA SHANTEL

37
NIGHTS
MONICA SHANTEL

37 Nights

Book Cover by Monica Shantel

Illustrations by Monica Shantel

ISBN 978-1-960696-94-6 (Paperback) ISBN 978-1-960696-01-4 (Hardcover)

Second Edition

For Ashly, because you always supported my writing even when I didn't.

Author's Note

This book deals with heavy topics. Including graphic violence, some self-harm, and the topic of abortion. This is a low spice book so there is some sexual content, such as mention of the topic and a few emotion-focused and fade-to-black scenes. There is also language. Please keep this in mind to decide if this book is right for you.

Claire's room
more offices down this hall
Nora's office
Monstrum Asylum

Emilie's room
Spence's room
courtyard

Nora
Witlow
5/14/20

"Spence Woods"
7/15/24

1

Some people didn't look death in the face. They'd walk on by, barely missing it by an inch. And just when he grabbed someone else, they'd halt and turn to him, begging for him to take them in place of their loved one.

I'd passed by him that night, and he took her instead.

I regretted it ever since. If I'd agreed to go with her, I wouldn't be on this damned winter drive into the mountains to an asylum secluded from all of society.

But she took my spot, and because of her, I'd be able to help so many more lives.

Just not hers.

Static came through the radio as I turned the knob to search for another station. For a split second, I caught a snippet of *The*

Air That I Breathe. Then it'd disappeared faster than I could catch it from its ultimate demise into the unknown. I let out a small sigh when nothing else came up clear. I was too far from the city to find a good signal out here anyway, and it'd been silly of me to assume otherwise.

Heavy snowflakes coated the road before me. My heater had been on full blast to keep me toasted during what had to be the coldest winter yet. This far from civilization, the temperature had dropped to single digits, and it hadn't been close to stopping.

I ducked my head to peer up at the sky outside my windshield. The clouds hung low and thick, the sun long gone for the night.

I pressed one foot against the clutch and the other against the break as I shifted gears, making a slow turn onto the dirt road that led to Monstrum Asylum. I slowed to a stop and turned the keys to the off position before stepping out of my bright red 1958 Cadillac Eldorado, buttoning up my thick coat. I unlocked my trunk, gathering my luggage and shutting it before glancing at the massive building I'd now call my home.

My boots made a soft crunch in the powdered snow. Monstrum Asylum overlooked the surrounding trees, its shadow looming over the winter wonderland.

The building had been built centuries ago, the age was displayed proudly. Most windows were barred to keep patients from getting themselves into trouble. At least two stories, possibly three if a basement existed, and from counting windows, ten rooms across.

I walked up to the doors centered of the ash-gray structure, ready to knock before I realized it was more than *just* a home. The snow had begun to melt into the curls on the top of my head.

"Nora Witlow, I presume?" a man in a white coat asked me.

With a smile, I shook his hand. "Yes, sir."

"David Harrison. I own and run Monstrum Asylum. I hope you find your stay to be welcoming. I wouldn't wish for the patients to scare you off before your first raise," he said with a chuckle.

My eyes wandered the hallway we stood in. The floor was made up of white tiles while the teal painted the walls. They had attempted to make this feel less like an asylum and more like home. However, it would be the people, patients and doctors alike, who would determine how I felt around this place. The looks of it had no bearing on my coziness.

"Let me show you to your room." David gestured for me to follow him.

I followed him down the hall. My eyes lingered on the names written on the doors.

When David noticed where my attention had gone, he added, "These will be your patients. Claire will be the hardest shell to crack."

"May I ask why?" I looked over at David.

He started walking again. "She fights back. But I'll leave the rest of the mystery up to your findings." Coming to a pause in his steps, he twisted to face me. "Before you get settled, I must explain to you first and foremost where the patients can go and during what time. The library, the entertainment room, and outside between the hours of ten and six. Nine is breakfast. One is lunch. Five is dinner."

I pondered on when would be best for my sessions with the patients. I supposed that was a question for another day.

We stopped at my room, and I peeked from behind the door. Inside had been furnished with a bed, a nightstand next to it, and a lamp sitting on top.

"Thank you." I closed the door behind me before setting my

bag on the bed and unzipping. I yelped and put my hand over my heart as a figure appeared in my doorway. “You scared me.”

“Nora, right?” the man asked me as he gestured to my bag. I hadn’t even heard him turn the knob.

“Yes.”

He unfolded his arms and pushed his weight off the frame. “Welcome to Monstrum Asylum.”

“Why is it named that? I tried to look it up, but the internet isn’t very useful. I feel it kind of insults the patients, does it not?” I gestured to the rest of the building.

“Maybe Monstrum doesn’t refer to the patients.” Something more sinister glinted in his eye as disappeared from the frame.

A shiver scurried down my spine as I shook my head to brush off whatever that’d been. Nothing would scare me away. I had a duty to the patients.

I left my room to take a tour around the asylum. The hallways were long and quiet as if they were the woods on a winter night. Every other light in this place seemed to be burnt out or turned off to save power.

My heels clicked against the tiled floor, up until my toe got caught on nothing and sent me packing. As my knees took the blow, I looked back at the empty hall for any obstacles. Rolling onto my butt, I took in a deep breath before I scrambled to my feet and continued on my way.

“Get yourself together, Nora. Nothing is there. *Nobody* is there,” I whispered to myself.

I stood and walked down the rest of the hall before stopping in a large, open room. A few small tables with chairs were placed accordingly, and a couch sat as the focal point for maximum lounging.

In the corner, a beautiful piano called for my attention.

I pressed my hand against my lower abdomen and grabbed the back of the couch for support. The tinge of pain was only the beginning of this horrendous cycle. I begged to be one of the blessed women who had it easy, but my prayers were never answered.

A whisper floated through the air and slithered into my ears like the cursed tongue of a serpent. Her eyes flashed in my mind, the fear overtaking my soul.

"Nora, don't do this to yourself," I mumbled. I came upon just the office I was looking for. "David, I was wondering if you have any painkillers." David's eyes displayed suspicion but that dissipated as soon as I blurted, "Cramps. I have to suppress the pain that is that of being a woman."

He waved me off. "Very well, Miss Witlow." He grabbed a bottle from the cabinet before dumping two pills in my hand. "Get some rest. You look like you may need it for the night."

"Thank you." I shot him a small smile before returning to my room and swallowing the drugs.

Taking his advice, I changed into my cotton pajamas and fuzzy socks. I found a bathroom down the hall where I removed my makeup, then I made it back to my room and got some sleep for the night.

I awoke to the sound of metal clashing against concrete tiles.

My eyes shifted to the bedroom door that separated me from the rest of the building. I dropped my feet over the edge of my bed and slid on my slippers, then I pushed myself off and left to see what the ruckus was.

"Miss Witlow, what are you doing up so late?" David asked as I rubbed my eye with the heel of my palm.

"I heard a noise."

"It's none of your concern. We've taken care of it. One of the others just dropped a bedpan." He faced the other end of the hall, just forty degrees to my right, as if he couldn't be bothered with my shenanigans at this moment.

I'd hardly call my concern that.

I nodded slightly and started to turn around, but paused. "Is there anything I should know involving the history of this asylum?"

"What do you mean?" His brows tilted inward, his lip beginning to curl.

"Forget I asked." I turned on my heel and headed back. I slowed as I passed the rooms with names on them. "Spence Woods…" I walked closer to the door, fingertips grazing the plaque.

A door opened a ways down. I stepped away from Spence's door and hurried to my own room. Closing my door behind me, I rested my forehead against it. I was far too wide awake to get back to sleep.

I checked my watch with a swallow. It was only five in the morning. I'd have to fill my morning with something productive.

As I lay back on my sheets, a stabbing pain erupted in my uterus.

Screams. The only sound for miles—the only noise clogging my eardrums.

Thump. Her body tumbled as her head laid propped up against the steps in a ninety-degree angle. A ball she became, but her life fled just seconds before that.

Blood. Her leg displayed crooked, her crimson bones poking out of her body. Her neck had snapped, and now every drop of blood pooled around her head.

I had wished for the memories to go away day in and day out. I desperately needed them to leave me alone. Mom suggested counseling. Ironic, given I was a licensed psychologist. I could deal with my problems on my own.

Could a doctor not diagnose themselves?

As the sun rose in the sky, I put on a dress in place of my cotton sleepwear. I slipped on some heels and took my mini bag with me to the bathroom. I touched up my lashes and lips with some pop before fixing the curls in my hair.

I dropped my bag off in my room, then searched for the dining hall. It hadn't been too hard to spot.

"Good morning." I flashed a smile.

A doctor served food at a table near the wall where three bodies occupied it, I assumed they were the patients.

"Miss Witlow, I thought you may like your own plate this morning." David pointed to a plate placed before an empty chair.

I was getting the impression that we were separated based upon our status within this asylum. I supposed it did make sense to keep the patients in their own space during this time.

"Thank you, Dr. Harrison." I sat down and took a bite of my food. My eyes did not keep it subtle as they moved back towards the patients.

Two girls and a boy sat before their breakfast—Claire, Spence, and Emilie, and not in that order.

"Nora, I heard you just graduated?" someone's voice carried across our table.

I twisted my head their way. "Yes. I just graduated this past spring. It was quite exciting to get my degree."

"Yes, I imagine," she said. She shoveled more food into her

mouth.

A man looked at her, his eyes falling on her meal. "I thought we agreed to not pry into private lives?"

"It's really no problem," I said to them.

She gestured to me. "She said it's no problem."

"She says that to be polite. She's a trained psychologist. She knows how to control her tongue." His gaze darted over to me.

I put my fork down. "While that is true, I am not afraid to be honest if that is what must be done. I said it's not a problem and I meant it. If I had a problem, I would mention how uncomfortable I feel. Do not be fooled, fellow, by my appearance. I may dress like I am submissive, but I very much have managed my own just fine. I am here to help patients and not make friends. I am not afraid to be the bitch if that is what I must be." I tipped my head towards him.

The woman beside him choked on her food. "I love her already."

"All right, pipe down everyone." David used his palm laid horizontally to lower the volume.

As we finished breakfast, I helped with the dishes. I heard a comment come from the asshole about me being in the kitchen, but I let it go. It was not a molehill I wanted to turn into a mountain.

"Has anybody died here?" I asked the woman who had come to my aid.

She twisted her body to face me. "You see a lot of talk that we're here to torture the patients in *inhumane* ways. They're not true. I mean, they can be. Not all asylums are piss-poor if that is what you're thinking. This asylum was only built within the last decade. It hasn't had many patients since. As you can tell, we don't get a lot of people here."

"Not a single soul has died?"

"Souls don't die. Bodies do."

I chuckled. "I see. You can call me Nora, if you were curious. I don't really feel comfortable going by Miss Witlow all the time."

"Will do, Nora. You can call me Monique." She put the pans away. "Next time, we are forcing the boys to do this. They eat off these dishes, too. Equality, am I right?"

I nodded, joy glued to my face. "Sounds great to me."

Monique grabbed my hand, patting it. "Welcome to Monstrum Asylum, Nora. I hope you enjoy your time here. We trust you to be a groovy fit for the staff and our patients."

II

"There's the last of your chores for the day," David said as he passed me a list.

I skimmed over it and glanced at him. "I'll get to it." I went on my way and mumbled to myself, "all right, cleaning the bathrooms should hopefully be easy enough."

Being the new staff member around here, it was no mystery as to why I was on toilet duty.

I barely looked up from my paper as a body smashed into mine. Before my butt could meet the tiles, fingers wrapped around my wrist, then a hand snaked around me waist to keep me on my feet. "Careful there, Miss…"

"Witlow. Miss Witlow." I peered up at the man before me, nodding while his icy hands dropped to his sides. My skin couldn't hide the tint of red burning my cheeks. Clumsiness was not a trait I was proud of. "I apologize. I should have been looking where I was going."

Black dress pants and a white button-up impressed me, certainly. Men did dress well around here, but I could still admire it nonetheless. His hair hung a little chaotic, and dark, but those eyes…

He was certainly no eyesore with such bright blue iris' staring back at me.

"No, don't be sorry. Mistakes happen to the best of us, Miss Witlow. It's nothing to be ashamed of." He gave me a smile, one big enough to show off the dimples in his cheeks. Dimples were just a malformation of the cheek muscles. How silly was that?

"I've got bathrooms waiting on me, so I'll see you around then." I averted my eyes downward, and towards the corner.

"Don't let me hold you back," he paused, "and if you want to know, I'm Spence. It was lovely bumping into you." He stepped around me and left me alone in the hallway.

Now that I knew who he was, confirming he'd been a patient and not an employee, my thoughts fell into uncharted territory. I could never admit to anyone that I uttered inappropriate thoughts about my own patient.

I was also well aware that I had been preoccupied by my list but what could he have been so distracted by as to not see me, too?

Redirecting my focus, I dusted the furniture in the main living area to start. After, I shoveled the snow off the cement in the back of the building. Patients needed fresh air even in this weather, and a place to sit or stand without acquiring a flu from snow in their shoes.

Darkness drifted across the sky as the sun had set just beyond the thick layers of clouds. If air could hate me, this would be pure loathing. The temperature was far below frigid.

I went back inside, peeking at my list again. I cleaned other areas nearby, leaving the bathrooms for last. I could now redirect all my focus onto the grimiest room of all. Most of the employees here were males and the urinals looked as if they'd never been cleaned.

The bathroom was big enough to accommodate the growth of people who'd be admitted in the future—with at least ten shower stalls forming an L shape from the back to the side wall. White ceramic tiles lined from floor to ceiling, leaving the scum to stick out like a sore thumb.

Every spray of cleaner and wipe of dirt would echo. No doubt the bathroom was mocking me for trying to keep it clean.

Dark, long strands of hair littered the floor, and those liked to snag no matter how many times I mopped over it. Before I'd even started, the floors were damp, but I wasn't sure where the water came from. Nobody had showered today.

Due to the lighting, I couldn't see every nook and cranny hiding in the shadows. My flashlight became useful, catching the spots of blood barely visible to the eye.

Muffled voices passed by the door. The thick walls around these parts were more for the employees, in case screaming and disturbed patients were admitted.

While scrubbing in a stall, I gasped as a shadow passed behind me, allowing me to catch it in the corner of my eye. "You scared me," I spit out.

I scanned the bathroom, but nobody was in here with me. Whoever it'd been, their purpose was to screw with my head.

"Who's in here?" I asked, the silence being sliced open by the echoes bouncing off the tiles.

Another shadow darted and I turned, placing my hand over my chest as I closed my eyes. "Nora, this is not real. This is not real. It's in your head." I inhaled and held my breath, exhaling after a moment. I repeated this process a few more times until my nerves had relaxed.

I yelled out at the sound of a knock on the bathroom door.

Monique peaked inside and shot me a strange look. "Nora, are you all right? I didn't mean to scare you."

I laughed off the fear and grabbed my supplies. "Yes, I'm fine. I just scare easily." I set my bucket a few feet away. "This bathroom is a trip."

"That's why I never clean it. David doesn't check this anyway." She shrugged.

I snorted. "It sounds like a wonderful idea, and I would gladly take it if my brain allowed. Sorry, Monique, but I can't leave a place dirty. I must finish *every* task."

"If you say so." With a sly smile, she closed the door, leaving me to fend for myself.

I got back to scrubbing.

After what seemed like forever, I finished and returned the supplies to the closet. I knocked on the office door just David opened it, not saying a word.

"I'm done with the chores," I said.

"Wonderful, you have the rest of the day to yourself. In a few days, you will have your first therapy session with one of the patients."

"Thank you." I flashed a warm smile before walking down the hall, stopping in the living area. I searched through the small selection of books, but my eyes moved towards the piano—where my mind really wanted to be.

I sat on the bench and leveled my elbows at an angle. I

touched a few keys, wincing at the awful sound. "Nora, you're a bit rusty."

I played a few keys with my right hand, starting out slow. I started on the bass notes and went up, pressing a few flats or sharps, depending, in between. "Not bad. It just needs some practice."

The piano was a lovely instrument. Something about the way life experiences translated made every tune sound wonderful.

Minutes later, I returned to the bookshelf. I was saddened by the lack of romance books. How could this be? Romance was addictive in our own lives. It gave us hope. It took us from our world and let us live out someone else's. I wished to live out a romantic fantasy I could not live on my own.

I needed to request more romance books for everyone's sake.

At the end of the hall was a set of stairs. Up, and down, and the ones descending hadn't been kept up with as wallpaper weathered and peeled, browning at the edges. A metal railing decorated the open side, also providing a little bit of support for safety reasons. Or I hoped.

As I headed down to explore the rest of the asylum, a room at the end of the hall in the basement caught my attention.

Dark, but I saw the faint outline of what looked to be a table. Walking closer, I stepped inside, catching sight of a machine that stood beside the table—a machine with knobs and wires attached to some metal tools.

Electroconvulsive therapy.

My eyebrows knitted together as theories ran through my mind. I was not blind to the methods people had used before. I could only pray that this method had been trained well in the patients' best interests. Everyone deserved humane treatment.

As I closed the door, I turned around and gasped, coming face to face with Monique. "You scared me again. I was just exploring some areas."

Every muscle on her face went rigid. "You shouldn't be down here. David doesn't like when his new employees go snooping around his asylum."

"I was not snooping. I was just finding a way to spend my time at my new job. Plenty of employees will spend free time getting to know the areas where they work. I'm sorry if I crossed any boundaries. That sign on the door said employees only, and I had been under the impression that I was an employee." I pointed to the door that led to this hallway.

A laugh erupted. "Nora, calm down. You look terrified. Come on, let's go find you something to do."

A nervous laughter followed while I sifted my thoughts for something comforting.

Monique took us up to the main floor, to the lounge area. "I know it isn't much, but it's all we got."

"I noticed." I dropped onto the sofa.

She gestured to the bookshelf. "Care for a book?"

"I would but I didn't find any good romance novels. That's something I want to ask about. If I'm going to escape into someone else's world, I at least want to read some kissing and hand-holding." I chuckled.

Monique sat with a smirk plastered on her face. "I see. We have a romance fan. And what do these romance fantasies involve, Nora Witlow?"

My jaw almost unhinged as my cheeks turned pink. "Excuse me, it's nothing like that. I just dream of meeting a nice man someday."

"Mhm, and sex? I'm sure you've had some thoughts about how you would like it." Her eyebrows raised.

I dismissed her question. "That's my business. And if you must know, I am not that big on those romances. I prefer to read about a man getting flowers. That's what I'm interested in. That's what makes my heart beat faster. I want to see more about a man that truly loves his woman and treats her like a queen, where a woman treats him like a king, and together they fight to keep their romance alive."

Monique laughed, her head rolling. "That sounds really boring."

"I want to see a marriage last…" I smiled a tad. "My parents are so happy together and I want to read love stories that end up like theirs, where they make it through the *I-want-a-divorce* stage—together." I hugged myself, being reminded of how cold this asylum was. The heater must have been struggling during this time of year.

She leaned forward. "You're not weird. It's normal for you to wish for a romance that lasts. It's normal to want a marriage that follows through with its vows. Most people don't go into marriage wishing to get a divorce."

I smiled at her, not aiming to start an argument. "Any special someone in your life, Monique?"

Her curls bounced as she leaned back on the sofa's arm. "No, and that is the way I like it. I am perfectly content with my life the way it is."

I put my hands up in defense. "It's all up to you. I'm not here to judge nor tell you what to do. I just want to get to know you more."

She shook her head. "You better not be judging me. I will kick your ass and I will win."

"That's what I want you to think." I winked.

Her expression changed as she stood from the sofa, lips falling flat and pupils shrinking.

I looked back as three patients came around the corner. My eyes lingered on Spence just a little too long, and he witnessed it. His striking blue eyes were different this time, but nearly impossible for me to read. That was just what I had come here to do, and certainly I would help him open up so he'd have a chance to live outside of these walls again.

III

"This will be your office." David and I stepped into a small room further down the hall.

My eyes lingered on the old files left on the cabinet. "Thank you. I'll be sure to make it my own, and a little cozy for the patients." Whatever it would take, they'd get to the point of being comfortable enough to tell me anything.

After David gave me some privacy, I closed the door and began to clean up the space. Papers had been strewn about with nothing left in order. Chaotic. But certainly not my tactic.

I had a small bag of garbage to take out when I was finished. The rest of the papers all had some interesting information that I wanted to keep, just in case. I organized those into folders inside the file cabinet, and there they would stay.

As I passed the entertainment room, I noticed its emptiness. Where were the patients? I walked towards the window and looked outside, watching as they breathed in the cold, dry air. However, only Emilie and Claire seemed to be out there, and I still had yet to figure out which was which.

My eyes landed on the beautiful grand piano, and once again, I sat and tried my hand. I focused on the melody as much as I did my muscle memory. Once I had gotten it down, it became easier each round to play on through. And play through I did. The notes jumped from my fingers and scurried up my arms before squeezing my heart.

Chills crawled up my spine, and as much as I wished to blame it on the music, I sensed something else. I put my hands on my thighs and turned to see Spence eyeing me. What was on his mind?

"May I help you?" I asked.

He shrugged. "I came up here to read a book, but I heard you playing. I dig it."

My cheeks heated from the embarrassment. I was still struggling to accept compliments as they were. "Thank you."

"Keep playing."

"I can't do that." I shook my head. "I'm not usually one to play for an audience." Maybe it would stay that way, but for now, I couldn't play for even one person.

Spence sat on the couch, leaning back against the arm. He placed his biceps behind his head as he prepared to yell encore. I did not need that kind of attention. One person was more than enough.

"All right, all right. I will continue to play, but you must know I'm rusty."

"That's what they all say." He smiled at me.

Facing the piano, I ignored his remark and placed my hands on the keys, feeling them out. I knew what I was going to sink my teeth into this time, and thus I began an older piece my father taught me. It was because of him that I took an interest in piano and classical music alike.

I pressed all the right keys, sliding my hands along in specific patterns that spoke to my soul. Each chord—each note rippled through my bones every minute I continued.

In some areas, the music slowed down. In others, it sped up. Goosebumps began to cover every inch of my skin as I became one with the harmony.

My father taught me music written by Beethoven first and foremost. That was when my love blossomed into something much more, and from that day forth, I knew exactly who I was and wanted to be.

As the melody came to an end, I pulled my hands away from the keys. I threw my legs over the other side of the bench, facing Spence. "That is all you will ever hear."

Something lingered in his eyes, but I couldn't quite catch it. Maybe one of these days I'd finally be able to do so. "I must say, Miss Witlow, that was even more wonderful than the first song you played. I'm honored."

"Honoring is over," a girl said as she rounded the corner. Her complexion contrasted with her dark hair well. "It's almost dinner time." She shot Spence a look, in which he nodded to and left the area to head to the dining hall. She gave me a look, studying my face for an awfully long time. "Be careful. Wouldn't want that pretty head of yours to snap from the lies." She, too, exited.

What did she mean by that? Was she referring to Spence or this asylum? I had no time to worry about it, so I made my way to dinner.

Monique saved me a spot beside her, which I gladly took. Glancing up at Spence, our eyes met for a brief moment, but his gave nothing away. It was impossible to get a reading on someone so reserved.

"Isn't that right, Nora?"

I swiftly redirected my attention to Monique. "Is what right?"

"Just say yes."

Stabbing some of my food with my fork, I gave her the side smirk. "I don't say yes to just anyone or anything. You may have to convince me to join your cause." I shoved the bite into my mouth. This food tasted stale. How could anyone properly enjoy this?

She rested her hand on my arm, rubbing. "Are you telling me to seduce you? Never pictured you as that kind of woman."

The guy across from us dropped his fork while his jaw hung open. "This is something I want to witness."

Pulling her hand away, she rolled her eyes. "You're disgusting."

"You take the fun out of everything and twist it into something it shouldn't be," I said.

He picked up his fork again and shrugged, piling food into his mouth. "I have the right amount of fun. Does this mean you two are lesbians?"

Monique narrowed her eyes. "Me? Lesbian? Never. Girls have fun and it doesn't need to be serious. We are allowed to have fun as we please without it meaning anything. You? Can't say the same about you."

He turned his head towards me, waiting for an answer.

"My sexuality is none of your concern. I came to do a job, and whether I'm straight, gay, or otherwise shouldn't have any effect. You will respect that." And once he understood, I decided to stay out of the conversations for the rest of the meal.

Once dinner was over, everyone went their separate ways. The patients headed to the entertainment area, and as much as I wanted to go and talk to them, I had other things on my mind.

I stopped by my room to grab a jacket before I went outside, admiring the way the looming darkness of the woods stretched out towards me like that of shadow claws. The tree branches reached out for my hair, and I stepped back to keep my distance.

Had I noticed when David came out to remind me the doors were locking, I would not have jumped. Instead, he almost had my skeleton leaving my body. I assured him I'd be back in soon, and I kept my word. I was back within the minute.

I found myself in my office with some background music to fill the silence. Record players made everything easier to digest. Everyone else had gone to bed when the patients returned to their rooms, but I had too much on my mind to worry about sleeping. Instead, I focused on my work.

The tunes were there to help me not trip myself out. If I believed anything easily, it was always the voice inside my head that told me I was haunted. Or that this asylum was. Whatever it'd been, I believed too easily in supernatural occurrences as opposed to everyone else in the living world.

They were quick to decipher every little thing and find the explanation for it. People debunked anything and everything they could.

Maybe it was an exaggeration to outright state that I was that gullible. I wasn't *that* credulous. I still questioned things to an extent, but when no easy explanation came, I never found it so hard to believe that something supernatural was behind it all. Since I was young, I'd always had an inkling that there was more to life than we could see.

A specific sound floated down the halls, bouncing between these heartless walls, echoing throughout the entire building. That couldn't be right, could it?

Moving the tonearm away, I stood from my chair and ventured out into the hall. My heels clicked, blending in with the melody ringing in my ears, daring to wake the staff and patients.

Coming around the corner that opened into the entertainment room, I made eye contact with the piano. Empty.

No, it couldn't have been possible. Was it? Certainly not. Ghosts didn't play pianos. Ghosts weren't real. Or so I told myself to keep my head screwed on straight. And yet, I had heard someone playing the same melody I had shown to Spence earlier. Unless he was a master of replicating music with his ear, there was no way it had been him. He'd also been locked in his room for the night.

"This isn't real, Nora. You know it's not real." *Did I?*

I spun on my heel and started walking the other way, and the music didn't dare start up again.

"Nora," a female whispered in my ear.

With a scream leaving my throat, I stumbled over my feet before catching my fall. I flipped onto my butt and scooted away. I searched the halls, frantic. I'd heard a lot of strange things but never was it that clear. Never so *close*.

"Who goes there?" I croaked.

Nobody responded. With nothing in my line of sight, I scrambled to my feet and ran back to my office, locking the door behind me. I sat in my chair and despite how freezing I was, I never left the room. My bedroom was too far, and I wasn't willing to risk my life.

I played records all night to keep the voices at bay.

To sweeten the milkshake, I thought about life back home.

My father, the man who had been so quiet and so in love with classical music himself. My mother, the woman who had been loud and outspoken in her own beliefs. And to add the cherry on top, my little brother Danny, who had a love for stories and all that was to tell about them.

Someone knocked on my door and when I opened it, the hallways had been lit up by the lights overhead. "I'm sorry, sir, I guess I got carried away with all the paperwork last night. I fell asleep here."

David waved it off. "It's all right. Just don't forget to get cleaned up for breakfast."

Knowing everyone was waking up, it was safe to leave. I went to my room and changed into a new dress, and then I touched up my makeup instead of bothering to remove and reapply.

Breakfast this morning had been silent. Everyone had heard my scream. They all knew I wasn't lucid. Would David question me? Would he question my ability to do this job? No, because I *was* of sound mind.

Or maybe their impression of my mental state would be exactly why they kept me.

David gave everyone some chores, and once I had mine all finished, I headed back to my room. Sleeping would do me some good. That could explain why I was starting to hear things.

The brain began to hallucinate after three days with rest, but I was not that blessed. I could begin as soon as twenty-four hours. Sure, I had gotten shut-eye, but staying up late in an environment with stereotypes nailed into my skull that asylums were playgrounds for the dead was enough to send my mind to the brink of insanity.

And elsewhere it had gone last night. Elsewhere indeed.

With the horrors far out of my sight, I could close my eyes and rest in peace. My nap lasted longer than I hoped for, but with my chores out of the way, David couldn't get onto me for taking some time to myself.

The *ghosts* here knew I most definitely needed it.

IV

He entered the room, taking a seat in the chair across from me. "Spence Woods, it's nice to *officially* meet you. I'm Nora." I gave him a nod paired with a warm smile.

He sat back in his chair with his legs spread and his arms folded across his chest. "Ah, yes. I do remember you." He flashed a little smirk. "I ran into you in the hallway and I heard your piano skills. I think we are a little more acquainted than that."

"Let's talk about you today. I want to know who Spence is. What brings you to this hospital?" I tilted my head in the slightest.

"Why should this need to be asked? Can you not check my file from previous psychiatrists? You could skip all this wasted time by catching up." He leaned forward a bit.

Shrugging, I casually said, "I could read your file, but I would rather hear it from you. I believe in getting answers from the source. Words from others could be formed in a way to make you look better or worse than you really are. This way, I can get the facts from you and cut out the middleman. Make my own opinions, I suppose you could say."

"Cut out, huh? Have you heard the rumors about how they get rid of the employees?" Spence lifted both eyebrows, entirely craving my answer.

I loved hearing rumors and legends but now was not the time. "Is there anything else you want to talk about if not how you ended up in this facility? I'm all ears."

Spence glanced out the window. Massive snowflakes coated the forest beyond in a record amount of time, sticking to last night's leftovers.

"Nora, I hope I don't come off the wrong way, but I don't feel comfortable telling you my life story. I barely know you." He faced me once again.

I kept the smile inviting. "This is what I'm here for. I will listen to your worries and your desires. My goal is to help you. Sometimes we need some support to get through it. There's no shame in that."

"Shame? There is no shame from where I sit. I just don't trust everyone to know everything about me. It doesn't matter what you do for a living. I have had plenty of psychiatrists and they all were the same. It is not strangers I tell my story to. I trust friends, very close friends. You are neither." His gaze locked on me.

I was unsure of how to respond to this. I could've corrected him that I was a psychologist, which had been different from a psychiatrist. I didn't hold as much power as he assumed. But now didn't seem like the right time.

"Don't take it personally, Nora. I'm just particular when it comes to my private matters," he added.

On one hand, I wanted to know what it was I could do to help. On the other hand, I wasn't here to tell anyone about my life story. "We still have another fifty-two minutes of our session left." I pointed towards the clock.

He shrugged me off. "What about you?"

"What about me? I'm here for you, not me. It is not I who needs any help." I was *sure* of that.

"Maybe I don't need any help either but here we are. You can't be certain that I need help because you don't really know why I'm here without looking at my file. Previous psychiatrists could have lied. They saw me in a different way and wrote their own notes. What they think is wrong may not actually be true. I could be normal, and you would have no idea. You expect me to be messed up in the head. I'm *not*, Nora. I never was." His eyes were reaching my soul in the sense that they brushed down my spine.

My eyes lingered on the door before landing back on Spence. "I know this is not ideal. You have to tell another stranger about yourself and it seems hopeless. You don't want to open yourself up like that. You don't believe this is going to help. I wish I could predict the future and say that this will, and you'll see brighter days but I can't. All I can do is offer to help and that's all I'm here for." I leaned forward. "I'm here for you. I may not know you, but you do have value."

He chuckled. "I have value? What if I'm a pedophile? Do I have value then? What if I've done terrible things to children?"

I kept a straight face, not giving him an upper hand. "Have you?"

He wiggled his finger at me. "Oh, I see where this is going. You got me. You're trying to get me to talk about myself and express who I am. Nice try, Miss Widow."

Widow—I was far from it. It wasn't far-fetched, though. That man had been dead to me in a sense.

I furrowed my brows as I averted my eyes towards the floor. "Spence, we ran into one another in the hall the other day. Then, you kept me company while I played a timeless piece from Beethoven." I lifted my chin. "You seemed so nice. That was who I met. That was your first impression on me. You didn't let me fall. You had manners. Tell me more about this man. That's all I ask."

"I just made fun of you, and you don't even flinch. I called you a widow." Confusion etched his face.

A small smile formed as I shrugged my shoulders. "But we both know it's not true. Your words are just words. Please, introduce me to the Mr. Woods I ran into."

He straightened his posture. "I apologize for making fun of your name. That was out of line."

"Is there anything else you'd like to add?"

"I'll give you a foot rub?" He cocked an eyebrow.

I let a laugh slip as I sat back in my chair. "I meant about yourself. You apologized after making fun of me. Is there any reason why you would be inclined to do so? Is there some inner battle between the angel and the devil?"

His eyes narrowed—darkened noticeably. I wasn't sure how such blue eyes could turn so black, but it unnerved me to no end. "What do you know about the angel and the devil?"

Swallowing my fear, I sit out, "It was a simple metaphor. There are always these jokes about people having mini angels and devils on their shoulders who tell them what to do. I was only trying to lighten the mood for a moment. I apologize if I've said anything to offend you." I put my hands up in defense.

"It's nothing personal, Nora. People always think they know about angels and devils. They know *nothing*." He laced his fingers together.

They called this a crack in his mind. I'd use it. I was finally getting somewhere. "What do you know about the angels and devils?"

His eyes shifted down to the floor. "I know that it's an ongoing battle. It never ends. They're two sides of the same coin but they refuse to believe it. Until they accept this, their feud never stops."

"Which side are you on? Good or bad?" This man threw every new mystery my way and it was as if I was getting another puzzle piece, only to realize the puzzle was growing larger quicker than I could put it back together.

"Both. Everything is not *black and white* like people make it seem. Each side has its downs. We never had a choice. We were automatically judged as inherently wrong." He shook his head.

"Is that what happened to you? You were judged wrongly? You told me you don't think you need to be here."

His fingers unlaced themselves as he leaned forward with his elbows resting on his knees. He went deep into thought, debating if he should even answer my questions. Then his eyes locked with mine. "At some point, we are all judged in the wrong way. Only sometimes does it affect our lives. Sometimes we end up in prison for crimes we didn't commit. We end up with scars or injuries based on false accusations. We end up with grudges against those who've made unfair judgments. We end up in Monstrum Asylum."

I swallowed the lump in my throat, fixing a strand of my hair. "I understand." A piece of his mind that opened new curiosities. I was seeing this place from *his* perspective. "And answer one last question, if you will. What do you see me as? I am an employee of this prison. Am I on the good or the bad side?" I hoped for the former, but I feared the latter. It would be much harder for me to gain his trust if he saw me as the bad guy. On the bright side, I would understand where he placed me, and from there I'd go about gaining his trust.

Spence fell silent for a few minutes, taking his time to respond with the most perfect answer he could pull from thin air. "It depends. You might work for the bad side, but you may not have any idea which side you're on. You've been deceived, Nora. Don't let them fool you." He stood from his seat. The session was over.

Shivers slithered down my spine as I walked over to the door. "I'm always around if you ever need to talk to me." I opened the door.

He approached the doorway but paused beside me. "You shouldn't be here. Things are never what they seem and a woman like you may never get out of here alive," he whispered.

Before I could ask him what he was talking about, he made his way back to his room. I bit my lip, rubbing my eyes. He was trying to scare me off. That was all this was. I didn't scare so easily, and he was going to learn that. I looked fragile by appearance, but I was not one to go down without a fight.

I headed down the hall, getting stopped by David. "Hello, Miss Witlow. How did your first session go?"

Smiling a bit, I answered, "It wasn't too bad." I turned on my heel and headed back to my room. I grabbed my notepad and recorded what Spence had told me during our session. As I left my room, I pressed my hand to my chest. "Oh, you scared me. Everyone seems to do that around here."

"That much is obvious," Monique snorted. "I heard from

Harrison that your first session wasn't bad. Spence is the easiest, believe it or not. Emilie is…close behind. Such a bummer."

Emilie would be my next patient in a few days.

"Is there something up with this place? I was just curious." If I told her what Spence said, I would not only be breaking a code between Spence and I, but I would make myself look insane if I let her know a part of me believed him.

"What do you mean? It's an asylum that has very few patients. It's been a slow year." She laughed.

I began to wonder if maybe the reason the asylum had fewer residents was due to the current times.

Maybe people had seen it for what it was, and took a little more care to help their loved ones. Slim picking wasn't an entirely terrible concept.

"I think I'll head back to my room for the night. It's been an interesting day and I'm going to wind down." I patted her shoulder as I retreated back to my room and closed the door. I looked at my small bed and sat on it with my notes in my lap.

As I studied my findings, my eyes began to grow heavy, and I hard as I tried to put up a fight, I struggled. I could never win against sleep, and I knew it.

After changing into pajamas, I lay in my bed for what seemed like seconds before falling into a deep sleep. Since arriving at this asylum, my sleep pattern had changed. I would wake up three times a night and my dreams had festered more into nightmares. Control wasn't an easy thing to grasp. The most I could do was force myself awake when I was about to die but I couldn't manage what I dreamt about.

In a few, I'd fall to my death. In others, I'd be murdered while my ghost continued to roam the earth. Nobody could ever hear or see me but somehow, these dreams were fun to be in. I wasn't sure if dreams had more meaning than symbolism, but I was left wondering if my demise was the warning I needed to heed in this place.

V

Music carried out of the gymnasium and into the hallways. Heels clicked against the tiles while laughter echoed into the air. Sobriety stood no chance, people were tripping over their own feet.

I stood in the stairwell, sipping some wine to keep myself company. This was the quietest corner I could find to give my thoughts a chance to run free.

"Nora, there you are! I've been searching everywhere. Why aren't you in the gym?" She pointed back in the direction of the gymnasium.

Shrugging, I kept my gaze fixed on the floor. "Too many people. I'm glad this is the end of one chapter, and I can continue my next journey, but I don't know these people. I don't care to know them. My focus is on my future and helping people who need it."

She walked up the stairs. "Come with me. I don't want to see you out here by yourself and I don't want to be alone. You're my best friend. Keep me occupied, please?"

I closed the gap between us and swept my arms. "This is where I like to be. I like quiet and empty hallways." A frown formed along her lips. "I understand your concern, and I love you, but I like to be alone, too. Sometimes we have to compromise."

"What does that mean? I don't compromise?" She crossed her arms.

I laughed a bit, and it filled the space in the spirit of an echo. "I'm an introvert, yeah? You're more of an extrovert. It's great and I love that we help balance one another but sometimes I want to spend one-on-one time with you. The whole crowd scene gets tiresome."

"This is our night, for us. This is a celebration of us getting our degrees. I want to spend it with you."

"So do I. I just don't care for the rest of the people in there. The music taste is horrendous. Why don't we go out for a nice dinner? My treat." I smiled.

"Nora, you're great. You just don't understand this will be the only party we ever get for this kind of thing. I want to live it." She huffed, her fingers loosening on the railing. "I guess I must do it alone." She turned, missing the ledge that led down to the first step.

I sat up in a hurry, wiping the sweat from my forehead. I glanced at the clock on my nightstand and read 5:14. I'd need to get up soon and start on some work around the asylum. I didn't have any sessions today, but I was sure David would give me chores.

***

Metal fences stood at ten feet tall as barbed wire spiraled along the top. It resembled a prison, which couldn't be ethical. Had any of these patients ever threatened another human? If the answer was no, they didn't deserve to be treated as criminals. Either way, rehabilitation was better than cruel punishment.

It had been proven through experience that rehab was a better method for even prisoners; otherwise, you would just get a repeat of the same crimes. Cages couldn't heal the root of the problem.

That's what I was here for. I was here to get to the source and help these people move on from what hurt them.

For the time being, the snowfall let up.

My eyes lingered on each individual patient to make sure they were not attempting to escape. As if they would, or could survive in this weather.

Emilie sat by the fence, but her gaze went far beyond the tree line. Something had her attention, and I was curious as to what had her interested.

Claire leaned against the side of the building, admiring her nails.

Spence stood in the middle of the field, lost in his own head. I wanted to peek inside, but I was sure he would never let me in.

"Spence keeps to himself. He likes it that way. He believes nobody here can be trusted," a female said beside me. I turned to see Claire right where I expected her to be. "I've tried to get to know him in certain ways, but even I can't do it and I'm on his side."

Nodding, I glanced at Emilie. "Is she quiet?"

Claire had barely worn a sweater paired with black jeans and a tight red top and black boots. What a look, and she did pull it off well.

"Thank you." She laughed. "Once you get to know Emilie though, she won't shut up. She whines more than anything."

I fixed my earmuffs. "We have the stereotypical group, it seems." I chuckled. "Spence, the reserved. Emilie, the observant. Claire, the gossip."

She narrowed her eyes. "I am not a gossip. And what about

you, huh? Nora, the doll. You come off as if you're perfect. You're not. I see right through you. You have no right to probe us for our personal secrets. You should be in here with us, right?" She spun on her heel and headed back to the other edge of the courtyard.

Claire was the mean girl. I gathered that much. She would be an interesting patient to get to know.

Spence stood out against the white background. His skin blended with the powdered liquid of this earth, and much like Claire, his dark hair contrasted it seamlessly. His eyes matched the shimmer of the snowflakes that laid atop the wonderland.

"Excuse me, may I see a nurse?" Emilie asked, capturing my eyes.

She wore a turtleneck dress in lavender, thick tights underneath, and a gray parka.

I looked at her hand as the blood dripped from her palm. "What did you do?"

She pointed to the fence and sighed. "My hand froze to the metal. I had to rip it off. I never seem to learn."

Whispers floated in the sky, inching closer to my ears. A bead stained the snow at our feet, where I noticed the black flatties on hers. 1957 Capezio. Who could afford such nice shoes when a patient here? What was her story? Had she come from wealth?

"Are you all right?" Her head tilted.

Spence arrived at my side while Claire twisted her head my way.

Dismissing their concerns, I shook out my hands, keeping my eyes glued to the crimson. "I'm fine." The whispers grew louder but her voice popped out like the dots of my dress. *I guess I must do it alone.*

I caught the fence as I stumbled in the snow. I gathered myself again, averting my gaze. "I'm fine." I stepped away from them before we returned inside, and Emilie went to see the nurse.

A pair of blue eyes watched my every move as I walked back to my room, closing the door. It was unprofessional of me to act that way in front of my own patients. I had to learn to gain better control of myself around the sight of blood.

It was a moment of weakness that they had witnessed. I was the psychologist. I was meant to be the strong one who helped them. They needed to know they were able to trust me.

A knock sounded on my door and I stood from my bed, opening it. "David, I apologize for what happened."

He smiled, but it lacked genuine joy. "No need—accidents happen. Emilie will be all right. I have some tasks for you."

"Does it involve being outside, or am I able to take off my warm clothes for the time being?" I turned, hoping he would give me a chance to remove my jacket.

"You can take off what you need. Meet me in the office." He disappeared down the hall.

I removed my warm layers and went to the office. David gave me some chores and I followed them. My best guess as to why he never hired janitors for these things was due to a budget cut, but if I made extra to clean as well, it wasn't the worst idea in the world. Cleaning didn't bother me all that much.

"And Nora?"

"Yes, Dr. Harrison?" I looked back at him.

"I appreciate the modesty. Sometimes people forget this is a hospital for the mentally ill and not a burlesque show."

Giving him a nod, I thanked him. However, my mind wandered to his comment. Was he referring to Monique just because she showed some cleavage? That wasn't his place to judge.

I shook my head and began cleaning.

A shadow fell over me as I was dusting the shelves in the lounge area.

I looked back, surprised by Spence's presence. "Did you want to have a session?" I stood, but my height never matched his. I couldn't come close even with heels.

He grabbed a book from the shelf behind me. "I wanted to ask about what happened outside. You looked so…terrified. I don't mean to pry, Nora, but it did seem a bit alarming as you nearly collapsed."

Every time he spoke my name, it sounded foreign. "Excuse me if I come off the wrong way but it's none of your business. I'm capable of handling myself."

"Does it seem odd that you claim you are who can help us but refuse help from others? We're all here *together* because we are never meant to do it alone."

"Spence, I'm here to help you. I am not here because I need help." I put down my cleaning bucket of supplies.

His eyes honed on me, sending goosebumps down my forearms. "Do you wish to help me? If so, let me help you."

"The gesture is kind, but I don't need it." I grabbed the duster from my bucket and swiped along another shelf.

"Are you a maid? A housewife? You sure as hell dress like one," a woman said, snickering.

I continued with my chores, refusing to give her the satisfaction. "Hello, Claire."

When I turned back to look at her and confirm my greeting was correct, Spence had disappeared from the area. Claire put a record on the player.

I finished dusting and turned around. I was on my way out of the lounge when Claire decided to ask more questions. "So, tell me, have you ever had sex? I mean, you have, right? You are an adult."

"That's a private matter. It's inappropriate to ask." I fixed the skirt of my dress.

She sunk into the cushions. "Is it? I'm just making conversation."

I shifted my weight. "I'm not comfortable discussing my private affairs with you. Thanks for understanding." I left the lounge before she could say anything more.

Chills covered my entire body as I passed by a familiar room in the basement. My eyes moved from the cleaning supplies closet and back to the door. I stepped inside the room, eyeing the machine that stood against the wall and faced the table in the middle.

As I approached the machine, I placed my hand against it. Pulling back, I choked and hoped my thoughts were deceiving me. The machine was warm as if it had recently been used.

I began thinking back to any of the patients, trying to remember if anyone had come back. Claire seemed to be normal, and I knew that due to her intrusive interview. Spence didn't seem out of the ordinary.

I hadn't seen Emilie since she went to the nurse, but I was sure they wouldn't use this on her after she got hurt. There was no reason to. There was never a reason to shock someone.

My eyes scanned the room for any evidence of my theory. Nothing stood out, leaving me to wonder if I was imagining things. The brain could be a miraculous tool in creating realities that weren't really there.

Walking towards the door, I accidentally kicked something and bent down to see what it was. A button must have fallen off someone's clothes. I couldn't be sure whose but there were only two options.

It was a button that popped off during shock therapy or an employee lost it while moving things around in here. I wasn't sure I wanted to investigate and find out.

As I left the room and returned the supplies, I remembered that one guy mentioned why this place was named Monstrum. Could it be because of the employees? No, no. I doubted Monique and David would be involved in evil practices. Decent humans knew shock therapy could never cure someone.

Just how many decent humans were there in our world? Did they end up running this facility? No, they would've been caught. Everyone here had no reason to raise my suspicions.

This place could mess with your mind in ways one couldn't comprehend and I refused to be its victim. I had to stay focused, not allowing the other worlds to cloud my better judgment.

VI

My knuckles nearly bled—beaming bright red—after knocking on the green metal door. "What," I breathed from confusion. The name on the door read Emilie Brooks, the second patient of the three I'd be counseling for a while.

"Come in," a soft voice said.

I entered upon her approval. I smiled while admiring the colors that shimmered throughout her room. Every shade of the rainbow that plastered her walls had an iridescent layer to top it off. As if she'd simply settled here and never expected to go anywhere else.

"You have a lovely room, Miss Brooks." I took a seat in a chair by the desk in the corner.

Emilie shrugged, sitting back on her bed to make herself

comfortable.

"Are you okay with talking about yourself?"

"It all depends on what you want to know. I won't tell you personal things that I'd rather keep dear to myself. Ask me anything else."

I nodded. "Where were you born?"

"Why does that matter?" She squinted.

A small upward curve formed on my lips. "I'm trying to get to know you. I want to know you as a person. I'm not here to judge you or make you feel lesser. I came here to make sure you know your worth as a person."

She grabbed a small book from her bed, rubbing the pages between her fingertips. "Well, it was a small town near the water. It was actually a water birth if you must know. My mother wanted me to be born in the water to make everything much more peaceful. People think that it's dangerous to have a baby in water but that's a lie. Babies grow inside the uterus and that uterus is filled with liquid until birth. The lungs are still collapsed until they take that first breath of air after delivery. So, if they're born in water, they don't die. They don't drown. The water only becomes dangerous to humans once those lungs are inflated. Then they can drown."

I furrowed my brows. "You refer to humans as they. Do you not consider yourself human?"

Her eyes snapped up to mine and something resembling fear flashed before disappearing. "Why? What have you heard?"

"Nothing. I just want you to know that being in this facility doesn't make you any less than the rest of us. You're still as valuable as we are. There's nothing wrong with needing some mental help. The brain is miraculous but it's not perfect, unfortunately." I shook my head, careful not to imply that imperfection was something to be ashamed of. "The downside to that comes from the trauma we face, and how it can deter our quality of life."

She eyed me as if I were telling her lies. It didn't connect the questions in my head. Emilie portrayed herself as a kind human on the outside but something much darker was scratching the surface just beneath her skin. "I see. They have you wrapped around their finger."

The hair on my neck stood on end. "What do you mean? Who does?"

"I don't want to talk about this anymore." She hugged her book and turned her body in the opposite direction, facing the wall.

"What do you want to talk about? I've got the time and I'm open to talking about anything you feel comfortable with." I gestured around me.

Her head lowered. "You should have left when you had the chance. You never should have taken this job."

"Emilie, I'm not scared of you or Spence, or even Claire. You guys won't scare me away. I'm here to stay and help you get better. I just need you to accept that." I rested my hands in my lap.

She kept her eyes glued to her lap as she said, "It's not us you should be afraid of."

I wanted to get off this subject, but it was the only way I was getting information from her. "Who should I fear?"

"You should go."

"We still have at least forty-six minutes left. I'm here until the hour is up. You were born in water. What else do you want me to know about you?" I leaned forward.

She twisted her head to face me. "Claire said we can't trust you."

It sparked curiosity in my brain when she mentioned Claire having a hard time with trust. As I recalled, it was Claire who claimed Spence had that issue. It was known that people could reflect their true issues onto someone else just to feel better about themselves.

"Okay, well, Claire is not here right now. If you are not comfortable answering, I understand. Where did you get that book?" I pointed.

She looked at it and turned her body to face me again. "It's special. Let's me write down my thoughts. Has a few poems, too, that explain how I feel. Some days get harder than others but they're always here, right where I leave them. The words never abandon me. My dad left it behind for me. Mom never wanted me to have it, and that's because she and Dad had bad blood with one another. This is all I have left of my father. I didn't let her take that from me."

"Is there any reason why your mom hated your dad?" I tilted my head.

She chewed her lip. "I think it's because Mom loved someone else. She never admitted it but there was another man that she would bring around every once in a while. I hated him. He was wrong for her. He seemed perfect but he was far from it. She wanted him to replace my dad, but he never did."

I frowned. "And you met your dad?"

"I never had the chance. He disappeared when I was little. Mom told me that he left to go do some huge business thing, but I think that's a lie. I never found anything that pointed to where my dad was. Mom was known for lying to me. I never could trust her. When I told her I wanted to live with my father, she got so angry. She tried to tell me he abandoned us and it was wrong for me to want him over her, but I did. I know she tried to take care of me, but I'd only ever asked for honesty. She never gave that to me. Her lies never matched up. She once told me my father worked for this huge company in some other country but when I did some digging, there was no company by that name." She let out a small sigh.

"I'm so sorry." I said nothing more to give her a moment.

After a few minutes of silence, she started again. "I left when I was old enough to move out on my own. I never looked back, and I haven't seen my mom since."

"Does she know you're here?"

Her brown eyes locked on mine. "Nobody knows we're here. Our names are kept confidential."

That didn't fit into the puzzle. Patient names were always part of the public record of any asylum. Why were theirs kept separate? Was visitation not permitted? Had they admitted themselves?

Speaking of which, I hadn't seen anyone try to visit them, or contact them at all. It struck me as odd that they wouldn't be allowed contact with the outside world. They'd have to be extremely violent towards others or themselves for that to make sense, but even then prisoners were allowed to have visitors, too.

"Do you think she would visit you if she knew you were here?" I kept my gaze fixed on her.

Emilie coughed. "I doubt it. She'd blame me for being here. She'd say it was my fault."

I straightened my posture as I sat up. "Why would she do that?"

She shrugged. "Mom didn't like me, and I couldn't really tell you why. My best guess is I ruined her life in some way. I'm not heartbroken that she doesn't know. The fear of how she'd react is far worse than my curiosity to know how she'd take the news. I'd shatter if she came here and told me it was all my fault that I ended up here."

I glanced at my fingers and exhaled the breath I'd been holding for a few seconds too long.

Emilie didn't deserve to end up in this life. She was troubled but only because she lacked the parental love she'd needed all those years. I was under the impression that she wasn't as unstable as others made her out to be.

"Are we done yet? If Claire knows I told you this much, she'll kill me." She scratched her nose.

I lifted my eyes. "Claire—you seem to mention her a lot. What's your relationship with her like?"

She shook her head and tugged at the book's cover. "I can't comment on that. I'm so sorry, Dr. Witlow. She would not approve, and Claire knows *everything* that happens."

"All right, that's fair. And you can call me Nora." I gave her a smile, but she didn't receive it in the way I'd hoped.

She placed a kiss on the book and gave me her attention. "What about you? Have you talked to the others yet?"

"I've had a session with Spence, but I can't say any more than that. I've taken an oath to keep my patient's information private if they told me something they wouldn't want others knowing. I have yet to talk to Claire, but I'll see her soon." I smoothed out the sleeves of my dress.

Her eyes lingered on my outfit a little too long. "That's a really pretty dress."

I straightened out the skirt with a nod. "Thank you. Do you wear dresses?"

Emilie looked towards the window. "Yeah. Sometimes, I do. I wouldn't wear any during this weather, though."

I chuckled at her remark. Maybe I was a lunatic for wearing dresses in the winter, but it was my style. There were tights out there that were thick and cozy. I was not too keen on wearing pants if I didn't need to.

"Do you like music?" I asked.

"Who doesn't?"

I shrugged a little. "You would be surprised. What kind of music do you like to listen to?"

"Music that most people wouldn't associate with a girl like me." She opened the book.

"What do you mean?" I focused on her hand movements. Her fidgety demeanor told me she was nervous but also remorseful.

She cleared her throat before saying, "People assume I'm a good girl. My music is not."

She glanced at the clock. We still had about twenty-four minutes left of this therapy session. I was making a dent with her, farther than Spence would let me go.

"What kind of movies do you prefer?" I asked her one more question as an attempt to open up some more about her secrets that she could subtly reveal to me.

She pushed hair behind her ear while her gaze stayed on me. "I like horror movies."

I hadn't expected that answer but there was always more than what met the eye.

"I like the adrenaline feeling it gives me when I get scared. I also enjoy watching people act stupid all the time. I don't understand how they are, but they are. You are not supposed to follow the noise. You don't hide where the killer is. We can't expect common sense where a plot it meant to exist, though." She shook her head.

I laughed. "You seem to really know a lot about horror

movies. Did you watch *The Tell-Tale Heart*?"

A gasp passed her lips. "You mean from Edgar Allen Poe's stories? They made a movie about that? It was just a short story, but it still gave me the chills!"

"I don't think I've ever read the short story, or any of his work, but I assume so? The man who hears a beating heart under the floorboards, correct?"

"That's the one! That's so far out." Her smile grew at the thought. The movie came out in 1960, but if she hadn't seen it, how long had she been here? Maybe it'd be incentive to get out.

"I'll make sure you watch it when you get out."

When. Not if.

"I wouldn't hold to that promise if I were you. None of the others before you made it out alive, and it's never going to be in the plot for us to get out of here. That was never the plan, and you should stop trying so hard."

Her expression transformed—pupils shrinking as her posture stiffened, watching my every move. "Take notes, Nora. You'll need to know how to survive a horror movie."

My nose scrunched up as a puzzled look spread across my face. Emilie knew more than she let on. Something strange was happening here and I couldn't begin to pinpoint where it came from.

VII

"Monique informed me she saw you in the basement last week," David said. He fixed a few papers before swiveling his body to face me.

"I apologize, sir, but I didn't see any signs that said I couldn't, and I thought I would get to know all my exit strategies," I said, cracking a joke. I pushed my cup across the counter, pouring coffee into it, and I would use it to warm up the emptiness inside my soul as I adjusted to my new life here.

He pointed to a few doors. "There's no reason to run, Nora, and certainly no exit in the basement."

My smile faltered as I sipped my morning brew. "Right, I will keep that in mind."

Dr. Harrison stepped forward—a little *too* close for my liking.

I appreciated my space, and I didn't need my new boss to invade that bubble. Not now, and not ever. "It's for your safety. The basement has been having a lot of issues, between the lights flickering, exploding, and some snow seeping in through the cracks, it's a floor that needs too many repairs. We wouldn't want to use that insurance you enrolled for just yet, right?"

A nod. However, I didn't wholly believe he was telling me the truth. Why? I couldn't quite put my finger on that answer. "It won't happen again."

"Good. The health of our employees is our utmost concern." David got himself a cup of coffee before leaving to go get his breakfast.

His words struck me as odd. If employees were the biggest concern, then who was caring for the patients? Shouldn't this have been about them and their health from the start?

I checked the skies outside, not at all surprised by the snow in the forecast. We were so far out of the city that the snow just never ended.

"What," I whispered as the lamp beside me flickered, then shut off. Within seconds, the rest of the building lost power. It wasn't unusual in a snowstorm, but it was for a lamp to lose it first.

With the power out, my first task was to gather all the patients and meet with the doctors. However, when I approached the entertainment room, I was taken back by the lack of people. Wouldn't everyone want to meet here? Who in their right mind wanted to walk around, alone, in a big asylum during a winter storm in the pitch black? It was beyond my comprehension.

"Hello?" I called out, spinning on my heel.

"Nora," someone whispered. Between the silence and lack of sight, their voice carried louder than it should have. Meaning it hadn't come from this room.

I followed the sound, but I stopped and turned back when the whisper came from behind. "This isn't a funny."

"Nora, I'm not playing a game," he replied. Spence. Where…

I felt the walls as my fingers brushed over a cold, metal lock. Right. The patients were in their rooms and Spence was calling out from his. "Where are the keys? I can't see shit in here." I squinted through the darkness as if it would help, but it did me no good.

Spence chuckled a little at my use of *shit*. "They're in David's office where they always are. Down the hall."

Down the hall.

I placed my hands flat against his door, sensing my direction. I twisted my body ninety degrees to my right and began walking. I dragged my fingers along the wall to keep myself on the right path but for a few moments, they brushed against the cold air as I passed the entertainment area, and then they returned to the texture.

One door. An office.

A second door. *My* office.

A third door. What was in this room?

After passing a few doors and counting them out, Spence told me to stop. I wrapped my fingers around the knob and let myself in after I assured myself nobody was inside. The beauty of not being able to see sent what was once used for sight to now amplify my hearing. When one of the five senses was taken away, the other four grew in strength.

Maybe that was why people became more paranoid, because they could hear sounds they weren't able to before…

I found the keys hanging in the wall, and I closed my entire fist around them so they would jingle. I left the office and followed the wall back to his room, but I ran right into someone else. I hadn't expected anyone else to be in this area, and I knew Spence couldn't have gotten out. Who was out here?

"I'm sorry. I was going to find everyone and get us all in one area. It would be easy with the power out," I sputtered.

Nobody responded. But dainty fingers wrapped around my wrist, pulling me forward. I expected to hit them, or even a wall, but instead I fell to the floor.

My hands slapped the ground as I rolled onto my butt and looked back.

"Nora, what's going on out there?"

I extended my leg and swiped it across the floor, but I never made contact with an ankle. "I'm not sure." I scrambled to my feet and tried the keys until I found one that worked. "Now to unlock the other rooms."

Spence guarded the hall while I let Claire and Emilie out of their rooms. Claire helped me navigate the dark corridor to return David's keys to his office. I wasn't sure how she could see better than I could.

I gathered everyone into the entertainment area, and from there I got out lots of blankets. I searched for candles, but there seemed to be only two. I lit them anyway.

Emilie snuggled up in the blankets.

"Why don't you cuddle with Claire or Spence? You need all the warmth you can get," I told her.

She just shook her head.

Claire gave her blankets to Emilie. "I don't need them. The cold doesn't bother me."

I wanted to question it, but I was freezing myself. Emilie accepted the blankets while Claire looked at the candles. Spence nudged her, shaking his head. Whatever she was thinking, he reminded her to be smart about it.

"What—" David rounded the corner. "Nora, what were you thinking letting the patients out? That is not your call."

Standing up, I walked over and glanced back at the three sitting there. "I apologize, David, but the power went out. I can't see anything and it's freezing now that the heat is off. I figured I could keep an eye on them and help them warm up, too. I'm just thinking about the patients."

David released a sigh. "You seem to really care about their comfort, don't you?"

"I do." I tilted my head, furrowing my brows. Was that a bad thing? And why was that such a surprise? That was my job.

He cleared his throat. "I can't fault you for trying to warm them up, can I? But next time you should come to me first."

I nodded. "Understood. Thank you." I returned to the chair and sat down with my one blanket.

David stood by the wall, keeping his eye on us.

Spence's blue eyes pierced the dark between us. "Did Nora tell any of you that she plays the piano? And she does it so well."

"It's nothing," I said.

"Piano? Why not entertain us? We have nothing else to do." David came in view of the flickering flame of the candle.

I clenched my jaw, thankful people couldn't see much of me. What was the reasoning behind telling everyone that I could play? There was nothing useful. Nothing of significance.

"Go ahead." Claire nudged her foot against mine. "Play us a piece, Beethoven." How did she…?

"I'm not confident enough." I shook my head as my cheeks heated.

Claire nudged again. "It's just us. Go on."

But it wasn't just them. It was eight eyes, eight ears all on me.

Judging me like spiders. It wasn't as simple as just them. "I can't."

She snickered. "What, now you're afraid?"

"Claire, that's enough." David shot her a look.

After one last glare, she pressed her lips together and said nothing.

I swallowed. "I'm sorry. I just can't."

Emilie reached over and patted my knee. "It's okay. There's nothing to be ashamed about." I sent her my weakest smile because it was all I could manage at a time like this.

Spence leaned forward, propping his elbows up in his legs. "What about a game? Don't you think we should play a game of some sort?"

"What kind of game?" I asked.

Emilie smiled. "I like games."

Claire, however, didn't seem too interested.

As soon as Spence said, "What about Never Have I Ever?"

Claire's eyes lit up, and it was seemingly noticeable with how dark they were.

"I've never heard of it," I said in a quiet voice.

He replied, "*Nobody* has." A mischievous vision planted itself right in his iris'.

David was ready to say something, but I cut him off. "It's a great idea. It'll be good for getting to know each of you."

Emilie squealed. "How exciting! Okay, okay, so how does this game work?"

Spence explained it to her, in which she nodded and sat back. "Are you going to join?" Spence asked David.

He shook his head. "In fact, I should probably go get the power figured out. Miss Witlow, I trust you to keep an eye on these three."

"Yes, sir." I nodded.

Once he disappeared, we all put ten fingers up. My heartbeat began to pound against my ribcage, reminding me how risky this was. I got to know them, but at what cost? They'd pick me apart as well.

Spence looked over at us. "We'll follow a counterclockwise direction. And as it's my idea, I'll begin." Clearing his throat, he straightened his posture. "Never have I ever lived in the city."

Emilie frowned as she put a finger down. "That was directed right at me, wasn't it?"

However, I also had to drop a finger. City life was all I knew before this.

Claire sat back. "Never have I ever given a blowjob."

Emilie laughed. "You're lying."

"No, contrary to popular belief, I haven't." She shrugged a bit. "What about you Spence?"

He snickered. "Claire, please, we're all adults here. You know very well my thing is for women."

However, I lowered another finger. Claire's eyes fell on my fingers. "Holy fuck, our innocent Nora has done the unspeakable."

Everyone else looked my way. I shrugged a bit. "Like Spence said, we're all adults here, Claire. When you're in what you think is a loving relationship, you want to make your partner happy."

They wanted to ask questions but that wasn't what this game entailed. It was about catching only a glimpse into each other's lives, rather than diving into the deep end.

"My turn!" Emilie sat up, knitting her eyebrows together. Her pretty head was deep in thought, looking for whatever leverage she needed. "Oh! I got it! Okay, never have I ever tasted blood."

Claire kicked Emilie's foot. "That was cold." She put a finger down, and Spence did too.

"You've never even once sucked blood from a papercut?" I asked her.

Emilie shook her head. "Nope, blood disgusts me."

That we could agree on. But I lowered a finger anyway. So far, I was the one losing this game.

We went around a few times, and eventually Claire and Emilie lost more fingers alongside me. It was refreshing to not be the one behind. I had a bit of a competitive side.

Claire lifted her chin, knowing she had the leverage. "Never have I ever been afraid of the dark."

Spence cursed under his breath and lowered a finger, as well as Emilie. It was understandable. When I dropped another finger, Claire smirked in the slightest. Was she targeting me, or was I tripping?

However, during the next round, my question got an answer. "Never have I ever been afraid of the sight of blood."

And so, I was forced to drop my last finger.

VIII

Blindness was not an option here. "I see you have a darker taste," I commented on Claire's choice in decorations.

Her room involved a lot of red and black, presenting her as a woman who preferred the colorless side of the spectrum. I could have perceived her as dramatic for a moment if I hadn't already known her to be tough on the emotional side of things.

"Let's get this over with, Norma." She chewed on a stick which threw me off guard.

I sat down on a chair across from her bed. "Let's start at the beginning. Mind telling me where you were born?"

She crossed her legs and folded her arms. "Why is this important?"

"Why is it not important?" I shrugged her off. "If you wish

to take nine years of schooling just to work in my field and tell me how to do my job, I will not stop you, Claire." I smiled in response to my words. "I apologize. It takes eight to twelve years for most. It all depends on the individual."

Her nose wrinkled as her top lip raised. "I hate school. Hell no. You must be so old by now. You wasted your entire adult life in school. You at least had some fun, right? College guys are better than high school boys."

I fixed the skirt of my dress. "My age is none of your business. Neither is my love life. This is about you. What are you willing to answer? Where were you born? How long have you been here?"

"Why are you afraid to talk about your age and love life? Are you a thirty-year-old virgin?" She laughed. "That's impossible."

The watch on my wrist told me we still had fifty-two minutes left here. "I could ask you the same thing. Why are you afraid to talk about your own life?"

Claire settled back in her seat and watched me like I had something to hide. "It's unrealistic."

"What is?"

"Adult virgins. It's not realistic for someone to go through puberty and get all these hormones and not do anything about it. Assuming you've had hormones for fifteen years of your life, you've had the urge to wanna be with a man, or a woman, and you did nothing about it. That's unnatural." She shook her head.

Something about Claire pushed the wrong buttons. I wasn't sure how to explain it. "They call it self-control. It's not a crime to not have sex. If you want to have sex, that is totally your business, and nobody is going to stop you. However, you also must realize it's their business to not."

"You refer to them from another perspective, as if you aren't a part of that group." She squinted her eyes at me and smirked a few seconds following. "You have been with a man, haven't you? Why are you so defensive of virgins?"

"I'm defensive of people who haven't earned judgment," I said.

She scoffed and looked away. "They've earned it. I've been called a slut countless times."

I leaned forward. "Have you been called that by every living virgin to exist?"

She shifted in her spot. "Well, no…"

It was too easy to point her towards her mistakes and take the better path. "Exactly my point. Judge the ones who shame you but don't group all of them together. There are virgins who don't care about what you do. There are good and bad in every group. There are nonvirgins who judge virgins, and ones who don't. You just need to be open-minded and wait for them to reveal themselves."

She pushed her hair back from her face and let out a small sigh. "It doesn't change how I feel. Calling me a slut isn't right."

I shook my head, waving my arm through the air. "Of course not. Calling anyone a name who hasn't done anything to you isn't right. Even calling them a name if they have offended you still isn't right." I sat back. "If it makes you feel any better, I'm considered a whore because I didn't stay a virgin until marriage. However, that still does not mean they're unrealistic. It doesn't make them nonvirgins just because they've insulted you."

"Sure, take their side." She threw her arms up.

I lifted my hands up in defense. "I am not taking sides. I am calling out what's wrong when I see it. You choosing to fight fire with fire is not going to diminish the flame. It's going to make it grow. It doesn't make you innocent if you retaliate after someone insults you. It means you both are in the wrong. If they insult you and you don't return the favor, it makes you the bigger person and then nobody can tell you that you did anything wrong. You can never go wrong with taking the high road." I put my hands back in my lap.

Claire rolled her eyes as if to reject everything I said. It didn't surprise me that she wasn't seeing an error in her ways. "You would never know what that's like. You're so perfect."

I laughed but it was too late to stop once I realized it was out of line. "No? Claire, I'm a blonde. I live with the stereotypes of being a dumb whore. A big part of entertainment likes to portray us that way. I've had people tell me it's impossible for blondes to be virgins because we were born to be whores as if our hair color affects our choices in life. I am not so perfect. Everyone gets judged for something in life. I also happen to be an unmarried woman at my age who chose to go to college instead of having kids."

This session was not going the way I'd planned at all. At least I knew David couldn't fire me over it. I was certain he'd support whatever I needed to tell them to get them to open up about their own life.

Claire scowled at me as if I'd called her a name. "I still don't like you."

I leaned towards her again. "That's okay with me. I only need you to understand I'm not the enemy. I know you think you can't trust me but I'm here for you guys. I believe in helping people who have mental health problems. I don't brush it off like it's no big deal. A healthier mind makes for a happier life. You deserve that."

"That would be great to hear if I had any mental problems, but my mind is good to go." She chewed on the stick more and it snapped between her teeth. She tossed it to the side.

The stick had been chewed on like it were a dog bone for a dog. Why would she even need it?

"Claire, I'm being serious." I gave her a stern raised eyebrow.

She grabbed another stick from the drawer and began chewing. "So am I. I don't have anything wrong in the mental department. Oh, my bad. I assume David doesn't want you to know there's nothing mentally wrong with us." She circled her stick, pointing it at me.

I wasn't sure where to begin questioning her. She was eating wood, and I wanted to get to the bottom of that but at the same time, I wasn't sure if she was telling the truth or not. "Why should I believe you? Patients can lie. They may tell me they are capable of handling life without any help. It doesn't mean I take their word for it."

She took a deep breath. "Look, Norma, I know you seem to think you run the show around here because you're above us but you're not our boss. You can't force words out of us. You're just the therapist. We are not obligated to talk to you."

An idea popped into my head. I had a theory I needed to test out. "No? What if I tell David you've rejected my help?" I folded my hands together.

I saw her muscles go rigid as she swallowed what I assumed was a glint of terror in her eyes. "Tell him."

Checking my watch, I glanced at her. "I can end this session now and tell David that I can't help you until you want help. Anyone knows that change doesn't happen unless the person themselves wants to reform themselves." I shrugged my shoulders. "It's the truth. I can't do much more for you here. I'm wasting my time if you are not open to therapy—therapy that I could be offering more of to Spence and Emilie since they're more willing to try."

Claire snapped her stick using her hands. "You have no idea what will happen if you do that."

I closed in on her, whispering, "Then tell me and let me understand."

Her eyes darted to the door. "Fine. I was born in a small town in Romania. You wouldn't know it."

"Romania?" I sat back against the back of my chair. "I never would have guessed. You don't have an accent at all. Were you there for a very short period?"

Her eyes narrowed at me as the corner of her lip curved upward. "I'm a lot older than I look."

"And I'm younger than I appear. I guess we both fooled one another." I flashed her the same smirk.

She pointed her stick at me, or at least one of the halves. "You're not like the other therapists."

"Glad to hear it. I try not to be."

I was making a small dent in this session and that was what mattered. Claire wasn't so bad. She just had firm walls and I couldn't blame her for that.

She pulled her legs up on the bed and threw her torn stick to the floor. "I've been here for at least seven years."

I almost choked on my own breath. "Seven years? That's quite a long time. I imagine you want to get out someday." She'd been here longer than my car had existed.

She leaned her head against the wall. "Wow, Spence was right. You have no idea what's happening."

"What are you talking about?"

Claire shook her head and ran her fingers through her hair. "We are never getting out of here. It won't be long before you either agree with it or they remove you from the staff because you don't. It always happens. I give you a month, maybe three weeks."

I furrowed my brows and let out a laugh at the wrong time. "What? I'm sorry for my outburst but I don't know what I'm supposed to believe."

The strong wind outside hit the side of the building, causing the silence to dissipate within milliseconds.

"You may not understand now but you will. I'm afraid that's time." She gave me a small nod.

I checked my watch. She was right; our session was over. I stood from my chair and gave her a smile. "You're not so bad, Claire. If you ever want to talk to me any longer than that, you're always welcome to let me know." I exited her room and kept a grin plastered to my expression. I made progress with her.

As I walked down the hall, I ran into one of the other doctors. "My bad, I'm clumsy sometimes." I fixed my clothes before looking up at him.

He gave me what was his attempt at a smile, but it was disturbed. Something about it made me feel uncomfortable in my own skin. "It's no worry. It happens."

I stepped around him and hurried down the hall, refusing to look back. Something about the malignant look in his eyes made my skin crawl and I was not about to take any risk in finding out where his problem began and personality ended.

My mind kept wandering back to what Claire had said to me about none of them being mentally ill. Why else would they be here if that wasn't true? They weren't physically deformed and disabled in any way. There was no answer that I could fit into the equation for this to make sense.

Part of me wondered if I was in a psychological movie. The questions continued to pile up, but the answers never surfaced.

IX

Passing by my office, I peeked inside. I almost jumped when Monique appeared behind me as I turned around. "I didn't see you there," I said. "In case you're wondering what I'm doing, I'm just going over the basics again to remind myself where things are and what gets done and when." I read over my list again.

Monique nodded as she nudged my shoulder with hers. "Understandable."

I stared at her shoulder before shaking my head. "Is there anything you need, or Dr. Harrison needs?"

"Nothing in particular. Although I was going to ask if you'd like to help me with something and we could get to know each other more."

"I suppose that couldn't hurt." I tucked my list under my arm. "What do you need help with?"

She pointed to the end of the hall. "There's a pesky rat over there and David tasked me with getting rid of it. But I know next to nothing about rats. Any suggestions?"

With a laugh, I shook my head due to her disgust. Most people were grossed out by rats. "Yes, actually. I used to have a pet rat when I was younger. Her name was Snowball because she was white, of course. Beautiful red eyes. Sweetest little creature. My parents let her stay with me, so I have a specific fondness of rats. We're going to get him out of that wall safely and find him somewhere else to live." I'd drive miles to the next town just to drop him off with someone who'd want him, if he was safe to be around that was.

"What do they like?"

I waved her to follow me to the kitchen. "Well, rats tend to go for berries a lot of times. Fruits. If that doesn't work we'll try cheese, and peanut butter."

Monique and I gathered the food needed to lure the rat out, and when we approached the end of the hall, I kneeled. "The key is to be silent. You don't want to let them think you're there. The more they know about your presence, the less likely they are to come out of hiding. They need to feel safe."

She laughed. "Do you use that same tactic on the patients?"

As I smiled cheekily, I laid out the fruits and berries before stepping out of sight. I put my finger to my lips, and after a few minutes passed, he slowly came out, headed for the berries. I leaned down and scooped him up with a small bag. "Can never be too careful. Rats carry many diseases."

She rolled her eyes. "That is why I came to you. I'm not touching that damn thing."

I carried the bag out of the building and looked at the rat. "Well, little guy, I can't do much from here on out. Winter is harsh this year, and it's not safe to risk bringing you into town *if* you are dangerous." Lowering the bag, I released him into the wild, certain he wouldn't survive long. But it wasn't my job to save everyone, was it?

I certainly felt guilt eat away at a small portion of my heart, but I had to put all these people's lives above that of a rodent with potential diseases. It wasn't personal. It was just simply survival of the fittest.

On my way back inside, Monique thanked me for getting rid of the rat. It had really been no big task for me. I was happy to help. However, she said the next step was to thoroughly clean the kitchen and check the food. It wasn't uncommon for people to find mice or rats in their homes, restaurants, or any building where food was.

And there was a chance some of that food could have been contaminated, sure. But the kitchen here at Monstrum Asylum was large.

Still, I helped Monique clean it. David appraised our success, and as much as I wanted to ask him for a little extra money for extra work, I didn't.

The day I walked through those doors, David reminded me of what this job entailed. Aside from talk therapy and the patients, chores came with it. I was tempted to turn it down, but something called me here. Something told me I needed to be here. I didn't believe much in fate, or maybe I did.

I stayed anyway.

Turning to leave his office, I stopped when he said something.

"Miss Witlow, I truly am grateful that you stepped up and

helped Monique. It's a trait I admire." He gave me a side glance. He filed a few papers in the cabinet before closing and locking the drawer.

"Thank you, sir. I intend to pull my weight around here. You took a chance on a psychologist fresh out of university."

"I do believe in giving everyone chances to prove themselves. This is America, is it not? Innocent until proven *guilty*." Something about the way his tone shifted sparked something deep down. It didn't sit right, but I couldn't quite place why. So, I dropped it.

He turned to face me. "But Miss Witlow, I do expect the utmost respect around here. You know my rules. I'm sure you won't stray far from them as they are there for your safety and the patients'. I know curiosity is a strong force to reckon with, but it did kill the cat. I chose you for a reason, because I have faith you are great at what you do. Don't disappoint me."

It was an odd thing to say, but I agreed to follow the rules.

When I left his office, I peeked at the stairs that led to the basement. Rules. Right. Rules are rules—meant to keep me *safe*.

I headed for bed but getting to sleep was a whole other problem. The temperature continued to drop by one degree every few minutes. I checked the barometer on my nightstand, and by midnight, it had dropped below zero. Not freezing, but zero, which was *well* below freezing. And the inside of the building wasn't that much warmer. It felt as if it were barely fifty-five in here.

I jumped out of the bed and headed to the kitchen for a snack. A warm snack, that was. Anything that would at least keep me alive through the night.

"Awake so late?" a female voice asked. Claire, of course.

I'd passed by her door so she could see me through the tiny

window to her room. "That is not any of your concern, Claire. Go back to bed."

"Hard to sleep in this temperature."

Unfortunately, she was right. "I can grab you more blankets."

She laughed. "They're not for me. They're for you. I prefer the cold."

"If that's the case, then it's best if you go back to bed. I promise not to be loud or keep you awake."

"Is that Nora?" Emilie asked, peeking through.

"Emilie, Claire, go back to bed. Please. I will not ask again. A healthy mind needs sleep."

"Says the woman who's up past midnight."

Straightening my posture, I started walking down the hall. "I do not need to explain myself to you. I am a grown woman." And all I was getting was something to help me get to sleep in the first place. The sooner I left them, the less of an excuse they had to stay up.

I found my snacks in the pantry and carried them back to the bedroom. Munching on spicy snacks was really the only way I could think of to get my core temperature up. On the plus side, spicy snacks were tasty.

After the snacks settled and I stopped shivering, I managed to finally get some sleep.

The sun was bright in the sky, but it made no difference the moment I stepped inside the new house I'd purchased. Well, new to me. Old to history.

The layout of the house struck me as odd. When I first walked in, I stood in a long hallway that went farther right than it did left. On the opposite side of the front door were other doors to rooms. No open layout. Just a hallway and the many rooms it carried.

However, exploring these rooms was last on my mind. On the same wall as the front door, to my left just a few feet down stood an elevator. Not the fancy new elevators you'd find in homes of the rich but rather the old style with the bar doors where you could see into the elevator as it went up or down.

So that was where my adventure took me.

The lighting in this house was dim. Dingy. Unpromising.

I took the elevator down to the basement floor. Every small sound echoed, and every loud one almost threatened my eardrums. But something felt off. Wrong.

Something sinister was lurking in the shadows.

I ventured further in, unable to control any real choices I made. Laughter bounced between the walls. Something squeezed my chest. I couldn't breathe, and I knew that something pure evil was hiding in this basement.

Taking the elevator back up, I found a doll sitting on a bench across from the entryway. My chest tightened and I ran for the front door as the darkness attempted to swallow me whole, to grasp my ankle and trap me forever.

I made it into the sun and dropped to my knees, allowing myself to cry. My father, who'd helped me move my things, ran to my aid. "Nora, what happened?"

"I can't go back in there. I can't live here." I had never felt stronger evil in my life, but something about it screamed not only to stay out of the basement, but to leave the house entirely. It wasn't safe.

My father wasted no time helping me with my bags and taking me back to the truck. I stayed with him for hours, afraid to move a muscle. I was starving, but it didn't really mean anything right now. I had put all my life savings into a house that had been cursed. A house built by demons. A house truly owned by the devil himself.

And no matter how hard I tried, I couldn't escape the feeling of pure anguish as I stepped into that basement. I could have run sooner.

I should have. But I had no control over my own body now. Not here.

But what could it mean?

What could it mean?

Losing a house in the span of minutes. Regretting decisions almost immediately. Being trapped with immense wickedness that I was suffocating.

Goosebumps rose on every inch of my skin, and I knew a part of it stemmed from my fear of going down into the basement. David warned me not to, and maybe he had a point. Maybe it was dangerous. Maybe there was nothing down there and it wasted my time.

Or maybe something else lurked down there, waiting for its prey. And much like my nightmare, it was tempting to find out what it was. Could it be something harmful, or was I really trying to paint ghosts onto canvas' where they didn't belong?

Checking the time on my watch, it read 3:15.

They said it was the most active time of the night, and just because I didn't know if I truly believed in that world, didn't mean I wasn't aware of its rules and superstitions.

3:15 AM. The devil's hour.

One thing I was certain about was my beliefs on coincidences. They didn't exist. Everything had a reason, and there was one behind why I had such a sinful nightmare at such a deadly minute.

Also known as the witching hour.

But certainly, witches weren't real, were they? Not the ones you heard about in movies. With magic. Power. Spells.

At this point, I couldn't be too sure about what I believed. I would leave anything up to chance when it came to a world that we couldn't see. Or maybe we could, and I had just been blind to it all this time.

X

"David, can I ask you a question?" I leaned against the frame of his office.

He looked away from his desk to meet my gaze. "What is it?" his space had been perfectly organized which struck me as odd, considering the few things I'd come to know about him thus far.

Shrugging, I asked, "Is there some particular reason why the names of the patients here aren't public? Every other hospital makes that a public record. I mean, these people have family that might want to come and see them."

He sat back in his chair and crossed his arms. "It's a complicated explanation."

I took a step forward. "I have time."

He stood up, attempting to intimidate me with his height.

"Nora, we should discuss this later."

"Why?"

"Because you are here to help them, and not question me. Go do your job." His eyes narrowed.

I was tempted to say something in return, and as much as I wanted to, it wouldn't have been a smart idea on my part. To put these patients first, they needed me *here*. I wasn't about to get myself fired.

Turning on my heel, I exited the office and walked towards the main area. Monique joined, walking alongside me. "Where are you off to?"

As I scanned the halls, I had to come up with an answer because I truly had no clue. "I was going to keep an eye on the patients. Maybe I could befriend them some more. They deserve some human interaction, more than they get."

"You really care about them," she said.

With a smile, I stopped in the entertainment room. "They're my patients. It's my job to care about them. Besides, I understand the basic needs of humans. Being loved is one of them. Maslow's Hierarchy of Needs is a great study of human beings and the mind. We all have five basic needs to survive here." I tilted my head at Emilie.

Monique gently hit my shoulder. "You just remember to be careful. I wouldn't want anything bad to happen to you." Her footsteps faded away as she disappeared down the hall.

Whatever she meant by that, I brushed it off.

I walked over to Emilie and sat down on the floor, planting myself beside her. "What's on your mind?"

She looked at me for a second before her eyes darted towards Claire. She turned her head away from me, focusing on the wall instead.

I glanced back at Claire and stood from my seat. It was her turn to talk to me for a bit, so I stopped in front of her, blocking her lighting.

She scowled. "What do you want from me?"

She came with *bite*, but I wasn't at all afraid of her. There was no way she could get rid of me.

"Are you the leader of this little group?" I gestured to Spence and Emilie.

She shrugged, gaze flickering from me to the window. "If you call it that. We aren't a group. We just have to stick together."

"I understand that. It's great that you guys want to support one another." I dropped onto the ottoman in front of her. "But I'm not the enemy. I just want to help you. It's safe to tell me how you feel. I won't use it against you in any way."

Claire responded by spitting at me, to which I closed my eyes and wiped my cheek. "Fuck you. We don't need your help." She leaned back, giving me the dirtiest look she could manage on her flawless face.

I bit my tongue to keep from saying something inappropriate. Claire was something else, but I had to keep my cool if I was to get anywhere with her.

I got up from my spot and fixed my dress. "Let me put on some music then." I walked over to the record player and laid on a record, fixing the tonearm until it came in clear as day. I turned, letting out a gasp at the body inches away from me. Spence had gotten too close, too fast. "May I help you?" I lifted my eyes to meet his.

He pointed back at Claire using his thumb. "Don't take it personally. She is always this miserable."

"Noted." I stepped around him just as my hand brushed his. It meant nothing, but it sparked something.

Something pure.

Unguarded.

Unblemished.

Dismissing whatever it was, I cleared my throat, taking a moment to study Claire, Spence, and Emilie. They all seemed to be just fine, yet my eyes grew heavier by the second. I couldn't explain why this was happening to me, and to me alone. I'd gotten wonderful sleep the night before, but now it was as if I hadn't slept in a few days.

"Nora?" Spence's voice echoed.

I blinked a few times and looked over at Emilie who had concern written all over her face. My ankle bent sideways as I lost my footing for a moment, but I grabbed onto the bookshelf for stability.

Nothing seemed to keep me awake at a time like this. My eyes were too heavy for me to keep open, but once they were shut, I was drifting away from this land and into another. No—I was *falling*.

I heard my name being called but the voices transformed into something more haunting.

A soft humming floated through the air as my feet pressed into a cloud-like surface.

My vision returned, but I wasn't in Monstrum Asylum anymore. I stood in the middle of a dark forest while tombstones formed a circle around a statue that served as a water fountain.

Fog rolled in, blanketing the ground until it became no more. The once pure water had turned to blood in an instant, contaminating the fountain and all those who had touched it.

I spun around, attempting to spot a trail back to the asylum but I came up empty. I had no idea how I ended up out here or if I could find my way back. The most peculiar part about it was the lack of snow on the ground. Where had it all disappeared to?

A bright light blinded me before my eyes adjusted. I took in my surroundings and noticed the doctors that hovered above me, invading my personal bubble. Had I died?

"What happened?" I sat up and threw my feet over the edge of the bed.

David came forward. "You passed out. We haven't been able to determine why this happened, but we hope it doesn't happen again. I suggest you get some rest."

It would have been risky to argue, so I took his advice and headed back to my room. After closing the door behind me, I settled into the pillows on my bed and pulled a few files I'd taken into my lap.

I tried to do some more digging, but it appeared too difficult to gather any crucial information on Monstrum Asylum.

I observed the clock like a hawk until enough time passed for everyone to head to bed. It was my turn to explore this place and uncover the dark secrets lurking in the shadows.

Before going further, I made sure to trade in for slippers while ensuring my clothes were toasty.

The darkness took hold of the empty hall, indicating it was safe for me to leave my room without being questioned. I shuffled down to the end where I found the stairs that led down to the basement. If they kept files anywhere, it would be the one floor that most people were too terrified to approach.

As my feet landed on the ground floor after the last step, I looked ahead of me and soaked in the view of pitch black. It engulfed me as I took a few steps forward. Minutes passed and as soon as that fourth minute hit, my eyes adjusted. Objects could now be made out in the abyss.

I entered double doors that were a few feet down the hall and to my right. I didn't see much aside from the outline of dozens of chairs. It took me a few moments to process where I'd ended up, but the red curtain soon told me everything.

This asylum had to be much older than I was being told. The entire basement had been abandoned—no employees to show this floor any love. The wear and tear on the furniture here was a result of years of decay.

There had been a time when patients could relax and watch entertainment in this auditorium. I wasn't sure why they would shut it down. Entertainment was always suggested for anyone wanting to get their mind off the seriousness for a little while. Life could be cruel.

Behind me, the double doors swung open, and I turned around to see who had caught me in my crimes. Nobody stood there but I had a duty to kill the *cat* within me.

I rushed over to the doors and poked my head out, looking both ways down the hall, not a single soul in sight. I backed away from the doors and inhaled. I held my breath for a few seconds before exhaling again. "There is nothing there, Nora. It's all in your head. You know how the mind can screw with someone's reality."

I'd seen enough horror movies in my day to associate old basements with it. My brain had been wired to see ghosts in these walls. I knew better. They weren't here; they were inside my head.

Leaving the auditorium, I headed towards the stairs, but something caught my eye. I approached the object, picking up the book that splayed on the ground. It was the same book that belonged to Emilie. Why had it been down here?

Voices echoed from the auditorium, causing me to nearly jump out of my skin. Nobody could be down here at this time. I was meant to be alone.

Walking through the doors, I looked towards the stage and widened my eyes upon the scene.

The stage lit up, all three patients present, having a conversation. Some furniture from the entertainment room on the main floor was set up to provide them with some props.

I stumbled forward and cleared my throat. "What are you doing down here?"

I received no response. They hadn't even reacted to my words. It was as if they couldn't hear me in the slightest.

Claire sat on the couch as she always had while Emilie curled up in the corner away from everyone else. Spence walked behind the couch, pacing across the floor.

"It was strange, don't you agree?" He turned and faced Claire.

She shrugged off all problems. "Why should I care?"

Spence shook his head in disagreement, glancing at something to his left. "Claire, I'm here to question the odd things. It wasn't normal the way she passed out like that. Something else is happening."

A small voice chipped in, "Is she sick?" Emilie's compassionate demeaner made my heart swell with content.

I had to remind myself this wasn't *real*.

They were talking about me, of course, but how was this possible? They couldn't see me. They weren't supposed to be in the basement. No patients were to ever step foot down here.

I wasn't to even step foot down here.

"There are two theories to this. Either Nora is sick and nobody knows, or the other doctors did this to her. If that's the case, she's on our side." Spence shot a look at Claire who snickered. "Not all of them are bad people. Maybe Nora is one of the good ones. We may be able to trust her."

Claire shot up and marched over to him, grabbing the collar of his shirt. "Don't you dare fuck this up for us. She isn't one of the good ones. If you tell her, I will rip your balls off and feed them to you. That is a promise, Spence. We have nobody to trust but ourselves. They put us here, and they won't be the ones to get us out."

He didn't dare push her away from him even if it caused something dark inside him to boil. "No matter which theory is true, she's not the bad guy. We don't have to treat her like one."

"They're all villains. When they took this job, they became villains. Emilie was taken away from the life she finally came to love. I was judged for my choices. You were judged for who your parents are. Never forget what they've stolen from us. Our freedom has been stripped away for their gain." She let go of his shirt and stepped away to return to him his space.

He ran his hands through his hair and glanced at Emilie who stayed in her corner. "I have a mind of my own, and I'll think for myself. If I conclude that she's able to be trusted, you can't stop me. I'm not afraid of you, Claire. You may scare Emilie, but you can't scare me into submission. Please, do not make me release my demon." His eyes fixed on her again.

A smirk grew on her face as she turned to face me. "Why not? It would be quite fun, don't you think? We could make Nora scream and run for the hills. It would solve our problem."

"She is not a problem. I don't think she even knows what's happening here. She's a victim as much as the rest of us," he said in a frustrated tone, his rage beginning to slip between his teeth.

Emilie added, "She doesn't. I spoke with her, and it really does sound like she has no idea what this place really is. She thinks it's just another asylum."

Claire's eyes locked with mine, and my heart stopped for a

split second. “You two have to ask yourself, which side would she choose if it came down to it? That’s a chance I’m not willing to take.”

XI

The wind whipped through my hair as I kept a close eye on all my patients. We came out here for some fresh air today, but I couldn't seem to erase the scene I'd watched a few nights before.

This breeze had been stronger and much more brutal. It slapped my face with its sharp, icy hatred. Although, I couldn't decipher whether it was the wind that despised me or Claire herself.

Spence came over to me, not giving me a single sign about the conversation he'd had with Claire and Emilie. None of them knew that I heard it. It was either that or I'd imagined it all, meaning the conversation never happened. If I had witnessed a true event, how was it possible? No logical conclusion could be made.

He approached me with caution as if I were a ticking time bomb. I was far from that, but I was certain that I was losing my sanity in this place.

"Nora, you seem very distant. Is everything all right?" he asked.

When I met his gaze, the look in his eyes was of genuine concern and nothing more. He knew better than anyone to judge my mind. He was a patient himself.

"Everything is fine. I've just been trying to think of ways to help you guys open up to me for your benefit." That was my best lie.

"Pardon my French, Nora, but that is bullshit and we both know it. Your mind is elsewhere." He glanced at Claire. "Is it because of what she said?"

It related to what she said, but I didn't know where to begin to explain that. I couldn't let any of them know what I saw in that auditorium. One thing was sure, and that was that I'd be visiting the basement again tonight. I had answers waiting for me.

I furrowed my brows, debating which direction to take this lie. "It would seem silly to admit what Claire said got to me. I have thicker skin, Spence. What is on my mind is my business. I hope you can understand."

"I understand the blind can't lead the blind. I also happen to understand that it's easier to open up to someone you can trust but if that person doesn't trust you, why should you trust them? I apologize if I've offended you, but I want to give you the perspective of being a patient here. We open up when you do." He bowed his head before turning and walking away.

It wasn't supposed to be a two-way street. It was not part of my job to reveal my life story to strangers.

And yet, you expect them to do just that.

When the time was up, I waved everyone over and followed them back inside. The cool air lingered on my clothes even after I'd been in for a couple of minutes.

I grabbed the collar of my coat, fixing its position. "Let me help," a male said.

"I've got it but thank you." I took my coat off before he had a chance. Inappropriate it was. He was a mysterious fellow, one that never failed to amaze me. One moment, he was telling me to reveal who I was but then he would offer his kindness through small gestures. I turned to head back to David's office. Someone called my name and I looked back at the three patients. "Did someone call my name?"

Claire laughed as if it was the funniest thing in the world. "Conceited much? Nobody said your name."

Knitting my eyebrows, I faced forward again. I swore I'd heard it. It wasn't unusual to mishear things. People did it all the time.

Someone whispered in my ear, "You killed her…"

I whipped around to see Claire, Emilie, and Spence heading the other direction towards the entertainment room.

Hurrying towards the office, I was colored with surprise when David wasn't there. Where he had gone was unknown to me and I wasn't sure where to even begin to look for him.

The whole floor seemed to be empty now. I had to peek into a file while I had the opportunity.

I opened the filing cabinet and found Spence's folder. I pulled it out and opened it up. A small gasp escaped me as I read the information on his admission to Monstrum—admitted a few years back. Was he so troubled or closed off that nobody could help him?

As my fingers lifted the paper to view the photos underneath, a voice startled me and the folder flew out of my hands, landing in a jumbled mess. "David, I am so sorry." I stood and faced him, shaking my head. "I just wanted to know a bit about Spence. He is a tough egg to crack open."

David reached down and picked up the papers and closed the folder before putting it back in the file cabinet. "You still know the policy. He must be able to open up to you himself. We need to know if he will trust you. Without trust, there is no cure."

I nodded and waited in the doorway. I was embarrassed to have been caught snooping. It was wrong of me to go against anyone's wishes to achieve my own. "It may take me a while. He is very keen on telling me his secrets if I expose my own. He has a hard time understanding how this works."

He looked at me and cleared his throat. "Well, if you can get him to open up by telling him about yourself, why not try it?"

"It's my personal life, and I don't want to have to reveal who I am to patients just because they can't talk to me. I will find a way to help them, but I won't tell them who I am in the process. That's for me to know. I don't get paid to tell my patients my personal business." I clasped my hands together.

He shook his head. "No, but you are being employed and housed to help these patients. And if it helps them, why is that wrong? What harm does it do?"

"With all due respect, Dr. Harrison, I don't need a hovering worry of Claire escaping and threatening my loved ones. She strikes me as the violent type. I would never put my little brother in harm's way like so. He does not have the physical capabilities to even hear her coming. Have a good night." I turned on my heel and headed back to my room.

It struck me as odd that David would even suggest I tell my

patients my private life. It was out of line.

I took a stroll past the rooms with my slippers, ready to take on the mysteries. Something out of the ordinary had happened the other night and I had to explain it.

"Where are you off to this late?" a voice asked to my left.

I fixed my eyes on the name of the door. "Why are you up this late?"

"I have a severe case of insomnia, Nora," he whispered. "What about you?"

I chewed on my lip for a moment, hesitating on answering him or not. "I just wanted to explore this place. It's grand and full of so many secrets."

Those blue eyes—the color of thin ice on a lake—peered through the small slot in his door. "Have you discovered anything interesting yet?"

My steps were careful as I closed the large gap between us. "As a matter of fact, I have." There was plenty in that basement calling out my name.

"What did you find?" Intense perfectly described his gaze, exposing my vulnerability. I swore he could see into my soul.

I fixed my robe a bit and glanced at the darkness growing inside the halls. "Why is that your business? If you excuse me, I have to continue my adventure."

As I started my way down the hall, something he said stopped me. "Let me go with you."

"That's a silly idea. I could never trust you to be alone, roaming the halls when everyone is asleep."

"Who says I can trust the doctors? You don't need trust in this place for some adventure. If you've seen my file, you would discover that I don't have violent tendencies. Claire is more likely to lash out if anything. If you want me to open up about my past, let me stretch my legs for a bit. I've never been harmful. Think about it, Nora. Being locked up in a cell is no way to cure the mind. If our mind is already a cell, being here just comes full circle."

Something about him intrigued me. His intelligence was a book I wanted to open and read. It was risky to even let him out, but he'd been right. He was indeed one of the calmer ones. I had never once suspected savagery. If that scene had been true, he never even used brutality against Claire when she grabbed his collar.

"All right. If you ruin this for us, I will…" I couldn't finish my sentence. My threat was empty, and we both saw past my lies. I'd never been able to hurt someone who hadn't hurt me first.

"Message received." He chuckled.

I left him while I made a trip to David's office. I turned the knob and looked at the wall behind the door when I peeked inside. I squinted my eyes as I grabbed the keys off the wall that had Spence's last name above them. I slowly closed the door behind me, careful to keep it quiet.

I hurried back down the hall and stopped at his door. My heart began to race as I put the key in the lock and turned until it clicked. I peered up at him, swallowing my fear. I refused to show him any of that.

When he hadn't opened the door, I pulled it open for him. "Are you coming?"

As he stepped out, he flashed me a grin. "I'm ready."

We made our way down to the basement, but my hands grew

clammy. This whole situation put me on high alert. Spence stayed by my side—cautious not to make any sudden moves as if I were some kind of cop. Either way, none of it explained why my heart was pounding inside my chest like it had been the first time me and my ex-fiancé decided to take our relationship to a physical level.

"What are you hoping to find?" Spence nudged my side.

I shrugged my shoulders. "Anything that tells me the truth about this place. There's not much information in the files and I have a lot of questions that David won't answer."

Something down the hall thumped and we both halted in our tracks. He'd heard that, right? Was I crazy?

"Nora, what is it?"

Shaking my head, I started walking. He must not have witnessed anything. If I mentioned hearing a noise, he would assume I was the one who belonged here, under the care of the doctors. They all believed that enough as it was. I didn't need to further prove them right.

I pushed through the double doors of the auditorium and kept my eyes glued to the stage. It was vacant and falling apart.

As if on cue, the stage light turned on and out came a woman. I gulped down the lump in my throat as her face came into view and I watched the same scene replay.

"I guess I must do it alone," she said. And just like that, she was gone. Her heart stopped beating and she would never return home to her family.

I used the back of my hand to wipe away a stray tear before looking up at Spence. "Did you see that?"

"See what?" My heart shattered at his question. It shattered into a million pieces. Again. And again. And *again.*

I leaned forward, the grin on my face growing wider. "Into the tunnel he goes; under the earth it blows." I blew my hands out to imitate an explosion.

Claire sent a snicker with a roll of her eyes. "Yeah, great story. Talk about explosions underground and give us more fears when we've got nowhere to go."

"Miss Anderson," David started, "do you think there's going to be an explosion in our basement?"

Emilie and Spence both turned to face her as her cheeks reddened. "Well, thank God for therapists then," Spence said with a snort. "We've got access to a free one if you need it."

Claire dismissed his insult and folded her arms across her chest, fingers holding her biceps. "I'd like to go to bed. Too much socializing for a day."

David checked the time. "I suppose it is about that time. All right then, everyone. Off to bed. Let's go."

Chairs scooted and feet shuffled as everyone else followed him to their rooms where he locked them in for the night.

At least I'd never have to worry about such a thing happening to me. Which was why I wanted to fight so hard to get the three of them out of here. Nobody deserved to be locked up in a cage for eternity.

I wasn't entirely sure how much time passed before I got up from the chair. When I did, I didn't head to my room for a good night's rest. I found myself standing at Spence's door. About to turn around and go back, someone coughed from inside. An overpowering stench of skunk drifted through the tiny, barred window. “Spence?”

“Yeah?”

“What are you doing?”

Silence. Then… “Nothing I'd feel comfortable telling my therapist.”

“Do I smell dope in there?” I kept my voice barely above a whisper just for his sake. Who knew what David would do if he found out.

Bare feet slapped against the concrete. “Maybe.” His blue eyes appeared, causing me to stumble back in surprise. “Am I in trouble? Claire gave it to me.”

Someone hissed a few doors down. “You’re too easy to chop.”

“Cool it, Claire.”

Tilting my head, I said in a quiet voice, “I’m not here to get you into trouble. I won’t tell David.” I ensured Claire heard the last part. I found myself believing the auditorium scene to be more and more true every morning. “As your therapist, all I ask is that you not bury all your problems with drugs. They sound nice in the moment, but running away is going to repeat this cycle of abuse.”

Claire snickered.

Spence’s eyes dropped as he said, “I’m not going to become an addict. I tried it, but it’s not for me. Besides, who says I’m running? I can’t go anywhere.”

“Exactly my point,” I whispered.

Quiet breathed life into this hall, and so did the footsteps that echoed down at the end where the stairs stood. I glanced over, but no face ever became clear. The footsteps hadn’t even moved. They never grew more distant, nor got louder.

“Goodnight, Spence.”

As I spun on my heel to head for my room, his voice stopped

me in its tracks. Deep. Gravel. Powerful, and chilling all at once. I'd never forget it.

"Nightmares are based in reality, Nora. Yours smell delightful to devour."

XII

Night fell—and hard. Winter left very little light to shine through the windows during the day, so when darkness came, it became almost pitch black as if a storm had rolled in. Snow was white, of course, but it never reflected it that way.

Patients returned to their rooms and doctors called it quits on the paperwork. I hid out in my room until the coast became clear, and then I was up and out. That stage was beginning to become an addiction. An infatuation. A mystery to be solved, and I wanted to learn more about it than anything else here.

That's where I headed. The basement.

Just as I took a step down, someone or something breathed on my ear. I twisted around too quickly, catching a faint glimpse of a woman as I fell down the steps. I managed to reach out and grab hold of the railing, stopping my fall.

As I lay across the stairs, my eyes darted back towards the top where she once stood. Whoever she was, she'd left now.

For a fleeting moment, I begged Spence to come to my aid and whisk away the fear. However, it was a transient thought.

I pulled myself back to my feet, keeping my fingers wrapped tightly around the rail. Maybe it would be smart to turn back now, and I desperately wanted to. But she was up there. I couldn't go back now, at least not without more answers than I had started with.

So I descended to the basement instead.

Voices echoed throughout the halls, whispering from every direction. I swear I'd heard my name, but I knew it was yet another hallucination. These walls spoke to me but as a psychologist, I knew how the human mind worked. Exactly as it was.

I found the double doors that led back to the auditorium, and when I stepped inside, disappointment coursed through my veins. No scene played before my eyes. Not Spence, Emilie, nor Claire stood on the stage with more secrets to pour out. The room was utterly empty.

The voices continued to bounce between walls, but this time, they came from another direction. I would have ignored them, but what was my other option? I refused to go back to the main level where *she* waited in the dark—like a predator stalking its prey.

I ventured deeper. Further.

The voices grew louder, and my suspicions heightened with them.

I stopped just outside of an unfamiliar door to a room I'd never explored. I reached for the knob, ready to turn, but I froze when I heard, "Monique, grab the blood bag."

Rustling.

"We could make this easier. All you need to do is simply give us what we want, and this blood is yours."

"Never," someone spat. I recognized that voice, but whose was it?

The male doctor said, "Suit yourself." David. No, that couldn't be right. Why would David be down here conducting something this vile? It sounded so inhumane from this side of the door.

Silence ensued, and moments later, the knob turned, and I stepped back. Before I could hide, Monique walked out with a bag of blood in her hand. "Nora."

My heart began to race, pounding in my ears. I almost couldn't hear my words come out of my mouth. "What's going on in there?" I hadn't planned to call out David or anyone else this early, not without knowing what the hell had been happening inside this building. I'd trapped myself. Now, I was required to prove to the patients that I was solely here for them. I'd choose their side.

"That is none of your business." She closed the door.

My eyes darted to the blood bag. She followed my line of sight. In seconds, I ducked when she attempted to throw her arms around me. I knocked my entire body into her legs, pinning them against the door. She groaned and dropped the blood bag right on my head. Blood spilled from my roots to my ends, dripping down my face as if it were my own.

Monique started pulling, but I twisted my legs and threw her into the wall across from us, backing into the door. I turned the knob and stumbled into the well-lit room, blinded by all the lighting.

"Nora," David started, "What are you doing down here?"

When my eyes adjusted, I blinked a few times and scanned the room. In the middle sat Claire, strapped to a chair. What the hell was going on in this place?

"I could ask you the same question, Dr. Harrison." Lifting my chin, I tore my eyes away from Claire's.

Gently, he set the needle down on a tray. "Why don't you tell me what you think it looks like?"

This was my chance to play my cards carefully. If I flipped the death card, it could go south in milliseconds. I could endanger my own life, and then who would back up these patients? They needed a man on the inside to pull the strings.

"Sir, it sounds like you brought Claire for a medical procedure and she's afraid of a needle." Wonderful.

Something flashed in his eyes as they flicked to a figure behind me. Monique.

I ducked down as she threw herself at me, flying over and knocking into the chair with Claire. I stood and grabbed a needle from the table behind me. I reached out, moving Monique's hair away from her neck as I pushed it into her skin. Whatever the liquid was, it forced a scream from her throat.

Her body slipped off Claire's, collapsing to the ground. My eyes met with David's, and he grabbed the needle beside him. "Nora, we can talk this out."

"What the fuck are you doing to my patient?" I grabbed a scalpel. "What did she do to deserve such treatment?" With my free hand, I grabbed a lamp and threw it at him. When he was busy missing it, I started cutting the leather straps from her wrists.

With one hand free, she grabbed David's and snapped it back at the wrist. He yelled out from the pain while I helped free her entirely. I swung open the door and started running, hot on

Claire's heels. David slapped a button, calling the help of others.

I navigated my way down the hall, climbing up the stairs. "Get the keys! The fucking keys, Claire! From his office!" I grabbed hold of the corner wall at the top of the steps, using it to swing my body around and run down the hall.

I heard the jangle of keys, and through the pale moonlight, I saw her small figure opening the door to Spence's and Emilie's rooms. "What's going on?" Spence asked her. Claire didn't answer him, but instead sprinted to the entrance.

My feet slid out from under me when I tried to turn the opposite direction as the other doctors came out of the rooms in front of me, blocking my path.

"Go!" I told the three of them. But unfortunately for me, Spence came running back in my direction. I made a beeline for the door to the courtyard, pushing my legs as fast as they'd take me. My feet began to beg for mercy as the snow tried to peel them from my body.

Shoving my fingers through the loops in the wire fence, I began climbing, ignoring the stinging pain as my skin clung to the metal. Bits and layers tore off with each grip.

"No, Nora!" Spence wrapped his arms around my waist and pulled me off the fence. "There's another way," he whispered in my ear as we spun to face the doctors coming towards us.

"Another…?" Spence set me on the ground and grabbed my wrist, dragging me behind him as he dodged the doctors like a bowling ball missing the pins.

He halted when we entered the asylum, and he closed the door, turning the lock. "There's something you need to know."

"Spence, what is going on? What is David doing in the basement?"

"Claire!" Emilie shouted, and Spence moved away from me

just as Claire pinned me to the door. The knob took a hit at my lower back, and I groaned, but Claire didn't seem too focused on my well-being at the moment. No, something darker lurked behind her eyes. Something pure. Primal. Hunger.

Something wet ran up my cheek, and when I registered that she had licked my face, Spence pulled her off me. No, she was licking the *blood* off me.

"That is uncalled for. She is trying to save us," he said.

Claire scowled, eyeing me like I was a snack.

Spence glanced behind him, calling Emilie closer. The doctors outside began banging on the door, and I jumped away from it, bumping a bookshelf. "We can't leave this asylum, Nora."

"Why not?" I spun on my heel to face him.

Emilie opened her mouth to say something, but David came around the corner, cursing under his breath.

"There might be a way," Emilie tugged Spence's sleeve. "The rooftop. We go to the roof and jump off that way."

Spence gave me a look, then Claire. "It's worth a shot!" He pushed Claire and Emilie first before grabbing my hand and pulling me along for the ride.

David reached out to grab me, but I missed his arm just by an inch. He grumbled as we ran towards the stairs and started climbing.

Up one flight.

Up two.

We headed up the last flight in the direction of the roof.

Just as Claire and Emilie opened the door, snow rushed in. It began snowing again, making it that much harder to see.

My wrist slipped out of Spence's fingers as he headed up the stairs, and he looked back with wide eyes. "Nora!"

A doctor had grabbed me by the hair and yanked me

back, forcing me onto my knees. "You think you could get lucky and escape with them? No, no, no…" David circled the doctors, blocking my view of Spence. "You've overstepped your boundaries. You've caused too much chaos."

Spence tried to tackle him, but he moved out of the way, glancing back. "My peripheral still works, son." He shooed his hand. "Do it. Now."

The doctor forced me onto my stomach, pulling my hair away from my neck. I struggled, trying to find any kind of leverage. A finger. Eyes. A wrist. His dick. I needed to break something. *Anything* on his body.

"Shhh," he said as he leaned down. Something poked my neck, and it stung when whatever he injected began to slip into my veins. I screamed out as the burning sensation grew, spreading like wildfire.

"What are you doing to her?" Spence grabbed David's shoulder, pulling him back, but David didn't answer his question.

My eyelids grew heavier by the second until I couldn't keep them open any longer. As every muscle in my body went limp, the darkness swallowed me whole like the blood had the day her soul left her body.

My mind swirled in a pool of memories, but none of them formed a coherent thought.

Spence Woods. Who was he? A patient, a man who believed that if I wanted him to open up, I had to spill my own secrets first.

Claire Anderson. A woman who despised me with no real reason as to why. What had I done? No, it wasn't personal. Someone had hurt her, and they intended for her to stay that way.

Emilie Brooks. A sweet girl, yet that became a sick game for someone to play and win. With the prize, they wanted to strip her of all that made her, her.

These were my patients. I had to remember them. I needed to be there for them, to promise to help and protect at any cost—even my own life.

So, why had they not run out that door? Why had they stayed back when David caught me? And why was I thankful that they didn't leave me to die?

XIII

As I entered the cafeteria, the pale man locked me in his gaze. Spence Woods. A man of mystery. Secrets.

He stood from the table and slowly approached, which wasn't out of the ordinary. All my patients came around eventually.

"Nora, I apologize about last night."

With my brows furrowed, I couldn't recall what he was talking about. The session? Maybe. "Mr. Woods, I say this with the least amount of disrespect, but my name is Miss Witlow. You do not get to address me by Nora."

His eyebrows knitted together. "Right, I didn't mean to offend you."

"That's all right. Now, what are you apologizing for?" I peered at the table where the other doctors sat. The food on my plate was calling my name.

"Last night. What transpired. With David. Do you not remember?" A tilt of his head, and his waves of black hair swept with it.

Clearing my throat, I met his eyes. "Forgive me, Mr. Woods, but I think you might have dreamt that. Last night I was in my office with my paperwork. If you'll excuse me, I'd like to eat my food before it gets cold." I stepped around him and took a seat at the table.

Conversations took place amongst the other doctors, but none of them caught my interest. Something seemed wrong, yet I couldn't put my finger on it.

Breakfast passed and the other doctors went to fulfill their duties while I was stuck in my office. Why did everything seem off?

I pulled out my files, going back over what I had gathered so far. Spence had barely begun to open up. Emilie was getting more comfortable with me. Claire? Wasn't so sure about her. She didn't like me, and that was normal from her end. However, that didn't mean the feeling was mutual. In fact, I might have liked her more than I knew. She was an interesting soul to explore.

To pass more time, I put on background music. The noise helped block out any paranoia.

I organized my files, labeling each one appropriately. I cleaned up the space and sat back, admiring the room I now had. Whoever had worked in this office before me had no attention to detail.

Someone knocked, and I paused the record as I told them to come in. Emilie poked her head in. "May I?" I smiled and gestured for her to sit, so she did after closing the door. She rubbed her fingers over her book's cover a few times. "Spence says you were working here last night."

"I was."

Emilie nodded in the slightest. "Do you trust Mr. David?"

"Mr. David? Dr. Harrison? I mean, trust is such a strong term. I believe he is doing what he believes is best for everyone. And I'm thankful I get to be here with patients that I have the honors of helping. That's all I've wanted. I knew the second I got my degree, I was ready to take on the world."

"Will you? Take on the world?" Her eyes widened a bit.

I creased my forehead as a puzzled look overtook my expression. "It's a figure of speech, Miss Brooks. I'm not a superhero."

She deflated. "Right. I knew that."

Leaning forward, I caught her gaze. "My point is that I'm happy to be here, helping you. That was why I studied. It sounds silly but when I was a teenager, I took psychology and I loved it so much I wanted to study to become a psychologist myself. The human brain fascinates me, and with an abundance of people struggling with mental health, it's the perfect job to get into. I want to see humanity find a way back to a healthier lifestyle. That includes helping people learn to manage their mental health so they can be happy more often."

Emilie picked at her book's spine. "Then you shouldn't have taken this job. Nobody here has mental health issues, and I say this in the kindest way I can, Nora, but we are not here to be your guinea pigs. We don't want our brains, or any part of us to be studied. We just want to love and be loved."

I opened my mouth to say something, but I realized it was not the time. My job wasn't to study them like lab rats. I was here to listen and understand. I was here to love them the way they wanted to be loved. Just as she told me.

She stood and released a sigh. "Spence wants to talk to you, too, if that's all right."

With a nod, I said okay.

Emilie began towards the door, but she stopped just before and turned back to flash a small smile. "You can call me Emilie, by the way. I like it when you call me Emilie." And so Emilie left me alone, disappearing for the rest of the day.

Spence entered next, taking a seat in the chair across from me. "Miss Witlow."

"Mr. Woods, what is on your mind?" I closed a file, placing it back in the cabinet.

"I want to apologize for the piano comment I made. I shouldn't have said anything to anyone, and I definitely should not have put you on the spot like that."

What piano comment was he referring to?

As soon as he caught the confusion in my eyes, he leaned back in the chair. "You don't remember that either."

"Remember what? I don't know what prank you're trying to play on me but it's not funny. I know you don't like me much, but this is going too far. You can't just go around making the doctors think they're insane. That's a bit harsh, don't you agree?" I crossed my knee over my other leg.

"Nor—Miss Witlow, we do like you. Well, most of us. I promise that we are not trying to play any games. Just forget I said anything." He cleared his throat. "What do you remember since you got here?"

"You ask me to forget what you said and then you ask me what I remember. Contradicting you are indeed." I cupped my knee, lifting my chin some more.

"How long have you worked here?"

I smiled, just to amuse him. "Fine, if you must. Last week. It hasn't been too adventurous but that's all right by me. Suppose it gets more exciting as the day goes on."

"It's been three weeks, Nora."

My smile faltered. I didn't even acknowledge him calling me by my first name. "What? I haven't been here for three weeks."

"You have. Check the dates in your patient files." His eyes darted to my cabinet.

Keeping an eye on him, I opened the drawer and pulled out his file. I opened it up to the first page, looking at the date. It was dated just a little over two weeks ago. I glanced up at him and closed the file. "Is this some sick joke to scare me away? I don't scare easily."

Yes, you do. You're terrified of blood and stairs.

"It's not a joke. That's your handwriting."

And when I looked back at the paper, it was mine. Something was wrong, and was this what I had been feeling off about? "But how? I don't understand."

Spence hesitated. "I wish I could say, but it would be too much at once. Just know that I'm sorry I couldn't stop him."

"Stop who?" I asked just as Spence stood. "No, please, tell me."

He shoved his hands into his pockets. "Dr. Harrison warned you to stay out of the basement. Maybe you should listen this time." He turned and walked out the door.

Stay out of the basement.

However, I didn't want to listen this time. I stepped out of the office and headed towards the stairs at the end of the hall. I made sure nobody was following before I hurried down, and since it was still daytime, it made it just a bit easier to use them.

My heels clicked, and I came to an abrupt stop. Too loud. What if someone heard me?

Taking them off, I held them by the backs as I passed some

doors. What was I searching for? Would I know it when I saw it?

Some music began to play behind a pair of double doors. I pushed them open and walked inside, looking at the stage. It had been lit up while the rest of the auditorium stayed dark, and empty.

What was this place?

Screams echoed, but the source was never found.

This auditorium gave me witchy horror vibes, and like something you would see in the basement of a church in an abandoned town, one with layers of fog you couldn't find your way out of. Everyone knew the one.

We'd all been to church enough to know.

A familiar voice floated from the stage and into my ear. *"Holy fuck, our innocent Nora has done the unspeakable."* Claire said those words, but when I whipped around, nobody was there. Where had it come from? And why had she said that to me? Or about me?

I didn't spare another second for the basement. I booked it upstairs and ran straight to my room, locking the door behind me. Was it my imagination or was this place haunted? It was too big to tell.

After a good thirty minutes, I slipped down the hall and found the landline on the wall, spinning the dial. The other line rang, and then she picked up.

"Nora? Nora, do you know what time it is?" she asked. From the sound of her voice, I called when she had already gone to bed.

I ran my fingers though my hair. "I'm sorry, Mom, but I have a question. When did I leave home? To come here?" I dragged my hand down my face.

A few seconds passed before she answered. "You left about a

month ago. Why? What is this about?"

A shiver scurried up my spine.

A month. Spence wasn't lying to me. If he had been, how could he have told my parents to make up the same lie? Where had my mind gone during the last two weeks? And who was the *him* that Spence tried to stop?

"Nothing. I just think this place is giving me the creeps." I looked up at the ceiling.

"Could it be related to Alicia's death?"

"Possibly. But I doubt that."

"You know, it's not unusual. It was a pretty difficult time for you, and she was your best friend. I'd understand if you came back home."

"No, Mom. No." I pinched the bridge of my nose. "I'm fine. Trust me. I just needed to hear a familiar voice is all."

I could almost hear her smile. "Danny misses you. We all do."

Warmth flooded into my soul. "Danny—how is he?"

"He's been doing good. He's made a new friend at school and they both get along well. I think he just needed a little push to get out there and you leaving gave him the courage. He needed someone to talk to."

"I'm glad he's good. I should go, but I promise to call at a decent hour next time. Time zones are messing me up. It's been snowstorms nonstop and I—" The line went dead. "Hello? Mom?"

I looked at the phone to find that the call had been disconnected. I was lucky to even get a few minutes with her. I flinched at the screaming inside my own mind, and not soon after a burning sensation spread throughout my neck. "What the hell?" I massaged it, pulling my hand away at the ache.

Monstrum Asylum. Something was very wrong here and I had placed myself right in the middle of it. Who had taken my memories from me?

Whoever they were, they did it intentionally. While I was going to get to the bottom of this, I would need to stay low and pretend I was unaware of my surroundings. If I could keep up the act long enough to uncover the truth, maybe I could be the hero that Emilie hoped I'd be.

Could I be the hero? Maybe not in this story.

XIV

Using a scraper, I wiped a couple feet of snow from the bench before sitting on it. I faced the patients just as my stomach grumbled. I'd skipped breakfast this morning and I shouldn't have, but I couldn't take that back now. I needed to wait for lunch.

Emilie clutched her book to her chest as she conversed with Spence. I couldn't quite pick up on what they were saying, but that was none of my business anyway.

Claire used her hand to wipe the snow off beside me, sitting down. "What's going on in that pretty head of yours?"

I glanced at her. "Too much for you to know."

She shrugged. "We all talk to each other. Maybe we don't talk to you, but we trust each other. Emilie believes you've changed. She said that…maybe now you won't be so forgiving or understanding. Spence, however, said you seemed to have lost your memory of the past few weeks. He believes you're the same Nora. You just have to find her again."

"The same Nora? Which Nora did you know?" Facing her, I furrowed my eyebrows.

Claire smirked a bit. "The Nora who gave a blowjob."

I shuddered. How did she know that? "Why does that matter?"

"It doesn't. I guess sometimes I just picture you as someone else. I make these…snap judgments. And when I first saw you, I immediately thought you were this good girl who would follow every order. You'd never harm a soul. You were so closed off that even a man couldn't faze you. But someone has…if you gave him a blowjob."

"We'd been together for years. It's hardly a big deal." I shrugged off the intimate moments that now tasted sour.

She released a sigh. I don't think I'd ever heard her sigh. It sounded so odd, and out of place coming from her. "I know. And I shouldn't have made you this poster child for the good girl. You have your secrets. You have your past. I need to…learn to respect that."

Did Claire just tell me she needed to respect my privacy? Or had I misheard?

Certainly I imagined the whole thing.

Claire looked at me. "Thank you."

"For what?"

Shaking her head, she looked at Emilie and Spence again. "Someday you'll remember, hopefully. And when you do, just know that I said thank you." She stood and walked over to the other two.

Just as the snowflakes began to fall again, I headed inside and the three followed. They went to the entertainment area while I headed towards my office.

As I sat in the chair, something sparked in my memory. Something…painful. A burning sensation spread throughout my neck, but when I touched it, nothing happened. It was gone as quickly as it had come, and I was left with not a single answer.

Who was the he that Spence warned me about? And what happened in the basement?

When lunch arrived, I took my seat at the table and scarfed my food down. It was unprofessional, and unattractive. But what more could I say? I hadn't eaten in twenty hours.

Monique warned me to slow down.

David approached us while clearing his throat. "Miss Witlow, I'd like to see you in my office when you're finished."

I swallowed my bite and nodded. "Yes, sir."

He left the table, and I feared I was about to get fired. For what? What had I done wrong?

As soon as my plate was empty, I took it to the bin and headed back to his office. Fingers wrapped around my wrist and yanked me until I spun around and faced whoever they belonged to. Spence.

I glanced at his fingers, and he let go. "I apologize, but I really should warn you to just be careful." Careful about what?

Something strange fluttered in my stomach, but I buried the thought. Spence was a patient. There was nothing appropriate about that kind of feeling around a patient. I needed to nip it in the bud, or I'd have to quit my job. I'd never compromise anything for a fling.

"Are you hearing me?" Spence waved a hand in front of my face.

I nodded a little. "Yes, but I don't understand why I should be careful."

"Just…trust me. Don't go putting all your eggs in one basket, all right?" He dipped his head to put his face back in my line of sight.

"All right." I backed away before turning on my heel and finding myself at David's office. He told me to come in after I knocked, so I went in and took a seat.

His office was far larger than mine, and understandably so. The walls were lined with desks and bookshelves. However, what caught me off guard was the abundance of books based on fantasy creatures. Why would he have those? He was a doctor, and one who dealt with mentally unstable patients. "Do you know why I brought you in?"

"To fire me."

He chuckled, assuming I was making jokes. But I wasn't humored by my words in the slightest. "No, I wanted to talk to you about a…promotion. A program that I've created. You've shown me some potential and I wanted to offer a spot for you, if you'd like it."

I wasn't so quick to accept. Spence warned me, did he not? "What kind of program?"

He grabbed a file and handed it to me. "This has all the information you need. I'll let you think it over for the night, and you can get back to me tomorrow. I hope that you choose wisely."

In other words, you hope I choose you.

I gave him a nod and stood. "Thank you, Dr. Harrison. I'll be sure to give it a lot of thought." I exited the room and headed back to my office. I plopped down into the chair and opened the file, smoothing out the papers. What was this program really about?

Immediately, my heart raced at the first line. David was suggesting that I join a program for psychiatrists, and I certainly hadn't studied to be one. He knew that. He saw my degree, and I knew I had strictly studied to become a psychologist. This was far outside of my field.

As I continued to skim the papers, I swallowed my fear and let it fester into anger. This wasn't legal. He couldn't make psychologists become psychiatrists this way. These patients needed more than that. They needed real doctors who had studied for those reasons. I didn't trust myself to medically diagnose or treat someone like Claire. I had no experience or training. I was here to simply let her express her feelings and talk it out through therapy.

I slammed the file shut and shook my head.

There was no way in hell I was joining any program that promoted something so illegal—something *so* unethical.

Whatever Spence warned me about, he was right. David was hiding something, and I shouldn't have been so quick to put all my eggs in one basket.

Someone knocked on the door and I rested both arms on top of the file. "Come in."

Claire came in and closed the door. "I was wondering if…you'd be up for a session."

Why would she be so interested? She had once been my hardest patient and now she was so willing. It didn't make sense. "Of course. Take a seat."

She sat in the other chair and scanned the office. "It's a cute little room. I'll give you that."

"What was it that you wanted to talk to me about? I'm all ears." I slid the file away.

She shifted in her seat, eyes glued to the floor. "Do you

believe people can change? Like if they fuck up, can they redeem themselves?"

"I do. I believe we all deserve second chances. I believe redemption is what keeps humanity alive." I swiveled my chair to fully face her.

She met my gaze and scooted closer. "What if this is their fifth or sixth chance? Do you still believe they can change?"

"I believe everyone can change, Claire, as long as their motivation for wanting to is strong. I believe that for certain people to change their ways, they must hit rock bottom. But I believe everyone can become a better version of themselves."

Her muscles relaxed as she sat back, nodding. "What's in that file you keep hiding?"

"Excuse me?"

She pointed to it. "You keep hiding it. And I'm curious as to why I'm not allowed to see."

I shook my head. With a shrug, I said, "It's nothing."

"It's not nothing. You can tell me. I'm not going to rat you out."

Something told me I could trust Claire, so I grabbed the file. "David wanted me to join a program, but it's corrupt."

"What kind of program?" Her eyes narrowed. Releasing a sigh, I gave her the file. She skimmed the papers, but it didn't seem to register with her. "I don't understand why this is bad. I mean, I'm assuming you don't trust him, but why is this so corrupt?"

"Psychologists and psychiatrists are two totally different professions. He's trying to illegally turn me into a psychiatrist when I have no license to be one. He wants me to go beyond my skills of therapy to diagnose you. To prescribe medications. I don't have that power, and that's not the kind of power I want."

Claire nodded a bit, putting the file down. "What will he do if you say no? I'm sure he'd ask why you said no and then if you told him, he'd fire you on the spot."

"I'm willing to take that risk."

"But what about us? Are you really going to leave us behind when you know a man like that is running an asylum?"

Damnit. She was right. I couldn't leave them here; that was selfish of me. It was part of my job to protect them and help them. "So what are you suggesting I do?"

She chewed her lip before crossing her arms. "I think you should join. Take it. You should destroy it from the inside. Isn't that what they do in books? They infiltrate the system, and the only way to truly help us and destroy this program is by accepting his offer. He'll never suspect you. But you already give everyone that good-girl vibe. So ask a few questions first, like you're still skeptical. Don't give off right away that you want to join, or it'll ruin your plan. After he answers the questions, give him a little surprise, and then say it sounds intriguing. It'll seem a lot more natural coming from you."

"What if I join and it's worse than I thought? I'm a terrible actor."

"Don't think of it as acting. Think of it as a lie so you can do the right thing and uncover the truth. Remind yourself that if you don't do a good job, you get us into major trouble." There she was, the Claire I knew. It made this feel a little more authentic coming from her. Maybe I didn't have much reason to worry. I simply just needed to give it a chance and rip the rug from under David.

I needed to expose that he was trying to criminally turn psychologists into psychiatrists, and if that was exposed, nobody would keep this asylum open. I would have leverage.

It sounded so cruel to want to do this to him after he had

given me a job, and I had hardly any reason to really dislike him. However, something fishy was happening behind this program and it was up to me to figure out what. There was nothing lawful about what he was doing to the other employees, and I feared it was far worse for the patients.

"All right. I'll join this program and see what happens."

"Good, keep me updated. It was my idea, so I deserve to know the ins and outs." She pushed herself out of the chair. "Just be careful, please. What happened last time really went south and if I'm going to be honest, it was heartbreaking to watch. Don't shatter my soul along with it."

XV

The doors had been double-checked a few times over until the windows were next on the list. Every opening of this building had been locked down as the blizzard outside picked up with strength, rattling the glass.

We gathered everyone in the entertainment room to keep a close eye. This storm wasn't letting up anytime soon.

I took a seat between Spence and Emilie—who was quick to grab my hand and I would have pulled it away if she were trying to harm me, but she was simply just scared of the storm.

Darkness engulfed the entire building when the blizzard cut our power. Emilie's hand tightened around mine. It wasn't unusual for strong blizzards to take place here. It was getting closer to Christmas and that meant the snow was becoming much more common around these parts.

I leaned closer to Emilie and whispered, "Do you want your book?" I noticed it wasn't in her arms, and I knew it could help comfort her. She appeared terrified of the dark.

So are you.

The large windows in the room let in all the lighting from the white outdoors, allowing me to see the movement of her nodding. "Would you?"

I stood from my seat and patted her shoulder. "I'll be right back."

I walked across the hall to her room. When I peeked inside, I had to facepalm at the fact I had expected to just spot the book.

Using my arms, I felt around me to follow my way to the bed. I grabbed something solid, and hard when closed. Touching the book sparked memories that I cherished for every day that my heart would beat.

We both sat on the floor of his room, and he scooted closer to me, bumping me with his arm. When I looked at him, he signed, Tell me a story.

I smiled at him and nodded my head. Danny loved stories and the way I told them. It made the light inside my soul grow with excitement when I caught that smile on his face.

I signed back so he understood.

There was once a beautiful girl, but she'd been stuck in a horrible situation. She deserved so much more, yet she'd never been given anything nearly close enough. Her father went missing when she was born, her mother the only one always around. Her mother had never been too fond of her father.

The girl had a secret, a secret she wasn't permitted to tell anyone. When she got her legs wet, she would turn into a mermaid. Her tail was breathtaking, but she wanted more out of life. One day, she met a guy and they planned to make a life together. When she turned eighteen, she was old enough to move out and together, they left her childhood home. She could finally be happy.

I finished.

Danny put his head against my shoulder. There wasn't anything I wouldn't do for him. He meant the world to me since the day he was conceived.

I placed a kiss on his head and wrapped my arms around him until a sweet slumber took him under for the rest of the night.

I held the book hostage in my hands as if it'd grow legs and escape me. I missed Danny so much, but I knew our parents had a good eye on him. He was living his best life.

I returned to the entertainment area and sat, handing Emilie her book with a small smile.

"Thank you," she whispered.

Something in my gut told me a famous pair of eyes were watching me, and when I looked up to meet them, I'd been right. For an unknown reason, Spence made me the focus of his vision.

To avoid an awkward moment, I looked away towards the hallway to my right. Footsteps echoed, and yet everyone here was present and accounted for.

They grew louder as the person got closer. They stopped just behind the corner, and a single red bead rolled into the room. My heart rose to my throat when I recognized it, then it hit the tip of my heel. So, I picked it up, rolling it between my fingers.

There was a letter on this bead—the letter *A*. I knew where it came from.

A whisper drifted into the area. *"Come with me…"*

Emilie leaned closer to me. "What is that?"

My head snapped in her direction and I choked on my own air this time around. "What is what?"

"The bead, and...that voice. You look terrified. You must know," she said in a low tone.

I swallowed the lump. "You hear it, too." They could witness what I could. I wasn't losing my mind after all.

Monique folded her arms, nodding towards the bead. "Why is it trying to get your attention?"

I knew why. I could never forget that night.

"Nora, honey, do you want to talk about it?" My mom wrapped a blanket around my bare shoulders.

The blue and red lights flashed, alerting everyone in sight that something tragic took place. A sheet covered her body as the paramedics carried her away on a gurney. The ambulance doors hid her from me before my goodbyes were cut short by the vehicle disappearing into the night.

"Linda, she needs a moment," my father pulled my mother away from me while my eyes stayed glued to the last place I saw the ambulance.

My cheeks had been stained by the tears that flowed with reason. My face had swelled up from the pain that festered inside me. She would never come home again.

I resented the words that left my mouth, "I have no idea why this is happening."

Everyone bundled up in extra layers of clothes while we got blankets to keep warm. The power wouldn't be coming back on anytime soon and the blizzard was still going.

Claire appeared unbothered by the lack of warmth. I was about to lose my toes to hypothermia and yet she could withstand this kind of cold.

I fixed my scarf some more to trap in the heat from my own breath. I wasn't sure how much longer this would go on for. We would freeze to death if the blizzard never ended.

Spence said something to break the silence. "We have to do something active to keep our temperatures up." His eyes landed on me.

Why was I always the center of his attention? Was he trying to prove to me he was willing to get better since I was his therapist?

Claire's eyes met with one of the doctors. "I can think of one way to keep active and warm."

David cleared his throat, not too thrilled with her suggestion. "We need something that won't require anyone to split up."

Something in the hallway made a clattering noise. Whoever's energy it fed off of, they'd brought such darkness with them. Such venom trailed behind like a snake, hissing only at times when it felt threatened. By what? Whom?

Emilie grabbed onto my arm as if I was her knight in shining armor. "What's happening?"

"I'll tell you what's happening. This is all part of some bad memory inside Nora's head. Her past is haunting her," Spence said.

Monique narrowed her eyes and a deep pit of confusion swirled around in them. "How would you know?"

I turned to face Spence and study his body language with what his answer would be.

He leaned forward, resting his elbows on his legs. "I know things and you can take a wild guess as to how I know them. Everything you've built this Asylum to be is what allows us to see what is terrorizing Nora."

I closed my eyes, afraid to face the truth. I did not want my fears coming back to ruin my life but now it wasn't just about me. Everyone else could *see* it.

"Why can't we see anyone else's fears? Or memories?" she asked.

Claire snickered as if this was all a joke to her. "Who knows the answer to that. So, Nora. We can witness what keeps you awake at night. Mind telling us more about it?"

"I'd rather not talk about it," I said in a whisper.

She jumped to her feet. "You have no choice. We are all going to be haunted if you don't tell us what the hell is going on." She closed the space between us, attempting to intimidate me.

Standing from my seat, I smoothed the skirt of my dress. "I'd rather not talk about it." I walked out of the entertainment room and locked myself in a closet when it was all clear, then fell to my knees. Nobody could begin to understand the pain that squeezed my chest.

My hands formed into fists as my lungs forgot how to accept oxygen from the memory. I opened my mouth to scream and let out a cry, but no sound formed. Everything that I buried inside me was begging to come out and it was becoming hard to contain it any longer.

The tears poured down my cheeks like a waterfall down a mountain. My heart ached while I begged her to come back. Nothing made me feel complete without her here. I had loved her whole, and yet I failed her that fateful night.

After a solid hour of crying into the void, tears stopped hugging my cheeks. They ran and hid, rejecting the idea of returning. There was nothing left in me to let go of.

I stood from the floor and exited the closet. Emilie had been waiting for me and the second I stepped out, she gave me a blanket. "I don't want to ask you to talk about it but if you ever do wanna talk, I can listen. We forget that even therapists need a helping hand from time to time."

I knew what came next. David was well aware that I wasn't in the right state of mind to help these patients. He would fire me in an instant and I'd lose my entire career. This was the one thing in my life that kept me sane for the moment. This career was something firm that I could grasp onto.

Emilie closed the space between us and pulled me into her embrace. I pulled away from her almost immediately, shaking my head. "I appreciate the comfort but that is unprofessional, Emilie."

"I'm sorry," she said in a small tone.

To this day, I couldn't explain why she haunted my thoughts. I assumed I had moved on, but she made it clear that I was far from where I wished to be.

I accepted the silence that filled the halls in all its entirety. It wasn't quiet in an eerie kind of way, but more of a peaceful way. There was no war inside my head. Everything had settled and I wouldn't be forced to confront the strangers who demanded what tore my heart open.

I whispered to Emilie, "I won't forget about you. You must know that. I really hope you get out and find your father someday. You deserve closure."

She gave me a crazy look. "What is this? Nora, you're not saying goodbye."

"I have no choice. I can't be of any help if I have my own demons to battle. The blind can't lead the blind," I repeated. There was nothing he didn't know. He was an intelligent man, and it was tragic that all his brain was wasting away inside this facility.

She pulled me closer. "No. I refuse to let you leave now. You're the first psychologist I actually like. You understand us the best. You have your own demons to fight and that makes it so much easier for you to relate to us. If we feel like you're just like us, we are going to open up more. David has to know that."

Removing myself from her grasp one more time, I dismissed the thoughts. "Why would David listen to you? From what I learned, it sounds like he doesn't care about you guys. He's getting on my nerves and I'm starting to think he's not the ally in this place." I pulled my scarf over my mouth and nose to breathe color back into my skin.

Claire stepped out of the shadows. "David may not be by your side, Nora, but *we* are."

Spence waited at the door for a session, so I invited him in and leaned back for a listen.

He started off with something more subtle, and sweet—dreams that left you desperate to climb back into bed for more. Somewhere, it took a turn.

A bummer, they said.

He began to carefully articulate his night terrors. The kind that ate one alive and devoured them until nothing was left but a hollow shell of a man or woman.

"And in this dream, David had been maniacal. Testing things. Taking our blood. All for one, single purpose, Nora—or, I'm sorry—Miss Witlow. We were fantasy creatures. The kind you'd hear about in books, and in movies. Mythical beings. Supernatural beings, too. The paranormal, to be exact."

"What kind of creatures would those be?" I asked in a quieter tone, desperate for an answer. Flashes of memories raced through my mind.

"Vampires. Mermaids. Angels, and even *demons*." His eyes locked on mine, sending chills down my spine as every hair rose on my body and goosebumps traced my skin. Something deep inside me lit like a match to its box. A flame burning. Crackling. Growing as its embers trickled in the darkness of my mind.

Spence adjusted himself in his seat and sat forward, dismissing whatever had been running amok in my head. "They're just nightmares. Nightmares become common in places like this. I presume you know all about them?" His eyebrow cocked.

My breath caught in my throat as I wrapped my fingers around the side edges of my chair, squeezing until my knuckles whitened. "Silly nightmares, I assure you."

Silly indeed.

Silly.

Anything but terrifying. Anything but real. Anything but the reality that my own best friend had been all but a flashback. A memory. A reminiscence. The picture you'd share every now and then to remind yourself that she was still in your heart where she'd forever stay, never wavering.

But she wavered.

The more intense these terrors plagued me, the further she wavered.

I was beginning to want nothing to do with her. Not a thought to remember her by.

Was this grief?

Far from it. A cry for help, even.

Grief could never be this cruel. It would never leave the survivor begging to forget a human being altogether.

"Miss Witlow," Spence's voice came out in a hush. Low. Deep. Almost a growl, as if I'd done something to offend him. Had I?

I inhaled, holding for a few seconds, before exhaling all the anxiety and doubts. "This may sound crazy, and I'm sorry if it does. Perhaps your nightmare was anything but that. Perhaps, Spence, your nightmare is something we're living through already."

XVI

Squinting my eyes, I read his name tag. "Aaron Smith?" I knew I'd never remember that name again, as terrible as that sounded. I found it easier to remember names that were less common, or less commonly spelled in certain ways. In other words, if they weren't my patients, I hardly knew them.

I'd try to remember, but sometimes even that failed me. I would feel bad about it in the end—I would. But what more could I do? I had so much going on inside my head that remembering basic names would not just fit.

"That is the name." He nodded. "So, the first thing I want to tell you is that we have a chart." He pointed me over to the chart hanging by the kitchen door. "We rotate every now and then since the nearest town is so far away." He handed me an envelope. "Dr. Harrison made a list and believe me, it will be long. He provided you with a credit card to pay for the groceries. Any questions?"

"Yeah, just one."

He waited for me to speak. All right then.

"How am I supposed to drive in this snow? I barely made it here."

"Check the envelope."

I opened it up to reveal car keys. "He's providing the car, too?"

"Yes. It should be decent for the snow. Plenty of space for groceries, too."

Grocery shopping seemed easy enough. It had been a while since I'd talked to anyone outside of these walls. It would be good for me.

Taking the envelope with me, I found the white 1960 Chevrolet Corvair off to the side. I got in and warmed it up for a bit, heater on full blast. "What was the saying? If you start to slide, turn into the swerve?" With a shake of my head, I started my long drive into town. Listening to the radio was a bust. I focused on driving safely anyway.

The drive took about an hour and when I arrived at the store, I hurried to the entrance. An older gentleman held the door open, and I thanked him with a smile before peeking at the list. "Shit, he wasn't kidding about it being long," I mumbled.

The piece of lined paper was full, front and back, two columns on each side.

I grabbed a cart and began shopping. I searched for the lowest prices and best deals. But that wasn't the best part of this trip. No, the best part was being surrounded by so many people. That was the moment I knew I was a city girl and always would be. Being too far from civilization was a nightmare—and *literally*.

An elderly woman stood beside me. “You look so cold, dear. Where did you come from?”

I flashed her a smile as I grabbed a few packs of bread. “I just started working at Monstrum Asylum. It’s about an hour up north, towards the mountains. Have you heard of it?”

“Oh, no, I’ve never heard of it.” She shook her head, her forehead wrinkles becoming more pronounced. “What brings a pretty young woman like yourself so far out of town?”

“I just got my PsyD, actually. My boss decided to hire someone with no real experience other than a doctoral degree so I can’t complain too much.”

The woman smiled. “A doctor are you?”

Laughing, I shrugged. “In a way. I’m a psychologist. I’m more a therapist than I am a doctor. I help patients with their mental health.”

She grabbed my hand, patting it. “You are doing wonderful work. God bless you.”

“Thank you.” I bid her a nod and grabbed my cart. I began rolling away, but her voice stopped me.

“You remind me so much of me when I was younger.” She came over and pulled a picture from her wallet. “That’s my husband, Herb. That’s me right there.” She pointed to a young woman. The picture had to have been taken close to 1910. But she was right. She had long curls and a long-sleeve dress—light top and dark skirt. She was a stunning woman, and she had aged so well.

“I’m glad you got to walk down memory lane. Memories are a wonderful thing that remind us of what life is worth.”

She grabbed my hand again, squeezing it. “I want you to have it.”

“The picture? Oh, ma’am, that is so sweet, but I couldn’t take that. You and your husband look so happy together."

She put it in my hand and shook her head. "Herb and I could never have children, so who would this picture belong to when I die? It's best that someone has it. Please. I insist." Her brown eyes sparkled, and I couldn't say no this time. So I thanked her again, took the picture, and went off on my merry way.

Little things like this were what made my day. They were the best parts of life.

When I finished stuffing my cart, and another, I headed to the checkout. A man bagged my groceries, loading them into the cart and ready to take them to the car.

I grabbed the credit card and handed it over. The cashier layered a slip over it before running it through the imprinter. However, my total had been over the limit, so he called up the credit card company for an authorization, which they would not give. Trying to explain that I was an employee for David Harrison at the asylum wouldn't get through to anyone.

Without holding up the line anymore, I stuffed the card into the envelope and used my own instead, which had been authorized. After I signed the paper slip, I thanked the merchant before turning away with a huff.

65.82.

I made sure to get a copy of the receipt so I could get reimbursed for the money. After the employee helped me, I sat in the car and furrowed my brows. "Why the hell did he give me a card that didn't work?" Paying $65 on the spot was not my idea of a good day. No, it soured my mood. I needed that money back.

On the way back to the asylum, I decided to snack on a small bag of chips. Since I did technically pay for it.

The wind picked up and the car began to slide. I tried to turn the wheel into it, lightly pressing the brakes just in case the tires caught friction again. However, all of my tactics failed, and I slid off the road. I didn't damage the car or get into real trouble, but I had gotten myself stuck in a rut. No matter what I did, the car wouldn't budge.

I checked my watch, and it'd barely been past midnight. No radio. And I had been too far from the city or the asylum to go for help.

Double checking that I had a good amount of gas left in the tank, I left the car on to keep me warm.

"Well, I suppose this isn't going to hurt the groceries. Not like they can melt under the sun," I mumbled.

Unsure of my next move, I got out of the car and tried to dig the snow out from around the tires. I hopped in the car and tried again, but I barely moved an inch or two.

I groaned in frustration. Trying not to get overwhelmed or overreact wasn't the easiest. I wanted to just break down and wait for someone to rescue me. But who would? Nobody else would be silly enough to drive their car out in this weather, would they?

It was easy to be the damsel.

After digging and trying to move the vehicle, it never worked. I repeated the process over and over, but it never made a difference. So, I sat inside and waited.

The late night had passed, and early morning was approaching as soon as I had given up. Winters grew so long while days shrunk. I missed the sunshine.

I turned the car off every now and then to save a bit on gas. Then I closed my eyes and let the exhaustion take over.

A scream erupted from my throat when someone knocked on the window. I opened my eyes and exited the car, facing Aaron. Ah, what a beautiful moment. I remembered his name. "I'm sorry.

I slid off the road and haven't been able to get myself out."

He chuckled and shook his head. "Let me help you push." He went back to the rear end of the car and I followed. We both began to push, digging our toes into the snow for more leverage. As soon as we got her back onto the road, Aaron got into his truck and headed back, and I followed closely behind.

We made it back to the asylum just as David asked what happened. I explained everything, and Aaron backed me up. This calmed him a bit and he dropped the subject.

I didn't though.

I told him the credit card company didn't authorize the payment and I used my own to pay, but I kept the receipt so I could prove that and get the money back onto that card. He took the envelope and receipt from me and promised to get on it.

Aaron helped me carry in groceries and put them away, and as soon as we finished, I pulled out the picture the woman gave me. I wanted to ask her what it was truly like to grow up during that era. What was the truth behind the perfect curls, the lack of woman's education, and no right to vote for anyone who wasn't a white male?

Sure, I could have read a history book or researched online. But no article could compare to the personal story of someone who experienced it. And certainly not someone I had met.

"May I ask what's in your hand?" Aaron asked.

I cleared my throat. "Just a picture is all. Ran into a good friend at the store and she wanted me to have it." I glanced at the fridge. "Well, Aaron, I should turn in for the night. Thanks again for helping me."

"It's no problem." He gave me a smile and headed towards his own bedroom.

I passed by the patients' doors and debated saying goodnight.

Would it be too forward? Out of line? Of course not. They were my patients, and I was meant to be friendly with them. To get them to trust me and open up.

So why didn't I say anything?

When I made it to the bathroom, I decided to take a shower. I grabbed a clean set of pajamas and stripped down before soaking myself in hot water. It felt amazing after getting trapped in the snow for hours. What didn't feel so amazing was the moment the lights went out.

"Hello?" I called out.

Nobody responded and so I decided not to say another word. It wouldn't be smart. They would have heard me the first time and responded if they didn't mean harm. Whoever was here surely meant to scare me.

I turned off the water and searched for my towel, but I couldn't find it. I felt for my clothes next, but it had all disappeared as if I were the young teen boy in a high school gym locker.

"Please give me back my clothes." Yes. *Please.*

Much to my expectations, they didn't.

Dropping my arms to my sides, I grabbed the door and stepped into the hallway naked. Most everyone had turned in, so the hallway was empty. And why should I have felt shame? It wasn't my fault, nor was the human body anything to be ashamed about.

I took a few steps and squared my shoulders as I walked down the hall.

"Holy fuck, Nora is butt ass naked," Claire said from the window of her door.

"What?" Spence asked. I thought I saw a flash of blue, but he wasn't at his window when I passed. "Nora, where are your clothes?"

“Spence, that is none of your business. I simply forgot to grab a towel and the power went out in the bathroom. Go back to bed.” That seemed easy enough. It gave me more dignity than saying a ghost stole them.

Claire laughed. “Sure, we’ll pretend we believe you. Goodnight, Nora.”

“Goodnight,” I said before I found my room. I dried myself and put on fresh pajamas. It was silly to tell anyone my clothes got lost, or someone took them. So I’d search for them tomorrow when the lights came on. I just hoped that my patients hadn’t seen me so vulnerable. Would they see me as less than their therapist? I couldn’t let that happen, so I’d go on to pretend it didn’t bother me.

XVII

Spence was taken by surprise by my quick pace upon entering his room. "I want to hear the truth and nothing but the truth." I sat down in the chair across from him. "When we were in the basement, did you or did you not see what happened on the stage in the basement?" Little by little, bit by bit—a few of my memories were coming back. They hadn't stayed away for long.

"Nora, you're a psychologist—not a cop." He shook his head.

"Answer the question." I wasn't playing any games this time around. "You said we could see my thoughts and what was haunting me. If everyone saw it, you must have seen what happened in the basement."

He straightened his posture. "So what if I did? I told a lie."

I laughed. "You didn't just lie to me. You made me feel like

I was losing my mind! I thought I was seeing things and I was afraid I would end up here like the rest of you. But it's not just me, Spence. It's a combination of…my past and something else. You mentioned something about this asylum being built for it and I want to know what you meant."

He smiled, teasing me with his silence. Those dimples were *so* prominent on his cheeks.

"Spence, I'm being serious. Something is happening here, and it doesn't make any sense. Why can we see into my head? This is no normal asylum." I narrowed my eyes on him.

"This asylum was built to contain, yet also unleash things of the paranormal world." He leaned forward, dropping his head as he used his elbows to support his weight on his thighs.

I swallowed. "Why?"

He lifted his head. "We… We aren't your normal patients." He got out of his seat and came closer, his height growing with every step he took.

"Why is that?" I feared that maybe I had judged all this the wrong way. Was I talking to an alien? A ghost? Were these dead people?

No, don't be silly, Nora.

He squatted down in front of me, grabbing onto my hands. "Don't run if I tell you the truth."

"That depends on what the truth is," I said in a low voice.

Suspense drummed against the walls as they closed in. Time slowed and I worried I'd never see my family again. I never said goodbye.

He said, "This asylum was built to keep us inside. Claire, Emilie, and I are not here because we are mentally ill. We're very healthy, in fact. We're here because we aren't human."

"I figured when you mentioned this asylum had paranormal

powers, you guys were…ghosts." My cheeks heated as I let those words slip. Saying it made me feel like I was the one needing mental help.

Spence laughed with the shake of his head. "We're not ghosts. We are creatures from other species. You'd be surprised to know this, but Emilie is a mermaid, Claire is a vampire, and I'm sort of a hybrid."

I choked. "Okay, whoa. That's…" I couldn't finish my sentence. This was outrageous.

"It's true, Nora. If you follow the clues, they add up. I'm a mix between an angel and a demon. Claire warned me not to tell you the truth, but it was going to come out somehow." He let go of my hands.

I remembered a few small things from observing Emilie and Claire. Claire didn't get cold during the blizzard. Emilie said she was born in water. It did make a little bit of sense. Spence had mentioned being an insomniac which would be true if he were a hybrid. Angels and demons never slept if I were to read the Bible.

My eyes stayed glued to the floor of his room. How could this be possible? Was I a fool to believe he was telling the truth, or did I think we lived in a world where other things did not exist?

"Nora, are you going to say something?" he asked me.

"How is this possible?"

"Well, when two people meet, sometimes they want to get naked and have sex—"

"No! Spence, I meant, how are you guys here? Why are you in this asylum?" I gestured around us.

He glanced at the barred window at the top of his wall. "David caught us. He's had us locked up since. He wants to know what makes us different from humans."

I scoffed. "DNA, genius. A lion is a lion because that's just its

DNA. It's not a mutation. That's beside the point." I sat forward. "You don't deserve to be locked up like a prisoner. Just because humans don't understand how you exist among us, doesn't give us the right to control you. You share this earth with us. You have a right to be here, and to be free."

"Saying that will get you killed." He straightened himself.

"Why?"

He turned to look at me. "Because David will have you killed if you try to go against him. He's done it to everyone who has worked here and defied his rules. Or almost everyone."

"What do you mean almost everyone?" I tilted my head slightly to the right.

Spence backed away from me as if I were a disease. Was I? "You. He never killed you."

With a shake of my head, my eyes darted over to the window. "No, that's not… He doesn't know that I know. Does he…?"

"Weeks ago, you went down to the basement. You found them with Claire, and David wasn't too pleased." He shrugged a little. "You had found out a little bit, and you tried to get us out, but David injected you with some kind of amnesia drug."

I hurried up out of the chair and crossed my arms. "Then I will lie my ass off. I will do whatever I need to do if that's what it takes to get you guys out of here without killing myself or erasing my memories. It's disgusting to lock people up just because you don't know how they were put on this earth."

Spence grabbed the edge of his nightstand. "Nora, that's dangerous. Don't be stupid, please."

I took a few slow steps toward him. "Don't tell me what to do. Nothing you say is going to stop me. Claire has been here for seven years. You've been here for three years. Who knows how long poor Emilie has been kept away for? You guys deserve to live your lives. This is not ethical."

He spun around in a hurry, facing me. I hadn't realized how close I got to him until he was peering into my gaze. "You can't go up against an entire staff."

I narrowed my eyes. "Watch me."

"To the outside, your death appears as one of us losing our temper and killing you. They will never know the truth because David controls what the public hears. Don't do this." His Adam's apple bobbed.

I let out the breath I'd been holding in. "That's not your decision to make." I circled him and left his room before he could protest some more. I had made up my mind. I wasn't here to heal their mental state. I was here to set them free from this prison.

A small part of me was thankful to hear that these patients weren't mentally ill. Trying to heal the mind was a tougher job than trying to break creatures out of an asylum.

I had to be the best actress I knew if I would get them out alive.

When people looked at Monstrum Asylum, they saw crazy. They thought of people who couldn't control their actions. They associated the idea with people who did not belong in society. Never did they come to think that maybe something more was going on inside.

People were so afraid of mentally ill people that they never questioned the ethics. When asylums had been much more popular back in the day, it was common for the patients to be mistreated. They were abused in ways people today could not accept.

They would try hydrotherapy. Forcing someone to handle freezing water was no sane way to treat anyone. They had tried electroshock therapy which everyone was aware of. Shocking someone into amnesia did not remove what made them mentally ill. It was torture for the patient. I couldn't forget about lobotomies. They would cut into the prefrontal lobe to remove pieces of the brain which always resulted in the patient losing a part of their personality. Sometimes, transorbital lobotomies were done just for the same reasons. It was depressing to think that these people had undergone such neglect throughout their years.

Every time I saw these patients, I would see the loss in their eyes. They had no reason to live while being locked here. They weren't patients. They were prisoners. They were the wronged innocent of the world. They had never done anything to others and yet we had to go and handcuff them to a life of—

What was this for? Were they being subjected to experiments as humans had been just seventy years ago?

I had to keep myself calm and collected as one of the employees walked past me. It made my stomach twist and turn at the thought of Emilie being forced to go along with whatever they did. She was half fish. How would they use that against her?

She already had legs. Emilie had her entire life plucked from her soul.

I couldn't say for sure. I didn't know the real Emilie. She could have been outspoken. She could have been a stronger woman and I never would have known. They stole her voice in a way. They took what didn't belong to them.

There had to be a way they were destroying Claire. She was a vampire, and vampires were dark. They lived and breathed in the shadows. In some odd way, they might have been forcing Claire into the light. I wasn't sure how, if there was no sun outside but it was my best guess.

The feline part of my brain wanted to see what characteristics she had from being a bloodsucker. Did she have red or gold eyes?

Or were they black? Did her eyes change at all?

I'd never seen her fangs, but they had to exist.

With a gasp, I froze in my tracks at the thought of what they could have been doing. David was probably pulling her fangs out to make sure she couldn't harm anyone. There had to be some reason as to why they couldn't overpower humans. David was *weakening* them.

Spence was the first one I wanted to discover more about though. Something about him pulled me in. I'd heard many stories about vampires and mermaids but the only stories I heard about angels and demons were the conflicting shoulders.

People believed we had an angel and a devil on our shoulder, influencing our decisions. Spence took that concept to a whole new level. He was a mystery to be solved and I would be the detective to crack him open.

Something about him piqued my interest and now I knew why. He was a charismatic man, and one that I could not seem to understand in the slightest.

The thought of him being treated like garbage made my head spin. He was two halves of a whole. How could they have used that against him? They'd get inside his head and turn himself against his own mind. He could be driven mad by the parts that did not see eye-to-eye.

The night I let him out of his room to explore the basement with me, my heart had reacted to it in a strange way, a way only certain men could make me feel. I had brushed away the idea at the time because I couldn't bear the thought of seeing my own patient in such a way.

The tables had turned. He was no longer my patient. He was a hostage here and the part of me that had shamed me for the pounding of my heart now had every opportunity to desire what it craved.

It wasn't unethical for me to be charmed by him. However, if Spence had my interest, I could not let anyone else know. If they knew me, they knew I could never go for a charge and as far as they were aware, I saw him at just that.

Spence had to be a secret. The way I saw him was now buried—hidden from everyone else. He could never be more to me if I didn't want to blow my cover.

XVIII

"Nora, would you join us tonight? We're going to have a meeting for the program," David said.

I nodded, not blowing my cover just yet. Whatever this program was, I'd find out tonight.

The day dragged on agonizingly slow as I waited for night to fall. With all the snow, it didn't look like daytime, but the clocks promised otherwise.

David sent the patients to their room after six, and then he told me to meet him in his office. Spence gave me a look, warning me to be careful. He didn't approve of this idea, but I'd concluded he didn't agree with Claire's ideas most of the time.

I met David and he handed me a key. "This is for the basement. It will help you get in and out of the area only psychiatrists have access to." Those words made nausea swirl in my stomach. Psychiatrists had access, and yet I was just given a key. I didn't have a license for this. Would it affect my permanent record?

"May I check it out now?" I asked.

David's eyes shimmered in delight. "I'd be surprised if you didn't. Let's go."

He led me down to the basement, past the auditorium. We walked by another door that seemed vaguely familiar, but I couldn't pinpoint the memory. We made it all the way to the end, and he used his key to open the door. "This is the night where we welcome you." I followed him in as he gestured to the other doctors. "Welcome."

Monique stepped forward and grabbed my hand, pulling me further into the room. "I am really glad you decided to join us. We needed another female brain around here."

I cracked a smile to humor her, but I didn't want to be here at all. "What is this program? I mean, it said that it's for psychiatrists, but what exactly is it that you'd want me to do as a psychiatrist specifically?"

She glanced at David as he stepped into my view. "That's why we need to do this first. We need you to swear an oath. This program is private. You cannot tell another soul about it. What happens in this room stays in this room. Is that understood?"

"Yes, sir." Not a chance.

David laid out his palm. "Give me your hand."

My senses kicked into high gear, but I gave him my palm. He used a sharp blade to cut into it, and I widened my eyes. "Is this really necessary?"

"Absolutely." He shoved his other hand out to the side and a doctor—or a fraud, I couldn't be so sure these days—placed a dropper in it. He stretched out my palm, dropping the liquid beads into my cut. "This will sting. Things will change. However, your senses will heighten. You will become a better version of yourself. When the process is complete, we will then discuss more about your role in this program. You're dismissed, Nora, and I wish you sweet dreams," he said as he finished wrapping up my hand.

I glanced at the other doctors and nodded a bit, unsure of what he was referring to. I left the room anyway and headed upstairs. Claire caught my attention as I passed her door. "Well?"

I wanted to tell her what they did, but I wasn't even sure. My heartbeat was racing in my ears and my entire body began to tingle. I needed sleep more than ever. "I..." I walked away before I passed out.

Claire whispered to Spence from her room, "They cut her. I can smell the blood."

When I disappeared into my room, I collapsed onto my bed. The world began to spin around me and maybe I was Alice for a split second, but as soon as my nightmares started, I stepped into the role of the Queen of Hearts instead.

Breakfast tasted extra bland, and I wasn't sure how that became possible. The wind outside rattled the windows, but it hurt my ears.

After we finished the dishes, I split up from Monique and took a stroll outside. Snowflakes nipped at my skin. I pulled my jacket tighter as fingers wrapped around my wrist and spun me. His bright blue eyes captured my gaze. "What did they do?" He examined the bandage.

My skin danced beneath his touch. "I'm not sure."

"What? What do you mean you're not sure?" He unwrapped the gauze and inspected the wound. "Nora, this isn't right."

I peered at my own cut to see what he was talking about, frowning. Sure enough, my blood had darkened, and my veins under the surrounding surface appeared more like spiderweb—black at their core.

"What the fuck did he do?" Spence's voice came out sharp as his jaw clenched. "I knew I should never have trusted Claire. Her ideas are shit." And I agreed. Whatever happened, it wasn't normal. I allowed David to cut me and put something right into my blood. How far was I willing to let him go so I could uncover the truth?

"Spence," I whispered.

"It's unacceptable. He probably poisoned you, and now you're going to die because she told you to join."

"Spence."

"What was she thinking? David knows what you tried to do the first time you found out. Why would he trust you a second time? He wanted a head start. He wanted to fuck with your mind first."

"Kiss me."

His demeanor changed, first freezing up before he shifted his weight. "What?"

I exhaled. "Good, you're still listening. I just needed to say something to get your attention."

His Adam's apple bobbed. "Right."

"I understand that you're worried, but I'm the one with the poisoned blood. It's my job to worry. Let me handle it." I wrapped the gauze back around my hand. "Thank you for thinking of me."

I flashed a small smile before heading inside. My cheeks heated up at the thought of kissing Spence. Would he have if I'd been serious? I was certain with lips like his, he was fantastic. His touch was gentle, and more than I'd ever experienced.

Nora, knock it off. He's your patient, and whether he's actually a patient is irrelevant. He needs you to save him. He doesn't need you to fall in love with him.

I entered the bathroom and examined the cut, watching as the black in my veins ever so slightly spread. If it was poison, I'd be dead by now, and it wouldn't have looked like this. No, David did something else.

The lights flickered. I closed my eyes, and long enough so nothing would pop up in the mirror behind me. When I opened them, the lights had completely shut off.

Someone whispered, but I wasn't quite sure who it came from, or which direction they were.

"Not again." I followed along the wall to find the door locked. "Damnit." I knocked. "Hello? Is anyone out there?"

A cold breath rushed across my ear.

I twisted around, pressing my back against the door. "Who the hell are you?"

No answer.

I started banging on the door, yelling and screaming for anyone to let me out. I couldn't let my fears control me, but I couldn't be trapped in the dark for long.

"Who is going to save you? Does anyone really care?" The voice became clear. It belonged to a female, but I still had no idea where it came from. Whoever she was, she didn't want me to identify her.

"Leave me alone!" I cried, backing away from the door.

"Do you really want to be alone again? No, you don't want

to endure all of that on your own, do you?"

Dizziness swarmed my head like buzzing flies, and I caught on a pipe, tripping and falling on my knees.

"Why did you have to do it alone? Do you think you deserve that?"

I covered my ears, shutting out the voice. "I was focusing on them! It's about them now!"

Through my hands, I could still hear her scoff as loud as a cannonball going off. "Were they too busy begging for your help to realize you were breaking into a million pieces?"

Dropping my arms, I slumped. "I was broken the moment I arrived."

"You have the perfect little family… Mom, Dad, little Danny… Yet, here you are, terrified of something so silly."

"It's not silly. She was my best friend."

Silence.

"You let her fall," she whispered in my ear.

I whipped around, waving my arms. Nobody was in here but me, and that was confirmed the moment the lights came on. The door opened and Emilie's head peered around it. "Nora?" She stepped inside. "Nora, why are you on the floor?"

I couldn't give her an answer. Whatever reason she came up with was good enough for us both.

Approaching, she kneeled before me. "Do you need a hug?"

Again, I didn't answer.

She leaned in and wrapped her arms around me, letting me seek comfort in another warm body. If I could say anything, I'd thank her for understanding.

After a lifetime, Emilie pulled away. "May I see?" She gestured to my palm. It certainly was the more appropriate thing to ask rather than rip it off.

I nodded.

Taking my palm, she unveiled the cut and furrowed her brows. "This must be their plan."

"Excuse me? What plan? Do you know what this is?" I scooted closer, eager to hear the truth.

She giggled. "Nora, I know a lot more than Spence and Claire sometimes. You'd just never know it because I like to hide the best parts of myself."

"Tell me. Please." I grabbed her wrist with my other hand, begging her to let me in on the secret.

Her smile dropped. "Promise me you won't get mad."

"Why would I get mad?"

"Promise me."

"All right, I promise."

"He's been extracting our blood. Studying it. Separating the blood from the plasma. It's like a toy." She scratched her inner elbow. "And I think he found a way to mix that with human blood safely."

My breath caught in my throat.

She waved her hand in front of my face. "Are you okay?"

"What does that mean?"

"It means that this program you're in, he's using our blood to give humans more strength. I'm not sure which blood he mixed into your body, but it's between Spence, Claire and me. It's likely you'll receive some of our characteristics, or abilities." I couldn't be quite sure of all their abilities yet, but it terrified me to know I could inherit some of that DNA. Did I want that? No.

I swallowed. "In other words, this program is only a ploy so he can experiment on the doctors using your DNA."

Emilie nodded a little. "That sounds accurate. I suppose we'll know soon who you'll get your abilities from. I kind of hope it's me. I'd love someone to share with."

Tempted to ask what mermaids could do, I opened my mouth to say something but now wasn't the right time. I had other things to worry about. I had to make sure I had this laceration under control before I saved the three of them from this monstrosity.

"Did you need help getting back to your room?"

"Yes, please."

Emilie walked me to my room and left me to ponder all the thoughts in my head. Claire knew he'd cut me. She smelled the blood last night. Spence knew something was wrong, prompting him to show me my wound. Emilie knew exactly why it looked like that, and the answer was what scared me the most.

Did I want to be more like Claire? Emilie? Spence? Did I want a reason to become a captive?

David was sick for assuming this was what I wanted. He never told me anything, at least not without saving his own ass first. He knew what he was doing when he made me make a blood oath before I could ask real questions.

He was molding me into his lab rat, and unfortunately for me, he'd succeeded.

XIX

I looked over at the body that plopped down beside me. "I know about everything. Spence told me what this asylum is really used for."

Claire shrugged. "I knew he'd eventually break. That's what he does. He's too soft. He hates keeping secrets."

I scoffed. "He was trying to help me out. And it shouldn't even bother you that I know because I'm not on their side. I don't support experimenting on innocent people."

"Who says we're innocent?"

She could be quite the trouble when she *wanted* to be. "Who says you're not?" Sighing, I faced forward. "Claire, I'm being serious. He did the right thing by telling me the truth, and I believe it because I've been seeing all kinds of things I can't explain."

"So just like that, you believe in vampires, mermaids, and the supernatural?" She laughed.

I rolled my eyes, dismissing her insult. "Why do you chew on sticks?"

"What?" This caught her off guard.

I turned to face her. "Why do you chew on sticks? When I have a session with you, you chew on sticks and I'd like to understand why."

Her cheeks burned. I hadn't noticed how pale she was until now, however. "I have to. David makes me chew on them when my temper rises. It keeps me from biting someone."

"And that's another question!" I put a finger up. "How are these humans able to control you? Don't you guys overpower humans? I may have just learned about this, but I imagine that you have more strength than we do."

She shrugged. "Well, some of us. Emilie is half fish, which means she has equal strength. Fish don't have more strength than humans, so…" She gestured to the air. "And I do, but that's because I'm meant to have superhuman abilities. Spence does, in a way but…" She rubbed her face. "Angels and demons are not much stronger than humans. So no, we can't just overpower David and his crew. There are more of them, anyway."

I patted her hand. "I'm on your side. And I may not know what to do right now, but I will spend my spare time coming up with a plan. I'll pretend that I'm just your psychologist and I have no idea that you guys are even different creatures at all."

Emilie's shadow fell over us as she stood, watching and hugging her book. "You know the *full* truth?"

Claire and I scooted apart so that Emilie could sit between us. I crossed one leg over the other and rested my hands in my lap.

"Yes. I know everything."

Claire gave us both a look, putting her finger to her lips. I wasn't sure why she was telling us to be quiet, but it became clear as Monique passed. When she spotted me, she rushed over. "Nora, we've been searching for you. We really need to talk."

"What's this about?" I furrowed my eyebrows.

She grabbed my hand and pulled me off the couch. "It's serious. Follow me."

Taking her orders, I followed her to the office. David stood from his chair. "We need you to talk to Spence. He's done something harmful, and I know he's been opening up to you."

"What did he do?" I swallowed the lump that had been forming the moment they mentioned his *name*. Why would he do something so stupid after I told him I'd help him? That was exactly it. He was trying to warn me not to save him.

David waved Monique away and led me to Spence's room. "Please, talk some sense into him."

"Of course." Nodding, I made sure he disappeared around the corner after unlocking the door.

I entered the room, my gaze falling on the broken man bent over the floor. It tore open my heart just to see him in this state. I didn't want to see any of them harm themselves. Prison could destroy the innocent.

My steps were slow and steady as I approached him. "Spence, it's me. Talk to me."

He kept his head towards the floor, his shoulders slumped. "Nora, don't bother."

"No. I will because that's what I came here to do." I circled him until I stood before him, then I kneeled. "You may not be here for the reason I assumed but you still need my help. You've been locked away from freedom for a few years and it's my job to free you. I take that very seriously."

"I told you not to bother," he mumbled under his breath, yet I still caught his words.

I settled on the floor. "It's too bad for you that I don't take orders. I fight to do the right thing." I got rid of the wavering of my voice. "Look at me. What did you do?"

Spence lifted his head to give me a look, but the result shattered me. Cuts covered his chest, cuts that ran deep and wide.

I shook my head in disbelief. Guilt washed over me, but it was a choke that squeezed my throat. "Why would you do this to yourself? Is this because of me? Is it because I told you I wouldn't stop fighting?"

He ran his hands through his hair and repositioned himself, lifting his knees and bringing them closer to his chest. "Every day that I sit in this place, I'm reminded of all the time I'm losing to be in the real world. It's a constant battle. I stay strong for Emilie because I know she's terrified but it's breaking me apart."

"Spence, I'm here for a reason. I firmly believe in everything having a purpose and I knew this asylum stuck out to me when I saw it. I moved all the way over and left my family to come here and help you guys. Maybe this is it. We can find a way to free you guys and I'll make sure David pays for treating you this way. I made that my promise," I said.

"Why did you make an empty promise?" He lifted his eyes to meet mine as sorrow swam through them.

I straightened my posture. "I don't make promises I can't keep, Spence. If you want to know more about me, that's what I'll tell you. Maybe I dress like a housewife when I'm an educated and unmarried woman, but that doesn't mean I act like one. I will stop at nothing to fight for justice. If it kills me, that's a chance I'm willing to take."

"You'd put your life in danger for strangers—strangers who also happen to be creatures that have a hatred towards humans." He looked away.

Chills ran up my spine, but I couldn't let them control my emotions. "Yes. That's who I am. I want you to know that some of us do care about you. Unless you've specifically attacked me, I have nothing against you. Tell me, Spence, have you ever harmed someone?"

His gaze locked onto me. "Yes."

Goosebumps rose along my arms, but I wouldn't jump to conclusions just yet. I had to hear him out.

He pushed some hair back. "I had no choice. My mom was being attacked and I had to protect her."

The words caught in my throat. I wasn't sure of how to release them, but I wasn't afraid. Something about Spence told me he was far from violent. He had defended his own mother. Surely he didn't believe he deserved to rot in hell for it.

"I'm sure your mother was very thankful. All moms love when their kids stand up for them. Well, all of them should." I released a deep breath I'd been holding in. "You did the right thing."

"I went against the council. I defied the people who were going to punish my mom for breaking the rules." He clenched his jaw.

Readjusting my legs, I leaned forward. "What rule did she break?"

"I'm a hybrid, Nora. What rule do you think she broke?"

I leaned back while focusing on the floor. He was a mix between an angel and a demon. That was against the law of nature. I wasn't sure what I was supposed to tell him.

He touched a cut across his collarbone. "It won't hurt me. I'm still half-angel. These cuts will cease to exist soon. I want you to stop worrying about me."

I stood. "That will never happen. I worry about you, Claire, and Emilie. It's who I am. Don't tell me to change who I am to make you feel better. I won't do it." I left the room and narrowed my eyes.

I'd bring down this asylum and I had to do it in a way without exposing what the patients were. It was time to start noting down everything that took place here. David was going to decay in a cell at some point.

I met up with David to let him know I had talked to Spence. When I ended up in my room, I grabbed the files and researched what I could about vampires, mermaids, angels, and demons. I got a lot of different opinions, but it was enough to give me a foundation to work with.

I'd have to ask them at some point more about their species.

David and the crew outnumbered the patients. We had to somehow become stronger. We had to think *smarter*. I'd ask Claire if she was okay with seducing the doctors and sucking them dry. It was one way to lower the staff.

Emilie couldn't do much, but she could possibly try to drown them in some way. It was an option I could work with. Hydrotherapy had been used as a medicine, and now it would be a weapon against the enemy.

I would have to find ways to lock employees in cold places where nobody could hear them. They'd freeze to death during this time of year.

Spence was half demon. Demons could influence humans, and not in the way humans should have been influenced. He could use that to push them to the brink of insanity the way they'd done to him.

We would have to do this in a subtle way. David could question us, but we'd need an explanation that wouldn't screw over the plan.

That would be the hardest part of all of this.

Then an idea popped into my head. My thoughts had been haunting me for quite some time, but what if I had used this to my advantage? If I could find a way to control the fear, I could turn it on the staff. They would be taken out by the memories that haunted me, and David would never suspect I was doing it on purpose.

A knock echoed throughout my room, and I opened the door to reveal Monique. "Yes?"

"David wants you to clean the bathroom. It's getting dirty again." She handed me the supplies and a bucket.

"Will do." I gave her a false smile. We went our separate ways as I headed to the bathroom. Was Monique part of this? Did she know the truth? Something told me she knew, if she was part of the program, and she was in on David's plan. It was becoming harder to trust people in this place.

I entered the bathroom and set the supplies on the floor, then I stood in front of the mirror, facing my own reflection. There would come a day when I could forgive myself but today would not be that day.

A face appeared behind me, a face that had once been so flawless yet now was bruised and covered in *blood*.

"Why have you been doing this to me? You're just a horrible memory that I can't seem to forget. I didn't mean it. I would do it over if I could. Do you not see how this is killing me inside?" A few tears rolled down my warm cheeks. My head began to weigh ten tons at the sight of the sticky, red liquid.

She said nothing more than, "*Come with me…*"

"I can't go with you! I have a duty here, don't you see? I was meant to come to save these prisoners. It's time for us to move on, Alicia." I wiped my tears away but that didn't stop my nose from running. "I can't live in the past anymore." I sniffled.

She lifted her hand and grabbed the back of my head, smashing it into the mirror.

XX

A throbbing ache pounded against my skull. The bright lights enhanced the pain, and I groaned in response.

"She's awake," someone said.

"We thought you had died for a moment." Monique hovered above me. "It scared us. What happened?"

The scene replayed. *She* betrayed me and tried to take my life.

"I slipped." I sat up and touched the ache. There were some white strips to keep the cut closed. It wasn't deep enough to require stitches, thankfully

Monique helped me off the bed and didn't say anything more. She didn't believe my lie, and I couldn't blame her. I wasn't in the right state of mind to argue over it. "Don't slip again."

"I'll try not to." I forced a small laugh as we both left the room.

She walked in one direction while I went the other.

David caught up with me. “Are you okay?”

He didn’t care. It was a front to keep me in check while he stayed in control. “Yes, I am. Anything you have for me?”

He hesitated for a moment but ultimately nodded. “Emilie needs another session. She’s been opening up with you and I appreciate that.”

It made me question what was so important about having them open up to me. Why would it matter whether they trusted me?

“I can do that. It hurts a little but I’m sure Emilie won’t make it worse. She’s a sweet girl.” I headed to her room without another word.

I took a seat in the chair just as she gasped at the sight of my head. “What happened?”

I was not prepared to have that conversation. “I’m fine. Let’s talk about you. I wanted to talk to you about a few things.” I fixed the skirt of my dress. “How do you feel about drowning people?”

The room fell silent, the air squeezing us.

“I’m not going to drown someone if that’s what you’re asking,” she said in a small voice.

I wouldn’t force her to do anything that made her uncomfortable. “I had an idea of how to pick the employees off, one by one. I thought maybe you could help but if you don’t want to, I won’t make you.” Shaking my head, I folded my hands together.

She took notice of my gesture, squinting her eyes a bit. “But you’re mad at me for saying no. I’m sorry, Nora, but I can’t. I’m not a killer. I won’t stoop to their level.”

The heater in this building was failing its duties.

“Tell me about mermaids.” I gestured towards her.

Emilie cleared her throat. "What do you want to know?"

I was quick with my response, "Powers. Abilities."

She coughed a bit. "Yes, right. Well, you can guess we grow tails. I'm considered a land mermaid. Not all mermaids can grow feet. Land mermaids can switch between land and water. I have limited control of water and land. It's a bit complicated."

I tilted my head. "How so?"

Her eyes searched the room. "I could show you but that's impossible to do without water or dirt."

"We have water in the bathroom."

"No, not the right time. And we don't have dirt anyway. I'd rather show you all at once."

"Dirt?"

She laughed a little. "Well, let me explain it. With water, I can manipulate it. It bends at my will. With dirt, I can do the same effect but it's not the same because of its consistency. It would be so much easier to demonstrate but it would be risky to sneak in water and dirt without David asking questions."

She was right. It wasn't a chance I could take. "Okay, so you have some abilities."

Emilie stood from the bed. "I hate being cooped up here. There was a time when I could go swim in the lake and be myself. Now I'm ashamed of who I am. I'd give anything to be normal just to be free." She came closer. "Do you mean it when you say you'll get us out?"

"I do. It'll be tough but that doesn't mean I won't try. I want to help." I grabbed her hands, warming them up in mine. "You'll get your freedom."

She pulled away to hug her book instead. "I once read this amazing story about a mermaid finding love. She was free to be herself. Well, that's a lie. She wasn't. But she eventually did break free."

"Tell me about it." I sat back.

Sitting back down, she went on. "Well, it was actually set in the past. Like, the far past. Anyhow, the story was about a girl. Okay, it was actually about a siren, which is different from a mermaid but still. Let me start over." She shooed her hand away.

I chuckled to myself. She was a mess sometimes, but it was adorable to the rest of us. She was like the cute best friend that everyone wanted in their life.

"So, this was a story set way back when. It was about a regular girl, one who had been trapped in this life she didn't want. She eventually escaped by becoming a pirate. It was unfortunate because pirates didn't accept women pirates. She had to hide. Well, sirens haunted them one day. Being a woman, she was the only one not affected by their singing. She saved them. However, she was bitten. She turned into one of them and left the ship, but she came back eventually because the pirate she'd fallen in love with was drowning. He convinced her to stay. It was so sweet." She sighed.

"How similar are sirens and mermaids?" I asked.

She shook her head. "Oh, not too similar. I mean, there is no special bite or anything. It's a gene. You have it or you don't. It's the same thing with all of us. You can't turn a human into a vampire or mermaid, or a demon-angel. When humans die, they go to this separate place. It's separate from angels. They're like ghosts. But humans can't just change their species. It's not like the stories you hear. David sure has been trying though."

I had to take a moment. That was something I'd never thought of. A lot of stories made it seem like humans could become these creatures but that wasn't the truth. You were born a mermaid or you weren't. You could wear blue contacts, but that didn't change your eye color. It covered it up. You could dye your hair all the time, but your natural roots would always grow in the color you were born with. Genes were genes. They were not interchangeable.

I cleared my throat as I asked, "Would that mean that regular mermaids can't be with a human? If they can't grow legs, they can't have sex. Do mermen exist?"

She nodded a bit. "Yes, they do. Mermen can reproduce with land mermaids when we are in mermaid form. We can also reproduce with humans. It's not encouraged, though. But water mermaids are not able to reproduce with anyone else but a merman. It's highly recommended that we reproduce with our own species."

I laughed a little. "Understood. So, when do you usually get your tails?"

"We're born with them. We always have tails. There is not a time when we don't. I mean, it is half of who we are, so it wouldn't be half of our identity if we couldn't even be mermaids until like eighteen, or something." She touched her legs as she swung her feet.

Part of me had to wonder whether or not she was getting a chance express herself at all. This was who she was meant to be. Had they stopped her from showering altogether?

"Do you guys get a chance to…" I was struggling with the wording. "Do you ever have a chance to express who you are? I mean, does Claire get to drink blood? Do you get to see your tail? Does…Spence have wings?" I furrowed my brows at the image in my mind. *Did* he have wings?

Emilie nodded slightly. "We do. Claire couldn't survive without blood. I still need a shower every other day. Spence… I don't know much about him. He likes to keep it to himself."

I knew that much. I never suspected how much pain he was in until he had slashed up his own torso. It crushed me to think he would bury his feelings and show them in a harmful way.

"What do you normally eat?" I asked her.

She choked. "Uh, I eat regular food? I don't eat fish if you were curious. But I can eat anything else I want. If I want a hamburger, I'll have a hamburger. Well, I don't eat meat. But either way, I can eat seaweed or a salad." She laughed.

"I guess that would make sense. I grew up with a lot of different lore." I snorted at myself, breaking out into fits. My giggles faded as I prepared to ask her something more personal. "How long have you been here?"

Her smiles turned into frowns as she attempted to remember. "It's been..." Her eyes grew distant, forming that glassy look. "We were separated when I was nineteen. It's been nine years now."

I swallowed the sorrow. "Nine years?" As far as I could tell, mermaids were not immortal like vampires or angels and demons. She'd spent nine years of her limited lifespan in this cell. The files had been older than I anticipated.

It didn't matter what Emilie said about stooping to their level. I was willing to go that far to bring justice. I would kill the employees working for David. I'd do anything to save them from a life of misery.

When she finished with her extra session, I exited her room.

"Would you want to help me cook dinner?" Monique asked me.

I couldn't say no, so I obliged, and we went to the kitchen. I washed my hands before beginning to chop the vegetables. I was careful to make sure we didn't make too much or too little.

"Nora, are you all right?" She turned to face me with a

worried look.

I looked down, noticing where her eyes were located. I'd cut my finger and it was bleeding all over the vegetables nearby. "Shit, my bad."

Walking over, I ran water over it before putting a band-aid on. I wore gloves after that.

"I'm fine," I answered. She didn't bother arguing and I was glad it was one of those days. I was definitely not in the mood.

Emilie had been here longer than the rest of them and it ripped open my heart, allowing crimson to gush everywhere. She had to be at least twenty-eight. That was *older* than I was. What if she had wanted a husband or kids? What about dreams? She was losing time to do what she deserved to do. Whatever it was, I was disgusted with David for tearing that away from her.

Something in his brain was not connecting if he lacked the basic compassion to see that these three wanted to live in peace. He refused to give them such a thing.

I was interested in carrying a conversation with Monique, but I wasn't sure where to begin. I could only ask her so much before she would suspect what I knew. I needed not a single soul to catch my drift.

"Nora, I know," she said.

"Know what?" I narrowed my gaze.

"Claire told me." She shrugged me off.

Claire betrayed my trust.

I sighed. "Monique, I don't want to talk about this."

"But it's loony!" She shook her head, laughing.

I tilted my head. "A little insensitive to say in an asylum, don't you agree?"

Her smile faded as she swallowed. "You're right. I'm sorry for using that word here."

I cleared my throat. "What is it that she told you?" It was smart to ask before I went on blabbing my biggest secret, only to find out that wasn't what Claire really told her. Why was Claire talking to Monique anyway?

"Oh, it's nothing important. I'm sorry I brought it up. Let's focus on the food, shall we?"

"Yes, let's." I watched her in haste while furrowing my brows. She knew something, didn't she? Why bring it up just to drop it? I needed to be a bit more careful with who I trusted around here.

As I finished with the vegetables, I slid them into the pot.

I could feel Monique's stare on the back of my head. Fear began to lay eggs inside me, allowing the terror to fester that I'd be caught in my lies, and that—that destroyed the whole plan.

XXI

The heater had been turned on full blast this morning as the temperature continued to drop outside. Snow piled up, one sheet on top of the other, covering the ground in a thick, white blanket.

I'd be the first to admit I missed the sunshine. It had been weeks since we last saw that giant star in the sky and yet, it would probably be gone for a few weeks more.

I approached the second floor as a distinct noise threw me off guard. Rabbits, or in this weather, two people without their pants.

As I got closer, I widened my eyes. Claire and one of the doctors were trying to make babies against the wall. I turned around as fast as I could and hurried down the stairs to the main floor. It wasn't supposed to be my place to tell anyone about their private affairs, but I would have to ask Claire about it one of these days. I had no idea she willingly gave it to the doctors she despised so much.

"Nora," someone breathed in a whisper. I faced the voice, looking up at Spence as he leaned against the wall by his room. "Can we talk?"

"Of course." I entered his room after he headed back in. Taking a seat, I asked, "What is this about?"

First, I noticed the heavy bags under his eyes, and I worried about how much sleep he was losing. What happened to him? I was witnessing this man deteriorate—and that was enough to steal my energy.

I thought back on his insomnia comment, recalling he didn't really sleep. If he didn't sleep, why did he have dark circles?

When he didn't respond, I made a big decision to move from the chair to his bed, planting myself beside him. "Spence, you don't look good. What's going on? What is David doing to you?" With a swallow, I held myself back from reaching for his hand. "This is scaring me."

He shook his head, grabbing it for me, like he could read my mind. I almost jumped out of my own skin from the icy touch. Could he get cold and feel it?

"Talk to me, please. Are you dying?" I knew it was a ridiculous question to ask but I had to get him to say *something*.

He laughed, but not in the cute or humorous way. Moreso it'd been pitiful. Pathetic, even. "I don't die." He cleared his throat. "Remember when I told you I was half-demon and half-angel?" his voice came out hoarse.

"Of course. I couldn't forget." I shook my head, snorting. "You don't forget something like that."

His fingers tightened around mine. "I'm two halves of a whole. I'm two halves of opposing sides. I'm in a constant battle with good and evil inside my own head. I just… I just need someone to comfort me. I need someone pure to calm down the demon side." His head fell onto my shoulder.

"I hardly call premarital sex that actions of a pure person," I joked in a quiet tone.

But I didn't have the heart to push him away. He'd been torn open, and picked apart for his worth, and I was meant to save him from the darkness that this asylum cast over them all. I couldn't abandon him in a time of need.

"Nora," he whispered, "don't look at yourself that way. You *are* pure."

I used my other hand to grab the exposed side of his that had still been wrapped in mine. "I'll take your word for it." Who knew better than a half-angel himself?

Spence's body temperature seeped through my smoldering skin, counteracting the flush in my cheeks. I could get hypothermia this way, but I still didn't have the guts to tell him to make like an egg and scramble. The searing pain lingered in his dull eyes—lacking their usual vibrant blue pigment. Instead, gray drowned all signs of life.

We stayed in this position for a while. I'd lost track of time, but he appeared to be asleep and I wouldn't be the one to wake him. I simply hoped his dreams were good and pure. He deserved something worthwhile in this horrid place.

David stood in the doorway, shooting me a look. I put my finger up to tell him to give me a moment.

After carefully lying Spence down on the bed and covering him with a blanket. I had a sneaking suspicion David was behind why Spence was in so much agony. An urge inside me grew as I glanced at my boss, craving nothing more than to bash his head in for doing this to *my* patients.

Once I'd exited his room, I cleared my throat to keep my anger at bay. "He was really upset about something, and I comforted him as his therapist. That was what he asked me to do."

David nodded after *learning* to believe that I didn't suspect him of any foul play, and so I followed him down the hall. "I wanted to talk about what happened in the bathroom. Monique told me you slipped but I don't buy that. You can talk to me, Nora."

If I didn't open up about it, he would get suspicious. I had to prove to him that I was on his side when I truly wasn't.

"It might sound a bit strange—although you did see it the night the power went out. She appeared in the bathroom and knocked my head into the mirror. I don't understand why, but I suppose that wouldn't stop her anyhow." I released a sigh. That hadn't been a lie. I *didn't* understand.

"Are you all right?" he asked, as if he believed he cared about my well-being.

"I'm doing okay. I just want to keep my job here. This place, in a weird way, distracts me from the bad memories. Having something that's constant and a passion of mine doesn't allow me to wallow in my own depression." I wasn't *exactly* depressed but I was still stuck in the grieving stage, somewhere, and this helped me keep my mind off of what could have been and what was.

David nodded, stroking his chin. "I'm glad to hear you're doing better. How has it been going with the patients?"

I tilted my head to my right. "Well, it's been…odd. Emilie has begun to open up a lot more. Spence is still pretty closed off, and he gets upset but he never tells me why, but I'm working on that. Claire… Well, she's barely shared anything with me. She likes me one day and hates me the next. She's quite an interesting character."

David grinned, but the curvature in his lips and wrinkles in his eyes made my stomach churn. "That's good news. I have an interesting task for you. We are running low on groceries. Would you mind going to get some for us?"

A chance to leave this place was exciting yet terrifying. If I left, they could be in danger. Yet, I was desperate to interact with normal humans who weren't good or bad—but rather just human. I craved something that resembled reality.

I just had to make sure what happened last time didn't happen again.

"I'll take you up on that offer, David. I'll go get groceries. Just give me a list and let me go get my keys." My smile appeared with ease.

He grabbed the envelope and shoved it into my hand where I then buried it in my pocket.

As I walked down to the main floor, something came over me. I passed David and shot him a deathly glare, muttering under my breath, "Fucking prick."

I quickly hurried from the building and slid into my car. I had no idea why I'd said that. He could have heard me. Why did that come from my tongue?

Could it be from *their* blood mixing with my own?

Driving down the long road, I listened to the radio for the few times it did come in clear, and I sang along. Relief washed over me, knowing it'd been a good move to get myself out of that asylum for a few hours.

I arrived at the grocery store in town after an hour of car rides and depressing tunes. As I walked inside and grabbed a cart, I peeked at the list he handed me. Something pricked my insides like a needle to the tip of my finger, and the comforting feeling of being out into the world with other people returned.

"I miss this," Spence said.

Whipping around to face him, I gasped out of fear. "Where did you come from? How did you get here?"

He chewed on his lip and rubbed his hand against the back of his neck. "Well, I, uh, possessed you."

I choked on my next words. "Excuse me?"

He was quick to pop in a reason. "It wasn't to harm you or invade your privacy. I wanted to leave the asylum and you're the only doctor I can trust to let me go with them. The asylum was built to keep us locked inside and I can't physically leave on my own. However, if I possess someone, I can. I'm walking in their shoes; therefore, the asylum doesn't recognize it's me."

"Spence, this is wrong on so many levels." I shook my head, pushing the cart down the aisle.

"I know, and I didn't want to scare you. I just needed to leave for a bit." He scanned the aisles of products and his eyes lit up at the sight of freedom. He had genuine solace in him for the first time in days. In fact, I'd never seen him in respite before.

Now it'd been my turn to chew my bottom lip. "Why don't you leave now? You're free. I won't force you to go back. I'll just tell them I have no idea what happened to you when they realize you're gone. I've come to realize I'm a damn good actress." I smirked a bit, pride taking over my being

He grabbed a package of green beans and threw it into the cart. "I can't leave. Claire and Emilie still need me. I won't leave them behind."

I stopped by the salads and picked up some of the kits. "I can never choose. What do you think Emilie will like more?" I glanced back at Spence.

He picked the one with sunflower seeds and balsamic dressing, then grabbed my hand to stop me from grabbing another bag. "Listen to me, Nora. I'm sorry. It was wrong of me to possess your body and I promise I will never do it again without your permission."

I gave him a small smile. "You have to do it again to get back inside the asylum, and I know you'll go against my wishes to save your friends. It's… It's not okay, but I can forgive you for this. However, I don't like knowing there's a demon inside me." I refused to admit that it didn't scare me as much when that demon was Spence. I *trusted* him. "I know that this is all new to me but I just… I've seen a lot of weird movies with demon possession, and I don't like it when demons make the person do something they don't like. I don't want to have sex with some stranger. I've seen that happen."

His laugh brightened the atmosphere around us. "That's not how it works. I mean, yes there are demons who do that but mine doesn't. *I* don't. My demon is concerned with hurting people. It's not a demon of lust. It's a demon of wrath."

"Wait, what?" Was he telling me that demons could only do what the sin told them to do?

I chewed on my lip some more as Spence filled up the cart with food that made my stomach rumble. "I still feel bad for using you like that. I'll make it up to you somehow. I promise. I don't make promises I can't keep."

"Tell me something. Did I call David names because of your demon?" I held up some fries. I couldn't choose between seasoned or unseasoned.

He put the seasoned fries in the basket, nodding. "Sorry about that. The demon in me might have an ever-growing scorn for

David and he's not afraid to hide it. So, Nora, now that we are out in the real world for a little bit, shall we go do something?"

I laughed and picked up some chips. "No, we don't have time. The longer I stay out, the higher of a chance you have of getting caught missing. I don't want to get you into trouble. But maybe one of these days I can sneak you out to do something besides shopping." I flashed him a smile.

He eyed some snacks on the shelf. "I would love that, Nora. This is why you're my favorite psychologist. Don't change, please."

My stomach fluttered at the idea of being called his *favorite*. It filled the void fermenting inside me, I desperate to feel successful in what I attempted to achieve in life—by being appreciated.

XXII

Claire pulled her legs up onto the chair, sitting crisscross. "You don't have to be afraid of me. Your blood, I mean."

I glanced at my bandage. "I suppose that's true. But I'm not quite afraid of…you." I unwrapped it, showing her the results. By now my wound has healed, but my veins bled black.

She furrowed her brows. "Do you mind if…I taste it?"

"My blood? You just said I don't have to be afraid."

"It's not for me. I can tell you which blood he gave you from each of us, or which of our DNA was used to create this new you."

"New me? Am I really new?" I chuckled. "I haven't changed."

"No, but you have new abilities."

Yes, I did, but they were slow-coming. Clearing my throat,

I handed her my palm. "Tell me, am I a vampire, mermaid, or angel-demon?" Was it wrong of me to hope I was more like Spence?

In seconds, she punctured my palm with her fang and tasted the black veins. She made a sour face and dropped it, releasing a sigh. "Just as I feared."

"What is it?"

"It's my DNA. That's why it tastes sour. Your blood is tainted for me." Claire sat back.

Sure enough, I was not part vampire, but I had specific strands of her DNA in my blood, which in turn made me more like Claire.

"Let's hope Spence doesn't find out."

Furrowing my brows, I tilted my head. "Why? What's wrong with him knowing?"

"Let's just say…you fascinate him. And I don't. Hearing you're more like me isn't exactly going to be the highlight of his day." She rolled her eyes.

It wouldn't be, but I wasn't going to act more like Claire. I also wouldn't drink blood, either. As far as I knew, I'd only get a few new abilities.

"If he dislikes me because David mixed your DNA into my blood, that means Spence was never good to begin with. I'd like to think he's more mature than that."

Her lips tugged upward on one side of her face. "Well, he certainly is mature."

Shivers crawled up my spine as the words spilled out of my mouth, "What do you mean?"

"Nevermind." She stood. "Can we go somewhere else? Your office is so ugly to look at."

We decided to head outside, in which case it was far colder

than normal for me yet bothered Claire not at all. Whatever her skin was made of, I wanted that. Unfortunately, it seemed I didn't inherit that ability.

"What abilities have you gotten?" She asked.

I took a moment to play with the question. I'd noticed a few things, but they only seemed abnormal because they had been so different before.

My hearing got better, and now my heartbeat would pound in my ears whenever my anxiety rose, or Spence came close. I could hear conversations as clear as day whereas I hadn't been able to eavesdrop before. Was it okay to admit this to David? He'd ask eventually.

I'd just been stalling long enough so he wouldn't ask, and for now it would suffice. It was hard to say how many abilities I'd end up with.

"The food lost its flavor. But that could be just my imagination."

"Could be but isn't." Claire twirled around and faced me. "In fact, I think it could have something to do with me. I'm not saying for sure that you will crave blood, but it's possible that you want something different. And human food is no longer going to be enough."

I groaned. "In other words, I need blood."

"*It could be.* Or you could eat tasteless food forever. You're not a real vampire—and never will be—so you don't need blood to survive. I do, but you don't. You just might crave it at some point."

Could I commit to eating boring meals? Possibly. It was better than the alternative.

"That doesn't make sense, or seem fair," I said. "David finds out about you and what you are, so he locks you up and treats you horribly. But then he tries to give us the same abilities and that's somehow better? Is he for or against this? Magic? Not even sure what to call it."

She shrugged, eyes roaming the gray sky. "We don't know. Magic exists, but not because of vampires. Witches have magic. Maybe a few other creatures, but we are certainly not one of them. We just have superhuman abilities and survive on blood."

That was not the answer I wanted, but it was the one I got.

"What were you doing with the doctor? I mean, I saw you two going at it like rabbits." I hadn't planned to ask but now was a better time than ever.

Claire leaned back against the wall. "I might be a prisoner, but I have needs, Nora. And these male doctors do, too. It's easy to seduce them. I enjoy sex, and I can't lose everything while I'm here."

Before I could stop, the next question tumbled out, "Is it easy to seduce Spence?" It could have made a bit of sense, since she craved blood and Spence would go out of his way to hurt himself.

Two peas in a pod…

Her laugh filled the space around us. "Are you jealous? I've certainly tried and succeeded a few times. But I never push them to do it if they really don't want to. I simply water the seed that's already planted." Her eyes lingered on my dress. "And Spence wouldn't dare hurt himself. He's resilient."

My face burned at the idea of Spence and Claire. Was she telling me the truth? Had they had sex? And why was it my business? More importantly, why did I care?

And why would I believe her about Spence? I'd seen the cuts. The proof was in the pudding.

She smirked as she came closer to me, trapping me against the wall. "Nora, I think you have a little crush on Spence. Don't worry, I won't tell."

"I do not." Yet the blush in my cheeks said otherwise. Why did this happen to *me*?

"If it makes you feel better, you don't need to worry all that much. Spence isn't fond of me, like I said before, but he certainly seems fond of you."

Was that true? Whether or not it was, it made no difference. I wouldn't pursue anything, and he wouldn't, either.

"Well, if you do decide to pursue anything, just know that he's a good guy. He'd never hurt a fly, even if he is half demon. That's why he doesn't like me much, and why you interest him. It's not normal for us to meet humans with so much good intent in their heart." One click of her heels and she was gone. Claire left me with more questions than I started with.

Had Spence really taken an interest in me? No.

But what about Claire? Had they both really had sex? I couldn't picture Spence as the guy who would want to sleep with her, but I supposed he was more unpredictable than I originally thought. Somehow, that intrigued me greatly.

After night fell, I took a walk to the entertainment room to read a good book. Maybe it wasn't the best idea to read romance after being told Spence may have liked me more than I thought, especially when I couldn't do anything about it. But I'd read anyway.

Romance was my favorite genre. It was also the only one I preferred to read. Everything else involved too much horror or darkness.

I avoided all dark genres like the plague. I had enough nightmares.

Picking a favorite book was nearly impossible. Every world I dived into became just as magical as the previous, and every couple I got to know were a blast. I fell in love with them both, so how could I be expected to pick *just* one?

I picked up a new book tonight, one that I'd never seen before. David must have ordered some new books. Claire and Spence weren't too concerned with reading, nor romance.

Emilie, however, could have been. It wasn't just for me.

Thirty minutes into the book, I had already become hooked. The characters were just a bit younger than I was, but still adults. And they had wonderful chemistry together.

The book took place during a historical time, when pirates once existed. They still did, but not nearly as much as they had during the 1700s. I enjoyed a contemporary romance just as I enjoyed a historical one. They both had what I craved.

Craved… No, Claire said I wouldn't need blood. It'd be odd if someone who was haunted by blood began to *desire* it.

Shaking my head, I returned to reading. During those days, only the rich could shower. Unless you bathed in the river, you'd only be allowed to bathe during warm months.

I certainly couldn't survive on showering only in the spring and summer.

The female character had learned to love the pirate life, and she learned to love the male love interest, too.

Must be a good book if she's up this late.

Furrowing my brows, I looked around. "Hello? You can come talk to me. I don't bite."

Not yet.

But nobody said a word, and nobody came out of the shadows. Whoever said that—they were messing with me. Maybe it was…

No. I wouldn't even entertain the idea.

The voice didn't come back. I continued with my book, but I

had to force myself to quit at one point. If I didn't, I'd never sleep and then tomorrow would be the roughest day yet. That said a lot for what I'd already experienced here.

I stood from the couch and began walking away.

She's up later than Claire. Maybe I should pick up a book.

I spun on my heel and faced the hallway, peering into the dark. "Who's there? I can hear you."

"Nora, what's going on?" Spence asked.

As soon as he spoke, the voice I'd heard became familiar. It was *Spence* who had been talking.

"Are you talking to yourself? Why are *you* up this late? That's the real question." I strolled over to his door, peeking through the bars. "Can't sleep?"

"I never can." His blue eyes shimmered before me and I almost leaped back. "But why would you assume I'm talking to myself? I addressed you, so I was talking to you. You sound like you're hearing the ghosts again."

"Ghosts…maybe." I glanced down the hall. "They're talking about me. But ghosts don't need to read, so why would they say that they should pick up a book?"

Silence hung heavy in the air while the storm picked up outside.

Spence cleared his throat after a good few minutes. "I don't have all the answers."

Liar. Just tell her that she's reading your thoughts.

This took me off guard, but I hid it well. The lack of lighting made it easy. "Neither do I. I suppose now I know that ghosts like to read and this one is spying on me while I'm at it."

Maybe it was another ability, meaning Claire could hear my thoughts and now I could hear Spence's. Was that wrong? Of course. Did it mean I'd stop? I should have but I wasn't sure how to turn it off. For now, it was comforting to know that there was more going on than met the eye.

With a shrug, I said goodnight and headed to my room.

Sleeping didn't come easy, or at least not that I now knew the truth. Did I tell Claire? What if she told Spence? She would. They were closer than I originally thought, and I wasn't about to take such a risk.

Instead, I'd keep this secret to myself. I'd use it on the right people. I'd learn to control it, and maybe I would be the one who bit the hand that fed me.

XXIII

I gathered up my clothes and threw them into the big bin outside my room. The doctor rolled it down to the next room, collecting the dirty clothes for the week.

Today, the snow had stopped falling and the clouds had decided to give the sun a chance to shine. Because of this, I was going to take the three of them outside for some fresh air—and a little vitamin D couldn't hurt either.

Once I had all my warm clothes on, I got the others ready and led them into the back where the fences kept them trapped. It wasn't ideal but someday soon they'd get out.

"Claire, you may want to stay inside," I said as I turned back and looked at her as she stepped out of the door.

She shook her head. "That's a myth. Vampires don't burn

under the sun. We're undead, not corpses." She rolled her eyes.

I scrunched up my face. "Uh, is undead not the same thing?"

She gave me a look. "No. I'm *undead.* Not dead. I don't have a beating heart because that would make me mortal. The dead are ghosts, like your friend who keeps haunting you. She was alive, then she died. I was never alive. I was never dead. I'm undead. I was born this way."

"Oh." I nodded a little. "Well, you would know yourself better." I walked in the opposite direction.

Emilie stepped in front of me. "So."

"So?" I lifted my head. "What's on your mind?"

She grabbed my wrist and pulled me closer as she whispered, "I see the way you look at Spence."

I pulled away from her, fixing my scarf to cover my burning cheeks. "I see him as I see you and Claire."

Emilie laughed. "Then you must have a crush on all of us because you can't lie about the looks you give him. I won't tell anyone. I think it's very sweet." She bumped my shoulder. "I can see why you like him. He's very cute."

"I do not like Spence. That's absurd." I coughed. "And even if I did, it'd be wrong."

"Why?" She tilted her head.

I looked up at the asylum, studying one of the windows as if someone were about to jump from it and I could save them. "My plan is to get you guys out of here. It'll be harder to make David think I don't know why you're here if I'm having any affairs with Spence." I glanced over at the man of the hour. "He also only sees me in a friendly way, and I wouldn't want to ruin anything now."

Emilie rubbed her eyes before shaking her head to dismiss my excuse. "I don't believe it. Spence would have to be blind to only see you in a friendly way." She shrugged before skipping away.

Spence stood beside the fence, his gaze lost in the trees. Something had his attention and I wanted to know what it could be.

I walked over and attempted to follow his eyes. The trees had been naked for months now—every secret they'd tried to bury exposed to the harsh winter.

"It's sort of nice outside, don't you think?" With both Claire's and Emilie's accusations running through my mind, standing close to Spence now posed awkward, causing my stomach to flutter and flip like a butterfly in a circus.

He folded his arms across his chest. "If you say so. Do you like winter?"

I had never actually thought about my favorite season. "I think it has its perks. You can make snow angels and have snowball fights. You can build forts and snowmen. You appreciate the warmth of a hot tub that much more. I also find it to be the most romantic season of the year." I had read enough romance books to know winter was the best at bringing two people together.

He shot me a side glance, chuckling. "Romantic?"

"Yes. It gives couples more of a reason to hold each other by the warm fire, drinking hot cocoa. There's a mistletoe above their heads." A small smile grazed my lips at the thought. "The most romantic sex happens in front of a fire. At least that's what I enjoyed." I could never forget that night. I may not have ended up with my ex, but that night was one that I always cherished.

"Ah, now I finally get to know more about you. It wasn't exactly what I meant when I wanted you to tell me about yourself, but I'll take it." He leaned against the wired fence. "I hate chocolate."

My jaw dropped, eyes widening in a playful manner. "What?

Who the hell hates chocolate?"

Spence laughed. "I do. Better send me to hell. Oh, wait, I'm halfway there." He gestured to the asylum.

A frown formed. "I'll get you out of here. I made a promise, and I don't break those. Please, trust me. I have a plan, one that may work if you're okay with murder."

He stiffened at the word *murder*. "I'm not going to kill anyone. I refuse to satisfy the demon in me."

It was my turn to cross my arms. "Well, you don't have to kill anyone. But Claire and I will. After seeing how broken you are and what David is doing to everyone here, I'm very capable of homicide. You don't treat people like this and live to see the light."

My stomach grumbled, filling the silence. Judgment radiated from Spence as his eyes burned into my soul. I'd felt exposed and not in a good way. He didn't like the sound of me killing the staff members, but it wouldn't change my mind. We had no other plan. David was set in his ways, determined to control and experiment on these people. He'd stop at nothing to get what he wanted unless he was rotting in the ground. Sending him to prison still put these three at risk.

"Can I show you something?" he asked me.

Our eyes met as I nodded.

He grasped my hand, pulling me towards the far corner of the fence at one end of the building. "We need privacy."

What would he need privacy for? Was this a big dark secret or was he going to show me his penis? I could've pried into his head to find out, but I hadn't mastered the control of that ability just yet.

He stopped and turned to face me, letting go of my hand. "I guess it's time to show you these." He pulled off his jacket, then his scarf and shirt. I had no clue as to why he wanted to show me his bare chest, but seconds later, he closed his eyes and large wings stretched out from behind him.

I stumbled back, too intrigued to look away. "Okay, so you *do* have wings."

Spence's eyes darted around the area, and he stepped away from me, assuming I'd been afraid of him. "Yes, I do. Maybe now was the wrong time to show you."

Shaking my head, I closed in on him in a hurry, reaching out before he covered them back up. "Don't put them away. I'm just shocked is all." My eyes were glued to the large feathers, mesmerized by the dichotomy. Opposing sides. Light and dark. One black wing—one white. It was unique, and I loved the idea of him being this extraordinary.

"Nora, are you okay?" Spence waved his hand in front of my face.

"I'm doing fine. It's really neat to see them." I wanted to touch them, but I felt that went too far. I had no right to touch any part of Spence unless he was coming to me for comfort.

He put them away and pulled his layers back on. Disappointment flashed across my features, but I flushed them away before he could catch it. "We should head back inside before David questions what's going on out here." He walked away from me and headed back into the building.

Claire and Emilie followed as I joined them inside the darkest place I'd ever stepped foot in.

As I strolled back to my room, a figure's movement caught my eye. It headed down towards the basement and I could take a wild guess as to just who it could have been.

Heading down to the basement, I searched for the ghost. "Alicia, I know you're down here. Do you want to explain to me why you keep doing this? I've already paid enough of my debt through nightmares and trauma!" I scanned the halls, but it was far too black for me to see anything obvious.

A whisper in my ear almost had me screaming. "Not enough, Nora. No, no—I've just been getting started."

"Why are you doing this to me?" I turned to face her, but she's vanished once again.

"Because I believe you should pay for your crimes," her voice echoed.

The pain hit me like a bird crashing into a window. Tears ran down my face, never letting go of me or what burdens I carried. "I regret it every single day. Do you not see that? I haven't gotten over your death. I haven't forgotten about *you*."

A door slammed and a wheelchair rolled down the hall, towards me. "You haven't forgotten? It's my duty to make sure you will *never* forget."

I wiped away the tears, facing the wheelchair that stopped squeaking as it halted in front of me. "What kind of friend are you? You want to make me miserable by haunting me after you've already died? My nightmares destroy me. I know it was all my fault. Is that not enough for you?"

It's never enough.

I realized the voice had come from inside my own head. It wasn't just Alicia making me realize I was a monster. *I* believed it myself.

I took a few steps away from the wheelchair. "I'm sorry for saying no. I'm constantly reminding myself to cherish the time I have with people still here. I want to do it over and say yes, I want to join you in that gym and dance with everyone we don't care about. I want to fix this, but I can't." Hands pushed against my back, forcing me down into the chair.

"Yes, you can." She rolled me through some double doors. Straps tightened around my wrists and ankles. "You can fix this, Nora."

"What is this? What are you going to do to me?" I cried out, screaming for anyone to hear me.

She grabbed a stick, placing it between my teeth. "You are going to fix everything when you spend the rest of your life in a facility. They'll send you away and I'll be there to haunt you every night. Nobody will believe you. You deserve to suffer for taking my life." She turned on the ECT machine, powering the electricity. "And suffer you will, Nora Witlow."

I spread my fingers, stretching them while I fought against the straps. Regardless of my futile attempts, I couldn't stop throwing myself against the weight of the leather around my wrists.

Terror nibbled at my brain as I forced images of help coming my way. My body shook, and I forced out screams that the stick muffled far too much for anyone to hear.

This would be my end. The last time I would see Claire, Emilie, and Spence. I never had a chance to tell anyone the truth, and yet, I never gave them that. They'd asked and I'd refused.

She connected two electrodes to my temples, one on each side. "I'll see you on the other side." Her cunning smirk embedded itself in my mind like a spider laying eggs as she powered up the machine, sending the volts coursing through my body.

I bit down on the stick in my mouth, a burning and tingling sensation seizing my veins. It stopped in an instant, but the electricity lingered even after the machine had been shut off.

"Better luck next time," she whispered in my ear before her ghost blended into thin air.

The world appeared so far from my grasp yet so close to reach out and brush my fingers over. I even tried to grab it but my wrists didn't budge. Voices called my name, but I was unable to make any of them out. If this machine hadn't been down here, I never would have been tortured with it—and by the one woman who used to call herself my best friend.

XXIV

My eyes were fixated on the wall across from me. My body convulsed for a second due to the memory of electric charges running through. "Bad habit," I said as I collected my sanity.

Spence was seated beside me, watching the same wall I was. "I should probably explain something to you."

"Explain what?" I faced him.

He cleared his throat. "Nora, we know what happened down there. You didn't strap yourself in that wheelchair. Someone else did, and if you just admit who it was, I can help make an understanding of this for you."

I swallowed my fear, looking away as a tear rolled down my cheek. "I wanted answers. I wanted to know why she would hurt me. She was supposed to be my best friend and when she died, my world crumbled to pieces. I followed her to find out why but when she wanted to make me suffer for what I did…" The words got stuck in my throat.

He wrapped his fingers around mine, warming them. He resembled that crackling fire in the dead of winter today, more than I'd ever seen of him before. "When someone is at their most vulnerable, their fears and emotions are enhanced. We all can see it in this asylum—a place built for the nonhuman abilities. You're vulnerable because you're in the middle of grieving. So, while you're grieving, we can see what is haunting your thoughts. *She* is haunting you."

My feet went numb at the thought of being exposed to everyone here. I couldn't keep anything to myself. My heels slipped off my feet, leaving my frozen toes naked.

"If my emotions are enhanced, why can't we see anything else?" I turned my head up to meet his eyes. "Anything besides the trauma?"

"For one, you blame yourself for your grief. That overpowers all your positive emotions. Two, she takes away those feelings. She wants you to be unhappy." He rubbed my hand between both of his.

She had been the closest person in my life who hadn't been related to me by blood. When her neck snapped, that changed. *Keep your friends close, and enemies closer.*

I leaned my head against the wall, unable to feel the cold bite on my skin. "Why does she hate me? Does dying turn someone wicked and spiteful?"

"That's just it. She's not—" He shook his head. "I didn't want to bring this up, but people are not safe even after they're dead. They're not safe from the evil that hides in the corners. If your friend strapped you into a wheelchair and electrocuted you, something tells me that she's not *your* friend. Death took her soul and replaced it with the sick version to mess you up."

I whispered, "So now I have to save you and her..."

Energy fled my body, but I could not even begin to fathom what she was being put through. My best friend had been locked away. She couldn't find peace even after losing her life—and that had been such a twisted version of the tale.

Spence leaned in. "Nora, you lost your best friend. You don't have to save anyone if you don't want to."

"That's just it, Spence. I do want to. I know that I'll be a shitty person if I don't save you or Alicia. Maybe this will help me get through grieving. Maybe I can finally have some closure if I save her from Death."

He nodded a bit as he leaned away. "I'm sorry."

"For what?" I asked.

A sigh escaped his mouth. "Sorry for how your life turned out."

"Don't you dare say that. My life is great. I lost her, and I will never forget her laugh. I at least got that with her." A small smile planted itself on my lips. "I'll try, anyway."

He gently nudged me. "Do you mind telling me what about it you love?"

Spence had begun spilling his own secrets. Now it was my turn. What harm could it do to tell him about the people who raised me?

I said, "I have a wonderful family. A mother, a father, and a younger brother. My mother was always there to kiss away the boo-boos and scare off the bad dreams. My father would play games with us when we were tired, and my mom got mad at him for keeping us awake so late, but we loved it. Danny was born when I was fifteen. He's my younger brother, the greatest person who has ever been in my life." I played with the hem of my dress.

"You and Danny are close, I suppose."

"Very close. I tell him stories to get him to bed. I taught him sign language so we could communicate. Danny was born deaf, but that never stopped us from loving him and letting him live life to the fullest. He's been bullied in the past, and I thank God he can't hear the cruel insults, but I'm always there. He's such a bright soul. He's the one who brings joy to our lives. He teaches us about love and happiness. I could never imagine my life without him." I wiped away a tear.

"I miss him, all the time. I love being here with you guys, but I also miss home. I miss the way Danny curls up in my side when I tell him a story. He's my best friend." I peered up at Spence, his eyes sparkling. "I would give my life up for him."

He smiled a tad. "He sounds like a really cool guy. Keep talking. I love that there's this little light in your eyes when you speak of Danny."

With the green light, I did keep going. "He didn't have friends for a while, but this really sweet girl decided to befriend him. She's been learning sign language to try and talk to him more, which I find to be the cutest thing ever. She'll get far in life. She's come over a few times and introduced Danny to baseball. He's actually come to really love baseball. He found something he loves to do and that's all I truly want for him."

He chuckled, pressing the back of his fist against his mouth. "Baseball? I'm more of a basketball kind of guy."

"Between you and I, baseball isn't that interesting but the kid wants what he wants." I shrugged. "I really love the friend he's met, and that's partly more of a reason why I felt okay leaving him. I don't like to leave Danny alone, but I know she'll have his back while I'm not there. I can trust her to keep an eye on Danny and make sure he's protected. I know it's wrong to always protect him, but I can't help it. It breaks my heart when kids pick on him."

He patted my leg. "Of course. Danny has his ability on his side. He can never hurt if he doesn't know what the kids are saying. And if he someday learns to read lips, he'll be smart enough to know how to insult the kid back without using words. He'll be unstoppable, and I know so because he's got as his role model."

I blushed a bit. "Am I unstoppable, Spence? Do you really believe that?"

He put his hands behind his head, between him and the wall. "Yes." He flashed me a sly smile.

As I stood from the bed, I tripped over my shoe and flew to the floor. I'd landed on my hands and knees, dropping my head against the floor in embarrassment. I had no coordination whatsoever.

Spence jumped from the bed and rushed to help me stand on my own two feet. Once I had my balance, he got down on one knee and grabbed one of my heels. "You might want these."

"I might," I said in a quieter tone.

He had expected me to understand where he was going with his line, but it became clear that I was lost with his intentions until he grabbed my ankle and lifted it up as he put my shoe on. He stayed there a minute longer than I anticipated.

"Spence?"

"I apologize, Nora. My mind went elsewhere. Sometimes that happens." He shook his head before putting on my other shoe for me.

A part of me worried as to why he got distracted so quickly.

Had David been using ECT on Spence? Was he losing bits and pieces of his own mind?

He stood and straightened his posture, observing me while I studied him. My back was against the wall across from his bed, my mind racing as I pictured Spence tied down with electricity pulsing through him.

While I'd been lost in the nightmare, Spence reached out and moved a strand of hair from my face, pushing it alongside the rest.

My breath caught in my throat as he leaned in, his lips barely brushing against mine. My heart had been ready to burst as my stomach did backflips. Having Spence this close was a maraschino cherry on top of the whipped cream.

"Oh, shit," a female said with a choked laugh.

I stumbled away from Spence, spinning to face him before looking over at Claire. "Nothing happened." More than nothing happened, and we all knew it.

I grabbed Claire's wrist and dragged her out to the entertainment area. "Don't say anything. David will kill me if he knows that—" The words wouldn't leave my tongue. If I said them, they would mean something.

My fingers touched my lips, the surface that Spence's lips had breathed against. It was soft and subtle, and it couldn't be considered a real kiss due to the lack of contact, but it was something that had my mind running in circles.

Claire pulled my hand away from my mouth, laughing. "Relax. I'm the last person who is going to tattle on you for being with a man who is supposed to be your patient."

"We aren't together, and he's not a real patient," I argued.

She gave me a look that made me feel like I had been born yesterday. "Yes, but David doesn't know you know that."

David.

I had almost forgotten about him for a moment. I'd been so caught up with Alicia's ghost—or what had once been her ghost—and the mysteries of this building that I spaced about David being behind it.

I scraped my teeth along my bottom lip, looking at Claire. She had been watching me with curiosity. "What?" I asked.

She tore her eyes away from my face. "Nothing. Are you and Spence a thing?"

"A thing? Before today, I had never even suspected that he would want to…do that." I gestured as I fiddled with the necklace resting against my chest. "I know you said he's interested but it's harder to believe, until he tries to…"

"Kiss, Nora. It's called a *kiss*." She closed the space between us, lifting my chin and inspecting my skin as if I were telling lies. Her eyes lingered on my throat a bit too long but she gathered control over herself. "What he did was almost kiss you. Say it."

"Why?" I was desperate to take a step back, fearful she might rip my throat out and suck my blood dry. No, she said she wouldn't. My blood was sour now, right? I could see the hunger in her eyes. I was a snack to her, and yet I couldn't get my feet to move.

She narrowed her eyes and grabbed the sides of my face. "Because if you don't admit it, how will you two ever end up together? Tell me what happened, Nora."

If I didn't bring the words to life, she would never put any distance between us. I could become dinner and I was not ready for such a thing. Swallowing, I whispered, "He *almost* kissed me."

The scene danced in my head while my heart pounded against my rib cage. Spence had moved that strand of hair away from my eye before bringing his lips towards mine. They had touched ever so slightly, and I couldn't deny what I knew.

Spence Woods had tried to kiss me.

XXV

Laughter filled the air, daring to go against the dread that drifted throughout this building. "I don't want to talk about me, Nora. I said this!" Claire shook her head. "I want to talk about you and Spence."

I folded my hands in my lap, desperate to keep up my professional status. "You and I both know that isn't appropriate. This session is about you."

Her eyes almost rolled into the back of her head. "Yeah, because everything here has been appropriate. It's totally *appropriate* for you to stand there while Spence is about to kiss you. If this was really just about keeping a patient-to-doctor relationship, you would not be getting close to him like so."

I pinched the bridge of my nose as I forgot to keep my cool

in front of her. "Can we please not talk about this? What about you, huh? I'm not blind. You were hungry, Claire. You wanted to drink my blood and that's what we need to discuss. We need to explore that."

The back of her head hit the wall, but she didn't seem fazed by it. "Yes, I wanted to drink your blood. Is that what you want to hear? I'm a vampire. Drive a stake through my heart."

"You told me my blood is sour. It's tainted. Do you not get enough? Why did you even feel the need to crave my blood?" I shoved my index finger between my bracelet and wrist, turning it around to keep my mind busy. Or to keep my sanity, whichever one preferred.

"Your blood has spots in it. Some spots are sour. Other spots smell like human blood." Claire pointed her finger at me. "This might come as a shock, but David hasn't been giving me enough. I got hungry. Why do you think I'm a sex addict? When people are turned on, their blood has this sweet taste. I screw my victims before I kill them because they taste better that way. Sex is just a bonus." She shooed her hand.

"I was not turned on." I scoffed at her excuse. I was not turned on by anything.

A smirk, subtle but present, appeared on her face. She folded her arms. "Nora, I have enhanced senses. I can smell you from here. Lust has a smell. Admit it. I'm not one to judge. You want Spence. I mean, can you blame yourself? He's got a great body and with him being an angel and a demon, he's gotta be wild in bed."

She didn't miss the gulp of air I took. I could not even begin to imagine Spence in such a way. It was wrong. It went against everything I stood for and believed in.

"And what might that be?" Claire asked, tapping her chin

with her eyes focused on me as if I were a concept she couldn't comprehend. "You're not a virgin so I know you aren't waiting for the right guy. You know he's not actually your patient." Her eyes lit up. "But ah, you tell yourself he's forbidden territory because it thickens the tension. Nora, you're a woman. You're a grown woman with plenty of hormones and you want him to grab you by the hips and ravish you."

I cleared my throat, loud and authoritative. "Claire, that's enough. We need to talk about you." I crossed my arms to put forth my firm hand. "Your words seemed to correspond to what had gone on inside my head, which begs the question, can you read my mind?"

Her eyes darted towards the floor before meeting me again. "Yes." She stood up in a hurry. "I told you I was a vampire with superhuman abilities. I don't just read body language. I read minds. I don't just run fast. I have a speed that surpasses the common *Homo sapien.* Human thoughts are so loud, too. You think we hear well? We hear so good that your brain screams to us." She put her hands on her little desk as she leaned over the top. "I do not want to be the bad guy. I never wished to be the bad guy, Nora."

I didn't want to correct her misuse of *good*, so I said nothing on that subject. But as she snorted, I remembered that she'd heard my comment anyway.

I tilted my head a bit to get more into her line of sight again. "In what way are you the bad guy? You're the prisoner."

"I survive off blood. What fuels me is the one thing that keeps other creatures' hearts beating, and I have to take it from them to stay alive." She pushed herself off the top of the desk and came closer, squatting to my level. "Even as a little girl, I never could control myself. I would attack vulnerable humans. It wasn't until hormones kicked in that I wanted to hunt men who were letting their other head speak for them. When my body developed, their eyes wandered. I could smell the lust radiating off their moist skin."

"Claire—"

"But I swore to only go after men I knew were using it the wrong way. I went after men who were cheating on their spouses. If I didn't teach them a lesson, who would have? He would continue to look for women who were not his wife. Yet, I helped them cheat. I still satisfied their needs. I guess that does make me a bad person after all." She let out a little sigh. "I've done horrible things."

My forehead creased at her statement. "But I saw you having sex with one of the doctors and you didn't kill him."

"If I had, David would have me put down like a rabid dog." Claire shrugged. "He was for fun. Sometimes I do want to enjoy sex for the sake of it rather than killing them. He wasn't that good. It's so hard to find men who know what they're doing. Although can you blame them? They're idiots. They don't know what a woman wants." She popped back onto her feet and turned away. "Women, however, do know." She glanced at me. "It's a shame that I can't get a real dick and a woman's knowledge of women's needs all at once. You can't have it all, I guess." She walked back to her bed.

I pushed some hair behind my ear before formulating a sentence that made sense. "So you have a very active sex life and your vampirism plays a part." The look she gave me was something else. I wasn't sure what to make of it.

Claire snickered. "Relax, Nora. I'm not going to seduce Spence. He doesn't have blood. Well, none that I'd be able to survive off of." She couldn't just read minds. She could make sense of unformed thoughts. "I mean, he is very tempting, of course, but I prefer…more bold males. At least now I do." Her eyes squinted as if she were picking through her own brain for more words. "So, Spence likes you, huh?"

"Excuse me?"

"Spence, he's into you." She lifted one of her perfect eyebrows.

My face heated up, but I attempted to keep my cool. "He's not into me. He probably just saw an opportunity and wanted to seize it."

She turned on her heel, pacing in the slowest of motions. "Riiiiiight, because that's how he is." One arm stayed crossed while the other was propped up to tap her chin some more. "I don't know him or anything after three years. He totally plays women."

Nausea was filling my stomach, threatening to send my breakfast back up. "Why would he be into me?" I kept thinking about why such a charming god-like man would bother himself such a simple human.

You're not simple, Nora. He opened his emotions to you, and you gave him a chance to express himself.

"I think you just answered your own question. Spence is…a complicated kind of guy. Even I can't get into his head, but that could be because vampires are locked out of angels' brains." She went deep into thought.

I had a vampire ability, and *I* could get into his head. But I still wasn't a real vampire. Claire made sure I knew that.

She continued, "I wouldn't say he's a sensitive guy. However, he does respect you in a way he has never respected another psychologist. He hasn't tried to kiss another psychologist, and trust me, plenty of them were attractive." She laughed to herself before shaking her head. "When he showed you his wings in the courtyard, I was surprised. He's never done that."

"You've known him for three years. How could you say he's never done that?" It had to be a sin to talk about Spence when he wasn't around. However, all morals flew out the window when I found out what Monstrum was here for.

Claire sat on her bed once again, running her hands up and down her thighs. "Spence and I had a thing."

I almost fell out of my chair when she admitted this. How had I never suspected a thing? She told me they had sex, but it was actually a *thing?* Spence never got angry with Claire when she grabbed his collar because he had once been with her for more than just a friendly movie night.

"It was a while back, Nora. I swear it never went anywhere. We were always fighting. He said I brought out the demon in him." For once, I'd seen Claire display a look of sorrow and guilt.

I had been there when Spence asked me to comfort him. He told me that he would always fight his demon side, and he wanted someone like me to make it go away. If I killed David and his staff, I would become the demon Spence was terrified to be controlled by. *Demon of Wrath.*

"So, how long did it last? Don't answer if you don't want to." I wanted to know. A part of me wanted her to tell me she was kidding, but the other part reminded me that he had a past and I had to accept that. They weren't together for a good reason.

"It only lasted a few months. We were on and off a lot. Our fights began with us screaming at each other. I wanted him to let me in. He would never reveal anything important, and I started questioning why he wasn't taking our relationship seriously. We would make up with sex. It was fun at first, but it got old quick." She rubbed her face.

My blood ran cold and my nerves went numb. It wasn't normal for me to feel this way. Their relationship was over a long time ago.

She sat back against the wall. "Angry sex is fun. It's rough and passionate, just the way I like it. But when all your fights are overpowered by it, it becomes meaningless. I wished we would communicate and talk it out. I wanted real solutions. I wanted to be that couple who apologized after a fight. Neither of us ever did. Our relationship thrived on toxicity. So, we called it off for good. Then you came in here and I could see how you interested him. I was a bit jealous, but I realized he deserves to be happy. If you can help him fight the demon, do it. He's a good guy."

"He's a good guy," I repeated. No matter how many times I said it, I was too afraid to do anything about it. The possibility of David catching us and punishing Spence made my stomach twist into knots. It was my duty to make sure we never ended up in that position.

Claire lay back on her bed with her knees raised. "I hope you make the right choice and find happiness. You really do deserve to be together. I know I drink blood and kill people, but I want to see him end up in a promising future. This asylum has torn him down and ripped away who he was. Help him. Please, do it for me, Nora."

I chewed on my lip, itching to get them out as if I'd let them stay in such miserable positions. I would never sleep if I didn't do what was right.

Yet, it would put him in harm's way and that was a risk I had to weigh in.

Getting off the chair, I patted down my dress and walked towards the door. I paused, tempted to look back at her and study her reaction. Was she upset? Was she smirking? I wanted to know but I couldn't bear to face her after what I said next, "I don't make promises I can't keep."

XXVI

"Is that such a good idea?" I asked Spence.

He didn't seem bothered at all, but he also hid a lot more than he felt. "It's only a terrible idea if you admit it is. I say we go down and explore. Find things that we shouldn't find. Things that we need to help us."

Going down to the basement wasn't my greatest plan, but it was the only one. We had no other choice. Sure, we technically did. We could stay up here where it was safe. Where our security was guaranteed and nothing bad could come.

But that only protected us for a few days. That wasn't to say it would protect us forever. And sometimes we needed to get our hands dirty just to make mud pies.

Spence and I headed for the stairs, and I stopped for a moment. He turned to look at me. "Do you need help?" He stretched out his hand.

"No, that's fine. I'm fine." I would do this on my own, and without the assistance of a patient. It wasn't right to ask them for anything. I was the psychologist here.

So I took it one step at a time. I meant that in a literal sense, too.

When we made it to the bottom, I pushed the thoughts from my head and looked back at Spence. "Come on."

He followed me down the hall. We tried a few of the doors but most of them didn't open. It made sense they were locked. Why would David have been so careless?

In the rooms that did open, they were empty. And only one room had the ECT machine. I wanted to ask Spence if David ever used it, but I knew the answer to that already.

"There's nothing down here." I closed the door quietly and turned on my heel, bumping into the man I needed to avoid. He stood just mere inches away, causing my heart to speed up a bit too much. "Sorry."

I'm not.

I couldn't determine if that was my voice or his.

Spence took a few steps back. "Nothing incriminating? Nothing worth our while?"

"Nothing," I mumbled.

We headed back upstairs.

"Thanks for coming. Not that you had to, or that I wanted you to. Not saying I didn't appreciate it or that I don't like you. I do like you. Not that way. Um, okay I should probably stop talking before I venture further down the rabbit hole," I said.

With a chuckle, he shrugged. "Relax, Nora. I get what you're trying to say. You'd never ask me to help, and you didn't. I offered."

I patted the skirt of my dress. "I should probably get some filing done in my office. I'll see you at our next session?"

His lips twitched as if he wanted to say something, but he chose not to. "Next session it is."

I headed to my office and got the filing done. Whoever had been here previously had no organization skills—and I meant that in the nicest way possible.

A half hour before dinner, I locked up my office and headed towards the bathrooms, but something caught my attention.

The sound of music. The way their fingers glided over the piano keys as if they'd been playing for centuries. Every note had been hit perfectly.

I turned the corner and stopped. "You never told me you could play."

"You never asked," Spence said without looking my way. I approached him with caution, and he scooted over. "Why don't you join me?"

"I only play classical music. That's what my father taught me."

"I can play some classical. I'm older than I look."

"It would be inappropriate to share a piano bench with my patient."

"I showed you my wings. We are far beyond appropriate." He tilted his head to look at me. "Stop making excuses and join me. We could make wonderful music together."

I cleared my throat, hiding the choking. Was that flirting? And was it as forward as I took it?

"I'm waiting, Nora."

Scanning the area, I concluded that most everyone was getting prepped for dinner. I slowly took a seat beside him. "One song."

"One song," he said with a smile. He focused on the treble notes, and I mirrored his movements on the opposite end.

Something slithered up my insides. It was one thing to play music in front of Spence, and another to hear him play as well. However, combining our talent was a whole new line I was crossing. And why had I given in?

His long fingers pressed the keys in one of many patterns. As much as I tried to follow his lead, I realized something was very wrong.

The keys were no longer making the beautiful sounds they were meant to. And as much as I tried to press the low notes, they didn't match my tone. They made their own, and a sinister song at that.

I pulled my fingers away and stumbled over the bench as I got up, moving away.

"Nora, are you okay?" Spence asked.

"Fine," I lied.

I was anything but fine. She did this. She had taken something so innocent and pure and twisted it into something so…disturbing.

"Fine implies you got up gracefully. It implies the song was over. I know better than that."

"Spence, please."

"I'm not trying to pry. But I'm not going to sit here and pretend I didn't just witness you try to run from the piano like it turned into a vat of spiders." He stood, closing distance between us. "What happened?"

After we had almost kissed, it was so hard being near him. Yet I couldn't tell my feet to move away. Not after that experience. Not after she stole the last thing once pure in my life.

I shivered, jumping back when he reached up and grabbed my face, running his thumb over my cheek. "Spence, don't do that."

He put his hands up in defense. "I'm just reminding you that I'm right here."

"That's what they all say," I whispered. "Before they disappear." I stepped back. "I'm f-fine," I sputtered. I turned on my heel and left the entertainment area before he could add anything more.

Alicia left me. Blake—my ex—left me, too. I wasn't willing to take that chance again.

Dinner was a bit awkward as Spence kept shooting glances at me. I avoided direct eye contact, mostly focusing on the conversation amongst the employees. I wasn't wholly in it, though.

When dinner was over, I attempted to leave the cafeteria, but Claire caught my arm. "What did you say to him?"

"Excuse me?"

"You said something to Spence to make him act this way. He's afraid of something. Did you not kiss him like I told you to?"

My eyes darted everywhere but her. "This is not important right now. We need to focus on releasing you guys. Starting a romance would be absurd and—"

"You two played the piano together? That screams romance if you ask me."

Crossing my arms, I finally met her eyes. "Reading my mind?"

"And you weren't hearing the same notes you played? Is this why you and Spence keep giving each other weird glances? You need to stop pushing away. Let us in. Let us help."

"Help with what exactly?"

She laughed at that. "Don't be that naive. You know what. We want to help you with whatever is going on in your mind. With…Alicia? Is that her name?"

"Claire, get out of my head!"

With a sigh, Claire stepped back. "Fine, but I'm not joking when I say you should stop being so quick to push everyone away. You should know better than anyone that letting people in is the best form of therapy." She headed to her room for the night.

How ironic. The patient was trying to lecture the psychologist.

"Nora?" Aaron asked.

I turned to face him. "Oh, right. Sorry, I'll be going to bed here in a moment."

He pulled something out, and my heart almost stopped. No. That damned envelope.

I still hadn't gotten my money back from the first trip. "Now? But it's almost seven. Surely David wouldn't send me out at this time, in the dark." And I'd just gone not that long ago. How could it be my turn *again*?

"He insisted. Sorry." He forced the envelope into my hands and disappeared down the hall.

My boss had been testing me. My loyalty to him. Why else would he send me to get the groceries three months in a row?

"David, you bastard," I muttered. It was at least an hour drive there, an hour drive back, and about an hour or so I spent shopping. I wouldn't be getting home until ten, and that was *if* I got lucky.

I went to the grocery store despite my distaste for the man sending me. I left my own wallet behind to ensure I didn't pay for the food again. If his card declined like the first time, I'd just return with no food.

The drive was long, and I was extra careful at a time like this. I couldn't see the road, so I had to drive a lot slower than I liked. But I did make it to the store, and I shopped for all the groceries he listed.

Much like last time, the card worked again. He must have informed his credit card company that I was an authorized user.

I returned to the asylum with the groceries and thanked God that I made it back tonight.

I got out and approached the front doors tugging them open. "What?" I pulled again but they wouldn't budge. They had been locked.

I knocked, waiting for anyone to answer.

When nobody came to the door, I started banging on it. "I just thanked you for getting me home in one piece," I said as I peered up at the sky. "And now this is how you repay me? It's freezing out here!"

No matter how much I yelled up at the sky, nobody let me inside.

I went to the car and unloaded the groceries in the snow to keep them cold overnight, then I hopped back in and turned the car on to heat up. I checked the time. 11:34. Almost midnight.

There was no way I was getting back inside tonight, and I had a feeling David had done it on purpose.

I eventually turned the car off when it passed midnight, snuggling up in my winter attire and laying the seat back as sleep deprivation raided my mind.

"Nora!" someone yelled. "Nora, wake up!"

I forced my eyes open and met Monique. She banged her fists against the driver's window, but as soon as she saw me open my eyes, she stopped.

"Open the car! Now!"

Every inch of me was frozen. I reached my fingers over, searching for the lock. I let out a small whimper as I smacked my finger against the wheel while pulling the nub up.

Monique ripped the door open and pulled me up from the seat. "Damnit!" She waved someone over and Aaron came over to help walk me inside. They dropped me in the entertainment area, right on the couch where the heater was.

The patients came out of their rooms for breakfast, Spence halting in his tracks when he caught a glimpse of me. He wanted to say something, but we both knew he couldn't.

Monique pulled off my frozen jacket first, then my socks. "Nora, what the hell? Why didn't you scream?"

I choked on my words and my teeth began chattering. "I tried."

"You're lucky to be alive right now."

"You're lucky I got your groceries," I said with a bitter tone.

Monique gave me a look. "Excuse me?"

I sat up as everything began to thaw—and dared I said it hurt like hell. "David made me go after dinner. What was I supposed to do? Say no to my boss?" As if he'd allow that.

Spence gained the courage to say something, knowing it would get him into trouble later. "What kind of boss locks the doors after sending an employee out into the snow for food?"

He had been right. There was no ounce of doubt David did this intentionally. Maybe he was hoping I'd freeze to death, and maybe I hoped so, too.

XXVII

David came to me early this morning during breakfast to ask about the cut, if anything had changed. I wanted to lie, but it wasn't something I could put off forever. Not now, when I knew my wound healed in record time.

So, I told him the truth. Partly.

He became aware that I could hear everything, and that food tasted bland, but that was as far as he knew. I was not going to tell him I could hear thoughts.

And I certainly heard his.

Not a damn useful ability. She's hiding something.

Just as David was about to walk to his office, someone new walked by with a doctor. She scanned the halls. "This place is massive!"

Right away, my heart broke. Yet another victim. "Who is she?"

He smiled. "I'll introduce her to everyone here after we get her settled." With that, he walked off and she disappeared to the basement.

I rushed over to the entertainment area, sitting in the chair. "He got another one."

"What? Who?" Claire hissed.

"I'm not sure. They took her to the basement." A shiver ran up my spine. "But I have a feeling that he has to do something to her before she can meet us."

Emilie shrugged. "He's only taking some blood. I mean, yes it is worse than it sounds. But that's what he does right away. Surprised I can remember."

"He's a monster. I'm starting to believe he named the asylum after himself." I glanced over at the hall.

Minutes passed, but she wasn't coming back up. I wasn't going to look at Spence, knowing that he wanted to kiss me as much as I wanted to kiss him.

My stomach fluttered.

Without trying, my ears tuned in to his thoughts.

How long will it be before he captures another? We can't expect to get out of here when more of us are under his control. It's impossible to expect one human to rescue us all.

I didn't give away that I'd heard him. Instead, I'd prove him wrong. I'd burn this asylum to the ground, with or without David in it. Preferably in it.

"Everyone, we have a new patient," David said as he stepped into the room.

A girl came out from behind him. She appeared young, but everyone here did. "Hello!" She waved. "I'm Riley."

"Be sure to make her feel welcome." David left after shooting me a suspicious look. What did he think I was here for? Did he suspect something else? I needed to be more careful, and I needed to assume *everyone* here could read my mind. My thoughts would be on lockdown.

Riley looked at everyone. "What is this place?"

"Hell," Spence mumbled.

Claire snickered. "He's just grumpy. You're young and naive." She shrugged. "He's Spence. I'm Claire. That's Emilie."

Riley nodded while I coughed. "And I'm Nora. Thanks Claire."

"Honest mistake. I'm not used to introducing the therapist."

"I'm not just a therapist. I'm a psychologist. Big difference. I didn't study for eight years to not go by my title." But she wouldn't care, would she? No, this was Claire.

She scoffed. "Give me a bit more credit than that. I'm *trying* to care."

Riley's eyebrows knitted together, but she shook her head.

Emilie stood, shaking Riley's hand. "Emilie. Mermaid, if you will. Spence is an angel and demon hybrid. Claire is a vampire."

Riley smiled. "Like me."

Claire grumbled. She didn't want another vampire.

"And what is Nora?" Riley asked, facing me.

I shrugged. "Human. Nothing special."

Emilie nudged my foot. "Except you have vampire blood in you."

Spence shifted in his seat. "So it's true. You have Claire's blood running through your veins now."

My face burned when I met his gaze. He knew, didn't he? Everyone did. "I didn't ask for it. It was Claire's idea to join and I didn't expect David to cut my hand, and I definitely didn't expect him to mix blood in it."

"Relax, Nora. I'm not upset with you." He assured me with an apologetic smile.

Riley's head shifted to her right, her brows furrowing and nose crinkling. It was far too much to dump on her now.

Emilie, however, picked up on the looks. "Oh my gosh, did I miss something?" She glanced at Claire. Claire sent her a smirk, promising to tell her later.

Riley sat on the arm of the couch. "I feel so left out," she joked. She stole a look from Spence, before making up her own conclusion. "What do you guys do for fun?"

"Fun?" Claire threw her arm over the back of the couch. "We don't have fun around here. You're a prisoner, Riley. Not a patient. You didn't come on your own will. David kidnapped you so he can fuck you up to make himself look better."

Her smile dropped. "I know that. But I have hope that I'll get out. Someone will find me."

"Who?" Claire sat forward. "Who is looking for you?"

Riley scanned all our faces. "My parents. My girlfriend. My sister. Everyone is looking for me."

Emilie dropped her bear. "Oh shit. David kidnapped someone from their own home."

"Maybe we do have a chance," Claire said.

"Has he never taken anyone from their home?" I asked.

Spence shook his head. "Claire has no one. I had my parents until I moved out. Emilie had to leave home because of her mom. None of us had anyone to ask questions if we turned up missing. Riley is the first to be taken from a family." He stood, walking over to the window and shoving his hands in his pockets. "David stalked us before he decided to kidnap us. He made sure we were alone in this world. Which means he rushed to kidnap Riley, or he was too desperate to care about the repercussions of taking someone surrounded by people."

"And someone is looking for her now," I said.

"Yes. Someone is looking for her now," he said in a quiet voice.

"I have access to the outside world. I can lead them right here." I nodded, pulling my coat on. "I will make sure they find us. I will devise a plan to get you out. Somehow, I will bring this asylum to the ground."

"Is this necessary?" Riley asked, looking around my office.

I shrugged. "If I want to make David believe I don't know about what you are, yes. So, let's begin." I sat back. "How old are you, Riley? You look young but all of you look young. You just appear to be the youngest here."

She gripped the edge of the seat. "Seventeen. And *actually* seventeen. Vampires stop aging at eighteen or so, physically speaking. Once they've hit adult age."

"You mean twenty-five or so."

"Do I?"

"The brain hasn't reached full maturity until twenty-five for most, a little later for some. That's when it stops maturing. Although I think it could differ for vampires. You have longer lifespans, meaning it could take longer or shorter for you to mature. The way dogs' lives are short and they reach adult age after two or three years."

Her eyes fell on the trash. "I suppose."

"What's on your mind?"

"I guess I just feel bad. I'm supposed to be upset but I'm not. Everyone here is annoyed by my optimism and I get that, but I'm hopeful in general. I can't just turn that off." She kicked her feet.

Taking a deep breath, I grabbed a pen. "Nobody asked you to. And I certainly wouldn't ask you to tone it down. It is a nice balance to have another hopeful soul around here. Nobody believes in me, which I can see to a point. Why should they? They have no reason to. But it's difficult to always be the rock. It's exhausting. I have to remind them that I have their backs and I'll get them out. But with you around, you'll help energize me. Remind me that I'm not alone."

Riley smiled. "Consider me your little buddy."

With a small smile, I grabbed a piece of paper. "Tell me about your life. What's it like?"

Her eyes sparkled. She wanted to talk more about it, but she was waiting for someone to encourage her. I understood that need perfectly. The need *to be loved*. Anyone, living or dead, wanted to be heard.

"Well, my parents try to say that they don't have favorites, but we all know they do. My sister is their favorite. It's either the first born or the baby. It's okay, though. Even if they love my sister more, they don't lack in loving me. They want me to be a little more like her, but they're finally coming around. I'm not my sister. We're different, and that's okay. And they haven't been upset with me, either, since I came out. I think they expected it. I never really went through a boy crazy phase, which I suppose can be normal, but I never had a crush at all."

I laughed a little. "Well, I'm sure some people do grow up without crushes. But go on."

Riley twirled her hair. "My sister and I were friends but then she went away to college for a bit. She dropped out, after she realized she didn't want to go into that field. I knew she would. She was afraid to tell our parents at first, but eventually they understood. Dad did, mostly. Why waste your money on a degree that you're not passionate about? It's not like you can forfeit your degree and get your money back. And it's not a small amount either! College is so fucking expensive. I don't blame anyone who doesn't want to give up their money to an institution for something they don't care about in return."

I laughed again, scratching my head. "I'm over thousands in debt so I completely understand the expenses. I don't blame anyone who doesn't want to go into that much debt." Eventually, I would pay it off.

She nodded and leaned forward. "Then there's my girlfriend. We only recently began dating, but it was… I don't know. She was dating this other girl, but I guess that girl kept gaslighting her about things. See, my girlfriend is human, and she's seen things. But this other girl isn't human. And she is things. So when my girlfriend found out those things, she brought it up and the girl kept telling her that she was delusional. It was pathetic to watch from the sidelines. But I swooped in and saved the day." She rested her head in her hands with a grin. "And now we're kind of a thing ourselves. It's not like she's going to hurt anyone. I read her thoughts. She's good-hearted."

I smiled, putting the pen down. It was certainly the kind of romantic story that belonged in a book. "She sounds a lot like a younger version of me. She got mixed up in this world and she just wants some answers. She has no plans to hurt anyone."

"She wouldn't even hurt a fly! That is what I love about her. And my parents approve, too. I was worried they wouldn't, but they've been teaching me to control my desire for blood. It hasn't been easy. She can be pretty accident-prone." Riley's laugh echoed. It was such a beautiful sound in such a desolate place.

"And your parents, they didn't freak out when you told they you liked girls?"

She shook her head. "Oh, no, vampires don't care about that kind of thing. We don't believe in a higher power, or really worry about reproducing."

I exhaled. "That's great. I've heard the horror stories, being a psychologist and all."

"She really is an amazing person. She gets me. Whenever she cuts herself on accident, she immediately leaves. It's not always the case, but she knows. By that, I mean she once bit her tongue from eating. I offered to—"

I tuned out the words for a moment. As much as I loved romance, I was not comfortable listening to an *underage* girl talk about making out with another underage girl.

"—and that was the best kiss I've ever had."

Did she breathe? Right, she didn't need to. She could talk forever if I let her.

"Riley, I absolutely love hearing about your stories, believe me. However, it's lunch time." I checked the clock hanging on the wall.

She tilted her head. "Huh. I guess I did lose track of the time. I am starving!" She stood.

Swallowing, I slowly got up. "I don't want to be the bearer of bad news, but David will starve you. That's what he does to the vampires."

"But that's dangerous. If he wants to keep us alive, he has to give us blood, doesn't he?" She crossed her arms.

"Claire doesn't get blood."

Her joy faded from her eyes. "But…that will kill us. If she doesn't get blood, she will drive herself insane." When she saw my confusion, she continued, "vampires who starve end up drinking their own blood. Vampire blood is poison to us."

Vampire blood is poison to us.

As soon as those words clicked in my brain, I didn't question what I had to do to keep Claire alive. I had a food source, and she needed access to it. I'd do the same for Riley, too. My blood was the key to keeping them from killing themselves.

XXVIII

I helped Monique finish setting the table for our Christmas feast. It could have been mistaken for a thanksgiving dinner had it not been for the red, white, and green color scheme.

The skin on the turkey was crisped to perfection, my mouth watering at the sight. Anyone who knew me knew I preferred crunchy and crispy food the most. I had always eaten my fries and meats with crispy, breaded skin. Something about the crunch between my teeth just made it that much tastier.

I glanced over at Monique who shot Claire a look. I furrowed my brows. What was that about?

When I hurried over to put on some Christmas tunes, I bumped into a certain someone I had been afraid to be alone with since a wild incident I was afraid to talk about.

Both of my hands firmly gripped the record as I lifted my gaze up at Spence and his piercing blue eyes. I was certain he could spot the anxiety displayed behind my wall.

What was I supposed to say? What were the right words in this moment?

"I'll get out of your way." Spence moved around me, walking over to the table.

This was what our relationship had come to. We couldn't even be normal around one another. If I didn't get my act together, David would begin to observe our odd behavior, then he'd decipher exactly why tension so thick it could be sliced with a butcher knife hung in the air between Spence and I.

I put the record on the platter and started the music. I headed to the table and sat across from Spence who now gave me a strange look. To clear the air, I said, "Have our sessions been helping you?"

Claire, who sat next to him, nudged him in his side and nodded in David's direction. Spence got the idea and cleared his throat. "They have. You're the first psychologist to get through to me."

David sat beside me, and I almost snickered as I turned my head to the side, away from him. "You're making progress? That's amazing news. I knew hiring you was the right choice—my little eager beaver."

That made my body recoil.

Monique sat on the other side of me. "You're an angel, aren't you?" She laughed. "Nobody else has been able to get through to these people."

Had anybody else known about their identities? Had they tried to help? If that was the case, why didn't Emilie, Claire, or Spence trust them?

I hadn't had any glimpses of Alicia, or what was supposed to look like her since that night she played my piano keys for me, taking what Spence and I shared for a brief moment.

The memory was seared into my mind like a letter burned into wood. The pain of that utter fear coursing through my body embedded to my skin like a memory.

"—ora?" Monique called. "Nora, are you all right?"

I blinked away the ill thought and looked at her. "I'm doing fine." I glanced at the piano sitting in the corner. It had been a while since I touched it. Since *she* tainted something so pure.

"Let's eat!" David clanked his silverware together and everyone began to dig in.

Everything around me slowed, all the noise passing through a muffled filter before reaching my ears. My eyes focused on the tablecloth with a pattern of holly berries. Alicia once sat at the table with me and together we'd laugh at the silliest of things. This became the first Christmas I'd spend without her and many more were on the way.

"Nora?" Spence's words sliced through all the filters clear as day.

I stood from the table. "Excuse me." I walked briskly to the bathroom. I closed the door behind me and once it shut, my emotions spilled.

I slid down the door with my hand over my mouth as waterworks streamed down my cheeks. The dull ache in my chest grew and squeezed what was left of my heart. I was lost without her. We had promised to do everything together after we graduated, and *I* broke that promise.

Someone pushed the door open and in came Claire. She kneeled, pulling me into her arms. "Let it out. It's okay to cry," she said in a quiet voice.

The tears didn't slow down anytime soon. They rushed like waterfalls looking for an escape. With every sob, my chest tightened. The pain latched onto every part of me. A lump formed in my throat, and my heartbeat went off course—irregularity becoming the norm. Yet it pounded so loud in my ears as I attempted to clutch my chest. I couldn't get even a scream out, but my cries were loose like a dog that'd escaped the fence. Sorrow flooded my veins. I was grief in the flesh.

Claire pushed my hair from my face, tucking it behind my ear.

This went on for thirty or so minutes until I'd been left with nothing. Not even hydration. My eyes were burned like a sip hot cocoa killing the tastebuds, and my cheeks stung from the prolonged exposure to the salty fluids.

I lay curled up on the floor with my head in Claire's lap and her fingers running through my hair for added comfort. "Is it about the ghost?"

"You could just read my mind to find out." My answer came out in a whisper.

"I could but I've learned when it's never an okay time to invade someone's thoughts. I want to hear it from you." She dropped her eyes to mine.

I had to give her some credit for trying to be better. "This is the first Christmas without her. It's a painful reminder that she's never coming back to me. I don't know how I'm supposed to live without her."

Claire let out a sigh. "You don't. You can't forget. You can't erase the pain. You have to let it all take its course. You have to go through the motions if you want to heal. It takes time, and it's different for everyone, but you can't rush this. You can't pretend it doesn't exist. Don't live without her. Tuck her into your heart for a warm place to thrive. You go on for her. Live the life she wanted you to live."

"It's my fault." I grabbed her hand from my hair and squeezed it. "If I had just listened…"

"Don't do that. You will drive yourself mad trying to think of the *ifs*. You can't blame yourself for this. Things happen. It's hard to believe, Nora, but we don't control everything that happens in life. Sometimes they just do, and we can't do anything about it." She lifted me off the floor using my arms. "I want you to remember that you aren't be at fault here. Sometimes life throws us flaming piles of dog shit, and we just have to dodge it or wash it off if we're hit. We take the blow and then we go forward from there."

I closed my eyes and swallowed whatever kept a hold on me. "How can you believe that?"

Claire got me on my feet, steadying me. "I've lived a lot of years, and I've seen so much death. You eventually learn that it's part of life and you can't stop it no matter what you do. It's tragic, yes, but it is not our fault unless we murdered the person. And from what I can see, you don't strike me at the type who was planning to kill her friend."

We stood there for a few more minutes before I washed my face. It didn't hide the puffy eyes. Those couldn't be covered up with water.

"Let's go." Claire grabbed my hand and pulled me back to the dining hall where we sat to eat our food.

After we all finished, I stood by the window to admire the decaying world covered in shimmering white. It fascinated me that death could appear so flawless and planned, and strike at the wrong moments and tear apart your very essence.

"I apologize for intruding if you want space or privacy. I

wanted to check up on you." Spence stopped beside me.

"Claire told you?" I gave him a look.

He shook his head, hands fidgeting in his black-pant pockets. "Claire hasn't told me what happened between you two. I just happen to be good at reading people and I can see the hurt in your eyes."

"Have you ever watched anyone you love die?" I gazed up at him.

He took a moment to think about his answer. "I've seen a lot in my life, and fortunately, loss is not one of them. I haven't been alive as long as Claire. I haven't had a chance to get close to most people besides my parents."

I chewed my bottom lip, tearing a piece of skin that'd dried up from the harsh weather. "You've been close to Claire. She…told me you two went out for a bit."

He ran his hand through his hair, pushing it back. "Well, yes. We did date. It didn't work out and we both decided to go separate ways."

Nodding, my hand barely brushed against his, but I pulled it back to my side. I had to keep my feelings under control. "It was toxic. I get it. She brought out the bad side in you… I'm proud to hear that you guys realized that was not a real relationship. Too many people in this world ignore logic and follow their feelings. The heart can betray us. It's not an exact science but feelings are temporary. They change at any given time." I clasped my hands together behind my back.

"What else did she tell you?"

"Nothing you didn't want me to hear. She told me that you guys fought a lot but never made up in a healthy way." I lowered my eyes to the floor. "You've never been open with her the way you are with me. I haven't forgotten the time you told me I bring a little kindness to this hollow world. Is that why you don't want me to kill David?"

Spence turned his head, scanning the area and rubbing his face. "It's complicated, Nora. It's so much more than you think."

"Tell me. I came here to listen. I have a degree that says I'm a fantastic listener, and far better at understanding the brain." I faced him. "I don't just want this to be about what I want. I want to hear your ideas. I want you to help. I just fear how effective it will be. I've heard of guys like David. Even if they end up in prison, they can hire people to work for them. You would never be safe. But if he's dead…"

"If he's dead, he can still walk around a ghost. Please, can we not talk about this right now?" he pleaded.

I exhaled a long breath. "All right, I won't talk about it." I picked up a book, inspecting it. I was in the mood to escape this horrid reality.

"I want to say I'm sorry for…what I did. I mean, in my room." He grabbed the book from me. "I didn't mean it." Our eyes met, and my mouth opened as I got ready to say something, but he beat me to it. "I can't lie to you." He returned the book to the shelf. "I did mean it. I'm not sorry. I'm *not* sorry for trying to kiss you."

Inside, I knew I wasn't sorry for letting him almost kiss me. I wanted it as much as he did but that trod in dangerous territory.

A small noise slipped from my mouth, unrecognizable. Clearing my throat, I said, "Spence, this is a bad idea. I already have a hard time not cussing David out for how he treats you guys. Nothing could ever happen between us. That could ruin our entire plan. I can't pretend to be on his side and hide an affair. I'm sorry, and I *do* mean that. This must stay strictly business. We have to be professional. I pretend I don't know about your secret, and we create a plan in our spare time."

Spence nodded a bit. "I understand. I won't do anything."

"Thank you." I smiled a bit.

He turned on his heel, pausing for just a minute. "I'll see you around, Nora." He headed back to his room.

A part of me stung, scolding me for letting him walk away like that. Spence had been the kind of man I'd wanted since I was a little girl. He had control over his anger. He was respectful. He got my heart racing and yet I hardly knew anything about him. I had never been more desperate to delve into a man's head than I had with Spence. And yet, I *rejected* him.

Claire would hate me if she knew what we agreed to. She wanted us to admit our feelings and jump into the deep end. But I never promised her I would do that for him. My one goal was to get them all out of this asylum for good and getting involved with Spence would make it so much harder to do such a thing. Feelings were temporary. They would eventually go away.

XXIX

"I'm gonna put a load of laundry in the oven." I furrowed my brows. "I mean the dishwasher. No, I mean the washer." I nodded, turning on my heel.

Claire caught up with me for a second. "He has you doing chores?"

"All the time." I faced her. "I've been meaning to say something. What if I offered some blood? I know David is starving you and I want to help."

She dismissed the idea right away, which I half expected.

I stopped and blocked her path, puncturing my wrist with my pen. It hurt like a bitch but that was nothing compared to starving. "Take it. I was being nice by offering it, but now I'm insisting. You need to survive long enough to escape, Claire. I won't let you die."

She forced a smile, but I said nothing of it. Releasing a small sigh, she grabbed my hand and brought my wrist to her lips. The sensation *sucked*.

Literally.

Having your blood pulled from your wrist with such force was painful in itself, which told me she had been starving for quite a while now. Eventually she stopped herself, making a face. "It's sour now. But thank you."

I took my wrist back. "Thank you for trusting me."

"I should be the one saying that. I'm the monster."

"No, you're not. David is the monster. Being a vampire doesn't make you a monster, the same way Spence isn't for being half demon. You didn't harm us. We harmed you. We stole you from your life. We plucked you like feathers from a chicken, then threw you in a cage and expected you to give us your eggs every day. Thank you for trusting me and seeing that I'm not like David, and I never will be." I left her alone while I went to the bathroom, searching for first aid. Once I found it, I wrapped up my wrist and started on my chores.

First was the laundry, then the dishes. I cleaned up the kitchen, making it look as good as it could in such an old building. I moved onto the bathroom next, beginning on the toilets first.

I turned to clean the sinks, but the showers behind me turned on, steam filling the air in a quick enough manner that my sight started to become useless. I spun around and held my head high. I wasn't going to be afraid of her, because she wasn't truly Alicia. She couldn't say anything *and* mean it.

I took hesitant steps towards the showers when something came over me. A sheet. I fought to get it off, but she only tightened her arms around my torso, shoving me under the shower. I took a big gulp of air as the scolding water soaked the sheet. All I breathed were water droplets.

Coughing and drowning in my mistakes, I struggled more, pushing my hands against the tile and forcing myself backward. I slipped and fell—and a cracking sound bounced between the tile walls.

Flashes of *something* filled my mind.

Spence had a hold of my wrist, and then he lost his grip. In seconds, I was forced onto my knees. The skin along my neck went up in what felt like flames as a burning burrowed under the surface. Spence asked David what he was doing.

My memory had been wiped clean, and when I woke up, they all pretended that nothing ever happened.

But it had.

And now I knew the truth.

I had almost brought them to freedom from the roof. It would have been the one way to pass the barrier. Unfortunately, it failed. I needed a new way out, and I knew what I wanted to do. If I lit the asylum on fire, the barrier turned to ashes with it. But I couldn't just start a fire and hope it would spread. It wasn't that easy during winter when the whole world was layered in frozen water outside of these walls.

The flame would fizzle out before it broke a hole in the prison.

"Nora. Damnit, she's not even conscious, and there's so much blood..."

My eyes opened after tearing my eyelids apart. Claire cradled my head, meeting my gaze. "You're alive! Holy shit, you had us worried sick."

I rolled over, groaning from the ache in my skull.

Spence kneeled but his eyes told another story. He was

terrified of all the blood coating Claire's hands. As soon as I caught a glimpse, my head felt woozy. Nobody lied. There was *a lot* of blood.

"Whoa, whoa, whoa, whoa, whoa!" Claire tugged me into her lap before I hit the ground again.

Spence pulled my body from her arms. "Let me." He placed his hand on the back of my head, and I wanted to cry from the amount of pain exploding throughout my whole nervous system. It felt as if the pain was being sucked out, dissipating and running along my nerves in the opposite direction. A tingling lingered where the pain had once squeezed, the subtle cry of an itch the only memory that I'd injured myself at all. It seeped out with the crimson, and then it was gone. "Should be as good as new." He scooped me into his arms and carried me over to one of the showers, sitting me against the wall. He turned it on. "What happened?"

As my senses began to slowly come back to me, one by one, it hit me as hard as I did the floor. "She tried to kill me, using a form of hydrotherapy."

Claire stripped out of her clothes and stepped into the shower in the next stall over. "Drowning?"

Spence grabbed some soap, helping me wash the blood from my body. He said, "Yes, that's what hydrotherapy is. Some people believe that if you die and come back, you can change the course of destiny. And then others believe you can cure illness that way. Don't ask me about the science behind that."

Claire laughed. "Don't ask you any *scientific* question. You tend to have…weird views. Like the fact that you don't believe in evolution." She poked her head around the corner.

He glanced at her. "I'm an angel and a demon, Claire. We are nowhere in evolution, so why would I believe in something that says I don't exist? If you believe in it, how did vampires evolve?"

"Easy. Elizabeth Bathory paved the way for us all." With a shrug, she turned off her shower.

Spence helped me up and wrapped a towel around me. "Well, she also only bathed in the blood of virgins. Are you willing to do that?"

She came out, not at all ashamed of her body. I could see why. Any woman would love a body like Claire's, flawless and blemish-free. Did vampires have deal with the same skin issues humans did? "Well, I was just bathing in Nora's blood. She's not a virgin, but I suppose it counts to some degree." With a smirk, she looked at Spence. "Oh, I wasn't supposed to tell you that."

Drying my head carefully, I was relieved that the severe—and likely fatal—injury had completely vanished without a trace. Was that the angel side of him? To be able to heal?

"Why would I care if Nora is a virgin or not?" he asked while crossing his arms.

"I'm an adult, Claire. I don't think it's abnormal that I'm not a virgin. And it wouldn't have been if I was, either. Everyone moves at their own pace."

"You two ruin all of the fun." Rolling her eyes, she put some new clothes on from the shelf. "You already almost kissed. Stop making this so awkward for the rest of us."

"You two almost kissed?" Riley gasped. "Oh my gosh, I need to know all of the details!"

Emilie smiled a bit. "I tried to stop her, but she insisted on coming to see what was going on." Her eyes darted to the blood washing down the shower drain. "How bad was it?"

"Spence had to heal her." Claire gestured to him. "Otherwise she would have died, considering it was a fatal wound. She barely came to."

Riley's eyes widened as she stepped in the pool of blood. "It…smells really good. I'm so sorry." She dropped on all fours and started licking.

"Riley, have some decency!" Claire nudged her ribs with her foot.

"I'm starving!"

She grabbed Riley by the back of the neck and pulled her up. "You're better than blood from a bathroom floor. Don't get sick before your family finds you."

Riley faced me as her cheeks heated red in color. "What happened?"

Emilie grabbed her shoulder. "Nora is being haunted by an old friend. Come, let's leave her be." She led her out of the bathroom.

Everyone's eyes were still on me, and then I realized why. I'd been wearing a *white* dress.

I grabbed the towel, covering my front. "I'm so sorry."

"What's to be sorry for?" Claire chuckled. "Spence certainly enjoyed the view."

He scowled. "I didn't look. I have more class than that."

After bidding my goodbye, I hurried to my room while they offered to clean up my mess. I changed into some dry clothes and tried to fix my frizzy hair the best I could. Without styling, it did its own thing.

It was easy for Claire to walk around naked. Spence had seen her many times, and I was a woman. She had nothing to even worry about. She had the body. But me? That wasn't so easy for me to say. I was small on top and on the bottom. Sometimes, it made me self-conscious. It'd been easy to tell women to accept their body, but it wasn't so easy when you were the woman who couldn't quite grasp it.

It was silly of me to be a grown woman with such insecurities. I'd been naked plenty before. I'd even had sex. So why did it make me blush to think that Spence had peeked at the most intimate parts about me?

Pushing aside those thoughts, I headed to lunch. Everyone participated in the conversation, but I kept quiet the entire time. Nobody seemed to notice too much, and I liked it that way.

She had tried to kill me so many times. If I wasn't careful, soon enough she'd succeed. She wanted me dead, and she would do anything she needed to to make it happen.

I had to find ways to fight back. Until then, I needed to be careful not to be alone.

Ever.

After lunch, I told the four of them about my plan. They all seemed willing to help, as much as they could. If David asked about it, I could say that they either had something they really wanted to talk about or that I needed to keep a closer eye on them, and that was why the prisoners were always at my side.

It would hold.

Although, I wouldn't say prisoners in front of David. They were patients as far as he was concerned.

Patients with no humanity, not allowed any decency. Patients trapped in these walls when nothing had been wrong with them from the start.

Spence wrapped his fingers around my wrist and led me off to the side. "I promised not to do anything to pursue you romantically, but I didn't promise to leave you alone. This has gone too far. It began as beads rolling and it escalated to murder."

"I know. And that's why I have a plan. Or I will have one."

"You almost *died*. You're allowed to be angry. Upset. Confused. You're allowed to have emotions. You don't have to hide it just because David is an asshole." He reached out, but pulled his hand back, shoving it into his pocket.

Sighing, I asked, "What do you want me to do? Cry about it?"

He snickered. "I never asked you to cry about it. Whatever you feel, don't bottle it up. Go deal with your emotions if you need to. I know you like to stuff everything into this box and throw away the key, and I know because we're the ones picking up the pieces of your grief. She's haunting you because you won't allow yourself to be human."

"What if I don't want to be human?"

"Pretending isn't healthy. Promise me you'll scream into a pillow or do something to relieve this trauma. Promise me." He stepped closer, not giving me any other option and no way to step around him.

Swallowing, I nodded just a little. "I promise."

His shoulders relaxed. "I'd give anything to kiss you right now. But I won't. Not against your wishes." He put distance between us again before leaving me altogether.

My heart did wish for him to kiss me. My brain was the one saying no and getting both to agree on something was like pulling teeth. And the more he didn't make a move, the more I *needed* him to do so.

"One day, he *will* give in. And so will you," Claire said so nonchalantly. When I shot her a look, she shrugged, adding, "I lost a coin toss so the first shift is mine." After seeing my expression, she laughed. "That's a gas! No, you need me to establish our rules. After all, it's my DNA running through your veins."

I grumbled.

"Oh, and Nora?"

"Yeah?"

"*Because* it's my blood pumping your heart, you won't be able to turn Spence away much longer. Even I never could resist him."

XXX

Someone knocked, then poked their head in when I told them to come in. "Claire. What's on your mind?" I asked.

She stepped inside and closed the door behind her. "Do you mean it when you say that whatever we say in private to you, it stays in this room?"

"Absolutely. I take patient confidentiality seriously. I also believe that it's not my business to tell anyone else about your story if you don't want it told." I swiveled in my chair to face her.

Claire took a seat and nodded a bit. "I don't have a life to go back to."

That much I knew.

"They disowned me," she said.

"Why?"

She shrugged. "Let's just say Riley is a lot better of a teenager than I was."

I leaned forward. "Tell me about it. I'm not going to judge you."

Releasing a sigh, she threw her head back. "When I was fifteen, my hormones were running wild. My parents were hellbent on teaching me to wait, and of course that just made me want to have sex more. Then this guy took interest in me…" A smile crept up on her face. "Made me feel pretty. He was mature. He was experienced."

I shifted a bit, getting the hint that this man was a lot older.

"He was thirty."

"Oh, damn," I mumbled.

She sat back. "My parents immediately disapproved. Rightfully so. But I didn't think so at that age. I was young and naive. I thought he loved me. Then we had sex. And for me, it was great. But when my parents found out, the police got involved. He was arrested on the spot. Charged. Went to prison. Sentenced, and then registered as a sex offender. He was human…"

"I'm so sorry. I know it can't be easy to look back on that memory."

"And do you know what is the worst of it all? I feel so guilty. I just wanted love, so I confided in him. I didn't even know better. I consented to the whole thing, but he was the criminal. They saw *me* as the victim."

I chewed my lip, trying not to step in. I had so much to say but I wasn't going to put Claire in the chair.

She gripped the edge of her seat between her thighs. "It's the men who get fucked over." Claire met my eyes. "Say something. I know you want to."

I exhaled sharply. "Okay, well, this is a bit of a tricky situation. Like yes, if a sixteen-year-old girl is with a nineteen-year-old boy, then I'd totally say the police should not look at it as just a victim-criminal situation. But this man was thirty! Thirty-fucking-years-old! He has no excuse. He's a grown ass man who should know better than to prey on young girls who don't know what they want. He *is* an adult with a fully developed brain. His mentality is far more mature than yours in the situation and he should have said no.

"He was right to be charged and arrested. That is strictly pedophilia. Okay, well, that's actually ephebophilia. Pedophilia is when the victim is pre-pubescent. My point stands! You were a minor. Aunt Flo was barely beginning to visit while you were going through puberty. You were figuring out how to be a woman. He took advantage of that, and I don't feel sorry for him. You are one-hundred percent the victim. You have no reason to feel guilty."

She rubbed the back of her neck, rolling it. "I suppose you're right."

I scoffed. "Not just right. I'm an expert. Psychology might constantly change but pedophilia and ephebophilia do not. There is no excuse for a grown man to pine after a child. None. I have the degree to prove that I'm an expert in this field. I've studied this stuff before. We've had whole semesters dedicated to picking apart criminals and pedophiles. We may not know everything, but there is nothing right or moral about grown adults who are attracted to children. That much we *do* know."

Claire rubbed her palms along her thighs. "After they arrested him, I ran away. I haven't seen my parents since. They'd be disappointed in me now. I'm still sexually active. Not married. They'd say I belong here."

Part of me wanted to tell her that they wouldn't hate her, to make her feel better. However, the other part of me didn't want to lie about people I'd never met. It wasn't right to tell her I knew her parents better. I didn't.

"Have you ever tried to reach out to them since?"

"Tried? No. They certainly tried looking, though. My parents have always been super strict. You wouldn't have thought that vampires would be so strict about sex and all of that, but mine were. They said sex is sacred. It's between two people who love each other. That's bullshit. They never loved each other, so according to them, they're in the wrong for having sex, too."

I folded my hands in my laps while nodding. "How would you feel if I contacted them to at least see if they'd be willing to help?"

"I'd tell you to fuck off."

I wanted to get more hands on deck, but I wasn't about to go against Claire's wishes. The last thing I needed was her to lash out and expose everything to David in a moment of pure rage. I wasn't going to do anything that would hurt anyone in the end. "Fair enough."

Looking down, she said, "Riley is lucky. She has everything you could need in parents." She shrugged. "They all accept her. She may not have been the daughter they pictured, but they accept and love her regardless. I mean, if my parents were so strict about sex, what would have happened had I been gay? Would they disown me themselves? Send me off to a conversion camp?"

"It's hard to say," I said in a quiet voice.

Riley told me that vampires didn't believe in a higher power, so why were Claire's parents so uptight about their morals?

"Hard to say for you. For me? I know them. They were happy I ran away. They didn't want a daughter like me to ruin their reputation. The daughter who slept with a sex offender. All these other daughters were allowed to talk to their mothers about having a crush. Could I? Never. I'd get the sex talk, and things like *'Claire, why do you need to worry about boys?'* Because back then, boys were cute. But they couldn't fulfill my needs. Hell, half the men my age can't do that either."

I snorted a laugh. "I'm sorry. I don't mean to laugh, but it's true. A lot of men are very uneducated about pleasure."

After chuckling, a smirk appeared. "Spence certainly isn't."

My smile faded as my face heated up. "Um..."

"Oh come on. I can tell you that. I can guarantee that Spence is no stranger to the woman's needs."

"Claire." I cleared my throat. "That's enough."

She rolled her eyes. "Yeah, yeah. Whatever."

I took a sip of my water. "We came here for you today. You came to me, in fact. To talk about you. I'm listening, so let's do just that."

"All right." She asked for water, so I gave her one from my mini fridge. I had so many stocked up. Coffee and water, my two loves. "And before you ask why a vampire can drink water, it's not going to kill me. Blood is good, but water can be refreshing, too." She chugged the entire bottle. "It distracts me from the fact that I'm so thirsty and hungry all at once."

Claire and I finished talking and as soon as she left, I followed behind. David stopped me at my office door. "How was she?"

"Good. She's been opening up a lot. I think Claire is finally learning to trust me." I gave him my best smile. Don't think of any thoughts.

Nodding, he gave me a measly thumbs up and disappeared around the corner.

As for me, I needed to figure out what else I would need to

do. I took a step forward but something got stuck under my shoe. I looked down and picked up the paper, opening the note.

Meet us in the basement.
Room at the end of the hall.

He wanted to expose more about the program. Finally. Had I earned his trust? Was I ready? Absolutely. But I was terrified all at the same time.

Following the note, I hurried downstairs and found the room at the end of the hall. I used my key to get in, closing the door behind me. Everyone had been waiting for me, and I didn't appreciate all the attention.

"I'm here."

"Welcome. We've given it some time to think, and we wanted to let you in on some secrets," David said.

Oh no. He was going to tell me the truth. What did I do? The only thing I could do. Pretend that I was on their side. But if I did that, I couldn't be friends with the patients at all. Could I?

"I know you're wondering what I put in your blood, but I'm here to tell you it's harmless. It's meant to enhance your abilities. You said you couldn't taste food, and you could hear better, correct?"

"Correct."

"And do you want to know what it was that gave you those abilities?"

Did I? I knew, but I couldn't let him know I knew and if I acted like I didn't want to know, he'd question me. "I do."

"Good. Sit down. It might be a bit to process."

Nodding, I plopped down.

"We used Claire's blood. Now, we know that mixing blood is fatal in any incident. But Claire's blood isn't your normal blood type. It's made of something different, and we were able to study it and manipulate it enough to make it safe to inject into our bodies."

"Do you all have her blood, too?" I asked.

David chuckled. "Some of us, sure. Others have some of Emilie's. We haven't quite figured out Spence's yet. Let's just say his is a bit more…supernatural."

Furrowing my brows, I folded my hands together. "What's the purpose of mixing her blood with ours?"

He tapped his pencil against a table. "I suppose you'll figure it out eventually, as close as you are to the patients," he mumbled. I'd only picked up on it because of my new ears. "Claire is not human, Miss Witlow. She's…special."

"How special?"

Monique came to my side. "She's a vampire, Nora. She survives on blood, and she has abilities that we want."

"So, you've been taking her blood and locking her up? To get some abilities? Why not just ask?" I peered up at her.

"You don't ask a vampire for blood," she whispered. "And now that you know the truth, we need to know if you're on our side."

They weren't aware I remembered everything they did to me. The way David forced me down and injected me with a drug to erase my memory of this asylum. I wanted to bash their heads into the windows for such a thing.

"I want to believe that what you're doing here is for the greater good. I can't blindly pick sides. Do you promise that all you're doing is taking some blood? You aren't harming the patients?" I had to play devil's advocate here. It was the only safe option. They knew me enough to know I wouldn't choose to hurt their prisoners, but if they convinced me it was helpful instead, maybe they could *win* me over. Maybe I could get away with this.

David stepped forward, flashing me his darkest gaze. "We promise. They are not being harmed. They're being taken care of. We just want to do this so that maybe someday, we can introduce them to society, and we can all coexist together. This is for the greater good."

Roll with it.

"Coexist," I whispered. "I'd like to coexist, too. Why shouldn't we be able to? If this…truly helps, like you say, then maybe I can get behind the idea. It doesn't hurt Claire that I have a bit of her blood in me, right?"

"Not at all. And if we can eventually introduce them, we can introduce ourselves. We will let the people know that having their blood in us doesn't hurt, meaning they won't hurt us. Then they can live amongst the humans peacefully."

I forced a smile. "That sounds kind of nice, actually."

Hook, line, and sinker.

XXXI

The doctors held Spence by the biceps, leading him to the bathroom in torn, bloody clothes.

Fear leaped in my throat as I rushed over and almost stumbled over my own feet. What had they done to him? "What happened?" I asked a little too desperately.

Cool it, Nora.

"He's afraid of needles," one guy said.

Needles. Right.

Spence would scoff at his own thoughts if he could.

Hearing them as coherent as they were at all gave me some peace of mind.

"Allow me to help him," I said taking another step forward.

"We need to get him a shower and change him."

"And?"

"And he'll be naked. A man will be naked in front of you."

I snickered. "Wouldn't be the first time. I'm an adult woman with needs of my own and ex-lovers. If an ass scared me away, could I call myself a psychologist? I'll get him showered and dressed. Professionally." I reeled my shoulders back, hoping that'd sell the act.

As if it were an act.

"We'll send someone back with a gown for him," the guy said as he opened the door and helped Spence inside.

I followed, getting a shower ready for him as the guys handed him over. I wrapped Spence's arm around my shoulder, walking him to the stall and setting him down, pulling the clothes off.

So stupid and naïve.

I dropped my jaw, holding back a gasp. How dare he say that? I'd been so tempted to tell him I heard that, but I wasn't ready to reveal my secret just yet.

He groaned as I lay him back and shimmied his pants off him with my eyes turned away.

Once he was left naked, I sat him in the shower, allowing the water to run down his body and wash away the blood. "How are you feeling?"

He barely grumbled a response.

I've been hit a truck, then sucked dry.

After he'd been washed and I succeeded in keeping my gaze on anything but his body, I took the gown the doctors brought and helped Spence to his feet, leaning him against the wall. I dried him with a towel, wrapping it around his waist and ready to pat myself on the back for making it through a whole shower without compromising the relationship we had.

I slid his arm through the sleeves and pulled it around his

shoulders. As I moved behind him to tie it, the towel slipped off, and I'd caught a glimpse as the nicest ass I'd ever seen on any man.

Turning away in a swift second, I stifled my gasp and fiddled with my fingers. "Um, I didn't see anything."

Lies. I heard the noise come from your lips. Your tempting kiss. The throat I'm dying to drag my teeth over. The tongue I'd love to explore every inch of.

My eyes grew to the size of the vinyl records in the entertainment area. Were those really his thoughts?

Glancing back at his shoulders, he slouched against the tiles. "Give me a moment and I'll find your robe and get you to bed."

Only if you stay with me and give me a taste of the delectable blood coursing through your veins. What makes your heart beat. What keeps you alive, I want what's mine.

The thoughts had been so dark, and I felt like a horrible person for prying at all. Private, indeed, and not meant for my ears. Yet I heard them all the same.

Before he could keep tumbling down this tunnel, I turned and tied the strings, ignoring the asset of his just hanging out the back. Without giving him another chance to think, I grabbed his arm and threw it around my shoulder, walking him back to his room where I tucked him into bed.

He turned away, drifting off somewhere. He didn't say another word.

I walked to the door, pausing, turning back to glance at the tortured angel. Just who the hell had that been in his head? Whose thoughts did those belong to?

Silence enveloped us. The air grew cold.

So much had changed after what happened between us and nobody could pretend it was normal. It would never be right. I'd seen far too much for a patient's therapist.

"Just tell me what would help you." It wasn't that he actually needed that kind of saving anymore, but this would be more believable if we followed protocol as usual.

David didn't want me to even hint at them that I knew what they were, and I didn't want him to know I'd known from the start. Lies slathered on top of more lies.

Spence shrugged, his gaze anywhere else but on me. I couldn't blame him. I refused to look myself in a mirror.

My hands had been folded in my lap while my legs were pressed together. I kept my eyes on Spence as not to raise any suspicion, as if that hadn't already happened.

"What about your parents? You haven't told me much about them. One was a demon; the other was an angel. Who was who?" I pulled half of my bottom lip in with my teeth.

He sighed a little before answering. "My mom's a demon while my dad's an angel. Mom was raised to possess people and influence them to make the wrong choices. My dad was raised to influence people to make good choices while he protected them from harm."

"I figured that was what they did." I laughed a bit. "I mean, angels are good, and demons are bad."

"Yes, but my parents defied nature. When they met, Mom would always tease Dad about his good deeds. She said he was boring and lived in this box. She taught him to live a little. He would do small things that were seen as crimes, but humans would see it as minuscule. In return, he helped my mom make better choices. They learned to balance one another. They fell in love and had me." He shrugged, his eyes locking onto mine.

My voice had abandoned me as he kept his focus on the one thing he seemed to want in this place. I was desperate to ask another question, but my mind had been simply a mess. I couldn't seem to form a coherent thought.

His voice snapped me out of my trance. "Nora?"

"Apologies. Back to the topic, your parents had you. What happened then? Have they stayed together all these years?" I shifted in my seat while moving my hands under my bottom. If I sat on them, they couldn't fiddle with things that made me look more nervous.

Spence grabbed a photo from the nightstand and handed it to me. He returned to his seat. "They did. They were their happiest after I was born. We had our family, and nobody could ruin it. David came and ripped us apart. I never know if my parents are still looking for me."

In the picture were a man and a woman, a woman who was happy while her eyes showed all the shit she had been through. The man appeared to be fragile and sensitive, his love for the woman blatantly obvious in his face. They were a beautiful couple, and nobody questioned how Spence had ended up with his looks.

"I know they are. If they love you, they're always looking for you. Parents don't stop loving you just because you disappear. I promise to bring you home to them. You deserve that." A small smile formed.

Spence grabbed the picture and put it back in his drawer. "Nora, I hate to tell you this, but David can't be stopped."

"Don't say that. Everyone can be stopped. He's an asshole, yeah, but he's not immortal. And don't say he will be when he's a ghost. I care about you guys. You've become my friends." I took a moment to observe his reaction to the label, to which he didn't seem to mind. He must have gotten over me or he was an amazing actor. "I don't give up on friends. You have barely gotten a chance to know me over several months. You don't get to tell me that I'm no match for him. I'm a lot stronger than I look." Fixing the collar of my dress, I shot him a stern look.

He shook his head with a smile, but half of it appeared to be missing. "I wasn't implying you're weak because you're a woman."

I stood up and gestured to myself as my skirt spun around me. "What were you implying? Do tell." I held a smirk.

"I was trying to say that David is also more cunning than he looks. You don't have any idea as to what's going on in here. You may think you know but you don't." His expression transformed into something more serious.

With my hands at my sides, balled into fists, I narrowed my eyes. "I'm aware you guys are tortured."

A laugh escaped him, but humor didn't lace his throat. "Do you know how? How do you stop a man if you aren't aware of everything that's going on? You can't. What the evil ghost did to you was just a taste of what David does to us. You could never understand what you're getting into."

I ran my hands through my hair, groaning due to my frustration. "Spence, you are never going to get it. I don't have to know the extent he's torturing you to be against it. I was raised to give a shit about people and how they are treated. I do not support this and I have a duty to save you guys. It is not something I can give up on." I took a deep breath before I lost my temper. Inhale, and hold it, then release it from my lips.

Spence popped to his feet. "I'm sorry. I'm sorry for making you upset." He tried to get close, but I backed away. Distance was all I needed.

Angry sex is fun. It's rough and passionate.

I could not even begin to ponder her words. If I was angry, it was even more crucial that Spence and I put space between us.

"I'm just so tired of you telling me who I must be. I'm not going to change my mind. I understand that you're worried, but you can't tell me what to do. If you want to make sure David doesn't hurt me, then begin by helping me come up with a foolproof plan. Telling me that I'm too stupid to understand the situation does not help anybody but David." I dropped my hands and turned away from him. The wall was just the ugly face I needed to see to keep all emotions under control.

From behind me, he said, "Okay. I'm sorry. I'll stop telling you what to do. And I never called you stupid."

I scoffed. "You might as well have when you told me I wouldn't understand the situation. I'm a human, Spence. I have a brain. Stop treating me like I'm a panda."

"Panda?"

Now who was the stupid one? "Pandas are very dumb animals. They only mate once a year because they have no energy to do it more than that. Even then, they don't know they're pregnant, and oftentimes, they kill the babies because they don't have the mental capability of understanding they just had a cub or two." I was a psychologist, and human brains were not the only ones I had studied during my years in school. All brains fascinated me.

Spence grabbed my shoulder and twisted me to face him. I would have slapped him if I was still angry but seeing his confused expression made me want to laugh. Feeling his fingers brush the exposed skin on my bicep made my heart flutter like a butterfly.

"I thought turkeys were the dumbest." He shoved his hands

in his pockets as a way of apologizing for touching my shoulder.

I giggled. "They're dumb. But pandas are considered far dumber. Pandas eat bamboo when they could survive on meat. Their brains are mush because they don't get their protein. I studied animals. I studied predators and prey. I love studying the brains of living organisms. Why every creature does what it does."

Spence frowned like a little boy who had been told he was a baby. "But… I have black and white wings. Pandas are black and white. Is it a coincidence that the dumbest animal has the same colors as me, someone who implied *you* were stupid?"

I choked on my own laughter as it erupted from my mouth. "Okay, what a happy coincidence."

He coughed a bit. "Well, I guess we should end this session. I'll try not to take your insult too personally."

"Aw, I'm sorry. I didn't mean to hurt your feelings." My fits died down, but a smile stayed glued. "Let's just come up with a good plan. That's all I ask of you."

He nodded. "Yes, yes. I can do that."

"Thank you." My hand reached up to pat his shoulder, but I pulled it back when I realized it wouldn't be appropriate. If we were to fight these feelings, we had to avoid contact. "Until next time, Spence." I bid my goodbye and vacated the room.

Echoes could fill the halls with how quiet they were, emptiness having a firm grasp on the atmosphere. Where had everyone gone? It was the middle of the day.

I walked to the office to ask David what to do next, but he wasn't there. Had everyone abandoned this place?

"Hello?" my word echoed into the abyss.

"Hello," a voice whispered in response.

As I turned my head, I could see her spirit at the other end of the hallway. She floated, watching my every move. Knowing what I knew about her intentions and that she *wasn't* Alicia, I rushed back to Spence's room and closed the door.

"Nora? What's wrong?"

I swallowed my fear, keeping my weight against the door in case she tried to push through. She was a ghost. She could walk through if needed—or could she? If this place was built for the nonhuman, were ghosts not in full control of their abilities?

"She's out there. I don't know what the hell to call her, but she was out there and watching me and everyone else is gone and I don't know where to go and I'm terrified. I cannot go through that again, Spence. I can't do it. I can't. I can't," I repeated the last sentence over and over.

He pulled me away from the door and wrapped his arms around my frame. Neither of us cared that we were supposed to be just a patient and his doctor. "It's okay now. She won't mess with me." His voice was low as he spoke comforting words into my ear so I'd never forget them.

I wanted to ask why she wouldn't do such a thing, but the words wouldn't leave my throat. Instead, I took refuge in his embrace, surprised by his warmth. He'd been so icy in the past, but now he was the equivalent of a heated blanket. He was two sides of the same coin: hot and cold—salt and pepper.

My arms rested under his armpits, hands gripping his shoulders from behind, eyes closed. If I opened them, she could be right there. It was a risk I wasn't willing to take.

"Until someone comes to get me, I can't leave this room. Everyone has disappeared and I refuse to be in the halls with that…that thing," I whispered.

Spence let go of me and took the blanket from his bed, wrapping it around my shoulders and securing it. "Then don't leave. You can stay as long as you need." He led me to his bed and sat me down. "I'll be here the entire time, making sure she doesn't touch you again. She'll have to get through me first, and in my expertise, ghosts aren't nearly as powerful as what I can do. If she tries anything, she'll beg me to take mercy on her. That's a promise, Nora."

XXXII

As I approached the doors that led to the rooms of the three prisoners, doctors were cleaning out Claire's.

"Where's Claire?" I asked.

A hand landed on my shoulder and I glanced back. David Harrison. "She was released. She went home."

"She went home?" I looked inside the room, heart breaking. David would never release her. I knew that. "Did her family get her?" I turned on my heel to face him.

"Indeed, Miss Witlow." His smile lacked sincerity. Something was wrong. She didn't have any family, but he had no idea that I knew that. He should have assumed I did, considering I made it clear she opened up to me. He saw our interactions outside of our sessions. How could he look me in the face and lie to me, and expect me to believe it when the both of us knew otherwise?

I picked up a pillow. "Do you need my help?"

He shook his head as he waved me off with his hand. "That's not necessary. We can handle this."

"She was my patient, too. I'd love to help." *Be pushy, Nora.*

His smile dropped like the music on a record going static. "It's not your concern. Claire was a patient and she's gone home. You can move on."

Move on? She was a person. I'd gotten to know her. I'd grown close to her, and I was told to just move on?

Nodding, I left the room and plopped onto the couch in the entertainment area. Nothing made sense. I knew things he didn't know I knew. Claire hadn't been released. Something bad happened to her, and my gut told me so.

Emilie sat beside me. "You heard about Claire I see."

"Something doesn't add up." I shook my head while pressing the edges of my hands against my mouth. "Why would she be released? I know why this place exists. I know what you guys are and yet, David says he let her leave? I doubt that."

She frowned and laid her head against my shoulder. "It's not crazy to think that he's lying. The things he does to us are brutal. David got mad at Claire last night and…things went very sideways."

"What do you mean?" My eyes shifted her direction.

"I mean he killed her and he's trying to cover it up." She let out a sigh. "She's not coming back."

I shook my head again, denying the words she let slip. "No. He just locked her in some secret room. Tell me this is all for show. Do not tell me that he killed her, Emilie. That can't be true." I couldn't bear the thought of David having murdered

Claire. Claire and I were friends. Right? She was the kind of person who held her walls high, but once you cracked them, she began to trust you. Once she did, she pulled you into her circle and never strayed from your loyalty.

Emilie grasped my hand. "I'm so sorry."

A laugh bubbled from my throat. "What? No. You're *lying*. You're just trying to hurt me. Maybe you work for David. She's not dead. He just moved her to isolation so she wouldn't have a chance of escaping." Why would I accuse Emilie of working with David? Why insult her just to pretend Claire was okay?

She put her head on my shoulder, wrapping her arms around me. "Do you hear how crazy you sound? Nora, I want you to stop giving yourself false hope. She's gone."

"False hope? Without false hope, people never look for their missing kids or friends or family. They give up. A lot of missing people were found because they hadn't given up hope and I know she's not dead. You didn't even see her body." I scoffed while crossing my arms. Without a body, was she really gone?

"David isn't just going to wheel her out here for everyone to look at. He likes to keep secrets." She shook her head, sighing once again. "No, I didn't see her body. But I also happen to know the things he did to her. She told me, Nora, and they were not humane."

I gave her a look with a cocked eyebrow. "ECT won't kill a vampire."

"No, of course not. But starving her would." She rubbed my empty shoulder.

"Starving her? But I gave her my blood."

"It wasn't enough."

"But I gave her *my* blood!" I yelled.

"Blood that's tainted with her own." She shivered. "What

does a vampire crave the most? That's what makes them a *vampire*. David was starving her because she wouldn't tell him what you and Claire talked about during the sessions. He wouldn't feed her. When a vampire doesn't drink, they starve. They lose their sanity. It's no different from a human going without water or sleep. You begin to lose all sense of self when your fuel is withheld. Claire was spiraling behind closed doors. She began drinking her own blood when nobody was looking, and I'm sure you know that their blood is toxic. Yours wouldn't be enough, and it's now mixed with what was her poison."

I wiped away the tears before anyone could see them. "No. That's cruel. Why would he need to? He wanted her blood."

"Think about it, Nora. Why wouldn't he? David has his own reasons that he'll never show anyone else. Without blood, she couldn't survive." She tightened her arms around me.

More pain came, and this time I didn't bother to hide the hot, salty tears. Claire was starving the moment she saw me after Spence almost kissed me. Her senses were heightened when she could smell the lust in my system, and yet I didn't think twice. If I had just asked her about it or offered her some *more* blood, and more often, I could see her. I had to see her. "This is my fault." I choked back the sobs. She wasn't gone. I didn't believe it.

"I know you guys were becoming good friends. I can imagine how much this hurts."

I lifted my chin to meet her eyes. "I promised her I would save her, and I didn't. I broke a promise and now it's costing me. It's costing you your minds." I used the back of my hand to wipe my cheeks. "We have to do something, Emilie. We have to stop David before he makes more drastic decisions, and while we're at it, we need to find Claire—wherever he's hiding her."

She shot me a pitiful look, but I didn't want nor need it.

Claire wasn't gone, and I knew so because even dead, where could she go? This asylum kept them chained. I didn't see her ghost running around. Vampires had ghosts right? Even if they'd told me only humans became ghosts, I didn't believe it. I didn't believe in what I couldn't see with my own eyes.

Coming up with a plan was not that easy around here but I had an idea. "I need to get to know your families. I have to get into contact with all your families. It's risky, and you guys haven't seen them in years, maybe even decades, but this is the only thing solution I have that makes us any progress. We have a chance if we get more people involved. We need an army behind us."

Emilie smiled a bit, internally grateful she didn't have to tear down my hopes and dreams anymore. "I'm with you on this one. I don't even care if I have to see my mom. If it could help, I want you to go for it. I'm terrified of ending up like Claire."

I stood. "It's settled. I need the names of your mother and father."

She jumped up, grabbing my biceps. "Whoa. My father is getting involved? I'm not so sure about that. He's long gone and he's never been in my life."

"I'm sure of it." I nodded while stepping away. "You and Spence need to write their names down. If any of you know Claire's parents, tell me those as well. Any family members are useful. We need all we can get. Then I will find out where they are and call them here. They're already vampires, mermaids, and angel-demons. It won't be hard to convince them what happened to you and what's going on in this facility." I grabbed a bunch of things, like a wallet, keys, my key to the room in the basement, and a few more things. "Tell Spence."

"That's a lot." She didn't budge, concern written on her face.

"It is. But it'll save your asses. And Emilie, please don't get caught. We've made it this far. We have to do all of this for Claire. She didn't give up her sanity in vain." With that, I headed out of the hospital. I wasn't sure where I would go but I needed answers.

As I drove down the road, I kept my eyes peeled for anything. I had no idea what to look for, but I'd know it when I saw it.

The snow had let up just a tad today, making the roads icy as the sun beat down. I drove with extra caution, because wherever Claire was, she needed me to find her sooner rather than later. All clues could help.

A house buried behind trees caught my attention. It would have been normal if it weren't for two factors: who lived this close to an asylum and not question anything, and why was this place the perfect depiction of a haunt house?

I turned down a road peeking out from the structure, the driveway long and narrow, but definitely no match for my baby. She got me everywhere I needed and never gave me problems.

I parked the car and got out, eyeing the large home. It was nowhere near as big as Monstrum Asylum, but it was still grand and oddly located.

Walking up to the front steps, I knocked. If someone did live here, I wanted to be polite and courteous. However, since nobody had answered after a few knocks, I walked right in. There were no neighbors to call the cops on me out here. As if the police would bother risking their lives in this weather for an abandoned property.

The place has been untouched for quite some time. Evidence was in the furniture left behind, layered in inches of dust and cobwebs. Did they leave on a whim? Nobody would disappear from such a lovely home without any legitimate reason.

Slow and steady won the race as I headed up the stairs and they didn't give way under my weight. The wood had bowed on some steps, cupped on others—its form rotting from the excess moisture and lack of upkeep.

I entered a small room, one covered in so much dust that the original colors could barely be made out in this poor lighting. This house hadn't just been left behind for a few years. It had been forsaken for almost a decade.

My fingers trailed along grain of the damp walls as I scanned the area. My adventures of exploration led me here, my interest surely piqued, and my promise to Claire coming true.

As I continued to trace the wood, my fingers caught on an uneven cut in the wall. I turned to face what did not match the pattern of how it'd been placed, slipping my fingers between the crack and pulling before stepping back as the piece of wall thumped to the floor.

I peeked inside the dark space behind the room, continuing to pull more of the planks down. A box became visible, and so I grabbed it and opened it, admiring what was hidden inside.

I brushed my fingers along a gold ring with an encrusted diamond before spotting a piece of paper underneath. A note—which I then unfolded.

The writing appeared old but not too faded to make out, telling me it couldn't have been here for more than ten years.

And I read on.

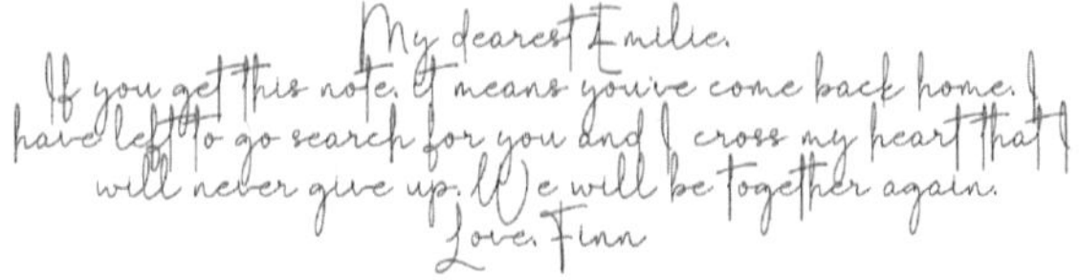

My dearest Emilie,
If you get this note, it means you've come back home. I have left to go search for you and I cross my heart that I will never give up. We will be together again.
Love, Finn

A smile slithered up my face, first reaching my lips and then eyes, as I pressed the paper into my heart. It had been a love letter—one meant just for Emilie. On the inside, I was squealing in delight, and sighing in awe. She'd found love, and with this, I could ensure the both of us would find that much more motivation to jumpstart the plan.

She deserved everything and *more*. David could not take away the promises Finn made to her and now that I was here, I would ensure they found each other again. I was going to set all of them free. Including Claire.

I picked up the ring, guessing and hoping it'd been what I thought it was. A love so pure that he wanted to marry her, and guarantee he'd wake up next to her until they both wilted like flowers. Full of life. Vibrant. Giving more than they took. Omitting a breath of fresh air in an otherwise mundane world.

As I turned to face the rest of the room, I realized this was where they had lived. This wasn't just an abandoned house. This was her *home*. She had run away with Finn and made a life with him here before David caught her and tore her from her dreams.

The story sounded familiar in a strange way. As if I'd heard it before.

When I looked out of the window, it hit me. Gasping, I almost lost my balance, using the sill to catch myself. I used to tell Danny stories about mythical creatures. I had told him a story of a *mermaid* who ran away with her boyfriend. Emilie had been that exact mermaid.

I once made up a world of a vampire who had to drink blood to live and yet she only did it to survive. That same vampire had been hundreds of years old, changing throughout the decades to match the time periods as if she were one of the humans, just to blend in.

There was a story about a man, one who was fighting his dark side and trying to protect what he believed in most. His parents were not bad people for what they had done, and *Spence* knew that. He lived it, represented it, and breathed it.

It occurred to me that I had told my brother all their stories as fables, mere fantastical worlds that I thought I had created. Yet somehow I had always known them.

It was no coincidence. I was involved in more than just being their psychologist. This had all been orchestrated from the start. I hadn't made my own choices. Someone here was telling me which X to stand on as if my life—*our* lives—were their own movie to direct.

XXXIII

After I'd arrived back at the asylum, David gave me a list of chores. Normally, I wouldn't mind doing them, and I'd even understand that I was the newest employee so I had toilet duty because of that. But these days, I was growing to resent David and his lists. I hated toilet duty after all that had happened in the bathroom thus far. He knew, too, who was waiting for me in there.

I hated grocery shopping, knowing what it would ultimately lead to. Whether he decided to have me pay exorbitant prices, or he "forgot" I was out while he locked up for the night, I didn't want to do it anymore.

I was done with his lists.

So when he handed me the paper, I shot him my fake smile,

left his office, then tore it up and dropped it into the trash.

Monique gave me a thumbs up, to which part of me took pride in after she'd been telling me to skip the chores for months. The other part of me itched to flip her the bird.

I didn't, but I wanted to.

Maybe the lists and grocery runs were David's way of reminding me who was in control. Or I supposed it could be his way of keeping me occupied while he did things right under my nose—things entirely illegal and unethical.

No longer would I be playing his games. I knew better. No more chores, and no more blindly following orders. He couldn't pull my strings and make me dance for show. He wasn't the puppeteer, nor was I oblivious to his practices.

I headed to the entertainment room, surprised to find nobody there. Although, with Claire missing, only three patients remained.

First, I put on a record, whichever music was handy. Then, I sat at the piano and attempted to play by ear and match what I heard. It'd been pretty shotty at best.

"Mind if I join?"

Spence. I should have guessed.

"I was just finishing up," I said as I rose from the bench "Have a go at it.'

"Bummer. I was hoping you'd play with me." His frown deepened the wrinkles in his eyes. I'd never noticed them before, but now it became apparent that Spence had been older than he appeared. Years of stress, and years of struggling in a crumbling world would do that to you.

Regardless, he sat down in front of the keys. While he attempted to match the tune of the song, he hit a few wrong notes before he found the right ones. And once he'd discovered the pattern, he played flawlessly, leaving my jaw on the floor.

Many beautiful melodies later, Spence stood, his long sleeve snagging on the edge under the keys. A piano shouldn't have had rough or jagged wood to catch on for safety purposes.

As he tugged, it cut into his shirt, but he couldn't get himself free.

"Let me grab scissors." I hurried to my office and grabbed a silver pair, bringing them back to him and maneuvering my way under the piano. I opened the blades and attempted to cut the fabric, missing by an inch. One more attempt, and I'd succeeded.

Climbing back out, I bonked my head, dropping the scissors, only to yell out as they embedded themselves in my arm.

I found my footing and pulled them out, pressing my hand against the wound to slow the bleeding.

Spence's eyes widened as he stumbled back. "Nora, what did you do? You can't see me like this. He'll lose control. He'll hurt you!"

I stepped forward with my hands out to remind Spence that I wasn't here to judge. "I'm sure that all sounds really terrifying. Why don't we just go outside for fresh air? Take a few deep breaths? It can help you relax."

His eyes darted to the blood dripping down my arm, nostrils flaring. "Relax? How can I relax, Nora? You're bleeding! Not lightly might I add." He growled as he turned away. "I can't look at you. For *your* safety."

With a failed attempt at pulling my sleeve down, I took a step back. "I'm going to clean up."

As I turned on my heel to head for the bathroom—where Alicia has targeted me before—fingers wrapped around my wrist. I halted and glanced back at Spence as his eyes fixated on my face. "I can't let you go alone."

"I'll be fine. Your fear of blood is a far larger concern."

And what about your fear of it? Did that just disappear?

"Not larger than your safety." He led me to the bathroom and gathered the first aid while I removed my sweater. He grasped my arm and swallowed, eyes glued to the crimson. "He's cruel, Nora."

"Highly unlikely. He's still you." I dipped my head into his view until his eyes locked on mine.

"You don't believe me? You'll see." His fingers dug into my skin as he dropped his head, grunting. After a few moments of silence, he lifted his chin until I met the soulless pits, his pupils seizing his iris'. Blacked out. The dark side of Spence Woods.

"Spence?" my voice came out small.

He clicked his tongue. "Nora Witlow. Nice to finally meet you." His eyes roamed down my arm until they lingered on the cut. "We should clean that up before you bleed out."

"You don't want to hurt me?" Confusion laced my expression.

He leaned forward, tsking. "He says things to make you fear me, to keep you alert." He reached for my wrist, yanking it towards him. As he applied pressure, his eyes flicked to mine. "You don't need to worry about me. I'd never hurt you, darling."

"I don't think it's entirely appropriate to call me that, given the situation and who could walk in at any moment."

"Not appropriate?" He tilted his head to his left. "Ah, that's right. You haven't even kissed yet. He wants to kiss you, too. The man has restraint."

"Good. All men should," I spat. "It'd be a shame if his lack of control got him hurt, or worse."

He choked on a laugh. "Oh, is that a threat?"

"If you see fit, so be it." I nodded towards the wound. "We're wasting time with chit-chat."

His eyes narrowed slightly, but he lifted the cloth to find only drops trying to escape. His gaze fell on me once more, careful and primal, never wavering as he lowered to the laceration and dragged his tongue across.

"You can't do that!"

But it didn't stop him from sucking the last of the blood. He wrapped it in gauze, ensuring that I didn't need stitches for this. It bled a lot, but not too much to require medical attention of any kind.

"How…" I couldn't get the words out.

"How what, darling?" He fixed my dress' sleeve. "How do you think Claire and I get along so well?"

Lifting my head, my throat bobbed. "Claire, right. And you're attracted to her?"

"She's attractive," he paused, "but I'm not attracted to her. We had fun for the time being, doing what we enjoyed in the sheets. We understood each other."

"But it was toxic."

"I suppose if you call angry sex toxic… Besides, I am half of him. Not a quarter, but half, and that means that I should get a say too. Her being able to bring me out just allowed me to live life, too. He never lets me do that, but she did. I can't hate her for that, even if he tries."

My eyes dropped to the tiles. "So do you want her?" He liked that she could help him feel free. Maybe like a friend with some sex from time to time.

"Want her?" With brows knitted together, he glanced at the mirror. "Are you jealous? I thought you didn't want me to act inappropriate towards you, and now here we are where you are so desperately trying to figure out if I like Claire more than you."

I scoffed. "No, I am not jealous. I'm a psychologist who asks these questions to get to know people. Come on, put two and two together."

"He told you I'm a menace. I'm wrath in the flesh. He said that I'm the bad guy."

"And?"

"And I need to know, do you believe that?"

"I don't know you. This is my first time meeting you, and far as I can tell, you're not a bad guy. You're helping me with my wound. However, you might just be a little too bold about it."

A cunning smile flashed at me. "I like bold."

"You want to be known as the kind of guy who ignores a woman's boundaries? Because that would make you the bad guy in this case. I set clear boundaries and the angel side has respected those. Now the question is, are you going to? If you cannot come to an understanding, then you know exactly why this would never work between any of us." I ran my sweater under the cold tap water to allow it to remove as much blood as possible.

"What boundaries have I crossed that you set?" he asked.

"Licking my arm was entirely unnecessary."

"That's it?"

"You called me darling after I told you it was inappropriate."

"Fine." He grabbed my shoulder, spinning me to face him. "Then tell me, looking in my eyes, that it was too far."

"You don't think that's an intimidation tactic?"

"Have I proved yet to you to be the kind of guy he paints me as?" His head dipped into my view.

I straightened my posture and locked eyes, expecting terror to slither through my veins. I even tried to open my mouth and say the words. None of that happened.

When I faced this version of Spence, I didn't fear for my life.

I didn't cower, or flinch.

He wouldn't hurt me. I knew that. He meant it.

I just couldn't quite tell him not to call me Darling. I couldn't quite tell him not to lick my blood like a madman. Why? Because deep down, it made me feel alive. For the first time in a while since my ex, I'd had the thrill of interacting with an attractive guy, and I didn't want to lose that. I wanted to see where it could go from here.

"I can't quite do that, Spence."

"Spence," he said, tasting it on his tongue. "Normally I don't get the privilege of wearing his name."

"Then what should I call you?"

"Darling is fine," he said with a grin.

"Spence it is." I turned away from him, walking to the door. "We should head back, and you might want to allow him to take control before David discovers this."

"And if I don't?"

"Then he'll finally have what he needs to do to Spence what he did to Claire."

The words slipped too easily. I regretted them, but I couldn't shove them back in and swallow. I couldn't reverse the damage.

"Claire? What did he do to Claire?" He stepped forward, concern evident. More than he'd ever feel for me.

Facing him, I shook my head. "Nothing. He's just been withholding blood, but it's fine because I've been supplying her," I lied. Thankfully, he couldn't hear my thoughts like I could his.

"You've been giving her your blood?"

"I'm the only one who can. She'll be okay." She had to be okay. I said it more to reassure myself that she was fine. What would I do if she wasn't?

In mere seconds, he closed the gap between us, hands on

my cheeks. "Promise me you'll be careful. She can't always stop herself, Nora. I'd hate to see anything bad happen to you."

Why did he have to say it like that?

"I promise," I whispered. "I'll be okay. Everyone will be okay, and once I save us all, we never have to worry again."

But it wasn't me I worried so much about.

"You need to hide, from David. Please."

For my sake, he bowed his head in obedience. "As you *wish*, Nora Witlow."

XXXIV

Wind whistled. Trees scratched at my window. It didn't stop me from climbing out of bed and slipping on a robe with socks. Tonight, I was finding Claire. I had to ensure that she was still alive, just to prove to Emilie she was wrong. For my peace of mind, she would be okay.

Sneaking to the basement was easy. During a time of the night where everyone had been fast asleep, I could go undetected.

As I made it to the bottom of the stairs, the dark hallway beckoned me, and I listened.

I searched rooms. I listened for any noise louder than my breathing. I used my key to get into the room meant only for our meetings, but nobody had been in there. So when I found myself in the auditorium, a sigh left my lips. Defeat. Despair, even. I thought I'd made progress, or maybe David had hidden her somewhere he knew I could never look. Maybe he discovered that I'd been venturing where I didn't belong.

And when I'd just about given up hope, she appeared, alive, on the stage.

It hadn't been her, entirely. Just the ghost of her in a way, a vision into where she was.

"Claire," I breathed.

She never responded to my voice.

Instead, she looked up, like she'd spotted someone. As David came into view, he held a cup. "It's yours, Claire, if you just tell me what Nora knows."

"She doesn't know anything," her words came out barely above a whisper. She had no energy left to give, and I ached to transfer her all of mine.

"And we both know that's a tall-tale you're spitting there." He swished the glass around. "I'll give you one last chance. I'm forgiving, but if you wish to dig your grave, I can't stop you. So, which is it?"

"I said she doesn't know anything. We talk about my parents and how much they hate me for my past crimes." Crimes? I'd tried to make her understand she was the victim. "We even talked about my relationship with Spence. She doesn't know I'm a vampire. She doesn't know more than what I've told her."

Or what David had told me in private, but she wasn't supposed to let him know that she knew about what they were doing with their blood.

"Yet she appears to despise my very being. She looks at me as though I'm the villain. I know what happens, Claire. I've hired enough psychologists to know how this ends. They figure our the truth, then I have to silence them for good before they ruin my plans."

"Yet you didn't kill her last time, did you? You erased her memories. With what, I don't know. But you can't be entirely sure that you're the one running the show." Her eyes shifted across his scowling features.

He stepped forward, pouring the red liquid—what I assumed what blood—down the sink. Her nostrils flared in response, mouth watering. "Spence's magic can mess with the mind. I've studied the blood of an angel to know that he can remove memories, which was exactly what I did. I've heard his comments in passing, too. I know he catches glimpses of the future." David pondered for a moment, contemplating the next bit of information. "I'm not sure why I kept Nora alive."

Claire moved in her seat, gaze falling to her lap. "Then do what you're gonna do. I'm done being afraid of you."

"Fair enough." David disappeared.

I turned away, only to hear someone yell out, "Restrain her!"

I glanced back at the stage, assuming it'd been directed at me. I badly wished it had been. No, instead, it had been directed right as Claire who now crouched in a corner. Growls echoed. Hisses bounced off the walls.

And when the group of doctors grabbed her biceps, brownish sludge dripped from her lips, coating her teeth and seeping from her arm.

Claire screamed.

I rushed forward, attempting to do anything but stand and watch. But I recognized the room as the very one where the ECT was. Which had been empty when I arrived here. If this was playing before me now, then what could I do?

The realization hit me, forcing me to my knees as I struggled for air.

I hadn't been watching the present. This stage played memories of the past. There was absolutely nothing I'd be able to do to save her.

They pushed her to the ground, pinning her arms as she trashed around. She yelled out, her screams tearing the insides of my eardrums.

They didn't help her. They restrained her, listening to her cries as pain ripped through her body.

She turned her head, begging for someone to make it go away. To feed her. To offer their blood to save her from a cruel fate.

Nobody did such a thing.

Her screams went on until her throat grew raw and she couldn't get any sound out. She shouted, but it came out stilted. Her eyes rolled back, hair clinging to her sweaty forehead. Arching, she writhed. Then, her body dropped, going still.

"Claire?" I whispered.

She didn't respond.

David nudged her. Kicked her side, even. But she never came to.

She never woke up.

She never opened her eyes or groaned from the aching in her gut. She didn't react to his hits.

Claire Anderson lay dead before me.

Long after the scene vanished, I stayed glued to the floor. Numb. Tingling throughout my legs, traveling up my arms until it took over my soul.

Until I lost all feeling.

Everything I'd fought for, gone.

Claire became a victim of David Harrison.

Her blood stained her own hands, and his as well. He had starved her so she had no choice but to poison herself to escape.

Because I couldn't keep my promise.

I attempted to stand on my feet before falling back into a chair so worn down a hole appeared in the seat.

How did I break the news? How did I tell Spence that she'd been starved to suicide? Emilie had accepted it. She knew the truth, yet I had denied it only to have to face it myself.

Why did I try to go digging around on my own? Why put myself through the trauma? Because what if Emilie had been wrong, and what if Claire had been down here—alive?

I risked watching her die in front of me just in case she hadn't been killed.

How lucky I'd been…

If Alicia found me down here to take my life, I'd beg her to. I'd tell her not to hold back. Selfish, sure. Definitely weak. Did I claim I was otherwise?

I was expected to walk back upstairs and pretend I knew nothing, to pretend I hadn't just watched them pin her down as she suffered an agonizing end. I had been expected to waltz back upstairs and go about my day as if I hadn't just witnessed something so soul-shattering.

So I didn't go back up at all.

I stayed in the chair, and seconds later, the tears began to coat my cheeks. Sobs racked my body. Lumps formed, making it impossible to swallow. My cheeks burned, the surface stinging under the warm and salty reminder that I no longer had my friend to confide in when things got too tough.

I no longer had my rock.

I screamed out, falling forward to the floor and burying my head under my chest. I didn't want to face anyone. I didn't want to have to go back up there and be the responsible one. I simply wanted to wallow and not be expected to walk it off like I had Alicia.

So I didn't go back up at all.

Darkness engulfed me. It wrapped me up in its cold arms and whispered that I didn't owe the world my sanity. How easy it'd be just to believe it, too.

How could David allow her to starve? Why the fuck would Claire save my ass over hers? I hated her for it. I wanted to go back and slap her for ever putting me above herself. Did she not know I wanted better for her? She was meant to stay alive for both our sakes, until I could get her out of this damned asylum.

Another cry harassed me.

"Fuck you, Claire. How could you do this to us? To me? To Spence? How could you be such a coward and such a knight all at once? I could've handled him a second time. I could've won!"

I rolled onto my back, my wails soon dissipating when dehydration washed over me. Snot built up to the point I became a mouth-breather, but I didn't bother to blow it. What difference would that make? She'd still be gone. I'd still have the urge to cry if I had any tears left to give. I didn't bother to make myself presentable.

I spent another good hour on the floor, and even if my cheeks had dried and the puffiness died down, I appeared a chaotic, useless, wanna-be hero when I found the bathroom after I made my way back upstairs.

I tried to smooth my hair. I tried to wash my face.

It still never brought her back from the tomb.

"Why couldn't you just tell me what David was doing to you? Why couldn't you let us figure it out together? You didn't need to go and make that decision on your own, for both of us. You could've asked for my help, Claire."

No sobs tormented me. I couldn't even muster up enough energy to be angry with a ghost.

I did have the energy to saunter back to my room and collapse as I was. Even as cold as the temperature was in this place, I didn't pull the blanket up. Maybe I could allow it to take me with her. Maybe I could give up and nobody would ultimately blame me.

Why did I have to be their savior?

Because Claire would slap me around to remind me that's who I was. Because I'd hate myself at the end of the night, and I wouldn't be able to sleep (as if I could sleep as it was) knowing I succumbed to the grief.

That's all this was—what the feelings were. Grief trying to tear me apart and claim its control. If I allowed it, what would happen to Spence and Emilie?

I loved Claire, but could I allow myself to put her demise above their hope?

No.

She'd remind me just the same that it was my one purpose in this asylum. I'd taken this job for a reason and to allow that to drown for the sake of my fleeting emotions, it was abhorrent.

It made me no better than David, and I'd be damned to drop to his level.

"Okay, Claire," I said in a quiet voice. "I'll keep going, just because your death should at the very least mean something. I won't let your sacrifice be in vain."

How would Spence react when he found out? Would I tell him?

Of course. I owed him that much after lying to him about where she'd been and what David did to her.

I just couldn't ensure the demon side wouldn't kill me in return for it. I deserved that much, however. I didn't deserve forgiveness or understanding. Claire wasn't given any of that, and I failed her, so it only seemed fair I took what she no longer could. She left it all for me to absorb.

The rock.

I'd be the stable and grounded one. I'd take all the abuse, and all of David's orders. I'd be the pushover, just to be the one who freed them. I'd allow whatever to happen, happen, if it meant keeping the three of them out of harm's way.

I'd go on pretending I was fine, because that was what everyone needed me for. No more weak Nora. No more wallowing, or pitiful behavior. I'd only exhibit what they needed me to.

In Claire's name, I'd be whatever the prisoner's required, and most times, what David asked.

XXXV

David stepped out of the office and right into my path. "Nora, I wanted to just let you know we have a new patient if you'd like to introduce yourself. His name is Taylor Moore." He smiled as he pointed down the hall, where Claire's room used to be.

My heart sunk at the thought of a new prisoner. We lost one and gained another. As I headed there, I noticed the new name plastered on Claire's door. She was gone but her presence would never falter.

Walking into the room, I forced a smile as I faced the guy who now invaded her space. "Good morning. I'm Nora, but also Miss Witlow works just fine. You're Taylor Moore?"

His eyes scanned my body as he leaned back. "I am, Nora."

He tsked, shaking his head. "What a shame."

"What's a shame?" I furrowed my brows.

He chuckled. "I was hoping my doctor would be someone else, someone more…open about themselves. I suppose you'll have to do."

Open? What the hell did that entail?

I was going to have to fight every reflex in my body to not punch him in the nose.

"Thank you. I take that as a compliment." His eyes honed on mine, and I stumbled back.

Choosing my next words with caution, I said, "Are you just good at reading what's on a woman's mind? Perhaps you have a girlfriend that you adore."

He shrugged. "No, I'm just a mind reader."

I leaned my shoulder against the frame, clearing my throat. "I suppose." Had they replaced Claire with another vampire? They still needed to experiment on a vampire, I assumed. They had Riley, but for whatever reason, they needed another.

He stood. "Claire must have been your friend. My bad. She *did* sound like your friend." He came closer. "Yes. I am a vampire. Thank you for noticing. Maybe you humans aren't so stupid after all." He stepped in front of me before placing both hands against the wall beside my head, trapping me.

I couldn't show him any fear. That's what he wanted.

No, you idiot, he wants lust. Vampires crave lustful humans.

I straightened my posture. "This is inappropriate, Taylor, and I don't want you. You're not my type."

He smirked a bit. "What do you mean? Species? Gender? I can work with either."

There was a small voice in my head begging Spence or even David to walk in at any moment. Unfortunately, my wish hadn't been granted.

Gathering up all my courage and strength, I shoved him, and harshly might I have added. He lunged at me before stopping himself as I cowered. I hadn't suspected the new guy to be so violent.

"I apologize for my behavior, Nora." He approached, pushing a strand behind my ear. When Spence had done it, it was gentle—romantic. Taylor turned a sweet gesture bitter. He wasn't being nice. It was a way of intimidating me and showing me he had control of this situation. "I hope it doesn't change things," he whispered in my ear. As soon as his finger traced down my collarbone, my hand met his cheek with a forceful slap.

"I said you're not my type," I said with a firm voice. I marched out of the room and ran into the one person who could calm my worked-up nerves. "Spence, I'm sorry." I shook my head.

He coughed. "No, no. It's not your fault. Is everything okay?"

"Um, let's talk in private." We entered his room, and I shut the door behind us. "The new guy is a douche. It's all wrong, Spence. He's trying to assert his dominance over me and it's disgusting. He tried to touch me and I'm not one to slap my patients but that was out of line. I swear it was!" I stuck my finger up, shaking it.

Spence nodded in response. "I can't imagine being a woman and having a guy hit on you when it's unwanted. He needs to respect your boundaries." He scratched his head while turning the other way.

I noticed his reaction to this situation, calming my nerves. "Spence, I did not mean it like that. When we first met, you didn't radiate this pervert vibe at all. You've always been respectful about things." It wasn't easy trying to tell him that his affection towards me was wanted when we were meant to be just friends. "You're not trapping me against the wall when I introduce myself to you. You're not whispering in my ear after almost hitting me—"

Spence spun on his heel and closed the space between us in mere milliseconds. "He almost hit you? Tell me his fucking name and I'll teach him a lesson."

I made the mistake of putting my hands on his chest, but I had to calm him down somehow. "He didn't hit me. He was going to, but he stopped himself. I'm not saying it was okay at all, but it's over with. I'm in a rut. I hate the guy—I do—but if I tell David about this or mention that I don't want to talk to Taylor, he may kill him. The guy is an absolute asshole, but he doesn't deserve to starve like Claire did."

The expression on his face fell, and he leaned against the wall for support. "What?"

It hadn't occurred to me that Spence wasn't aware of Claire's death yet. Wouldn't he have been the first to know? Wouldn't Emilie have told him by now?

"I'm sorry, Spence. I didn't realize… I…"

He sat on the bed, running his hands through his hair. "Tell me the truth, Nora. Please," his words had come out quietly as he begged for answers. "No lies this time."

He knew.

It broke my heart when I said the next words over again, repeating the tragedy. "Claire is dead. David starved her, and she drank her own blood. They found her that way." As much as I wanted to cry, it wasn't my turn. Spence needed my support and I had to be his shoulder. He knew Claire in ways I hadn't. He had every right to be torn by her death.

The silence lingered in the air, then a sniffle cut through. It had come from Spence. A minute later, he was sobbing over the loss of someone he had cared about for a long time.

Sitting beside him, I let him lay his head in my lap as he expressed his pain. I had to hold back every tear, going against all my better instincts, not to follow his trail. Claire left me to be the rock now.

I brushed through his hair, stroking along his temples. If Claire were still here, she would remind me that he found comfort in spilling his feelings to me. It made me feel special to know he felt safe to be himself around me. I wanted him to always know he could tell me how he was doing. I would never judge.

When the tears passed, Spence sat up and pulled his knees up, resting his arms on top of them. "I'm sorry, Nora. I didn't mean to do that. I had no idea…"

"No. Don't be sorry. As a good friend once said, it's not your fault. You can't erase the pain or pretend it doesn't exist. We must live through it and let ourselves heal through time. Claire meant something to you. She meant something to me, and I understand your grief. I may grieve for our relationship, but I still know that you must grieve for yours and it's okay. Remember her for the person she was—a beautiful soul." I gazed up at the ceiling.

He didn't respond to anything I'd said but I couldn't blame him. What could he say at a time like this?

"Spence, where do people go when they die? I mean, I know that we are taught to be good people, or we will burn in hell or something, but then you guys mentioned that ghosts are dead people so… I'm just curious. If Claire and Alicia died, where did they go?"

He took a moment to think before answering, "Heaven and hell aren't for humans. Heaven is for angels and hell is for the demons. When they die, things happen. There are places considered paradise and other places that are the opposite. They're like a prison. If a criminal gets death row and dies, he's going to those bad places. More prison for him for the rest of forever. If someone dies in peace, and they're ready to leave, they go to paradise more likely. As long as they weren't a horrible person on earth, otherwise, they'd end up in those prisons. In Alicia's case, she was young. She wasn't ready to die. Her death was sudden. She stopped in the middle, per se. The ones with unfinished business haunt people, places, or things that keep them back. She was probably haunting you."

"So, that's it? But if she was taken by this thing, what happened? Death stole her and replaced her? How does that work?"

He shrugged. "Death is like the keeper of the prisoners. Alicia was wandering around, so he took an opportunity. He likes to screw with the living by replacing ghosts with awful versions of themselves."

My head began to ache at the knowledge. How could that be? If that were true, there had to be hundreds or even thousands who had been kidnapped and replaced just because they got stuck in the middle.

"And Alicia, this is the awful version? Her darkest secrets?"

He didn't respond, and I assumed it was because he didn't want to tell me the truth. Alicia, deep down, truly did believe I was the cause of her death. Spence didn't have to say that, but I pieced it together on my own.

And that was what hurt so much worse. All legends were based on some truth, and I supposed legendary evil ghosts were, too.

"How did all this start? Angels and demons." I gestured to him who just so happened to represent both.

He rested his head back against the wall. "Seeds. Seeds were planted. It sounds really weird. That's how we're created, which is similar to humans. Depending on how you grow that seed can determine the outcome. Demons can have angels and angels can have demons. I'm not just a hybrid because I have both parents. I'm a hybrid because my dad was afraid of nurturing me as I was growing inside the womb as a seedling. My mom made up for the other half, which is why I'm both. If demons nurture theirs, they can have an angel. That's why they try hard to neglect the seedling while it's growing. It's the same with angels having babies."

This was a whole new way of reproducing. I had no idea angels and demons could have different babies. I supposed hybrids were far rarer, and an abomination for more reasons than one.

"So are hybrids rare, then, but more common than I thought?"

He nodded a bit. "They can be. I'm not the only hybrid. I'm just an abomination because they can't decide if I belong in heaven or hell."

"So it's bad for demons and angels to have babies together and it's bad for babies to also be born as hybrids. Well, that sure doesn't complicate things." I snickered.

"Yeah, it's a complex world." He took a deep breath. "Have you prepared for the dance?"

My mind searched for any mention and came up empty. "What dance?"

"There's an event that David likes to host every year. I don't understand much of it but all the doctors dress in white while the patients dress in a color of their choice. It can be anything as long as it isn't white, of course. I think he does it as his way of giving us some fun or whatever. If he controls when we have fun, he can make sure he has control over everything. But it's coming up in a few weeks. You should definitely prepare." He smiled a little.

What was I meant to prepare for? It was just a dance, right? "I'll look into it some more." I grinned, nudging him.

I stood by my words, too.

Regardless, there was one person I was going to avoid at all costs, and he went by the name of Taylor. If he dared to touch me again, he'd feel more than a slap. I wouldn't allow a man like that to run the show around here.

He'd be quick to learn respect and know this was my body. He wasn't permitted to be anywhere near me from here on out. If he didn't accept that message, I'd make it loud and clear for everyone in the hospital. No more games.

I came here for business, and that was where it'd stay.

XXXVI

As I passed by Emilie's room, I found her curled in a ball. I stepped inside, waving at her. "Hey, are you all right?"

She shook her head. "I'm losing…memories. I don't know what to do."

I sat on her bed, scanning the items in her room. Nothing popped out or seemed out of the ordinary. "What do you mean?"

She let out a long sigh before sitting up. She grabbed her head, wincing as if she were in pain. "I can't… I try to remember how I got here but I have no idea. Is that supposed to happen?"

I pulled her into my arms. "No." I rubbed her back. "I need to know, Emilie, what is David doing?"

Her entire body slumped, and I'd assumed she had no energy to hold herself up. "One of the doctors died. He was murdered, and David thinks we did it… He tried to get us to confess but I couldn't. I didn't do it, Nora…" She rested against me.

"You need to tell me what David was doing to you." I lifted her face, holding her cheeks.

She whined a little. "I'm so tired. I just want to sleep." Her eyes fell shut as she let all her consciousness go.

I lay her down and tucked her into the blankets, then I stood.

I was going to get to the bottom of this.

After leaving her room, I headed downstairs to the office, stopping at the door when I saw David at his desk. "What's going on? A doctor ends up dead and you assume a patient did this? They didn't, and I know you've been using the machine on them, and shouldn't that be enough to tell you they physically couldn't kill a man? It becomes obvious when Emilie tells me she can't remember how she got here. I also know Claire was never released. I know that she poisoned herself from insanity. You let her starve, David. You murdered her."

He swiveled, folding his hands together while his elbows stayed propped up on the arms of the chair. His eyes met mine. "I see you're upset."

"I'm not upset. I'm furious. You said you weren't harming them. You are abusing your power. They deserve to be treated better. ECT is meant to be a last resort thing, not a weapon against them if they don't tell you what you want to hear. What you want to hear may not even be the truth. Even then, ECT is meant to be used in very controlled situations. I know you aren't using it that way." I planted my heels together.

"Miss Witlow, we shouldn't have this discussion right now. Your temper is clouding your better judgment, hindering your ability to speak like an adult." He pressed his clasped hands against his mouth.

I took a deep breath to keep my frustration to a minimum. "I've been an adult for seven years. I am pissed off because these people I've devoted my time to are being treated lesser than humans. That's disgusting, and you know somewhere in your twisted mind it is." I pointed my finger at him before turning and walking out of the office. I had to figure something out, and stat. By the day, things were dwindling and I didn't have much time left.

With a plan in mind, I waited by the closet until David exited the office. He was protective of something in there and I intended to find out what it was.

Entering, I pulled out their folders. I made sure to keep my eyes peeled for the monster himself—the facility name now clear as day. It wasn't named Monstrum due to the patients. It was at the fault of the doctors who played a hand in torturing innocent creatures.

As I found Claire's folder, my breath caught in my throat. I flipped it open, peeking at the contents inside. Her picture stared me dead in the face, and so did the date she had been admitted. Flipping through, I found more photographs. They'd taken pictures of her fangs, studying them as if there were some way he could attain it themselves. *He couldn't.*

Coming upon the last picture, my heart stopped. Claire lay on the floor with her hair sprawled around her. Her eyes were glassed over—empty and void of all life. Her arm had been punctured by her own teeth while brown ooze spilled out. That same ooze left stains on her lips, stains that made her death much more valid. What I'd seen had happened, and David took a picture of the proof for some sick game of his.

I closed the folder and put it back in its place, holding in the pain of what I had seen. I couldn't lose my chance now.

So I flipped open Spence's, going through the images and stopping when something stood out. It was a paper that talked about his *tests*.

My theory had been confirmed: the patient struggles upon the sight of blood. Woods battles the inner demon. If we continue this routine, he'll lose control. The demon must be released.

Closing the file, I covered my mouth. I was going to be sick. I slipped them back into the cabinet and closed the drawer before sprinting down the hall to the bathroom. I bent over the toilet and let go of my entire lunch.

I had never even imagined it would be as bad as I thought it was, yet I'd been proven wrong. Spence had told me that he hated giving into the demon. He avoided anything or anyone who would bring it out of him. Yet David was trying to do just that.

And now everything began to make sense, things coming to light that I never wanted to believe.

Inside Spence's head played a constant battle against himself. I could never begin to understand the pain he was going through, trying to make it all stop. I'd have to fight harder than ever to help him keep it locked up. I would never let him lose to himself again.

I planted my butt on the cold tiles, leaning my head back. "There is so much to do," I whispered to myself.

Everything on my plate piled up. I had to get everyone out of here while keeping them sane. And during this battle, I had to somehow save Alicia from the grips of Death himself.

I closed my eyes to get rid of that image of Claire, the one of her on the floor in such a horrifying position, up close and personal as if I hadn't watched it from afar first. When my eyelids went black, the scene became that much clearer. They starved Claire and I was going to make sure all the vampires and her family knew about it. I had to get rid of David and his army without destroying Spence in the process.

After I picked myself up off the floor, I headed to Spence's room. I knew it was time to talk about what was happening. He needed saving and I was the only one who could remotely help.

"We should talk," I said, my words coming out hoarser than I intended.

He seemed to be lost in his own head, and we both knew that was never a good idea. "What is there to talk about? Claire is dead. We will be soon."

My eyes locked onto his as I stepped in front of him. "No. You won't be. Claire was my friend, and yes I am pissed off and torn over her death, but I won't let them do the same to the rest of you. You're going to fight with me. You will fight against the dark parts of your mind. I refuse to allow the demon to control you." I closed the space between us as I squatted down and grasped his hands. "I know I can help."

"Why are you so sure?" His voice had barely been audible.

Multiple scenarios played out in my head. I could kiss him here. I could give up on our agreement. It would be so easy to give in and let all our worries fly away through passion.

That was why I was so sure of myself, because I cared about him in more ways than one, but I couldn't get the guts to do something that had been based on terribles ethics. Something so abhorrent that just the mere thought made nausea swirl around in my stomach. I couldn't ruin what we had in hopes of something that might never work out. I was just a human.

I'd never be anything more.

I squeezed his hands. "I just know, Spence. There is a fire burning inside me. It's growing and the flame gets brighter each time. I know David blames you for what happened to his doctor. Emilie already told me, and it sickens me that he is doing this to innocent people. Come on." I stood. "David won't stop me from taking you out for fresh air."

He tugged his hand away from me. "Nora, please."

"Spence, snap out of it. This is what he wants. He wants you to give up on hope. Don't let him win. Get off your ass and come outside with me." I waved him over. "Don't let *me* down."

Taking my advice, he got off the bed and followed me as I gathered Emilie, Riley, and Taylor, leading the four of them outside into the frigid winter air.

Taylor walked around with his hands in his pockets. "I knew you would come around, Nora."

"That's Miss Witlow to you." I went over to Emilie. "I know about Finn."

Her eyes met mine and a small light began to glow inside her. "Finn?"

"Yes. I found a note. He left it for you. You deserve to read it for yourself." I handed her the letter.

She unfolded it and her tears built up in the rim of her eyelids, but never spilled over. "Oh Finn… He's still looking for me, Nora." She hugged it to her heart, sniffling. "I miss him so much."

I smiled a little as she cherished their unspoken memories. "He is, and I want to get you home to him. That's what matters.

Your undying love is what will end David and his plans. Hold onto that."

I turned and glanced back at Spence. As I walked towards him, Taylor blocked my path. "So, Nora. About that threat…"

"Miss Witlow." The thick air made my temper that much more reliable. "I still meant it, Taylor. I do not appreciate when a man hits on me unwanted. You don't respect me. You just want to fire up my hormones so you can drink my blood." I grabbed his finger, squeezing and entirely ready to snap it back. "Don't test me. I am not in that kind of mood."

Pulling free, he put his hands up, stepping away. "Message received." He faced the building and mumbled to himself.

Spence stood by the fence, admiring something out there beyond the forest. While stopping beside him, I nudged him. "I know things are going wrong. I know that—" I swallowed. "Claire's death has made it feel much more hopeless. I can't tell you it's going to get better or it's going to get easier. It never does. Life is a bitch. I even know what it's like to lose someone close to you, someone you care about. It feels like the universe is forcing the breath out of you every morning when you wake up."

The trees attracted my gaze, but nothing was really out there during this time of year. Still, Spence wouldn't say a word.

I continued, "Somehow, you learn to live with the pain. You realize there are other people in your life who also need you in their lives. Claire knows you'll never forget about her. She wants you to be happy, Spence. She told me herself that she just wants you to be at peace in your life. It takes a lot of courage to let someone you care about be happy even if it's without you."

He turned his head after a while with a frowned. "Don't lie."

"I'm not. I would never. I'm telling you the truth. Claire told me she was jealous of me when you…tried to kiss me. She wanted to be that woman, but she realized she was your past. She just wanted you to be happy. She was the one person who was most supportive of us getting together. She begged me to make you smile. I just couldn't make that promise. She would slap you for moping around and giving up because of David. She never gave up. Instead, she fought. She fought until her last day. Learn from her." I stepped between him and the wired fence.

He rubbed his eyes with his thumb and forefinger, groaning. "It's so hard, Nora."

I nodded my head. "It is hard. You struggle with your dark side, and you told me that I'm nice enough to help you fight, so let me do my job and help you win that battle." I pushed against his chest to put some distance between us. "They need our weakness, but we must show them our strength if we are to win this war."

Spence lifted his head. "Okay… I'll try."

I gave him a smile, assuring him that everything would somehow work out.

***

Everything did not in fact work out.

At least not later that night.

As darkness crept over the last of the moonlight, screams pierced the halls. I jumped up, assuming someone had been getting murdered, and without throwing anything extra on, I rushed from my room and towards the patients' rooms.

A male scream.

Particularly Spence's.

Without thinking, I found the keys in David's office and hurried into his room, pulling him up from the mattress while yelling his name to wake him up.

When he opened his eyes, he found me with shallow breaths

and hair falling around my face. Then, he pulled me to him, arms around my waist, as he buried his head and sobbed.

"Spence, what happened?" I asked in a whisper.

He didn't answer for a few moments.

"Spence?"

"It felt so real, Nora. I don't usually sleep, and I thought this was real." He pulled his head back, looking up at me. "They were everywhere. Demons all around, clawing and trying to tear me apart." *Trying to bring out his dark side and make him do such horrid things.*

But he'd never say that out loud.

"It's okay, Spence. It was simply a bad dream. I'm here now."

Was it just a bad dream? I couldn't promise that, but I'd fight anyway. To ensure his safety, and always make sure he never felt alone.

"Do you want me to leave?" I tried to ask in the gentlest way possible, considering I didn't want him to assume I wanted to go back to my room. I'd do whatever was best for him, but if he also didn't want me here, I'd give him that, too.

Sweat coated his skin as his chest glistened under the low lighting seeping from the window. "No."

He lay back down, and against all morals, I pulled his blanket back and climbed in with him. He didn't even give me a chance before he pulled me to his chest, and not in the sense that he wanted more out of this encounter, but he did it like a child would cling to a bear for comfort. I was the only person to ground him in reality from the night terror.

I attempted to ignore the coolness of his skin. The way his fingers drummed on my shoulders to find some stability.

But pretending not to bask in his musky scent couldn't be helped. I just thanked the universe that he had been too affright to notice the brushing of my nose against his neck.

XXXVII

Riley chewed her lip, ignoring the blood that followed. "Why is Taylor any better? I mean, what was the point of starving Claire?"

Sitting back, a lump formed in my throat as I swallowed. "I don't think he planned for Claire to drink her own blood. I think it came as a surprise and he was mad for letting it happen. I believe that Claire…just wanted out of here. She had no family to return to and so she decided to…give up all hope." I didn't dare say the word, because I didn't want to. It would mean that this had been her fault, and her choice. It wasn't. David drove her to it. David Harrison was responsible for shattering her spirit to the point of death.

Riley nodded a bit.

I lowered my head as a few tears slipped from my eyelashes, and I quickly wiped them away. It wasn't the time to cry. Riley was here to talk about her life some more, and my only job was to listen.

"Hey," she whispered, coming close and wrapping her arms around me. "It's okay if you let it out. She was your friend."

I peeled her away from me. It felt wrong to allow her to comfort me the way Claire did, like Riley was her *replacement*. "But she wasn't. I don't think she saw me that way. Besides, she knew Emilie and Spence way longer. I don't have any right to cry over her."

"Spence and Emilie don't strike me as the kind of people to tell someone they can't mourn the death of a friend—and she *was* your friend. I believe she really was." She rubbed my back.

I choked on a sob, and soon the dam flooded, making the town its victims with nothing but destruction littering its tail. Everything inside me bled, my emotions entirely obvious.

Claire had been opening up and *trusting* me. How could I have let her go? How could I allow David to be alone with her? I knew what I saw in that basement the night we almost escaped. Claire had been the victim, and I barely even tried.

What about Alicia? All those years we were best friends. We planned to grow old together and live our best lives. We were going to be the maids of honor at each other's weddings. We would be the first ones we told about a new promotion or a new job.

But I ran. I didn't want to look at that home anymore. I spent barely four months at home before I fled the city. I came out here to get away from everything but the further I ran, the bigger the avalanche that chased me. And eventually, it would take me down with it.

The tears fell until my entire soul begged for water. My cheeks stung. My vision blurred even long after the fact. Inside, my entire chest ached, and with that my limbs shook involuntarily.

Sniffling, I gripped the sides of my seat, looking away from the person who walked in the room. Regardless, his perfect face with those damn dimples kneeled right into my view. "Nora?"

He pulled his shirt over his head and lifted my chin, cleaning up my face. As much as I didn't want to, he made me blow my nose into his shirt. The last thing I wanted was for anyone to see me like this. Especially Spence.

Riley barely knew me, so it wasn't as terrifying. Yet at the same time, I was her savior. She was supposed to count on me to be her foundation.

However, it wasn't even about Claire. It was, but not entirely.

This was also about Alicia.

Spence wrapped his arms around my shoulders, pulling me into his chest. I wanted to resist. I wanted to suck it back up and pretend I was fine. But now that the gates were open, it was that much harder to close them.

So I relaxed in his arms.

He brought his hand to my face, pushing hair from my eyes. "We will mourn together. As much as it hurts right now, we make it bearable to live with," he whispered against my temple.

The words squeezed my heart with a warm hug on a cold winter night.

Inviting.

If I hadn't been so weak, I'd kiss him here and now. I'd devour the taste of him to remind me of why I kept fighting.

I didn't do that, however. I just relished in his safety net for the moment and held onto that bit of hope. I wasn't completely alone. Not yet. And if I played my cards right—not ever.

He pressed his lips to my temple. "We'll get out of here, Nora. We will do it for Claire. Alicia. We'll do it for everyone who's ever loved us as we are."

I placed my palm flat against his chest, pulling away ever so slowly. Spence placed his hand on top of mine.

Kiss her.

He didn't make a move to inch any closer.

No, we made a promise. We keep our promises.

I tried to tune out his voice, and once I did, my own took over.

Kiss him.

It would be so easy for him to grab my bottom lip with his thumb and show me how he really felt. And for a second, I wanted that. But the more he resisted, the more I appreciated how great he really was. He'd endure anything not to jeopardize our friendship, to hurt me.

A true gentleman.

Riley cleared her throat, and then footsteps echoed in my ear. I yanked my hand away from Spence, blushing just a tad.

David opened the door and looked at both Spence and Riley. "I need to talk to Nora."

They took that as their cue to leave. I begged them to stay, but all Riley could do was give me an apologetic look. She couldn't defy David's command, and I knew that. Nobody really could.

David closed the door. "We need to talk about your outburst, and the way you treated me. There are consequences, Nora. Do you understand?"

"But if I could—"

"Do you understand?"

I forced down my rage. "Yes, sir."

"Good. What happened with Claire was an accident. It was not my intention. You must know that. As for your punishment, we have a few new rules. You are out of the program. Completely. You will be taking most of the chores every day of the week. We have also decided to restrict your hours. You are only to be out between ten and seven unless I say otherwise. This punishment will last until I say it's over. Is that clear, Miss Witlow?"

Taking a deep breath, I nodded. "Yes, sir."

"Good." He flashed his wicked smile. "As for today's chore, you will be shoveling the snow from the driveway. We need to clear enough spaces for the dance that is coming up. You better be on your best behavior."

"I will be." I stood from my chair. "I'll get started right away."

He left my office.

With a sigh, I rubbed my face. I didn't want to do this, but I had no other choice. I had no energy to even argue. I had to prove I wasn't completely rogue, otherwise he'd fire me, and then I'd *never* have a chance to save them.

I put on my best clothes and spent hours upon hours getting the snow off the driveway. My fingers had gone numb hours before I finished, and my toes had started to believe they didn't exist. As if I hadn't needed them to walk on.

I stumbled through the front door and headed straight for my room. I shoved my toes and fingers right in front of the vent, groaning from the sensation as they began to thaw. The best way to explain this horrendous feeling was that it was made up of three-quarters of aching and a quarter of tickling. The equivalent of stepping on a puncturevine.

David had no remorse for it. If he could force Claire to drink her blood, why would he feel guilty from almost giving me hypothermia, or frostbite?

In fact, he had no remorse for anything he did. I'd love to watch him burn to the ground. As much as I wanted to promise Spence I wouldn't kill him, I couldn't. David murdered Claire. He didn't deserve to live, and maybe he would become a ghost, but if he did, wouldn't Death just kidnap him and hold him prisoner? I would never rush to save him.

I needed to somehow rescue Alicia, but I needed to also keep these four from impending death. Alicia was dead, and as disgusting as it sounded, she couldn't suffer any more from being a prisoner. These four were very much alive and at risk of being murdered.

It was my job to help everyone, these four being priority.

Sure, it was going to be much harder now that I wasn't allowed out after hours, but I'd find a way. I would always find a way. For Claire—and for Alicia.

Breakfast was quiet today. None of the doctors said anything, and I assumed it was because I wasn't treated like one of them anymore. I was halfway between prisoner and prison guard. Even Monique didn't say a word to me.

I'm sure David told them what happened and their trust had diminished. Did it bother me? Not in the slightest. As long as David didn't throw me out just yet, I could live with a few less friends. I never needed these employees to help me out anyway. They only got in the way.

The entire day dragged on. I said barely a word to the

prisoners, and they barely spoke to me. It helped David believe I was on his side to an extent. But deep down, I had no reason to talk to anyone.

Riley and Spence saw me at my most vulnerable and I was ashamed by it.

Taylor was still just a prick that I barely wanted to interact with. I'd get him out and that would be the last of it.

Emilie was busy thinking about Finn and his love letter. I wasn't going to overshadow that. I didn't really need her to talk to me anyway. I'd leave her in her happy little bubble for a bit.

This was the routine I followed the next few days. I strictly followed the schedule and had no conversations. It gave me time to plan the escape. Could I possibly make it happen at the dance? Maybe. But then all those casualties would be involved. I couldn't burn it down with innocent people inside. Most of them didn't know what was really going on, so it wasn't my place to say they would support such cruel practices.

I needed to do it soon, though. My time was being limited, and David was escalating. I couldn't allow anyone else to die at his hand.

That wasn't the hardest part yet. I still needed a way to burn it down without killing the four of them, but keeping David locked inside. Could I lock him somewhere? Possibly.

That was hard to answer, though.

What about Alicia? Would she follow me if I left? Would she burn down too? I couldn't even guarantee that I'd have a chance to save her after I fled with the others. What was I supposed to do then? Drop everything and rescue her first?

I was stuck between a boulder and the base of a cliff.

While the four went outside, I stayed in and played some piano to keep my head level. What would my parents have done?

They'd tell me to save Alicia first. She was the one who got the ball rolling on this entire road and I had to go back to the source to solve it. Maybe if I saved her, it would open better opportunities for me to help the rest.

As my fingers glided over the notes, filling the air with a harmony meant for the dead, my senses heightened in mere seconds. Alicia was watching me. That much I was sure of. And who was going to save her if I didn't? Who else loved her as much as I did?

I would create a plan to help her first, then I'd put it into action and go from there. I could only hope on her grave that it worked, and that it paved the way for the asylum to crumble.

XXXVIII

He stood by the wall, eyeing me. "Waiting on me, Nora?" Taylor shot me a smirk.

"It's still Miss Witlow." I glared as I leaned over in the chair. "The whole bloodsucking thing turns me off."

"He's asking for you," David said as he came to the entertainment area where I was sitting. He glanced at Taylor. Something heavy and wicked hung in the air. Bad blood between the two of them, at the very least. Taylor was a newbie and in the defiance stage. He could snap and attack David at any minute.

So why didn't he?

Standing up and walking between them, I gave Taylor a look. *Keep your cool, or David will kill you like he did Claire.*

He swallowed whatever anger he had and walked away

before he lost his temper.

I spun to face David. "I'll check on him now." I headed towards Spence's room and closed the door behind me. "Fuck, Spence. Not again." I knelt on the floor and inspected his cuts. "Why? You said you would try."

He lifted his eyes. "And I meant it. This is not my fault, Nora. I didn't do it this time."

If it hadn't been for these prisoners who needed me, I would have choked from the rage. "David did this? He's going to pay." I squeezed my hands into fists. "Why cuts? Why?" I racked my brain for answers.

"Blood makes me…lose control." He ran his hands over his hair. The file came crashing back. David wanted to unleash the demon, and this was his only method.

I got off the floor and left the room, heading to a closet where I found some first aid to help tend to his wounds. When I returned, I took a seat in front of him. "If this is true, then let me clean it up. You can't lose control if you don't see it. I said I was here to help you."

I pondered the last time he cut his chest, and I'd been questioning it. Had David been behind that, too? Spence might have taken the fall to keep me from lashing out at David.

He nodded, leaning back against the edge of the bed. "It's going to hurt, isn't it?"

I pulled out alcohol wipes and patted them against the cuts. "I'm sorry." I winced at the sound of him inhaling and exhaling rapidly. "It will feel so much better soon."

"Right, right. Soon." He groaned in pain, clenching his fist.

When I finished with the last wound, I discarded them in a bag. "No more blood. You can relax. The demon will go back into its cage." That was about all the hope I could muster up.

It faded when he placed his hand over mine. "Nora, this is hard."

"I know. It wasn't going to be easy, but it'll be worth it when this is over. You'll be free. You'll all be out of this horrid place." I was starting to wonder if my own words could be taken as a promise anymore.

His hand lifted from mine as he grabbed my chin, forcing me still. "I mean *this*. It's hard to pretend I don't feel anything." He let go of me. "It's impossible to be this close to you and not do anything about it."

I lowered my head, sealing the bag of bloody wipes and closing the kit. "I understand the struggle. I do. It's getting dangerous though. Taylor is not on our side. If we give in to our feelings, he will read my mind and destroy the entire plan."

"Don't let him get into your head." He tucked a loose strand behind my ear. "You can lock him out." Shivers ran down my spine as his fingers brushed behind my ear.

"Spence, you don't understand." I met his gaze, admiring the purity shimmering in his eyes as I studied his soul. "I want to but it's far too risky."

He repositioned himself and it wasn't until then that I realized his fingers were under my chin and guiding me closer. "I know you want to kiss me as much as I want to kiss you," he whispered.

Our faces centimeters apart, I needed an escape from his grasp, so I said the one thing that came to my mind. "I was engaged once." My heart scolded me for destroying the moment. His lips seemed so tempting—so *enticing*.

Spence pulled back, furrowing his brows while creases crossed his forehead. "Engaged?"

I rubbed my eyes. "I'm sorry. I didn't mean for it to come out like that." I ran my hands up and down my thighs. "I just thought you should know. I… I had been engaged to one of my previous exes. We were in love, and we wanted to be together forever."

He nodded a little, folding his arms. "So why did you end it?"

I released a sigh. "He fooled me. I got suspicious of late nights at work. I told him I was going out of town for the weekend, but I'd lied. When I came home after the first night, I found clothes all over the place. I knew it wasn't my bra. The sight was horrifying. He had been cheating on me with some woman…" I closed my eyes tightly.

"Nora, you did not deserve that."

I snorted. "And that's just it. I blamed myself. I thought it was my fault, that maybe I wasn't giving him enough sex or something. This woman was beautiful. She had the face of an angel and the morals of a demon. No, I'm sorry for saying that. She didn't know. She had no idea he was engaged. He screwed us both over." I shook my head. I twisted my body to face the same direction Spence was, my head resting against his shoulder.

My voice went quiet as I continued, "That was years ago. Alicia was the one who helped me use the engagement ring to scratch his fancy car. It wasn't who I was, but she convinced me that he didn't deserve his money back for stealing my heart and destroying it. He destroyed what was mine, so I did the same to him. I know you're not that kind of guy, Spence, but it's still a fear of mine."

"I can understand that. It's hard to trust people with something so fragile." He leaned his head on mine.

"I get insecure. I doubt myself and my relationship at times. I question if my partners are attracted to me. Finding him in bed with someone else stripped me of all security. I never felt more worthless in my life. It's tough trying to build myself back up, to believe that someone great could come along and find the value in me. I fear that someday I won't be good enough for him and he will find it in another woman. Again."

I took comfort in the quiet atmosphere. Our thoughts settled down, tucking themselves in for the night.

Spence broke through it. "I would never stoop so low."

I lifted my head, looking at him. "That's not what I'm afraid of with you, Spence. I'm afraid of finally having something good again and having it torn away. If David finds out, I'll have to see something I could *never* live with."

Day in and day out, I had been the one around to see the toll this place took on Spence. He would come to me and cry when he lost someone he cared about. He had once fallen asleep against my shoulder, expressing his most vulnerable parts. He—or David—slashed his chest to get his anger out, anger that David was trying to expose to the world. I had seen the rawest parts of him and he had seen everything about me, too.

My thoughts had opened and my secrets stripped, every part of my brain naked in front of Spence Woods.

I had loved a man once, a man who tore my heart to shreds. I had promised to love him forever. It was I who said yes when he got down on one knee. Why had he done it? What was the purpose of marrying me if he was just going to screw the next best thing?

I asked myself this all the time. I examined every inch of my mind, studying and observing. Had I not given him enough sex? Did I not listen to his problems or accomplishments? It was possible that the sex wasn't satisfying.

I'd refused to ever try anal, and she gave him exactly what I never could.

Still, other pieces of me would suspect it was her. She had something I never offered. Beauty. Gorgeous eyes and full breasts. I wasn't ugly and I was aware of that, but I could never compare to her. Her hair flowed like the waterfalls on a romantic getaway. Her body curved along the edges while mine flowed more subtly than that.

I would have no reason to be jealous if I knew it was all for show, but it never was. Her looks had been natural. She had been gifted with a body most women dreamed of. My ex-fiancé simply took notice of that.

"That dance is in a few days. David invites others as a way of letting the outside world have a peek inside the building. This way, they can't question us or anything. He knows we aren't stupid enough to tell others we're not human. Well, Taylor may not be so bright," Spence joked.

It wasn't a shock to me that David would do such a thing. He had a reputation to keep up with. This dance could be our way out, somehow. I just needed to get the attention of humans without exposing them for what they really were.

"I wish I could say it got better." My eyes fixed on the wall across from us, lost in the cracks and crevices. "I'm fighting, Spence, but I'm beginning to lose hope."

"You can't lose hope. If you do that, how do we believe in you? You promised to get us out of here. You never make promises you can't keep." He nudged my side.

I closed my eyes, picturing her face and those glass eyes. I didn't want it to be true, but it was, and my heart yearned for her to come back. I missed her encouraging words and even the ones that used to mock me for what I did to aid them.

"I promised to save Claire. I didn't do that. She was hungry, and she had even told me that David was withholding blood and I never helped her. I'm culpable. How can I keep my promises after that?" I brought my hands to my face, attempting to rub away the guilt and shame that held me tight within its grasp.

He grabbed my hands, warming them up with his own. "You're Nora. I know you. You will keep them because you know it only gets worse if you don't. You could never give up on us because it would send you into oblivion if you knew we ended up like Claire."

I stood. "This is why I could never tell Claire I could make you happy. That's something I can't promise. I'm sorry, Spence. This just can't happen between us. We can't get close anymore if we are going to fight it. We tried, but we have no self-control." I took the first aid kit with me as I exited his room.

I returned it to the closet before walking to my own room for the night. I had my dress ready and prepared for the dance coming up, but I would use it as nothing more than an escape plan from this place. I would use it to get the prisoners out of here. Emilie was going to go home to Finn while Spence returned to his parents. Taylor would go back to wherever he belonged. Riley would see her family and her girlfriend again.

As I sat on my bed, Spence's words rang through my mind. He was ready to let go of his worries and give in to temptation. I couldn't lie to myself and say I wasn't persuaded by his lips and his soothing voice. I weakened under his touch, waiting for him to kiss every inch of my skin.

However, I lived in reality. Reality taught me that things that seemed too good to be true were *always* just that.

XXXIX

He folded his arms across his chest, watching me. "I'm not going to tell you anything."

I shrugged. "I expected that, Taylor. But it doesn't change the fact that we are here for one reason. You. If I don't crack you open even a little, David could take that as an invitation to try it himself." I wasn't one to use threats, but Taylor seemed to *only* respond to them, so it was worth the shot.

He grumbled. "Fine, under one condition. Emilie told me you were part of a program for psychologists and psychiatrists. But I thought you were a therapist. Is that not what this is?" He gestured. "So what are you?"

It was a fair trade. It didn't give away too much information, thankfully.

"Well, we'll start by explaining all of them. Then I want you to take your best guess at what you think I am." I smirked a bit. What a fun little game, testing his intelligence and how well he paid attention to me.

"Therapists generally are only skilled in one type of therapy. They usually work with patients on the regular, and a lot of them work in the city. They also may know some psychology but they're not the exact same. All psychologists can be called therapists but not all therapists are psychologists." By the look on his face, he was utterly confused. "Let me break it down. Catholics are under the umbrella term Christians, but that doesn't necessarily mean Christians are Catholics. It's the same with therapists and psychologists. Psychologists can work in a broader field than therapists, if they choose.

"As for psychiatrists, they are the closest to doctors you get in this field. They are the ones who sign medication to patients. They specialize in illnesses and treating them. Psychologists provide therapy. This is considered talk therapy. It's a type of psychotherapy which is used to help patients change and overcome their problems. So, I ask which one do you think I am?"

Taylor searched my mind. "I don't know."

"Psychologist. I went through eight years of schooling to study the brain and behavior of humans so I could provide them psychotherapy. And now that you know that, it's your turn to tell me a little about yourself." I leaned back in my chair, crossing my legs.

What he didn't know was that I had some of Claire's abilities. I could see into his head without his permission, and maybe it was a bit wrong. But was it so wrong when the man I was invading had tried to violate me?

Groaning, he threw his head back. "Fine. I'm not as bad as you think."

Yet in his head he said otherwise. He knew he was nothing more than a disgusting womanizer. He said those exact words, too.

I drank some water. "Why do you say that?" I cupped my hands around my knee.

"Because you think I'm this pervert."

"And you don't think you are?"

He snickered. "Okay, so I hit on you."

"Hit on me. Almost *hit* me. You trapped me against the wall. I think you need to go into more detail about why that's okay and doesn't make you a pervert."

What I saw next in his mind was pure filth. He had a fantasy playing between him and I, and it was much too graphic.

Taylor shifted in his chair. "I have a hard time controlling myself. I see something I like, and I want it."

The contents of my stomach rose in my throat. "That is not an excuse. I'm a human being. I'm not food."

"Well, you are in a way." He chuckled. "Food…" His eyes lingered down my legs. "Among other things."

"Taylor."

"But think about it, Nora."

"You do not get to call me that."

"Don't you want someone to grab you by the hips and kiss you? Do you miss the feeling of a real man? Imagine all we could do. All that stops us are your panties."

Clenching my jaw, I slammed my water on the desk. "That is enough. I am not attracted to you in the slightest, Taylor. Do you know why? Because you view women as objects. You look at me and see sex. You don't see a person. You don't treat me with any respect. You don't listen to my wishes. Do I miss the feeling of a real man? Absolutely. But you are certainly not him and you never will be. I'd never be desperate enough to stoop so low."

"Ouch." He patted his chest. "Message received. It's Spence, isn't it? I've seen the looks. If only it were so easy, right, Nora? To kiss him. To rip his clothes off."

"Stop it."

"To ride him into the sunset."

I stood, opening the door. "This session is over. Out. Now."

He got up and grabbed the frame, turning to look at me. "I put something in your head. I tend to do that. I'm not a pervert, Nora. I'm a monster. I'd steer clear of me."

Taylor believed that much. What he didn't say out loud was that he had been the son of the same monster. It wasn't any excuse, but it told me where he learned his poor manners from.

His own father.

"I do try," I said.

He grumbled and walked out. I closed the door behind him, locking it. After taking a few deep breaths, I closed my eyes and fell against the door.

Spence's fingers trailed up my thigh, pulling my dress with him. His lips brushed my ear, whispering sweet nothings. I gripped the wall and the cabinet, sliding down the door.

No—this was wrong on every level.

I shook the dirty thoughts away and pulled my knees to my chest. Taylor was a piece of shit. There was no doubt in my mind about that.

Was he worth saving?

After I'd been certain he had left, I went to David. It wasn't pleasant for me, but I needed to prove I wasn't behind anything.

"Anything you need help with for this dance? It would keep my mind busy."

"No, no, shoveling the snow was more than enough. Thank you." He shooed me off.

I didn't know where else to go, so I disappeared into the basement and found myself in the auditorium. No more scenes played before my eyes, and for that I was glad. I was afraid of witnessing Claire's death all over again.

While on my stroll, I checked the same doors I always did. The ECT room had been locked now. I'd lost my access to the meetings when David took my key back.

Just as I tried another door, the knob turned, and it creaked open.

It'd never done so before, but I didn't waste any chances on checking it out. Maybe it wasn't entirely smart, given that it could've been a trap. Still, I had to try.

Stepping inside, I flicked a switch and the lights barely lit up, a few flickering here and there. In front of me were rows of seats, much like you'd find at a university in a classroom.

Down in the center, a table sat—where patients would lie to become a display for onlookers and those too curious about mental illnesses.

It disturbed my mind as nausea began to climb my throat.

Before I lost my breakfast, I hurried from the room and gently closed the door behind me as if I'd never went inside at all.

Then I headed back to the auditorium.

I took a seat in one of the old chairs. "You know, Nora, this would all be easier if you had your shit together," I said. "But you don't. No, instead you decided to ignore your feelings and here you are. Your lack of grief is your biggest flaw."

It wasn't so easy to let myself *feel*.

I'd grown up with loving parents, but it had never been so effortless to show people my emotions. And then at some point, it became hard to express them to myself.

It was unhealthy, but I couldn't change overnight.

I shivered as something flowed over my feet. I looked down to see a sheet of water, and when I turned back, I saw it seeping in from the double doors.

I got out of my seat and immediately went to the exit, pushing against it. They were locked. "Hello?" I shoved harder but I couldn't get them open.

Banging on the door, I began screaming, hoping anyone could hear me. But nobody was coming. I was far into the basement, this asylum too massive. Even the vampires couldn't hear me.

I scanned the room for another way out. First, at all possible doors, then at the ceiling to see if any trap doors existed. Vents. Anything. Unfortunately, this was the basement, and there were hardly any ways out to begin with. It was built to be inescapable.

The water rose to my calves by now and I threw my heels off, wading through to the double doors once more. I grabbed my heel and started smashing it against the window, and it cracked, but I hadn't paid enough attention to see what waited behind it.

More water.

The crack began the road downhill and the window shattered, all the water pouring into the room. "Fuck!" I scanned the area again, for anything that I could use to make enough loud noise. I hurried to the stage, grabbing some metal and banging it against the pipes.

I screamed as the pipe burst and *more* water began spraying everywhere.

Grabbing hold of the curtain, I jumped up and began

climbing, but it ripped from age and I collided with the wooden floor. I struggled to breathe for a few seconds before the wind rushed back in, along with spurts of water.

I rolled over and got back on my feet. “I’m gonna die down here. And nobody is going to even know.”

Was it pathetic to give up so easily? Maybe. But what other plan did I have? I had tried everything.

Keep screaming until you can’t. Don’t give up so easily.

Taking my own advice, I began screaming at the top of my lungs, but after a few minutes, my throat became hoarse and I couldn’t keep up with it any longer.

The water seemed to be rising faster. How was that even possible?

Alicia.

In mere minutes, I was already swimming. As the water got closer to the ceiling, I started kicking and banging on it to anyone up there, yelling against the floor.

Just an inch of space was left between me and the ceiling, and I took one last gulp of air before I went under. I held it as much as I could, but my lungs burned and I gave in, letting the water take over. I began sinking as I choked, watching my world slip away. Fingers wrapped around my wrist and pulled me through the current.

When I broke the surface, I lay on the stairs and coughed up all that had gotten inside my lungs. It was a miracle that I survived every attempt Alicia threw at me.

It was a *miracle* that someone knew to come looking for me.

I lay back, closing my eyes and taking deep breaths. Fresh air. Such a beautiful thing.

Feeling around, I grabbed the hand of my hero. “Thank you. I’m not ready to die. I swear I tried everything I could to get out of there. I couldn't find an escape. It was stupid to go down there alone, I know. I know I shouldn't have. I just didn't want to drag anyone else with me. I didn't want to get them into trouble. And seeing you wasn't an option because we both know we can't be together."

He didn't say anything.

"I'm just grateful you saved me despite all our differences, but I've concluded we must do something about Alicia first. If we don't, there's no telling if I'll have a chance to save her after I do you, so I need to figure out where Death keeps his prisoners so I can go in there and bring back the real Alicia, the one I know. Or the one I did know…"

He pulled his hand from mine.

"Can you help me?" I waited for an answer. "Spence?" I sat up, opening my eyes and facing him. But it hadn't been Spence who saved my life.

Taylor.

I immediately moved up the steps, putting distance between us.

He didn't look my way. "Nobody else could hear the screams. I could have let you die, but…you're our only key out of here."

I narrowed my eyes.

He sighed. "I'm a monster, Nora, yes. I saved you for my own selfish gain, and I'm not going to lie to you about that. But you should know that I don't want to be a monster."

"Then change."

"Easier said than done. It's a habit to say what comes to my mind."

I crossed my arms to hide my nipples. "So why do you say you don't want to be a monster?"

"Is it hard to believe I want to change?"

"You're asking the wrong woman."

He nodded a little. "You have no reason to believe me, and yes I did save you for a selfish reason, but I saved a life instead of taking one. Does that not count for something?"

"Hardly. You don't get to overshadow your poor morals with being a hero. Now answer my question, Taylor. Why do you say you don't want to be a monster? You don't give off any vibe that you care to change."

Taylor turned his head and met my eyes. "Because David promised me more blood if I was a dick to you. I don't want to be this way. I don't want to be persuaded by blood. But when you're so hungry, it's hard not to be. It's not as simple as a human skipping meals. Our blood is both our fuel and our hydration. And we both know humans last three days without hydration before they die, and during a period of that, they can lose touch with reality."

With a snicker, I looked away from him. "I'm aware of that much. I'm not stupid, Taylor, even if you treat me like someone worth nothing more than a piece of meat without a brain."

"When you kill one, two more take its place. Claire's gone, but now Riley and I are here to replace what David lost in desperate times." What he said next confirmed my biggest fear of David. "He despises you, Nora, and he's using me to make you scream."

XXXX

I smoothed the skirt of my dress, turning my hips as I examined myself in the mirror. I wore dresses every day but never were they this long. The skirt itself had flowed out around me in a puffy-like manner with long sleeves and a backless bodice made of silk, flush against my skin.

I curled my hair, my makeup a bit more glamorous on the eyes and lips to make them stand out. On a normal occasion, I wore red lipstick and mascara. Tonight, I had gold eyeshadow to go with the mascara, and a little eyeliner to shape it.

Leaving the bathroom, I headed to the entertainment room where people hung out. The halls were crowded with bodies, and the open areas had been cleared of furniture so people could dance and mingle.

"David, you are never getting away with this," I whispered to myself. As I twirled around, I noticed someone who stood on the other side of the crowd. His black hair had been combed back, his blue eyes popping against his black suit and a navy cardigan under his jacket, tie tucked in. He appeared a man straight from a modeling agency.

He scanned the area, and once he spotted me, those dimples flashed at me. He was coming this way. No, this wasn't right. I told him we had to avoid each other.

I ducked behind a woman dressed in all pink, heading through the crowd like Cinderella. Yeah, as if she would be working at an asylum.

I pushed my way through the people until I ended up at the end of the hall, just on the outskirts of the dance. I didn't see the black suit anywhere, and I knew I had lost him. I wasn't here to dance or mingle. This was my one chance to search for a way to bring David and Monstrum Asylum to the ground.

"Need some help?" his voice echoed behind me.

As I turned to face him, I mentally cursed myself. I was one of the few females wearing white. I wasn't hard to find. "Spence, we can't be near one another."

He chuckled with a shrug. "I won't tell if you won't."

I searched for David, but I couldn't find him. "We can't be seen here." I grabbed his hand and I dragged him down the stairs to the basement. The water had been long gone now. And with Spence by my side, the basement didn't seem so scary. "I found a surgical theater down here the other night. If I can use that… I'm searching for a way to expose this place for its lies, without exposing what you guys really are of course. If I can just somehow prove you guys are being mistreated, that's enough to get this shut down. This is the modern age. Nobody here supports these inhumane methods used on you." I searched the rooms. "Unfortunately, they'll care more if they think you are just humans." I shot Spence an apologetic look.

He nodded a little, peeking into a room. "I understand. That's how most human minds work, is it not?"

His words rang in my ear. I stopped in my tracks and turned to face him. "I wish I could say no, but yes. Humans are notorious for judging what they don't understand."

"But you didn't." He shook his head.

I laughed a little. "I'm a woman, Spence. I am well aware of what humans are capable of. Just a few decades ago, I would have been locked up here with you, and not for any valid reason, but simply because I'm a woman and I have my own opinions. If I'd married, my husband could admit me without my consent. Women like me get locked up all the time. By their families. By their husbands. We aren't real people. And many of the people who play a part in that monstrosity still linger in the morals of those alive today." I grabbed the skirt of my gown.

"Have you ever been judged? I mean, for something you could never control? Personally?" He gestured to me.

I frowned a bit, thinking back to my junior high years. They were the cruelest of them all. The kids were quick to warn everyone that high school would be so divided and judgmental. High school was a breeze. Junior high was anything but that.

"When I was growing up, I was a slow developer. Late bloomer." I leaned back against the wall. "All the other girls were forming their figures and I was still flat-chested. That wasn't the worst part though. I was a skinny girl, and I couldn't seem to put weight on. I ate a lot of food, but it never mattered. People would make fun of how boney I was, or said I was anorexic and when I told people I ate like a pig, they never believed me." I swallowed the bad memory.

Spence stepped forward, stopping in front of me. "People are mean. Nobody seems to understand this world would be a better place if they just kept their ugly opinions to themselves."

I exhaled. "Yeah, and that's just it. I tried to be different from that. I'm not saying I was a perfect child. I wasn't. I was a monster at fourteen, Spence. But I've tried hard to grow out of that and become better for myself and those around me. That's why this means so much to me. Getting you guys out of this place is like me trying to redeem all the wrong I did or what others did unto me." I peered up at him, searching his eyes for his heart.

He shook his head, glancing down the hall to make sure nobody had followed us down here. "You don't have to make up for the sins of others. Those are theirs to bear."

"And yet you get punished because your parents broke the laws and had a hybrid child." I cocked my eyebrows. "You're bearing their sins."

He smiled a bit. "You could say that." He shrugged as his smile faded. "But I'm serious. Even your ex who cheated on you doesn't get to dictate your life now. His sins are his own. You're not to blame for what he chose to do. Don't let him destroy your happiness now."

I lowered my gaze as I nodded in the slightest. "Sometimes, it does happen. I let things ruin my happiness and I wish I wasn't like that but I am. It's not so easy to act happy all the time. I begin to feel like it isn't earned or deserved."

His finger brushed against my cheek. "You've helped me so much, Nora. Isn't it time I return the favor?"

My eyes met his while the oxygen caught in my throat. His hot breath feathered across my lips, inviting me in to taste what Spence had been so willing to give all this time.

My brain told me to stop him, to do *something*. But I was out of confessions. He knew everything there was to know. My heart begged me to stay—to keep my lips parted just enough for him to take charge.

When I hadn't moved or said anything to resist his touch, he closed the last of the gap as he moved his lips against my own. My heart pounded against my ribcage, my legs going numb in seconds. Inside my head, the world began to spin. I didn't have a second to spare for anything else.

Only for Spence Woods.

He deepened the kiss, his hand grasping the underside of my chin to keep my head from falling. It could have, too, given how weak he made me. I became a pile of mush.

Spence pulled away just enough to say, "I would apologize but I can't lie."

"Then don't." I took this small window as an opportunity to get some air. Breathing wasn't something he needed to do but he knew it was something that kept my heart beating—and for him nonetheless.

He brought his lips back onto mine, pouring out every ounce of passion he had been holding in for a while. He pulled at my bottom lip with his teeth, opening my mouth just enough for him to explore with his tongue.

I could have stopped him, but I didn't even want to. Claire knew what I had been thinking. Spence was a gentleman to me for so long. Tonight he would be anything but.

Gripping the tie to his attire, I slipped it off him when I loosened the knot. He traced his lips along my cheek, down my jaw, planting a few kisses along the side of my neck. "It might be a better idea if we take this somewhere more private," he whispered.

I barely got a nod in before he tugged my hand and led me into a room, one that didn't come off as creepy as the rest of them.

His fingers found the buttons on the back of my dress, but he didn't attempt to struggle quite yet. "Just to be sure, I want you to want this. I am not one to overstep my bounds when it's not wanted."

My fingers played with the edge of his jacket, pulling it off, and then his cardigan. Brushing over the buttons of his shirt, I undid the first one. "Spence, I know you've got a gentleman persona to keep up, but I am asking you to drop it for just a little while."

He cursed with every button he fought on my gown, finally sliding it off my shoulders and letting it drop to the floor. "Your wish is my command."

While his lips trailed along shoulders, I wrestled to get each button free from his shirt as his finger messed with the strap of my bra. As soon as the last button was undone, I pushed his shirt off.

The next forty-five minutes were spent well, this room was no longer freezing to the touch. Our breaths coincided as one, and my soul now stood complete. We'd soaked up every ounce we could of once another in all the ways.

We both knew we could never go back to the relationship we had before, not after we had given each other every promise that I'd once denied and told Claire I could never hand over.

My brain and heart both agreed on this one thing; we could never be just friends even on the outside of the building.

"Don't you think we should go back up before people suspect where we went?" he asked in a hushed tone against my ear.

I laughed a bit, leaning my head back against the wall. "Sounds like the right thing to do, but we've proved tonight we are not following the right thing to do."

He let out a sigh filled with content. "You're right. I like where we are now with our bare chests mushed together."

My eyes fluttered shut again as I drew in another deep breath. "Spence, I'm wearing lipstick that doesn't hold up against sex. It's on your lips, and mine. We can't go back to the party. We have to go to the bathroom to clean up."

He dropped his head and pulled his body away from mine. "Okay." He grabbed his boxer briefs from the floor, putting them back on.

He got his pants up, buttoned his shirt, pulled his cardigan on, and fixed his tie. Spence came over to help me button up—although he whined a few times—and I cleared my throat to get his attention. "We still can't tell anyone. I'm serious. If David even thinks we have something between us, he will put you through hell and I can't live with that guilt."

"I dig you, Nora Witlow." He turned me around and pulled me close by my wrist, fixing parts of my hair that appeared astray. "And my lips are sealed. Of course not for you." He gave me a chocolate kiss.

"No, no… Not for each other." I patted his chest, running my finger along his jaw. "I'll see you when I can." I flashed a smile before turning on my heel and leaving him in the room. We both went our separate ways, finding the bathrooms upstairs to present ourselves professionally once more.

Our eyes locked from opposite ends of the hall, but the connection was lost as soon as he disappeared into the crowd of people. I had to avoid most women because I was sure I had that sex glow all over me, and if anyone suspected it, they would question who my lover was.

I lingered near the table with snacks and drinks, eating my

worries and drinking away the satisfaction. If Claire had still been here, she would be so proud of me for finally stepping up and making Spence happy. I regretted not promising her that I would do that for him but I'm sure wherever she was, she knew that I came through.

As I wiped under my lip, I smiled to myself. Spence was the kind of man I needed in my life. He had been nothing like my ex, and I intended to keep it that way. If his demon had control, there was a chance he could show to be like the fiancé I once loved.

XXXXI

I halted in my tracks as I passed by his room but he wasn't in it. I checked the entertainment area, furrowing my brows. "Spence?"

Searching every room on the main floor, I concluded he wasn't up here. As I walked downstairs to the basement, the faint sound of buzzing tickled my ear.

I quickened my pace, following the sound to the room a couple of feet down. The ECT room. My heels clicked with every step, alerting the staff and I didn't even give an ounce to care. My heart hammered against my ribs as I pictured his vacant eyes matching Claire's from her last night alive. I couldn't lose him. Another one. I wouldn't survive if they took him from me, too.

Rushing into the room, I widened my eyes. "What the fuck

are you doing to him?" I yelled at David.

I wasn't ignorant of how afraid Spence had been. I knew that fear from experience.

A few of the other doctors were hovering around him while he'd been strapped down to the table, attempting to reject every electric charge coursing through his body.

"This is none of your concern, Nora," David said with a threatening tone.

"He's my patient! This is very damn well my concern! I know without a doubt he doesn't need this!" I turned off the machine. "Get out. This is wrong, and you know it. Don't torture a man just because you're sadistic." I unstrapped Spence from the table and sat him up, keeping my arm around his torso. "We're going to his room before you shock him into oblivion."

Monique stepped forward to grab me, but David's hand shot up to hold her back.

"But David—"

"Let her go." His eyes met mine, promising that he'd get his revenge.

I helped Spence back to his room, making sure David wasn't following us. I had never meant to defy him or rebel, but it was beginning to show that I was not here for him. I was here for the prisoners he locked away, and if he didn't figure that out by now, it'd be a miracle.

Sitting Spence on his bed, I grabbed the blanket and wrapped it around him. "I am so, so sorry. I wish I would have gotten there sooner. It pisses me off that he would do that!" I balled my hand into a fist.

Spence swayed, a bit disoriented. "He wants to put my angel to sleep… It's…" his words faded.

I squatted in front of him and grasped his hands. "No, it's not working. Tell me it's a stupid idea. Please."

He leaned back against the wall and closed his eyes. "I can't lie."

I wasn't in the right state of mind to argue or comfort him. Neither of us were. "Get some sleep. You need it more than ever." I helped him lie down, tucking him in. "And when you wake up, don't hate me for what I might do." I placed a small kiss against his forehead before leaving the room.

A fire blazed inside me, stirring alongside hell. Seeing Spence in such a confusing place of his mind let loose *my* demons. I wasn't about to control them.

Stopping inside David's office, I crossed my arms. "What the hell was that? Care to tell me why you're trying to destroy my patient?"

"This is not your concern," he repeated.

I said, "This is my concern because you hired me to help them. I am doing my job. You're failing at yours. How much is it going to take before you realize you've gone too far? When he loses core memories? When he forgets his parents? When you kill him?" My voice began to rise.

"Nora—"

My hand shot up, palm facing him. "No. Don't make excuses. You killed Claire and you know damn well that was your fault. You can't pretend it was an accident. She didn't leave. She wasn't doing better. I know because I'm her therapist! I'm the psychologist, here. I'm the one listening to these people talk about their lives. I'm the one who listens to their problems and fears, and I help them. You cannot replace me. You cannot perform inhumane treatments on them. What kind of doctor are you?"

He stood from his chair, stalking closer. "I'm the best. I run this asylum. I'm *your* boss. I can have you removed in an instant. Don't question me. Do not think for even a second that me letting you take him is my weakness, because it most certainly is not, Nora Witlow. You are not in charge here. You do *not* tell me what to do." He raised his hand before bringing it against my cheek, and a slap echoed throughout the small room, barely leaking into the halls. "Get out of my office before you're fired. Now." His eyes had turned to what appeared black—soulless—while his features stiffened.

I backed out of his office, walking quickly to Spence's room. I checked Emilie's to make sure she was still there, which she was. Then I sat in his room while he slept just to make sure nobody touched him again.

He groaned as he opened his eyes, rubbing his head. "Nora? What are you doing here?"

"Protecting you. I have a lot of questions but a lot to say at the same time." I looked over at him.

He sat up in a hurry and pulled my chair closer by the front legs. He inspected my cheek. "What did you do?"

I let out a sigh. "I got mad at David. He hurt you and that didn't sit well with me. It's one thing to know he's doing it but seeing it happen is another experience. I lost control of my temper. I'm sorry. I just… I wanted to rip his head off."

He brushed his knuckle against the red mark. "That was stupid of you."

"Then I wear stupidity with pride. My blood boils at the sight of someone I care about being tortured. You were suffering. He was *hurting* you. I will never be okay with that." I shook my head as my eyes fell to the ground.

His fingers were gentle while they lifted my chin. "Now I have to see you suffer. That doesn't look soothing."

I straightened my posture. "If he hurts one of us, he hurts us both. We're a team." I wanted to say we were a couple, but I couldn't confirm if that was true. Were we actually together? Was that what we agreed to?

He closed his eyes. "Please never challenge him again. I'll never control my demon if this is what I'm forced to see."

"Don't tell me what to do." I sat forward. "I make my own decisions, Spence."

The fingers that once held my jaw now traced down my neck and collarbone. "Every time you get hurt, I'll have to make up for it." He unbuttoned the first button of my dress.

I leaned closer to him and I expected his lips to land on mine, but he had brought my chin higher so he could plant kisses down my neck instead. He wrapped an arm around my waist and pulled my entire body onto his bed, laying me back.

He got a few more buttons undone and trailed kisses down my stomach.

"Spence, we can't." It took all my power to say those words. Every part of me wanted this as much as he did but it wasn't a good time.

He crawled up, his mouth hovering above mine. "Why not?"

I buttoned up my dress. "Because anyone could walk by and hear us, and we have way too much to talk about." I sat up, facing the wall opposite his bed.

He moved my hair to the other shoulder, placing kisses along my skin. "Talk about what?"

I grabbed his hand before it could reach that first button again. "I'm being serious this time. We have to talk about what we're going to do here. David is out for blood, trying to kill you all. As if he doesn't seem to care about keeping you alive and just attaining your DNA to mix with ours. He wants more. He wants to chase that high he first got when he walked in on Claire drinking her own blood."

Spence pulled back. "What can we do?"

I twisted my body to face his, laying one of my legs on the bed and the other hanging off the edge. "I'm not sure. But I've come to realize something strange is happening here. It feels much like a movie, like someone here is trying to place all the pieces where they can." I pulled a brochure from my pocket. "This. I found this at my college when we were having one last party after graduation. It was put there like a promotion. Someone put it there to make sure I saw it because they wanted me here."

He opened it up and made a face. Brows knitted downward, and lips twisted together. "But Monstrum Asylum doesn't advertise. David is very strict about who gets to come here. He doesn't have a job application anywhere. You know it's here but it's very hard to apply here for patient and employee purposes."

I nodded. "Exactly. That's my point. And it goes farther than that. Okay, before I ever wanted to be a psychologist, I would tell Danny stories. I told him stories about mythical creatures. I told him the story of a mermaid who had a bad home situation. She wanted her dad, but her mother treated him like a bad guy. So, she ran away with her boyfriend when she was eighteen. Spence, I told my brother Emilie's story before I ever knew she existed. I told Claire's story. I told *yours*. I knew about you guys before this."

He gave me back the brochure, shaking his head. "What? That's impossible."

"I used to think vampires and mermaids were impossible but

you're very real. I'm telling you, something weird is going on here." I scanned the room as if I were searching for cameras. I found none.

I'd applied for Monstrum in mid-July, sure. Whoever wanted me here tempted me and put me here in the dead of winter. They knew I wouldn't take the job right away, right? I'd taken months off before I started working here. Before I trapped myself in the mountains during a harsh winter.

"Who do you think did it?" Spence leaned forward as he lowered his voice.

"Maybe David chose me. Scoped me out. Maybe that's why he didn't kill me when we tried to escape that night." I skimmed the lines in the brochure, searching for clues. "Someone evil or someone good. It's someone who wants control, someone who *knew* this was supposed to happen. They must know about our future. They have to know how this ends. If they're wicked, they know this kills us all. They want us to die. However, if they're moral, they know I'm the key to helping all of you escape. You could live outside of this place, and they had to get me here to ensure that'd happen."

"Do you believe that?" He lifted an eyebrow.

A smirk rose. "I believe you're real, don't I? Listen, if they knew that I told stories about you, they knew I would be more understanding of your species. I would want you guys to be free from this horrid asylum. Someone must be behind this, surely. They brought me here to save you, which further proves we have a real chance. I want to know who they are. Tell me, are there any creatures you know of that can predict the future?"

He took a moment to search through his brain for answers. "There is one, but they're harder to find. The world isn't very friendly to them, the Salem Witch Trials being your great example."

"Witches." I swallowed. "How would I find one? How do I summon one?" I jumped up from the bed. "If I find her, she can help us escape. She can tell me how to save Alicia. She knows everything that's going to happen and that already has."

"It doesn't work that way, Nora. Witches can't just predict the future whenever they want. It comes to them at random. They get important visions, or premonitions if you will. She may not want to be involved with us at all. She doesn't have a choice when it comes to your influence in this place, but I assume she'd rather stay out of it as much as she can help." He attempted to stand but his body was still convulsing here and there from the ECT.

I grabbed his shoulders, keeping him seated on the mattress. Then I said, "She's involved. She was the one who brought me here, and now it's time to ask her for more. She can guide us. She knows the outcome of our war. I don't really care how little she wants to be involved, because she already is and I'm aware of it. I'll sweep every possible means I need to, to ensure your safety. She brought me here. She forced my hand. Now I'm going to do the same to her."

XXXXII

I searched through the endless articles about witches and where they liked to hang out most. How could I contact the one who had brought me here to begin with?

An idea came to my mind as I glanced at my bag. I pulled out the brochure *she* left behind for me to see, opening it and searching for anything that could tell me how to get her here.

One of the words looked different from the rest, the font style out of place. "Aha, I found you."

The word was *mental* as in the mental state of being. I knew it had to do with that word given where I lived and my profession. I took the brochure with me and walked down to the basement, entering the auditorium.

"Come on out. I know you're watching us. And quite frankly,

I don't think it's working. I'm planning to leave this place for good. After being harassed by a vampire, seeing another die, and being slapped by David, it's time I saved myself." I walked up to the stage, climbing up and looked at the seats that were left.

When I got no response, I pulled out a small matchbox. "Don't make me burn this place to the ground. I will." I lit one of the matches and set the brochure on fire, dropping it on the wooden floorboards.

"Stop!" a voice screamed.

I didn't heed her orders until she came out of the darkness, then I doused the flame with my shoe. "There you are. So, I assume you're the one who led me to work here?"

She didn't dress in the way I expected. I had assumed she would come out in a large cloak with many piercings and tattoos. She looked just like any other girl in a button-up and pants. "What do you want from me?"

I climbed down from the stage and approached her with caution. "I want to know why you did this. I want to know what you saw."

Her green eyes popped out against her tanned complexion. "I'm not supposed to tell you what I saw."

"No, but you can change the course of the future by planting seeds to achieve the outcome you want. I'm simply recognizing that this is your doing and not destiny or fate. I want to know what you saw." I paced a little "I lied about wanting to leave, but I'm sure you know that. I'm here to get them home to safety and I know you can pitch in." I was begging her at this point. I had nowhere else to go.

She released a sigh. "I'm not supposed to be involved like this, Nora. If David finds out about any of this, I will be trapped here too. I'm here to make ensure they go home, and not to make the situation worse."

Swallowing my fear, I took a seat in a worn-down chair. "I'm not trying to make it worse. I'm here to save them, and I have no idea how. All I'm asking for is some guidance on which direction to go. I'm lost. I want David dead, but I can't be the one to kill him. It will destroy Spence if I do it. I need to know how to take this place down without exposing them as creatures while allowing David and his staff go free."

She rubbed her eyes as she shook her head. "I'm sorry. I can't. I don't know how you took him down. I just know you did. I see the outcome, not the journey. I only help you find the start of that journey." She headed towards the exit doors.

I jumped out of my seat, following closely behind. "Help me! Please, help me or I will burn this place down. It's the only plan I have in mind and I'm not sure how to get them out of here before you burn in the fire." I ran around her, stopping in front. "Do it or I will tell David everything I know."

She scoffed. "You wouldn't do that. You know you'd put them in danger. Besides, you would do that to Spence? I know you're a thing now. You're not very subtle."

My cheeks burned red. "What?"

We both walked down the dark hallway. "Nora, don't take this the wrong way, but you're terrible at hiding your feelings." She stopped, turning to face me. "You're in love with him."

I laughed, covering my mouth before someone heard me. "Whaaaat? Love Spence? Noooooo."

"I've been in your life a lot longer than you think." She shrugged, moving again. "And I know you, Nora. You don't have sex with a man unless you love him. That's the kind of woman you are. It's okay to admit it. He's a cute guy. He struggles with his inner conflict, but he does his best for you. I think he loves you, too."

I tapped my chin. "Let me get this straight. You think I love him?"

She glanced back at me with a smirk on her face. "Correct. You love him and you know without a doubt, if he proposed, you would say yes in a heartbeat. You feel it, Nora. Your ex-fiancé may have taken a year to propose, but he was never right for you and that's why you hesitated. But with Spence, even after five months, you know how you feel. You would say yes without a second thought and that tells me you love him. He is the exact man you've been wanting. You just haven't realized that yet. I've studied you like a book."

I choked on my word and grabbed her arm, pulling her back. "You've studied me? What?"

A smile graced her expression. "Nora, relax. I'm not harmful. Witches are like every other living creature. It's not all black and white. We aren't good or evil. We mess up. We make good decisions just like bad ones. We're humans with magic." Her eyes darted to the floor. "But fine, I will help you. I'll help you figure it out. Also, next time Taylor doesn't listen to you, knee him in the balls. That teaches them in seconds. Vampires are like undead superhumans, but they can feel pain. Especially in the crotch."

I mumbled, "Yeah, knee him in the balls. Great idea."

He had told me David wanted me to suffer, and that much was clear. But why had David never fired me? I'd lashed out many times. I'd even almost saved everyone, but it never made a difference. He kept me around regardless, despite how much he wanted me to bleed—my insides staining the floors of *his* hard work.

I'd undo all of it.

We walked up the stairs to the second floor and I waited until it was clear to take her to Spence's room.

"Spence, meet…" I furrowed my brows, realizing I never knew her name.

She clasped her hands together and nodded a bit. "Catalina. My mother loves cats. I know you're Spence. I'm essentially the one who put this plan into motion." She gestured around us.

I glanced at him, taking notice of shaky hands. He seemed on edge today. She'd mentioned he had a lot of inner conflict. "Spence? What's wrong?" I sat beside him, taking his hand in mine.

When he looked at me, his eyes held every ounce of sorrow. "I worry, Nora. What happens when we leave? Do you know why I try to be such a gentleman? I have to make up for the demon stirring inside me. If we leave here, we can't be together. I'm supposed to be with someone of my own species. I'm dangerous."

"Spence, one problem at a time, please." I patted his hand. "You and I will figure out how to be together. I can't just leave you. This is the first time I'm happy with someone."

Cat plopped down on the other side of him with a big smile plastered on her lips. "Yes, and that's her way of saying she loves you."

"Cat!" I yelled.

She laughed and patted his cheek. "I'm not sorry for saying it."

Spence wrapped his fingers around mine. "Is it true? You've fallen in love with me?"

I chewed my lip. "You know, I'm not sure. Cat says I have because she's studied me like a book or something but…"

Cat narrowed her eyes at me.

My face heated. "I do love you. I've fallen for you, Spence." I couldn't believe those words left my mouth. Now I was prepared to be rejected.

He placed his empty hand against my cheek. "I care about you. You let me express myself and you never judge. I also appreciate that you don't hate me or Claire for being together when she was still alive. I can't say I love you just yet because even my own feelings confuse me, but when I know, I will tell you."

A small piece of my heart did ache, but I understood exactly what he was saying. "It's okay. I'll be here when that time comes. I'm not afraid of commitment. I just worry about my partner backing out after my last ex decided he couldn't promise me forever." I laughed a little and looked down at our joined hands. "On a new subject, Cat will help us figure out how to make it out alive."

She got up and paced around the room. "It'll be a tough situation, but I know I can do it. Maybe. I've never actually done this before. I'm not a very well-trained witch." She laughed with a hint of nervousness in her voice.

I shooed her. "That's all right. We're all learning in this process we call life." I sent her a small nod. "I have a great idea, but it's still a work in progress." I met their gazes. "My idea involves burning down the asylum with everyone inside, except the prisoners."

"Nora," Spence said, disappointment lacing his voice.

I took a deep breath. "Yes, I know. It's going to be rough but there's no other option. David will never quit. Trust me on this. I'm not a genius but I get by. This is me trying to get by. I am getting sicker by the day just seeing what you guys endure."

He grumbled, "I know. I know..."

Cat halted. "Wow, you actually meant it when you said you

would burn this place to the ground. I'm surprised. I'm also impressed. You've got so much fire—and I love it—and that is why I'm pleased to work with you."

"The fire comes from a lot of bad experiences." I shook my head as I sighed. "I do what I can to make my life worth living. I don't want to look back and regret it. Although, I regret saying yes to Blake. Suppose that was my mistake to learn from. Trust me gut, which is exactly what I'm doing here. Burning down the asylum is trusting my gut."

She laughed. "Ah, yes, he was quite the catch. Don't mind him. He's not doing so well now. He lost his job and now he lives with his parents who constantly nag him."

A sly smile crept up on my face. "Karma is a bitch."

Cat looked out of the small, barred window. "It will be when David and this asylum no longer exist. What goes around comes around. He's a rat from the sewer, bathing in people's feces and feeding on garbage. He's nothing more than a piece of crap from the trash can, which ends up in the dump and *never* returns. So, Nora Witlow, let's make sure David Harrison never does return even from beyond the grave."

I liked her thinking.

XXXXIII

"The things he does to them…it's all just so cruel. Inhumane," I said while lowering my head. "And he's such a vile human being. But what about Death? He stole my best friend. Now he's keeping her locked away, and it's up to me to save everyone. Can you imagine being this weak little human and being tasked to be the hero?" I glanced at Cat.

She sifted through papers. "That certainly is a lot to do. I wouldn't want it to be me, but then you dragged me into this."

I slipped behind her, looking through the file cabinet. "I can't do it alone. Besides, you put me here, so you must help get me out. You don't get to put my life in danger and then bounce."

"I didn't put you here. I merely pushed you in this direction. You put yourself here."

I laughed. "You wish. You put the brochure in my face, knowing damn well I'd end up here. My options were limited." My smile faded. "Did you know Alicia was going to die that night?"

The tension thickened.

I'd gotten my answer.

"And let me guess, you aren't allowed to intervene," I whispered.

Cat came into my view, leaning against the cabinet. "It's not that simple. Changing the course of history is a big no-no in my world. I'm made to see the future. I'm not allowed to change it. As much as I wanted to stop it, I couldn't. If I did, you'd end up at another job and you'd never come save everyone. It sounds selfish to say that she had to die so you could be the hero, but…it's the only way you'd leave home. I let nature take its course."

"My only two options in this world were to either have Alicia or Spence. I could never have both."

She scratched her arm. "Yes."

"Then I was allowed to make a new friend. Claire. But she was ripped from me too. So, I must ask, Cat, what am I getting out of this? I get to relive my trauma all the time. I'm escaping the clutches of death. It sounds like I was dealt the rotten apple."

"I know it sounds bad—and it is—but you're strong, Nora. That's why you've survived three attempts now from Alicia trying to murder you. Well, the evil version of her anyway." Cat smiled, but it never got through to me.

Sitting down, I pulled a blanket around my shoulders. "One thing is certain. I'm never going to live in the mountains again. Winters are brutal."

"They can be, but spring is a beautiful season," she pointed out.

I spun around in my chair a few times as I tried to forget my worries. I wanted all of this to be over already. "Why do you live in the asylum? You don't want to help but you live here?"

"I don't live here. I simply visit, to make sure that you're doing the right thing. Or that everything is going accordingly. The portal is in the basement." She shrugged. "I might have told a small lie, but only because you keep changing the course of things."

"Excuse me?"

She cracked a smile. "I have had to intervene a little. With you freaking out on David. Finding out about them being creatures before you were meant to. You keep getting into these traps and I have to get you out. I might have helped a little with Alicia trying to kill you. Meaning, I may have saved you."

"So much for being strong."

"Hey, you still are." She nodded my way. "Your body has put up with some wild shit. My point is you keep changing course, and I have to simply redirect you back." She cleared her throat. "When you found Claire in the basement the night you almost freed them, you weren't supposed to know yet. I don't know how you veered off the path but here you are. David wanted to kill you, but I had to persuade him to erase your memory. Every single time he's let you slide, that's my doing. He wants you dead. Gone. But something inside him can't quite do it…" Cat lifted her fingers playing with a bit of magic. "Careful though. I can't save your life when it comes to the final battle. That's going to be all you."

"Fair enough. Why do you want to help me so badly?"

"Why wouldn't I? I wholeheartedly believe in you."

"That's not a valid answer."

She groaned.

Cat began at the start of her story. Her childhood. Her father and mother had always disagreed about how to raise a witch. Her mother was encouraging Cat to train and learn, but her father said she wasn't ready at that age. It caused this major fallout, and thus they divorced.

Cat got stuck with her mother.

Over the years, she was taught small magic. Harmless magic, like changing the colors of things. As she mastered each step, she moved up. By the time she was eighteen, her mother said she knew enough to take on the family heirloom.

Catalina was gifted a pendant that would keep her protected in certain instances. Like this one. She was able to hide herself from David much easier, and it was a valuable thing to have with a monster like that walking this world.

She left home and decided to take her own journey, and on that journey she met Mateo. He was supposedly the most romantic man she ever met. Unfortunately, she had to leave that journey and he stayed behind.

He taught her about love and kindness and helping those in need. Most importantly, he taught her that she had magic and it was to be used for good.

That wasn't to say her mom's advice was useless or she didn't follow it but letting go of a man she loved to come and use her magic for good was certainly a huge step. That was why she chose Monstrum Asylum. She wanted to help save the prisoners here, and when she saw the final battle, she tracked me down and pushed me in that direction so I would do what I was meant to.

"May I ask what plan I might have for this?"

Cat laughed. "Um, not my place to say. I shouldn't be revealing details about any future. That's dangerous. I must let you figure it out on your own."

"Does that mean when it's over, you'll tell me?"

She tilted her head to the left. "I mean, if I have to? But I probably won't. I think you're done changing course. We're not far off from it now."

Correct she was. With the way David had been taking things, I had to make my move soon. He'd been torturing the prisoners and now that he knew I was rebelling, I couldn't risk letting David them out of spite.

"Hey, you won't fail. I'm sure you won't."

"That's easy for you to say. You can't tell me anything, so it saves your butt. I'm the one who must go up against David. I'm the one who has to worry about the man I love losing himself to a monster. I found one man cheating on me. I don't want to find the other one dead."

She rubbed my shoulder. "He can't die. Demons aren't living, and angels are…kind of the opposite? Hard to explain. But Spence can't die, Nora. The worst that would happen is that you lose him to the demon and he doesn't come back from it."

She made it sound so innocent. So easy.

It was anything but that. All I wanted was to be promised a happy ending. I'd seen too much loss by now and every person that I let die was another piece of my heart torn from my chest.

I was amazed I had any heart left.

What would happen if he had lost to the demon? Would I see him again? Would he still want me? Would the angel ever get control again?

That's what made it worse than death. Living without him, and knowing he was trapped in there with no way out. Watching him screw other women just to break my heart every day. I could never live with that. If his demon side took control for eternity, I wasn't so sure I could stay in Spence's life anymore.

We'd be forced to go our separate ways. How would I find a love like that again? I wouldn't.

I'd vow to die alone, because he would be the one to kill me where I stood.

Cat and I went our separate ways for the night. I followed the prisoners outside and observed Spence from afar. He caught my gaze and approached me, waving for me to follow.

I took the chance, and he took me to the little spot where David couldn't see us. Spence grabbed my wrist and gently pushed me up against the back of the building. "I've missed you immensely, Nora." He pressed his lips to mine, taking hold of whatever I would have said in return. It didn't matter right now. I relished the taste of *him*.

We intertwined our fingers as his lips trailed down my jaw. I laughed, shaking my head. "This is a bit inappropriate with everyone around."

"Everyone?" He glanced at the others, who were pretending not to gawk. "Emilie and Taylor are no strangers to sexual acts, and I'm sure Riley isn't, either."

"Spence, I know you did not just suggest we makeout in front of a minor," I managed to sputter before he kissed me again.

"Shh," he breathed. "Kissing is not a crime. I'm sure she's witnessed it plenty before."

One of his hands slipped from mine, dragging his finger along my jaw and down my neck. He popped open a button. I widened my eyes, grabbing his hand. "Spence! What the hell? You can't do that in public!"

"They went inside." His lips found their way to my neck.

"If that's true, then we should go, too. Otherwise, David will get suspicious." I grabbed his chin, making him look at me. "Please. Don't. Not now."

His eyes lightened up, and his features softened. "Oh, I'm sorry. I didn't mean to push you." That was the first moment I questioned if his demon had a little bit of control. But he had a demon of wrath—and not lust—right? At least that's what he'd told me...

Spence backed away, giving me some space. "We should head inside."

Just as he turned, I grabbed his hand and pulled him back to me. "Wait. I want to ask...can you choose how much control your demon side gets?"

His icy eyes lured me in, and Cat had been right. If Spence proposed to me, I wouldn't hesitate to say yes. "It's a bit risky, but yes. Too much control though, and it'll be hard to put him back in the cage."

I'd suspected that was the case, and when I thought back to the time he possessed me just to leave the asylum for a night, it further confirmed my suspicions. He had to have some form of control over him to use him to possess people. Only demons had that ability—didn't they?

He was two halves of a whole, and not the same two halves. Both halves were opposing sides, fighting for dominance. They were two brothers who wanted to prove to everyone who was better. They were twins, both born of the same sperm but separated by morals.

I was tempted to poke around in his head, but I knew how wrong it was. If I could just know what he was thinking so I could answer my questions without the shame...

As I chewed my lip, I fixed my button. "And how does he feel about me?"

I wasn't one to tell him to let his demon have control. I fell in love with the Spence who stood before me. I didn't need any other version of him to come and destroy what we had—including his dark side.

But what if his dark side completes him in ways he doesn't acknowledge?

Spence stepped forward and snaked an arm around my waist. With his other hand, he pushed hair behind my ear just as I closed my eyes and placed my hands against his chest. In an almost inaudible whisper, he said, "I think you already know the answer to that, Nora."

XXXXIV

My leg thumped repeatedly against the chair. *Fire.* I had to light the asylum on fire while getting out the prisoners and keeping the employees in.

My biggest problem was finding the right plan.

"Nora, are you all right? You seem so…stressed," the words slipped out of his mouth far too smoothly.

My eyes moved to multiple places around the room. I knew how to get Spence out, but the others couldn't quite leave.

A shadow fell over me. I looked up to see Spence standing behind me. He leaned down, placing his hands on my shoulders. His fingers moved in wonderful ways, massaging the stress out of my muscles. "You are far too worked up over this."

"I can't help it, Spence. I want you guys to walk free. I'm

losing my mind here. Everything makes less and less sense every day." A shiver ran down my spine as he continued to work at a knot near the base of my neck.

I sunk in the chair, relaxing in his touch. "You always seem so sure of things. I don't know how you do it."

He chuckled against my ear. "You're the optimistic one." His lips traced down from the back of my ear to my throat.

"It's your turn to be optimistic," I said in a breathy tone.

He walked around the chair and squatted in front of me. "I will be." He snaked a hand behind my head, pulling me closer as our kiss began with the driving hunger we'd ached to show each other for days on end—agonizing even. It had only been seconds before his lips found something else he liked better. They moved against my skin, down my neck and chest.

I wasn't sure what his plan was, but my mind embodied a chaotic disaster. I had no chance to think a single thought.

His fingers brushed my collarbone as he unbuttoned my dress from top to bottom. All day, this office had been chilly in ever ounce but once his lips trailed every area of my skin, the heat rushed in to comfort me.

There was a plan needing to be formed but that had escaped my mind the closer his mouth got to my underwear line.

I was in another world—all my worries slipping away. Everything that had me on edge for the past few months no longer existed and the only person on my mind was Spence. He made everything okay. When I was with him, we were invincible. We could take on the world together.

Footsteps echoed in the halls, growing louder.

Spence jumped to his feet and headed to the door, keeping his shoulders in front of the small window so they couldn't see inside. "And that is why I've had issues with my parents in the past," he said to throw them off guard.

When they disappeared, he stalked over to me, admiring me as if I were a science project.

It all began with a spark and grew into a bonfire. "I have no idea how to explain this without sounding crazy. My heart is pounding and my hands are shaking. We could be caught doing what we do, and yet somehow, the idea of that makes it so much more thrilling."

His fingers hooked into the top of my underwear, pulling them down my legs and over my heels. "I don't think you're crazy, Nora. I think you've never experienced a little rebellion in your life." He planted a few kisses along my left thigh. "And sometimes, it's acceptable to break rules."

"If we get caught, we'll probably be killed." I gripped the sides of the chair as he kissed my inner thigh.

His chuckle vibrated against my skin. "That's what I'm here for. I'm already an abomination and this just adds to the list. Relax and enjoy. You stress too much as it is, and it isn't healthy for the mind, or arteries." He sent me a wink before kissing the most sensitive part of me.

Heaviness weighed on my eyelids, so I let them fall shut. If I had ever been in such a situation with Blake or anyone else, it would never have been worth getting killed for. There would have been no question that I would have ended things just to stay alive.

It was not that way with Spence. He made my mind race and my heart flutter. He fueled the fire within me. He didn't make me feel like I would never be enough for him. I knew without a doubt that with him, I'd always be safe. It wasn't an easy explanation as to how he made me feel like we would conquer the world but something about him just hit all the right notes to my music.

Maybe it'd been the logic from my brain raising all the green flags, or maybe my gut instincts from my heart. Or possibly both. There was no clear answer.

He was the kind of man who could cause me to go against the grain—to defy authority. It wasn't easy to fight my feelings and pretend we had nothing between us. Every inch of me needed him nearby. He completed me, balancing out parts I never knew I had to have.

With his fingers wrapped around my thighs, he peered up at me. "I think our session is over."

It had been my most embarrassing moment yet, finding that I made a mess on the chair. Was I to blame? Hardly.

"We are in so much trouble." I pushed myself out of the chair. "I have to take a shower. If Monique catches me, she'll know what happened. She'll see this all over my face." I started at the bottom of my dress, buttoning it up.

He looked around his room and shrugged. "I wish I could clean it up, but I don't have anything and if I use my sheets or something, it won't be hard for the employee who washes them to get what we did."

I groaned. "You make this so much more complicated than it needs to be."

He came closer, helping me fasten buttons. "You were stressed. I was required to relieve you of it." He placed a gentle kiss on my nose. "I hate seeing you stressed." His striking blue eyes searched my secrets, hoping to find answers. I couldn't seem to find them *either*.

"I have to get something to clean up our mess." I made sure he knew it wasn't my fault alone that this happened, even if I took partial blame for what he seduced me into.

Leaving the room, I found a bunch of paper towels and a plastic bag in the closet down the hall.

As I bent over to yank the trash bag from the box, a breeze hit the spot between my legs and my eyes grew to the size of saucers. I wasn't wearing any underwear.

I rushed back to his room and shoved the supplies in his hands. "Clean it up. I need to find my underwear." I dropped to my knees and searched everywhere. It was a tiny room and yet, they ceased to exist.

Spence dropped the plastic bag beside me, tied off and filled with the soaked towels. "I thought maybe I could keep it as a souvenir."

My eyes shot up to him. "Souvenirs are for people planning to leave." I climbed to my feet. "Are you planning to leave? You're the only man who has ever cared about me."

He laughed with his entire abdomen. "Souvenir, yes. I just meant I want to keep it to help remind me of why I fight. Is that weird? Do humans not do that?"

I fixed my dress before sighing. "Yes, we do. I guess it's not entirely weird. We've had sex; I've confessed my love for you." I huffed. "Fine, keep them, but it's the only pair you get." I fixed my hair next. "I still like wearing underwear," I mumbled. I hurried from the room and dropped the bag off in the trash bin before going to mine.

Once I'd gathered fresh clothes and a towel, I headed for the bathroom.

I stripped down and turned the temperature to warm, careful to wash every part of me well. I had to make sure I smelled like watermelon and not a woman who enjoyed the gratification from her lover.

The lights cut out.

I knew it was useless to ask who was there. This was the doing of one person—Alicia's evil twin.

I grabbed the towel off the wall that separated my shower from the next, wrapping it around myself and walking towards what I hoped was the door. "I know who you are. You need to stay away from me now."

Her face appeared in one of the mirrors on the wall. "Why would I do that?"

I tightened the cloth, knowing I was utterly vulnerable. "Because you were once my friend. The real Alicia wouldn't want this. I already suffer enough from what I said to her, and you're not Alicia. You are the darkest parts of her, the parts she had always refused to let out. She was my best friend and I know her far better than you ever will."

"You *killed* her."

"I did not kill her!" I shouted. "I didn't push her down those steps! She slipped off the top and broke her neck. If I had followed her, the same thing would have happened because sometimes, you can't change the outcome. I had no control over this. I'll admit to Claire's death being my fault, but Alicia was not. That was a horrible accident." I broke down sobbing into my hands.

"An accident you caused. You walked up those stairs and she had to *follow* you." A hand landed on my shoulder.

I shook my head, sniffling. "No. It was not my fault. Claire taught me that there are some things you cannot control. I could not have predicted she would slip. I did not push her. She died as the result of an accident and even the police knew that. Alicia deserves to be happy."

She leaned down. "And what do you deserve?"

I swallowed my sniffles. "I deserve some peace and quiet." I stood, spinning around to face her. "I deserve to be left alone, to live my life, and get through my grief without you ruining it." I took a step forward. "You will pay for all of this. You're going to be destroyed because you are *nothing*. You are not real. You're a copy of her, but you're not her. You are a coward. Death is a fraud. He sends you to do his dirty work but you and I both know you can't do it because you are still part of Alicia and Alicia's love for me is always going to be far greater than you can ever muster up as hatred."

"That is not true." She narrowed her eyes.

Now centimeters apart, I asked, "Is it?" I spat. "You run on my fear, and I'm not afraid of you. How could I ever be scared? You look like her. You are the exact replica of Alicia, a best friend of mine. Seeing you makes me miss her, but it doesn't make me fear you." I shoved her. "There is nothing to be terrified of anymore. She is gone. I must accept that."

"You may not be afraid, Nora, but that doesn't stop me from taking away what you love most." She reached out and pushed back, causing me to slip on the water all over the floor.

My body fell back, and I reached out to catch myself before my head cracked on the tiles as a pair of arms slipped under mine to catch me from a fatal blow. "You forget whose side she's on," a woman said.

I looked up to meet Cat's green eyes, thankful she had walked in at the right time. It was time to burn Monstrum to the ground and everyone who was inside. There would be no going back.

XXXXV

The walk from the courtyard to the asylum was short—or could have been had I not slipped in the snow and scraped my knee on the freshly shoveled cement.

"Fuck," Spence and I both uttered at once.

"It's fine," I said. "It's just a scrape. I'll clean it up in the bathroom."

"Ah, yes, where Alicia keeps harassing you." He tilted his head. "I don't think so. Let's go." He waved me to follow.

As badly as he itched to grab my hand, he fought the urge just in case one of the employees saw us along the way.

Once we made it to the bathroom, he sat me on a toilet and grabbed first aid. "Damnit, Nora. You're always getting yourself into trouble." His fingers wrapped behind my calf, pulling it upward to straighten my knee as he used alcohol to swab it. Bloody had trickled down my shin, and what I once said was just a scrape looked far worse.

"I know, and I don't mean to. Spence, maybe you should leave." I nodded towards the door, placing my hand over the blood to block his line of sight.

His brows shot up as he met my gaze. "Afraid of the demon coming out?"

I shrugged. "Afraid? Not particularly. More worried for your sake."

He reached for the gauze, placing it over the wound and softly taping it to my skin. "A little blood won't faze us. Relax. And try not to trip." He patted my leg.

With a small smile crawling onto my lips, I replied, "I don't make promises I can't keep."

He made sure I could stand without any wobbling. Once I was on my feet and steady, he turned away and left the bathroom with I hot on his tail. Immediately, I jumped back when he closed his bedroom door in my face without another word. Had I said something wrong? Did I do something?

I opened my mouth to apologize, then closed it. Apologize for what? I didn't do anything wrong, did I?

"Goodnight," I mumbled, heading back to my own room.

Sleep came too easy that night, and I supposed it was good that it did.

For when I woke up...

"Bummer," Monique said as she shut my door.

I curled up in the blankets to try and trap as much heat as I could, but it didn't make me feel any better. At least not at the moment.

Instead, aches gripped every bone in my body. My appetite disappeared, and with it, my sanity. It was far too hot, yet I had chills, and my throat? Entirely inflamed. I couldn't utter a word.

That was how Spence found me, too.

I tried to tell him not to bother me too much or David would suspect, but I didn't think he got the memo. He brought soup, and more blankets, and proceeded to sit with me while I groaned. The soup did wonders going down my throat, even if I didn't particularly crave food.

When I'd finished, Spence handed me a glass of water which I forced down despite the agony. *Fluids, fluids, fluids,* he said.

As I propped myself up against some pillows, I met his eyes—and a gasp left my lips. "Spence?"

The corner of his mouth tugged upward. "I do love when you say my name, Nora." He reached out, brushing my unkempt hair from my eyes, not at all bothered by the sweat coating my forehead.

"What are you doing here?" I whispered. My fingers itched to reach out and touch him, but I held back.

He scooted closer. "What ever do you mean?"

I mean *you*, Spence. This side of you. How... The words formed, yet never dared to leave my tongue.

Eyes black as night, they searched every wrinkle on my face, studying the beads of sweat that dripped from my hairline. Why was he looking at me like that?

He leaned in. "How did the demon escape the cage? Go on, Nora. You can say it. I won't bite."

He said that, yet the smoke swirling in his eyes still gave me goosebumps.

His fingers trailed down the blanket, above my knee. "He said it wouldn't faze us, but he lied so he wouldn't have to leave you on your own. Can't say I blame him, either."

"David." David will get suspicious.

"David's far too busy with his own shit that he couldn't care less about you today." He tilted his head. "I mean that nicely of course. I care about you."

Is that why he brought me soup?

I scooted further back, just in case I was contagious. Maybe not to vampires, but I couldn't confirm if Spence was immune or not.

A chuckle vibrated in his throat. "You scared you'll get me sick? Hardly. Humans can't really pass on illnesses to supernatural creatures. Given our impeccable health that is." He fixed the blanket around my body. "So now that we've answered your two questions... Let me take care of you."

My brows knitted together as I attempted to inhale a large breath.

"You think you can take care of yourself?" He clicked his tongue. "Hardly. You're a mess. You're in pain, and you can barely breathe, let alone speak. I wouldn't expect you to take care of yourself when you're compromised. Your health is taking a hit and that's what I'm here for." He gave me the water, which I sipped.

I wanted to tell him I could breathe fine. My throat had swelled, but I didn't feel like it could close on me either way. It was moreso that my throat was on fire and I wanted honey to soothe it.

I'd give my life for honey...

Although that's what I was doing in a sense.

He brushed more strands back. "You should lie down. Come on." He gestured to the bed, in which I scooted my bottom down until my head rested on the pillows. Spence tucked me in, but he didn't move from his spot. "So, since you can't talk and there's not much to do, allow me to tell you about *my* fondest memory."

His? As in, the demon's?

"We always knew our parents were an abomination. We knew from the time we had conscious thoughts. Everyone always reminded me everywhere I went. I guess it made sense, given my black and white wings. But I didn't realize this..." He gestured to himself. "I didn't realize that this side of me wasn't the same as others. Not everyone struggled with a dark side. Spence always heard my voice in his head, and when we confronted our parents, they told us. He has two sides. The angel and the demon. So I began to talk more, and suddenly he...shifted.

"People hammered the notion that I was wrong on every front. They made us feel just as filthy as they did our parents, but of course Mom combated their words. She wouldn't allow her own son to feel like a mistake when we had no choice in existing as we are."

I twisted my head to look up at him.

"I was always just a voice, but then I convinced Spence to let me take over. He never knew what it meant, or that it was possible for me to do that. He thought I was simply a voice in his head. I talked him into it. Convinced him to place cuts along his chest, and the pain with the blood...it fueled me, Nora. I was fully born that day. And with power, I attacked the person who consistently shamed us. She tried to press charges, too." He laughed at the thought. "But my mom let her have it. She said the lady was asking for it by always bullying an innocent child. I was only seven at the time." He dropped his chin, eyes focused on me as he began stroking my hair, sending small jolts from my head to my toes. "That's my fondest memory. Sticking up for myself. Showing people not to mess with me. They're the same people who try to tell us our morals are so twisted, yet they have the balls to bully children into sin. I am what they made me. Am I truly to blame?"

I opened my mouth to say yes, but he shook his head, a grin apparent. "Don't answer that. I know that I'm a grown man now. I know I'm aware of my choices and I have the power to control myself. That doesn't make them any less wrong, though. You want to kill David, don't you? That's your end goal. I will help you. He might not, but I'll be around. Listening at all times." His fingers danced along my temple as shivers slithered down my spine. "You have no idea, Nora. You don't understand the hold you have on me. Claire was a good time, sure. But you, you're the one who..." He pressed his lips together.

I inched closer, pressing my cheek against his thigh, begging him to finish. "Please," I forced out in a hoarse whisper.

Even through the layer of clothing, coolness radiated from him, and not in a way that would've made the virus raging inside my body worse.

He sat forward a bit, his black wing curling around me. “Hopefully, that should warm you,” he muttered.

Spence admitted I kept the demon at bay. But if that side of his had confirmed it...

I was hopelessly in love with Spence—and *all* of him.

He became my lifeline.

After a few more minutes, he finally responded with, "You're the one who taught me that there's something better than wrath," in a quiet voice.

My heart exploded. My very being became millions of

butterflies. My bones became mush, and I knew I belonged to Spence Woods. I'd said it before that I would say yes to marriage in a heartbeat, or that I couldn't survive happily without him out in the world.

I meant it, too.

Here, and now, I was *his* and nobody else's. And damn how I wanted him to be mine all the same. To utter how much he needed me and my warmth. To remind me that I was his medicine.

I loved him with my every fiber and I couldn't wait to call myself his wife. To become Nora Woods.

To become the one promise he made and kept in this big, bad world.

Until I had the green light, I'd never mention it to him. I didn't want to scare Spence away now, even if I knew what I did. He wasn't going anywhere, but I feared it all the same.

"People fear me, more than they used to." He hummed gently, tracing his fingers along my cheek. "They used to curse me. Avoid me. Insult me. They'd do everything, but they never really feared me. They feared what I might become, but without belief, I guess they never truly were scared. If they had been, they wouldn't have had the balls to insult me at every turn. But when I showed them my colors, they flipped. They never spoke to me. Never talked about me to my face or behind my back. I just became the monster under their bed. Then David found me. And when I disappeared, nobody asked questions. I know that for a fact. Maybe my parents wonder, but nobody else cared. They only celebrated that the boogeyman was gone."

My heart cracked. He might have been the shadows that lurked in the corners and closest of people's bedrooms, but he wasn't inherently bad for existing. I believed people made their own choices.

He'd admitted to me that his fondest memory was beating a woman, but I didn't believe that entirely. Because he also told me that I taught him something better existed than just anger.

I'd grasp whatever I could and keep it close to me.

"Sweet dreams," he whispered as he moved down the bed and placed a kiss on my forehead.

Ironically, my dreams had been sweet. Sugary. Filled with all the child-like wonder in the universe, because of him. He'd managed to do to me what I did to him—make the nightmares go away and replace them with hope.

We kept each other grounded.

And forever was what I vowed to him.

XXXXVI

I chewed the skin on my lip, ripping it off with my teeth. "Okay, since David has created a shield that keeps you inside. How do we get rid of this shield? The plan is to sneak them out. Spence will possess me, but we have to sneak Taylor, Riley, and Emilie without anyone else's knowledge."

Cat shrugged. "I'm not even sure at this point. You'll take them all to safety, driving in your car. I'll be the one who stays behind while starting a fire in the basement. David has no idea I'm here. He won't see it coming."

I glanced at Spence. "Any ideas? Do you know what it is that keeps you all locked in?"

He grabbed something from his desk. "Yes. There are certain things in this world that are kryptonite to each of us. David studied those and mixed a potion with those ingredients, locking us inside. He used it to go around the entire building so no matter which way we go, we can't leave. That's why Cat can leave. He has no idea she's here and what it is that repels witches."

I grabbed the photo from his hand, admiring his parents. "Tell me why you can leave when you possess me."

"The kryptonite harms my angel form. He never gathered anything for the demon because he knows I follow my angel morals. It's going to sound stupid, but…coal is an angel's kryptonite. Hell is filled with it." He rubbed his neck, giving us both looks.

I frowned. "So much for a barbecue."

Cat cleared her throat. "Emilie's kryptonite is plastic. She's a mermaid. And yes, even land mermaids count in this scenario because plastic is a danger to all creatures. Taylor's kryptonite is…his own blood. I figured you knew that after Claire died. It's also the same for Riley."

There had to be a way to bring down that barrier.

"But we need to change our plans," she interrupted my thoughts. "Alicia, or whatever we call her, is trying to kill Nora. If I hadn't been there, she would have ended up with her head split wide open. We can't save them if Nora is dead. We have to get rid of the evil and save the real Alicia. I have an idea on how to stop Death. You need to lie to him. Life stops him. Nora, you and Spence have to tell him you're pregnant."

I furrowed my brows. "But I'm not. He'll know in an instant that it's not true."

She put her hand against my stomach. "No, he won't. You've barely had sex. It would be too early for there to be a heartbeat so he can't tell you it's not true. This lie will get you access to the underworld. It will give you a chance to go find Alicia and save her. If you can bring her back, her evil form will vanish. She can't survive if Alicia isn't being controlled by Death. Death loves nothing more than seeing unborn children die."

I glanced at Spence. He nodded, saying, "It's true. The unborn are the most innocent and killing the innocent is like an addiction. And I don't have a heartbeat so it's very possible for our child to not have one. They'll never even know we had sex only three weeks ago."

Nausea swirled around in my stomach, reminding me that I would be facing Death. This was not my best option, but it had to be done for *her*. "Okay. Let's go save Alicia." I nodded in agreement.

We headed out the door, but Spence pulled me back. "Are you sure you're up for this? I want to double check if you're uncomfortable."

"I appreciate it, but I'm sure."

"I just…" He cleared his throat. "This is a delicate topic. And I know it sounds like a nasty solution, and I wouldn't want to suggest it if we had another plan, but we don't."

"Spence." Reaching out, I grabbed his hands and pulled him closer to help calm him down. "I get it. It is a difficult situation. But I'm not actually pregnant. This is a life we're talking about. Okay, well, a soul. My best friend has been kept prisoner and she deserves to be free. Yes, it sounds terrible. Yes, there is some shame in this plan. But I will pretend to be pregnant and get an abortion if it saves Alicia. On the plus side, there isn't any real harm done because again—I'm not actually pregnant."

But what if you are?

I pushed away the thought but a second later I realized it wasn't my own voice I'd heard. I'd heard Spence's mind.

Taking a moment to process what he was feeling, I closed the door and sat down. "I understand. You think maybe I could really be putting myself in danger, or even…" I couldn't get the words out.

He released a sigh. "I'm not trying to add stress. But it's possible for you to already be pregnant. You just wouldn't know it yet, not until a little more time has passed. And if you are, I wouldn't want to send you into a plan that could get either of you killed."

"Either of us?"

"You, or the…baby." He frowned. "We should talk about it, Nora. If you are pregnant, we should do something about it. I'd hate myself if I allowed you to get pregnant with my child. And if you aren't we need to take a lot more precautions to make sure it never happens."

"Who says I wouldn't want to have your baby? No, that is not the point right now." I shook my head. "I'm not actually pregnant! Come on. Let's not make this a bigger deal than it is. I'm just going to go in, act the part, then find Alicia and bounce."

Cat tilted her head but said nothing.

Well, out loud.

She knew it wasn't her place to talk about our decisions or our future. Well, maybe… She was the one who influenced my future after all. There was no real decision behind me being here.

In her head, she was confused as to why I was talking the way I was, but I think part of it was because I had spent so much time around Alicia that I picked up on it subconsciously. Now that I was going to see her one last time, I was slipping back into her lingo.

Cat went to the store and brought back the supplies I needed. Using her portals made it a faster journey, and right now, I was all about that.

Spence tried to give me the same talk again. He wanted to make sure I was okay with this, but what if I was? Was that so hard to believe? It was common for women to go this route back during this era. However, I told myself that it was all an act and it would bring me back Alicia. That was enough to make me go through with it.

Everyone kept reassuring me I didn't have to do this, but it got irritating to listen to, so I eventually left Cat and Spence while I locked myself in the bathroom.

I did pee on the stick first to make it more legit. It came out negative as expected.

What would I have done if it was positive? I couldn't be too sure, but I probably wouldn't have gone through with this plan. It was a whole other ballpark—bringing in a whole new soul.

I wasn't so sure Spence felt the same way I did though.

Did I want kids with him one day? Maybe. I still hadn't fully decided yet if I wanted to have children, but I had time to figure it out. I had around ten years, and there were people who would say I had less than that. They'd tell me I needed to know now because this was my prime age. But it wasn't their life. It was mine.

In my experiences, I wanted to look back and say I didn't regret any of my big decisions. I wasn't going to have a child I didn't want just to appease the old-fashioned people who thought my only job was to reproduce.

The world was plenty populated. And if I did decide I was content with enjoying my life at my pace, that would be the end of it. Was I prepared to give up my dreams for a child? Not likely. There were so many things I still wanted to do. I didn't want to give up my sleep for a baby. I didn't want to give up my free time. And the more I pondered the idea, the quicker I realized I would not be a good mother. I'd spent so much of my life pleasing others and making sure they were taken care of.

Now I wanted to live for myself at the very least.

Some would say Spence took away from that, but I knew him enough to know he added to my life. He never sucked joy from it.

So, I stood in the bathroom contemplating my entire future and what *I* wanted from it. If Alicia had been here to comfort me, I'd know the answer. She always asked the right questions.

Soon, I'd see her again.

Soon, I'd get to say goodbye.

Soon.

I paced around the bathroom, holding the stick. I had already drawn a red line, making sure it seemed legit.

"What's wrong with you?" She appeared out of thin air, glaring daggers.

It took me a moment to collect myself so I could put on a good act. "I'm worried now. I mean, what will happen? This is a whole other ballgame." I set the stick on the counter. "I'm pregnant with his baby."

She stepped back as her eyes darted to the test, confusion written heavily on her face. "What? That's impossible."

"I wish it were but it's not." I wondered if it were possible for us to have children someday. It was a nice thought if I wanted them, but I had too much going on to think about that now. "This is going to ruin way more than I can handle."

She lifted her eyebrows, eyebrows darker than Alicia's had ever been. "Ah, do you have an idea in mind?"

"Yes, I do. But here's the problem. This baby is part demon and angel. Getting a regular abortion won't be easy in the human world." I shook my head, running my hands through my hair to seal the deal. "You can kill me later. Right now, I have my own problems."

She came over, grasping my hands. "I have an idea. Death can help you. Come with me, and he can do the job for you. It'll be so simple—so easy."

I chewed my lip, hesitating. "I don't know if that's a good idea."

She put her hands against my stomach, pushing. "Trust me. Nobody else knows how to abort the fetus better than Death himself."

This was all a big lie, and I was thankful it was. I had too much on my plate to worry about having a real child, or even trying to protect a real child from Death himself.

"Okay, let's go. But Spence cannot know about this." I tugged her wrist.

She shot me a cunning smile. "That's exactly what I was thinking." She yanked me into a dark corner.

I gasped as we walked through, entering a place so dark that even my pitch-black room appeared bright. "Holy hell."

She laughed, but her laugh didn't echo like one would suspect. It was cut short, lingering right in front of us. "This is far from holy, or hell. Hell is on a different level. This is where Death lives." She led me through the hallway, stopping in front of a door. She knocked, then a voice granted her permission to come inside. We walked right in and paused a few feet before him. "I brought Nora. She says she's pregnant, but she can't get rid of it with a regular abortion because it's Spence's."

Seemed like Spence had a name down here people couldn't forget.

Was I making a mistake with this plan?

He glanced at me, eyeing my form. "Nora. I've heard of you.

A pleasure to see you come to *me* for help." His iris' studied me a little too long, and a part of me worried that I wouldn't be able to get away with this.

But I had to, for Alicia's sake.

XXXXVII

Part of me asked why I didn't bring Spence, but I knew the answer. It wasn't exactly an option, yet doing this… It didn't stop me from feeling so alone. Isolated from the world. It was the last place I wanted to be, but it was only a glimpse of how Alicia had been feeling for over six months.

He waved me over and began heading back down the hall. "I will make sure you are taken care of."

I scanned the area, trying to figure out where I would find Alicia. Where did they keep the souls?

"I'm a bit hungry. Is there a snack?" I asked, catching up to him.

He chuckled. "We have some…strange snacks around here." He stopped and opened up a door. It had come out of nowhere, appearing in the darkness. “This is our snacking room. I’ll give you a few minutes.”

I walked inside and closed the door, almost choking from the sight. “This is…” I saw multiple jars of souls, souls that were just drenched in sorrow. “Alicia.” I searched the shelves, hoping to spot her.

Finding a familiar face in a room full of thousands of souls was exhausting. Overwhelming, even. I needed a faster way to search.

As soon as I came up with a plan, Death returned. “Let’s get this started.”

“I haven’t found a snack yet.”

“Am I supposed to feel sorry for you?” He waved me out of the room.

While leaving, I was blocked by Death. “Did you get anything to eat at all?”

Shaking my head, my stomach grumbled. Perfect timing. “I didn’t, no. Which is why I change my mind. I don’t know if I have the strength to do this on an empty stomach. I hope you understand.”

He stepped forward. “You mistake me for an entity that has compassion. I’m Death. I’m the result of so much gone wrong in the world. You made your bed and now it’s time you lie in it.” He shoved me back into another door and I stumbled against the wall. Beside it was a table and a tray of tools.

“You can’t do this.” I turned around, attempting to walk around him.

He pushed me again. “I can, and I will. I follow no rules.” He forced me back onto the table, his strength far superior to mine. He tightened the straps over my wrists and pulled my legs up onto the stirrups while pushing my dress up against my stomach.

"You have no choice now, Nora."

It was only a matter of time before he figured out I was lying.

And I still hadn't found the real Alicia.

He used a pair of scissors to cut my underwear off and grabbed a speculum. I looked away, unable to face something so invasive. And much to my dismay, I could feel *everything*. "Is this not so bad?" he asked.

Pap smears were terrible as they were, but this was certainly no pap smear. This was unwanted.

Cruel.

Inhumane.

I needed a way out fast.

The sound of gloves slipping on pierced my ears. Uncomfortable was an understatement. "Are you sure you're pregnant? I'm not seeing or getting anything at all."

I could have responded. I could have kicked him in the face, but with my wrists restrained, it wasn't a risk I could take. I needed to be smart about my escape, even if I had to endure this for a minute longer.

Anything for Alicia.

And I'd never tell her what I did to save her. Her response would be anger for such a stupid move, like I'd sacrificed my sanity for her safety. It was fine. I was fine.

I loved her to no end, and I would prove it by putting up with anything to set her soul free of this and give her the chance to see paradise.

"There's nothing. I think you've lied to me," Death said, snapping me out of my bubble.

"I didn't lie. I didn't." Desperation laced my voice. So pathetic that I thought I could get away with this. It was no wonder he didn't believe me, and I saw it by the look in his eyes. I humiliated him—tested his intelligence—and he fell for it. Now it was my turn to bear the consequences.

"Yes, you most certainly did, Nora. You thought you could fool me, and for what?" His eyes narrowed. "Are you here to save your little friend?"

"You have a lot of confidence to assault Nora," someone said behind him.

Death pulled back. "Ah, Spence. So nice to see you again. I'm sorry you had to find out this way."

Spence marched over, yanking back on his collar. "Fuck you." He ducked as Death swung his arm around, missing his face.

He brought his knee up and sent a blow to the gut and brought his fist to Death's jaw, causing him to stumble back. Death lunged.

The two of them tumbled to the ground and Spence kicked him off, throwing him into the wall. "I'm sorry you had to find out this way, too." He took another swing at his face, pummeling him until Death could no longer fight back.

Spence rushed over to me and pulled the straps off, helping me down. "Did you find her?" he whispered.

I shook my head. "No, but I know which room she's in."

I led the way while Spence took me to the room a few doors down. I closed it behind us. "Quickly. I don't know how to narrow it down, but I'm certain she's in here. I can feel her calling to me." I could hear her begging for me to rescue her from a horrid fate.

Spence nodded as he looked through the jars. Upon realizing her voice was tugging at my ears, I followed the cries for help to a jar in the corner on a low shelf. "Here! I see her!" I grabbed it, but the jar wouldn't open with my strength.

He hurried over and allowed his demon a little more control as he unscrewed the lid. His blue eyes seemed so impure—so tainted to the core. "Here." He handed the jar back, not trusting himself to touch her in this state.

I nodded, holding her close to my heart. "Let's go."

We ran out of the room.

She peered up at me with the most depressing look I had ever seen. "I'm going to save you." I put her into my dress pocket.

Before we could make it to the corner, I was tackled to the ground. Yelling out, Alicia's evil twin ripped my hair back and grabbed a fistful of my best friend from my dress. "Not so fast," she hissed in my ear.

"Alicia!" I shouted, flipping onto my back as Spence growled and jumped for her.

Despite our best efforts, she tossed her soul back to Death who now stood in the doorway. "You're going to regret this, Spence Woods." He squeezed, crushing what was left of her until she became nothing but ash.

I squeaked out a cry, every inch of me deflating as my heroism ceased to exist.

Worthless. That's what I was now.

I couldn't even save my friend.

Spence pulled me back through the dark wall, and shortly after he lured me into a hug. "I'm so glad I went in after you. He's ruthless, and far stronger, Nora."

Choking on a sob, I asked, "What happened to Alicia?" I studied his expression, waiting for his eyes to return to a vibrant blue. Spence had given him a little power to help me fail. I still had to keep his demon from gaining full control, even if I'd lost her for good.

His hope drained from every crevice. Color lost. Pale, like a ghost. "She returned to dust. She no longer exists, and I'm so sorry I couldn't save her."

"Save her? I'm the one who lost her." I wiped away vigorously at the never-ending waterfalls on my cheeks.

"Don't you dare say that," he spat. "You're not to blame for trying." Smoke clouded his non-pigmented iris'. "You did everything you could, and you put yourself in danger and paid the price. She'd never blame you."

"How would you know?" I screamed at him. "How the fuck would you know what she would or wouldn't say to me?"

He cupped my cheeks, bringing me just mere centimeters from his lips. "You've told me enough about her that I picked up on the kind of person she was. I am so sorry." He buried my head in his chest, planting kisses as a few tears hit my temple. "Nora, fuck, I am so, so sorry." He swallowed his cries.

Still, I whispered, "Alicia, please forgive me."

We stayed in silence for a few minutes.

Another question dawned on me. "What did he mean when he said you'd regret this?"

"It's nothing you need to concern yourself with." He brushed his fingers through my hair.

I pulled my head back to tilt my chin his way. "Tell me. I have to concern myself with you, whether you want me to or not. At least keep me in the loop."

"It means he plans on revenge." His smile dripped with sorrow. "Someday, if I can be killed, I'll belong to him. It's my inevitable end for being an abomination."

"Then we'll make sure you'll never die," I said as a matter-of-fact.

Easier said than done, but I loved him and he knew. It meant I'd take a bullet for him without any hesitation.

"She always forgave you," he whispered to my hair. "I know she did. I felt it, even as small as her soul was. She radiated with the love she felt for you."

Those were the words that I needed to hear, and yet they still didn't make the pain go away. It just reminded me all over again that she had lost the war and I could never visit. Never again would I get to see my best friend.

Nora, the voice in my head echoed. *She's not mad at you. You must know that.*

Did I know?

Of course. Because as Spence said, I knew her. She was never the kind of person to hold a grudge even if she easily flustered.

Did she blame herself? This entire time I had always painted myself as the culprit but never would I get to ask how Alicia felt about it. It was her death. Her own accident. It had been the loss of her life and it couldn't have been effortless for her to just accept the truth. I grieved over the death of my best friend, but she grieved over losing absolutely everything she ever had.

Her friends. Family. Jeff. Her entire career. She had barely begun her life and it was ripped away too soon. How could anyone be okay with that?

And I'd just let her vanish into dust.

I could never forgive myself, even if she would have.

It wasn't the feasible thing to do.

More tears slipped from my eyes as her memories tucked themselves into the folds of my thoughts. A big piece of my heart was forever torn, knowing she was no longer an existing soul. *Gone*—but certainly never to be forgotten.

"Whatever you decide, we'll do it," Spence muttered. "Funeral. Memorial. We'll do it in honor of her. Her spirit might not be alive anymore, but we'll keep it that way for her."

Damn, I loved him so much. How could he be so perfect?

Why was I forced to choose between him and Alicia? Why couldn't I have had both?

Life sucked, just as much as Death. Together, they were polar opposites, yet they worked together so flawlessly. If anyone asked me, they were simply brothers who thought we were games to be played. Won and lost. Forgettable, and nothing more than a code meticulously formed.

Alicia had been their victim, Spence the pawn, and I the ignoramus.

XXXXVIII

I knocked on his door before opening it.

Spence hunched over at the edge of the bed, staring at the floor. Something was wrong. I could sense it.

A bit of blood seeped down the edge of the bed, onto the floor.

I rushed to his side and kneeled before him. “Spence.”

“Don’t fucking touch me,” he said in a low voice. It didn’t sound like him. It sounded…

“Look at me. Now,” I demanded.

He met my eyes, but they weren’t his eyes anymore. Not those baby blue eyes that once captured my heart. They were wrong, like his pupils had dilated so much that it was all he had left. His eyes were pure *black*.

"David did this, didn't he?" I stood. "Didn't he?"

He clenched his jaw. "It's humiliating that you still ask these questions as if you don't know what goes on around here. I don't know what he sees in you."

That stung. Hearing that his demon side despised me was heartbreaking. But that wasn't important right now. Not to Spence.

"I'm going to clean this up." I left in a hurry and grabbed the kit, bringing it back to Spence. "Sit back."

He slowly leaned back onto his hands. "Do you ever read his mind when you don't think you should? Do you know what thoughts he has about you?"

I cleaned the blood using the alcohol wipes. He grabbed my wrist, teeth seething from the pain.

His grip loosened when what I assumed was the stinging disappeared.

"His thoughts of you are much dirtier than you'd expect for a little angel." I focused on bandaging his wounds, and when I finished, he grabbed the top of my dress where the buttons came together. "They're very immoral," he whispered as he ripped my dress open.

I gasped and stumbled back, pulling the fabric back together. "What the hell are you doing?"

Spence slowly stood from the bed and grasped my wrist. "I'm showing you what he's afraid to show you." He pulled us towards the bed and sat down, sitting me on his lap. "All those thoughts…" He gripped my waist.

I wanted to fight the feelings, knowing that he'd be so angry at me if I didn't. But even if it was his demon side, it was still Spence's body. Still his touch. It was still the same man who made me weak. He was just hiding beneath the surface—and fighting these feelings wasn't so easy.

He pushed my sleeves down my arms and began licking my neck. His feelings for me conflicted with one another. This side of him was always confusing, terrifying, yet mesmerizing all at once.

Was it so wrong of me to be attracted to both?

His lips trailed down my chest as he removed my dress entirely. Tracing his fingers up my back, he ripped my bra open and slipped it off, throwing it at the wall.

Spence was going to kill me. Why couldn't I make him stop? Because demons had charm. Because the way his lips moved was intoxicating. Because he was still *Spence.*

He moved his lips up my neck. "You taste divine, sweetheart."

"Sweetheart? Spence never calls me that," I said quietly. "What happened to darling?" I gasped a little when he pressed my body against his. I could feel his bandages, which brought forth feelings of guilt.

"Sweetheart. Darling. I'll call you many names, if you just ask."

"I never asked, yet you still do."

Using his thumb and forefinger, he grabbed my chin and lowered it until our lips were just millimeters apart. I could practically relish his scent.

When he crashed his lips onto mine, I devoured him. I didn't care about the rules or whatever could go wrong. All that controlled my mind was hunger. That same hunger must have dominated him, too, because he kissed me hard. As if his life depended on it. As if he would lose me if he didn't take all that he could. I'd give, too.

This feeling mimicked him sucking my life from me. It

exhilarated me to say the least.

Then someone knocked on the door. "David is on his way so you two better wrap it up," Taylor said.

I pulled away and struggled to catch my breath.

"Such a shame," he whispered. "I was having delicious fun." Spence kissed down my neck again.

"You heard him. David is coming."

With a sigh, he leaned back and stole a good look at my disheveled form. Swollen lips. Dilated pupils. Hair falling from its pins. "Later we will finish what we started."

I didn't verbally agree with him, so I got off his lap and found the rest of my clothes, putting them back on. "I need to talk to David about this."

He stood and lifted my chin. "This? You don't want to see me?"

"I don't want to see so many cuts on your chest."

Spence placed his lips to mine, but instead of kissing me, he rubbed his thumb across the bottom. "But I would love to see them on yours."

With wide eyes, I stepped away from him.

"It's called a kink, sweetheart. We'll unlock yours very soon."

David entered. "Nora, what's going on in here?"

I shook my head and looked away from Spence. "I had to fix his cuts."

Spence let out a dark chuckle. "*Fix* my cuts is a perfect way to put it."

I knew David wasn't ignorant towards the look on my face. The way my throat thirsted for more. My eyes raking over Spence's body, begging to have all of him—including his demon side.

David jutted his chin. "Nora, come to my office. Now."

I followed him.

"We do not fuck the patients," he hissed. "That is well below your pay grade. I did not hire you to whore around."

My fingers ached to slap that sickening look off his face. If only I could find the courage. "You hired me to care about the patients. All I was doing was bandaging his cuts, sir."

"I was not born yesterday. In fact, I was born many years before you. I know what sexual attraction looks like. I know what lust looks like, Nora, and it is written all over your face." He pointed his finger at me.

"Dr. Harrison, I—"

"I understand that you have needs. You've been cooped up here for almost eight months. This is not the way you fulfill them. If I catch you with *my* patients like this again, I will have to terminate you. Is that understood?"

"I—"

He raised his voice a few notches. "Is that understood?"

"Crystal clear." I swallowed my fear.

After I left his office, I stopped by my room. What had he meant by termination? Firing me, or worse?

"What did he say?" Spence asked.

I didn't need to look at him to know that his demon still had control. "Nothing. It's not your business."

He reached for my wrist, but I pulled away. "It is my business if we were about to do things we both dream of."

"Drop it," I spat out with venom lacing my tongue.

He didn't say another word.

I did my best to avoid Spence in my spare time. I wanted to help him, but I didn't want to lose my life before I had the chance. And I knew every time I glanced his way, the demon was still in control.

Passing the bathrooms, someone called out my name. I looked over, knowing full well that Alicia was gone and there was no reason to be afraid. Spence was leaning against the frame. "You've been avoiding me, sweetheart."

"For our safety. You got me into a lot of trouble."

He pointed to himself. "I got you into this? That doesn't seem fair. You enjoyed every second of it. And if that douchebag hadn't interrupted, we could have had the best sex you've ever experienced."

"That's not very fair to Spence. He doesn't even like you. I can't be having sex with you," I said in a whisper. I slipped out of the hall and into the bathroom with him.

"But what about what *you* want?"

I let out a sigh. "What I want is to make him happy. I don't want to hurt him."

He approached me. "So avoiding me altogether is your solution now? As if I hadn't taken care of you when you were sick?"

I tried to put space between us, backing into the sinks. "Spence—his angel side—told me that you struggle with wrath. Yet the first time I met you, you seduced me by licking the blood from my arm. Which is it? Do you struggle with wrath or lust?"

His lips curved up into a smirk. "What if I like both? Angry sex seems to be our favorite." He meant *our* as in his and Spence's. Claire had once told me that's what they used to do.

"So the angel side lied to me?"

Spence's smirk faded away. "Not so much as lied as he did

just not explain the whole truth. Sure, wrath is my biggest flaw. But what you must understand is that demons can still love. Still lust. Even if their biggest sin happens to be something else. Our mother's biggest flaw was envy. But she still lusted after an angel, correct?"

Of course he was right. Not even humans had one single flaw. I needed to remind myself that not everything was so black and white. Maybe in Spence's case, sure. But certainly not in mine.

I brought out the gray in everyone.

Even if it'd been for Alicia's sake, I couldn't shut down the small voice inside me that hated herself for what Death had done. It wasn't as easy to forget about it as I'd hoped. I thought maybe I could just move on since my best friend was no longer trapped and in pain. But I wasn't safe. I didn't feel safe inside my mind, or in my own body. I'd been violated.

"Are you all right?" he asked in a quiet voice.

"I'm doing fine."

"You're not. You can't hide your feelings all that well."

"I don't want to talk about it." I never wanted to. I'd been humiliated. Ashamed. And talking about it only made me relive the horrid memory, which is exactly what I didn't want. So for the rest of my life, I'd bury it down and pretend it never happened to me in the first place.

I wasn't a victim, or a survivor. Because it never happened to me, right?

Changing the subject, I said, "David knows what we were doing. And I'm not about to screw up our plan for one good time. I'm not going to wreck our future for that."

He scowled. "What the fuck did he say to you?"

"Excuse me?"

He closed the distance, pressing his chest to mine, grabbing my face in both of his hands. "What the fuck did he say to you, Nora? Don't tell me lies this time." He might have been showing love through his gentle caress, but his eyes told a whole different story. I couldn't run.

"He said he didn't hire me to whore around. He'd terminate me if it happened again," I blurted.

He growled and moved away from me, punching the wall. "That fucking asshole. He's going to pay for talking to you like that. Nobody gets to talk to you that way."

"Spence," I slowly approached, careful not to scare him. "We need to get you back."

"What?" He snapped his head towards me.

"I need the angel side to come back out. That's the best way for this plan to work. We both know it."

He snickered and stepped away. "I worked hard to get here. I am not going back in."

I wasn't sure how to convince him, but it was my job to save him. If I didn't, he'd never forgive me for this. I wasn't willing to risk everything for the demon side.

"Please," I said. "For me."

"Didn't you hear me the first time? I said no." He gave me the most poisonous look I'd ever seen.

Heading to the sink, I grabbed one of the shards that laid broken. "And I told you we need him. If he doesn't come back, I can't go near you again. David will terminate me—whatever that means. Do you really want to be the reason that I'm killed?" I faced him. With his demon side, the one way to get through to him was to act like him. Blame him. Make him feel angry.

"Don't say that."

I placed the shard against my arm. "This is what he'll do. If you don't let him have dominance, this is what he will do to me just to hurt you and punish me for wanting you. You know you and I can't contain ourselves. Your demon half lacks self-control, but with your angel side, we can at least pretend to be nothing more than a psychologist and her patient. You're putting me in danger."

"That is not at all true!" he shouted.

"Is it?" I yelled back. "You'd rather let me die than give up power. Do you hate me? Because I love you, Spence. I love *all* of you."

He shook his head, fighting whatever it was he was telling himself. "No, I don't hate you."

"Then fucking show me. Show me that you don't loathe my guts and want to see my blood all over the place. Show me before I have to prove it to you." I pressed the edge into my skin, drawing beads of blood.

Spence glanced at the shard, heading towards the wall. "Stop it, Nora! Stop doing that to yourself!"

"Stop me! Bring him back and stop me!" Why did this feel so wrong? Why was his demon half so stubborn?

He backed into the wall, dropping to the floor. "Sweetheart, stop," he whispered.

I dropped the shard and rushed over to him, dropping to my knees and grabbing his face in my hands. His eyes were back to blue, and my heart beat red. "Spence?"

Looking directly at me, his shoulders slouched. "I am so sorry for giving in. I'm sorry I failed you."

I pulled him into my chest. "Don't say that. You never failed me. David failed you. He got you at your weakest and he is the only person to blame here."

He wrapped his arms around my back, clinging to me. I rested my chin on top of his head and closed my eyes. If I let go,

I might lose him forever.

In one breath, he said, "I'd die for you if you asked me to."

XXXXIX

White knuckles.

Sharp, shooting pains.

Fatigue.

This was the norm for every menstrual cycle of mine, and while I was aware that it wasn't healthy, I had no money to go to a doctor and find out what the real problem was. Women's education was horrible when it came to such things, because nobody ever told girls when to see a doctor about their visit from Aunt Flo.

Only last year did I find out that Aunt Flo was a health concern, and I was in my mid-twenties. They pushed us to get mammograms and check for breast cancer. They told us about pap smears to check for cervical cancer. They never once stopped to teach us when pain was and wasn't normal for a cycle, and that was why so many young women went undiagnosed with endometriosis or PCOS.

Instead, we were told that every girl had menstrual pain and we needed to suck it up. We needed to do better.

And it wasn't a coincidence that Aunt Flo visited right after being assaulted by Death himself. I'd had pap smears before, but nothing had ever been as invasive as what he did.

Maybe Cat and Spence were right to triple question me about going through with the plan. Alicia was *safe*, but my body was not.

Shivers ran down my spine when fingers brushed my ear as they pushed hair behind it. "You look like you're in pain," Spence said in a low voice.

"Aunt Flo is here. Nothing serious."

But it is serious.

His thoughts somehow comforted me.

He released a sigh. "I'm sorry. I wish I was able to help."

I was about to tell him he could by running to the store and getting me a few things, but he couldn't quite do that. "I'll be okay," I whispered.

Spence did the next best thing he could think of. He brought me into his arms and rested his chin on top of my head. "I'll be right here."

Wrapping my fingers around his bicep, I squeezed when pain shot through my uterus. "I know. Now that Alicia is at the very least free of Death, we need to put the plan in action."

"Right now?"

"Well, not now. But soon. Eventually. Right?" He nodded a bit while I squeezed again. Spence cursed under his breath, and I pulled away, looking at his arm. "Oh, shit, I'm so sorry." I grabbed the skirt of my dress to clean the blood I'd drawn.

He pushed my dress down. "It's okay, Nora. You don't need to ruin your nice dress. This is only a sliver of what you're feeling. I can survive a little discomfort."

"I'm not worried about the pain. I'm worried about the blood." I placed my thumb over the small cut to hide the blood. Something inside me ignited as an urge overcame me.

I wanted to *lick* it.

He grabbed my chin and pulled my head to look at him instead. Before I could ask questions, his lips were locked with mine, moving in sync. Did he know what I was thinking? Of course not. He couldn't have.

He dragged his lips down my neck. "It's okay. This is a good distraction. All three of us can enjoy this."

Three. He was referring to both sides of himself. It was odd to hear him say it that way, but it wasn't less accurate.

He unbuttoned halfway down my dress, pushing my sleeves down until it all hung from my stomach. Dragging his tongue across the exposed area of my chest, he lay me back on his bed.

A scream ruptured throughout the whole asylum, shaking the walls.

"What the hell was that?" I sat up, pulling my dress back up and buttoning it.

Spence swallowed as he got up. "Let me investigate."

"No, no. Let's both go." I followed Spence out to the hallway. Footsteps drew closer from the direction of the stairs and Spence whipped around at the speed of light, yanking me into his chest before we were trampled. "Cat?" I yelled as she tripped and face planted. I pushed myself away from Spence and scurried over to her. "What the hell happened?"

She sat up, scooting away. "He found me."

"Who?"

But my question was answered as soon as David's feet came into view. "Nora, out of my way."

I immediately stood and faced him. "David, what is the meaning of this?"

"Out of my way, now!" he shouted at me. It gave Cat enough time to run off and split out through a portal. "Damnit, Nora!" He shoved me into the wall using the front of his arm, but he glanced over his shoulder to give me one last menacing glare. "I'll see you in my office later. We'll deal with your consequences." He disappeared down the hall.

Spence rubbed my shoulder to provide some comfort. "Are you okay?"

"How can I be okay?" My eyes watered before I could even gain control of myself. "He knows about Cat and now I'm in huge trouble. I'm fucking screwed."

"Hide."

"What?"

"Hide. Just hide out somewhere. Pretend to have a family emergency and leave for a bit."

"Where am I going to hide?" But it hit me. The empty road.

The last place I wanted to be was the dark, cold mountains. But I had to put aside my fears for a moment just until I could get them out of the asylum. On the bright side, Alicia was in a better place, and I didn't have to fear her evil ghost coming to suffocate me. No, I just had to worry about David instead.

He kissed me one last time. "Go. I don't want to see what he will do later."

I did as Spence suggested. I went to my car and started it up, driving a little bit away from the asylum until it was out of my view. I parked my car and sat back with the heater on full blast. What kind of mess had I gotten into now?

David would be looking for me, waiting to erase my memory again or worse.

"That was close," Cat said beside me.

I jumped, still not used to her being able to get into places with ease. "Damnit. Cat, what happened?" A ringing in my ear bothered me but I didn't have time to worry about that now.

She leaned back in the seat. "I didn't do anything. Okay, well, I was practicing my magic so I could possibly mask them while we escaped, you know? Like masking them from the barrier. But David must have heard or seen something because he came in and before I had time to think, I was running."

"So that scream was you?"

"Precisely. I scare easy."

I snickered. "And now I'm here."

"What?" Cat looked around at all the snow and empty roads. "Is that why you're out here? David threatened you?"

"I let you get away. And without you to persuade him, he told me we'd deal with my consequences."

"Let me try and persuade him again."

Shaking my head, I pulled my jacket tighter. "No. No, that's far too risky now. You've already been caught and now he's expecting you to come back. He'll be looking for you. It's fine. I'll hide out per Spence's suggestion, and we'll somehow have to make the plan happen without my help from the inside."

Cat dropped her head. "This is my fault. I screwed everything up. My mama is going to kill me. She told me to do good and I carelessly practiced my magic. I shouldn't have."

"Whoa, whoa." I faced her. "This is not your fault. We just didn't anticipate how much time we had. I took it for granted.

I spent it with Spence instead of working on the plan. I need to resist him."

She leaned in and furrowed her eyebrows. "Well, I can see some lipstick smudging. And your buttons are lined up wrong."

Widening my eyes, I looked down at my dress. She was right. I had buttoned them the wrong way. I undid them and fixed them while clearing my throat. "I'm sorry."

"For what? Nora, you've spent the past six months focusing on all the prisoners. You've been stressing endlessly about where to go next with your plan, or what plan to even make. I'm not going to fault you for wanting to get a little frisky with the sexy angel-demon. Spence is quite the catch, and I'm going to help you get back in there so we can bring it to the ground."

I got out of the car and looked over as she followed suit. "This is now or never. We must get the ball rolling."

She shrugged. "We do. I can sneak you back in right now but what's your plan?"

"You'll have to wait and see."

I glanced to my left just as a snow squall hit us full blast. I was sent flying into the snow piled up on the side of the road and Cat had to dig me out. She helped me into my warm car, and neither of us said a word.

This journey alone had been one long rollercoaster and I was more than ready to get off the ride. Being fired only made it much harder, yet at the same time it also motivated me that much more to kill David. Spence didn't want me to, but it was for his safety and the safety of others. And if I did kill him, I had to make sure he never escaped the asylum himself.

Months ago I wouldn't have considered such a thing. But this wasn't months ago anymore. This was the present and if I had seen things other humans could never fathom. I had witnessed the cruelest of treatments. I had fallen in love with a man so pure of heart that nobody would have assumed he was half demon. And in some twisted way, his opposite-colored wings only made him that much more enticing.

Cat was right. I deserved a little break. Spence reminded me that through all this stress, he was always there to support me. Claire was gone, and Alicia had finally escaped in some ways, but he would always be right there.

If someone asked me the question: if you could go back and change anything, would you—I'd tell them no. Because if I changed anything, would I still have Spence? Would I still have saved Alicia? Those weren't results I was willing to give up. Not now, and not ever.

David hated me, but he hadn't been able to break my spirit. He hadn't erased my memory. Those two things alone were grave mistakes, and I was coming back for blood.

It was a good thing I had found Cat and discovered that someone was behind all of it. She was my key to getting in and out of the building without one. But David would know I was coming back. He would be waiting for me. Could I take such a risk? Never.

"Well, once this snow squall passes, we need to get back into that asylum," I told her, staring out of the window.

"I can do that. I'm very good at that in fact. Portals only took me like three years to master." She laughed. "But they make everything so much easier."

"That's what we need right now. Easy. I promised Riley, Emilie, and Taylor. Spence is also somewhere in that mix," I joked. Even then, my jokes felt hollow. It was impossible to feel otherwise with so much responsibility hanging over my head. If I didn't come through for them, David would kill them all.

He wouldn't hesitate, either. He knew ways to get around their deaths and use their blood for his gain regardless. But I wouldn't let that happen. I couldn't.

If I did, I'd become the villain of their story.

XXXXX

"I'd like to apologize for what I said." David nodded towards me. "About you whoring around. It was extremely out of line, and no boss needs to treat their employees that way."

Why was he apologizing?

"It's been brought to my attention that nothing happened between you and Spence. I was jumping to conclusions."

Who told him that?

"I'm also sorry that I got angry after that girl got away. Accidents happen, and sometimes we make the wrong choices."

Was he implying I was too stupid to move out of his way?

"As a way of saying sorry, I'd like to give you a new task to prove that you're here to help." He flashed a smile, but it never reached his eyes. "I would like to ask you to bring out Spence's demon side again. You managed to turn him back and I've never seen anyone do that before. So I would love to see you do the opposite. If we can get a handle on both, we can possibly try to find a solution. We could even cure all the demons in this world. You would be a hero, Nora Witlow. You would be our savior."

What the hell was he going on about?

"I knew I chose you for a reason."

"You chose me?" I patted my skirt. "But I came for an interview, and you said that I had potential."

That's precisely how interviews work. Disappointing that someone is that pretty enough to be so dim.

Shit. I think I'd heard his deep personal thoughts for the first time, and they were disgusting.

He gestured to me. "This is that potential. Can I count on you?"

"You're asking me to put him in danger just to save the world?"

"What is one life to the rest? Would it be well worth it?"

What if I said no? What would he do then? I didn't exactly want to find out. "I can certainly try, but I can't promise I'm any good at it."

"Any good at bringing out the darkness in people? That's up for debate but thank you."

As foreseen. Consistently setting low expectations and failing to achieve them.

I turned on my heel, ready to leave this damned office.

"And Nora?"

"Yes?"

"Don't breathe a word of this to anyone. It could destroy our whole plan, and maybe even you."

My airway closed for a second. Was that a threat, or was he

trying to keep me safe? No, of course it was a threat—and one disguised at that to keep me safe. "Yes, sir."

I left his office and headed to the cafeteria for lunch. What was I supposed to do? He asked me to bring out Spence's demon side again. I could never do that.

Sitting at the table, I made sure to eat my food with no room for talking. Bite by bite. Mouthful by mouthful.

Monique tried to talk to me, but I gave her a smile with stuffed cheeks. She took the hint that I wasn't in a talking mood, or in her mind I was just starving.

When lunch was over, I took it upon myself to go to my office and figure out why David really chose me. Anyone else and he would have fired them in an instant. He would have even killed them.

But no, not me. He erased my memory and tried again. He kept giving me chances. So why had he given me chances over and over, and why wasn't he trying to get rid of me for good?

Someone knocked on the door, but when I didn't answer right away, they knocked louder.

"Come in," I said.

Cat hurried in and closed the door. "Sorry, didn't want to get caught again."

I nodded and furrowed my brows. "I need to ask you something. And I need an honest answer."

"Shoot."

"What would have happened if David never hired me?"

"You know I can't see that kind of future."

"What kind?"

"The alternative kind."

"If I never came here, what would have happened to the patients?" I folded my hands together and rested my chin against them, elbows propped up.

Cat slowly took a seat after locking the door. "He probably would have killed them out of desperation. Yes, he killed Claire. But Spence, Taylor, Riley, and Emilie? He would have gone mad. He would have killed them shortly after."

Nobody else would have come to the rescue but me.

"So in other words, I'm essentially the reason David is sane?"

"Hear me out, Nora. You are the hero and he's the villain, correct? But David doesn't see it that way. In his eyes, he's not the bad guy. He's doing what he thinks is best for this world. I'm not in any way saying it's right. I'm not defending him, but he doesn't see himself as the villain, and without a hero to keep him grounded, he would have gone insane."

"Is David afraid of me?" I asked quietly.

When she chewed her lip, that told me everything.

"He's afraid of me, and what I can take away from him." I leaned back in my chair. "And what does this man love most? What is he afraid that I can take away?"

His life's work, of course. I could bring everything here he worked so hard for crumbling to the ground.

"When David brought out Spence's demon side, he believed he was being the hero. When he erased your memory, he believed he was playing the good guy. And when he held that ball to give outsiders a glimpse at his work, he was acting heroic. He wants to believe he's good. And you know more than anyone that we can choose to see ourselves differently than we really are."

Sure, Cat made a great point. He was threatening me because in his eyes, I was the threat to his heroism. I never said it had to be right, but it made the most sense.

With my hands in my lap, I asked her, "What do I do? He wants me to bring out his demon side and I can't. He said I could save the world."

"He's using innocent people for his project. Of course he thinks you can save the world." She spun around in the chair, leaning back.

I swallowed, facing the door. "How do you change a man's perspective? How do you make a villain see himself as a villain?"

Cat halted in the chair. "You can't. He's in too deep now."

"I have no choice but to kill a man because he thinks what he's doing is right but it's really wrong?"

She reached over and pulled something from her pocket, unfolding it. She pushed the paper over to me on my desk. "I went home and printed this up. But it might provide some insight."

I looked at the article of a little boy by the name of David who once found a mermaid suffocating from the lack of water. That was his story, anyway. He said that the mermaid tried to attack him.

Claw him.

And so he saved the town by letting her die.

"This is brutal."

But I had a feeling this mermaid was reaching to him for help instead. Nobody believed he saw a real mermaid, so he had to set out to prove he wasn't crazy.

Then he got his doctorate and opened his own asylum. Monstrum Asylum. "He found the proof he needed that these creatures were real," I whispered.

"So what did he try to do?" Cat asked. "He wasn't in it for fame. He didn't want to prove to everyone that they were real. That's why he hides them here, Nora. No, what he wants to do is rid this world of these creatures."

"Why keep them locked up? Why not just kill them right away?"

"Because curiosity killed the cat."

And David couldn't help that he wanted to know where they came from and why.

David once thought a creature was trying to kill him, so he let her die. But it forever plagued his mind, and so he took it upon himself to save the rest of the world from them. He opened an asylum just for them, to collect and study them. To kill them. But he also wanted something more from these creatures. I just didn't know what.

"Why me? Why am I here if he thinks I'm the villain?"

"Isn't it obvious, Nora?"

Yeah, isn't it obvious?

"If he believes he's the hero, he believes he can redeem you. He's trying to redeem you."

I shook my head. "But he's never redeemed the others. The patients told me that."

"The other psychologists fled from fear. They didn't stick around to save us. You're trying to save us."

Save us.

That was it. "Oh my gosh, Cat. I know what David is trying to do." I stood from my chair.

"What?"

"He isn't trying to kill the patients. Not intentionally, no. He's trying to *cure* them." Just like in the early days of wards, doctors tried to cure people of everything through insane methods. David was no different. He truly believed he was the hero, and he was using these patients as his experiments. He didn't see the error of his ways. He saw hope. He sought a way to remove their DNA and what made them, *them*.

He was trying to make them human.

"That's why he's been so desperate after Claire died. He feared he was losing hope. Control. So he hurried to capture another, two more vampires to take her place. He asked me to bring out Spence's demon side because he wants to use me to make him human. He said he wants to find a way to remove the demon and I'd save everyone if I could help, because I'm the only one who has any real power over Spence."

Cat jumped at the sound of a loud boom in the sky outside my window. A thunderstorm was rolling in. "He wants to rip away what makes us unique."

Maybe when he was a child, he felt guilty for letting that mermaid die. He wanted to be the hero, and that's why he was here to make up for it by taking the DNA out of the design.

However, he still wanted to be like them. Maybe out of envy—but he wanted to take what was theirs for himself, and yet he thought what made them sick would heal him in return. *Heal humanity.* And simply because these creatures could live in harmony better than we could. He saw them as the cure, but he couldn't let them take all the credit, either.

He was so frantic about curing them and being the hero that he couldn't see clearly. He thought it was okay to hurt them just to save the rest that he could possibly cleanse. After all, what was one life to the rest?

With all this information to process, I safely got Cat back to the basement while I hurried to the entertainment area. I was searching for someone. Spence. Emilie. Whoever was around.

But I couldn't find any of them.

"Damnit," I whispered.

I grabbed the landline, but I got no reception, so instead I went to David's office, knocking. Why was I here?

He called me in and I opened the door. "Dr. Harrison, I know what you're doing."

"Do you?"

"Yes. You're trying to save the patients from themselves. You want to make them like you and me." I softened my face, attempting to make him believe I was on his side. That he *redeemed* me.

"I just want to save the world, Nora."

"And I want to help you."

"Then bring out his demon side."

"If I do that, can we grab it and rip it out of him? Do you know how to do that? Separate his demon from his vessel?"

David leaned back in his chair, tapping his fingers together. "I have an idea, but I need you to bring out the demon and remind him that we aren't here to hurt anyone."

"And then will he be safe? You'll let him go?"

"I promise," he said with a small smile.

If he survives, that is.

I despised hearing his thoughts. Even Taylor's were better than this, and his were purely perverted.

I nodded and left the room, knowing he was lying to my face. But if I could make him believe I was on his side, our plan could work. And he'd never see it coming.

Would I be willing to bring out the demon side just to prove to David I was not his villain? Could I be certain that I'd be able to get his demon back under control a second time?

I had to make myself bleed just to make his angel side come out. How ironic was that? Bleeding himself brought the demon out and bleeding me dry was what put him back in that cage. Could I do it again?

It was impossible to answer that question, but I needed to find Spence and tell him what I knew. I needed to form a plan with him, one between just the two of us. One to fool David and lure him into the ultimate trap. I needed Spence's help to make David believe that his demon side had control when it would be Spence all along.

Just where the hell was he?

XXXXXI

The only thing echoing in the halls were the clicks of my heels as I headed towards my room, only for fingers to wrap around my wrist and pull me into my own office. I opened my mouth to yelp, but a hand covered, and I relaxed as Spence pressed against me, trapping me between him and the door.

When he lowered his palm, something in his eyes shifted. "I know what you feel for him."

"What?" I swallowed the lump forming in my throat. How could he not know? I wore my heart on my sleeve, apparently.

His fingertips trailed down my jaw. "You think I'm going to be angry with you. Why? You're in love with me, Nora. And even if I do struggle with that side of me, would I not feel flattered that you love us both?"

My eyes dropped from his to the wall behind him. "It's pretty simple, actually. I love you, and I wouldn't jeopardize what we have just because he's a bad boy version of you. I don't want you to think I'd ever love or want him more than you at any given moment."

"Oh," he paused, "but he is me. Maybe another side. But because of you, he's kept under control. He has something to live for. Why would I not give you the chance to have both of us? I'm not going to be jealous, because you will have always fallen in love with this side of me first. The other side—he's just a bonus." His fingers danced up my neck, grabbing my chin. "I'm giving you permission to do whatever you want with him. That's how a healthy relationship functions."

My breath caught in my throat as he traced his hand down my dress, slipping it into his own pocket and pulling something around. A blade. Where the hell did he get that from? "What's this?"

"Go on. Cut me." He placed the handle in my palm, tightening my fingers around the metal. "Summon him."

"David wants that to happen. I'm not about to make it any easier for him."

"Fuck David." He squeezed his own fist around mine, bringing the sharp edge against his chest. "Do it. He does it all the time, and it sickens me. Weakens me. Makes me feel less than. But you... If you do it, it'll empower me. I can take back control in ways he could never fathom. Allow me that. I trust you fully, Nora Witlow."

Releasing a small breath, I pressed it into his skin, slicing downward. He shut his eyes, wincing from the pain, but when they flew back open, charcoal smoke clouded his better judgment. The icy iris' had taken a backseat.

"Spence," I whispered.

Instead of uttering a response, he smashed his lips to mine, hand reaching up to grip my jaw as he devoured me. Tasted me. Consumed everything that I was.

I allowed him that, too.

His other arm snaked around my waist and whipped me around, placing me on my own desk. I wasn't permitted to be out this late, past my bedtime. Breaking the rules for him, it made my heart pound against my ribcage. He left a blazing trail of kisses along my skin as he worked his way down. Drumming his fingers, he undid the buttons as quickly as he could move, planting soft kisses to my stomach.

His eyes flicked upward as he asked in a low tone, "Will you let me in?"

"Take whatever you need from me," I managed to get out.

He didn't hesitate. He took my underwear. He took my vulnerability and gave so much more in return. Even in this form, as rough as he could be, he made me feel whole.

I'd feared that if this ever happened, all I would've done was compare him to Spence's angel side. But I didn't do that.

His hold was tight, afraid to let me go in fear I'd change my mind. Or maybe because he'd been craving this moment as much as I had. Possibly both.

He was still the man I loved. Still his tongue. His lips. The only difference was Spence had been in a different headspace, so he knew a few new tricks. I'd learned that I enjoyed both ways for their own reasons.

"You're lucky all of the important notes are locked in the cabinet," I said in one breath. He wasn't all that different from the angel side in this situation.

"Am I lucky?" Grabbing the edge of the desk, he pulled

himself to his feet and leaned in, tangling a hand in my hair. "I'm lucky, sweetheart, because I can finally confirm for myself that your ex is a douchebag for ever letting you go. His loss is *my* gain." He captivated my kiss, all of the darkness that made up who he was transferring between us both, thick and bitter, yet so addicting. His hands fit perfectly under my thighs as I wrapped my legs around him.

I lowered my hands to his pants, undoing the belt and the button, and the zipper. Undoing him until I saw even the most sensitive parts about him. Everything he was—it became mine. His pain. His trauma. His burdens. I'd take all of it because I inescapably loved him.

He allowed me to experience love in the purest form.

Just as I threaded my fingers in his hair while he kissed my neck that resembled his favorite pie, the door swung open.

And there stood David Harrison. My boss.

"Fuck!" Spence cursed and turned away, fixing his pants and buttoning the rest of his shirt.

With wide eyes, I slid off my desk and grabbed my dress, pulling it on and trying to keep it closed. "David." It was exactly what it looked like, so I didn't make excuses.

His jaw clenched as he glanced at Spence who barely looked his way. "My office. Now."

I hurried out of the room and followed him, trying to fix the buttons as best I could. Discomfort was an understatement. Walking into my boss' office with no underwear feeling all warm and sticky. Wow, what a way to leave a mark on the world.

He closed the door. "You were out past your curfew. You were quite literally fucking my patient. Do you have any class Miss Witlow? You're not even married."

I shook my head, afraid to speak.

"I've given you chance after chance. I've spared your reputation, but now I'm not so sure that was intelligent on my part. In fact, I'm not so sure I ever made one good decision that involved you at all." He closed the gap between us. "You're nothing more than a whore. You've sold yourself to Spence and for what? Did he promise you answers? Tell me, was sex going to get his demon side out of him?"

I shook my head a second time. "No, sir."

"You lied. You spat in my face when you said you were here to help. When you claimed to understand why I was doing this. Fraternizing with the patients is not on your degree, and I don't know who taught you such vile acts, but it will never happen again."

"It won't, sir."

"No." His hand met my cheek, leaving an evident mark and a sting in the air that rattled my ears. "It won't. Because you're fired, Nora Witlow."

I struggled to get the words to leave my tongue. Fired?

Fucking bitch.

He despised me so much, even his thoughts said so. If I was fired, why wouldn't he just say it to my face now?

"Get your stuff. I want you out of my asylum this instant. You'd be so lucky if you so much as landed another interview after what I'm going to say about you. Consider your name smeared amongst the public." He stepped back and opened his door.

I hurried out of his office and went to my room, throwing everything into a bag.

"Nora?" Barely audible.

"Spence, you should go. David fired me. I'll become the town harlot."

He approached me, every-so-gently grasping my chin. Still his dark side. He hadn't lost control. "You're not a harlot for falling in love and trusting me with all of you."

"You should go to your room before he does something to you. Worse than what he probably has planned." I threw the last of my things into my bag, locking the clips. "Please."

His hand slid up my jaw, the other one coming up, too, as he grabbed my face. "No. I'm not staying without you. What he has planned will probably kill me."

"Doubtful. He needs you alive. You're a project to him. While vampires are easier to replace, you're not and you know what." I gulped my tears back. "Spence, don't do this. I'll find a way, okay? No more relying on Cat to persuade him. I'm a grown woman. I'll find a way."

He leaned in, kissing me sensually. Slow. Showing me exactly what I meant to him. "If you leave, I can't sleep."

I can't sleep without you. You're the sole reason insomnia doesn't bother me. I feel safe. At peace. I can dream. I need you, Nora.

I cursed myself for needing him the same.

"I can't take you with me."

"Yes you can," he said quietly. "If you give me permission to possess you, I can leave. At least then I'll be safe. David doesn't have anything on this side of me. He can't stop me, and he certainly can't conclude that I escaped with you because it wouldn't make sense."

My gaze fell. "Are you certain?"

"To be with you? Without a shadow of a doubt." He captured my lips again, enticing me—convincing me to say yes. I had no reason to say otherwise.

"Yes," I breathed. "Only because I can't live without those kisses." A small smile formed. "But we will get the others out.

I'm not running.”

"No, not running. Just protecting yourself while you find a new plan."

"Then I give you permission."

He nodded, teetering forward until he jumped in and took control of my body. Wore my skin. Shrunk into my skeleton.

Still, with him, I felt safe. Just as he trusted me entirely, I felt exactly the same way.

With my bag slung over my shoulder, I exited the asylum and hopped into my car. It wasn't under I'd driven a mile down the road that Spence detached from me and sat in the passenger's seat. "I'm never going back to that place, not without you." He reached for my hand, intertwining our fingers. "Do you understand?"

"I wouldn't ask you to." I glanced at him before returning my eyes to the road.

Snow covered every inch, hugging the trees and promising death if we weren't careful out here. So beautiful yet so deadly. Flawless. Like a ballerina who used her grace to kill and leave no trail.

Yet I never feared driving in the snow. Sliding was inevitable at times, and yet my parents taught us to enjoy such things. Spinning in parking lots. Reminding us we still had control, but we could also have fun.

That alone took away the dangers of driving in the snow, or at least significantly reduced them.

“We can't stray too far,” I reminded Spence. “And it must be soon. Now that I have no money coming in, and no food and no place to stay…” We had limited resources which made the plan much more difficult to execute.

“Noted.” He squeezed my hand. “But now that I'm free, I can

manage to keep us alive. You know longer need to worry about that stuff, Nora. I know my way around. I have my secrets, and they come in handy."

There was only one place to go now.

The abandoned house where Emilie and Finn once believed in happily ever after.

XXXXXII

"Emilie used to live here?" Spence asked, winter eyes warming my soul. "No wonder David found her so easily. She was only about five miles down the road, give or take."

"With Finn." I nodded, running my hand along an old windowsill.

He glanced out of the dirty glass, searching through the trees.

Approaching, I rested a hand on his back shoulder. "What's on your mind?"

"Survival. Forming a plan. David must know I'm gone by now. I have to also keep you alive seeing as this house has no power or gas. Gather food. Whatever supplies you'll need, such as water for cooking or washing. Going to the bathroom. Products for your monthly cycle."

"You know about that?" I furrowed my brows. "I mean, of course. But most men find it repulsive and quite frankly know little about it."

"Most men are also humans who fear women in general. That's why you hardly have any rights." He brushed my hair from my face. "I know some things. Blood doesn't scare me anymore, thanks to you."

A tear slipped down my cheek at the thought of Alicia. "We both wobbled at the sight. Now here we are." I turned to face the window. "Helping one another overcome our fears. Do you believe in fate? Destiny?"

He blinked a few times. "I suppose I do. I believe in things happening for a reason. I believe things work themselves out. I believe I met you to fall in love and now I'd never go back. I'm not particularly fond of changing the course of things. Even if Cat did persuade David countless times. Even if she brought you here, I still believe that all had a purpose. She was given the power to bring you, and that in itself is fate. Your life isn't a film, nor is it out of your control. You fear that maybe nothing was ever your own doing but that's not true. It is because you make it so. Cat may have planted the seeds and guided you, but it was your perfect compassion and heroism that made all this possible. Your life isn't a film—no. What it is, is a novel."

I choked on a laugh. "A novel? And what makes you so sure about that, Spence?"

He shrugged, a sly smile tingling on his lips. "I just know these things. I can't tell you why."

I'd concluded that he could heal, and possess, and…see the future? Maybe? The extent of his abilities, but mighty useful indeed.

"While we're staying here, we should clean up as much as

possible. At least make it livable and when Emilie and Fin live here again, we won't have made a mess. We'll have cleaned one," I said.

Spence nodded. "With what supplies?"

As my eyes darted back to the bathroom in the hall, I chewed my lip. "How easy would it be for you to get some? If I give you an address."

"Depends on the distance and if I can sneak in and out."

"My house. While I was in college, I stayed with my parents. There are cleaning supplies, and they're both at work during the day and Danny is in school there, too. It's hours into the city though."

He unbuttoned his shirt, his wings spreading to full span. "You underestimate my speed." He cracked a smirk. "I'll be back soon." He pressed a kiss to my temple and exited the house before shooting off into the sky. I opened the window, leaning out and watching as he spun a few times, his laughter vibrating against the sky. Then he disappeared beyond the trees.

Something deep down, all that tension dissipated. Spence was free. He'd been my responsibility, and I had come through.

I loved him so much that it ached when he wasn't near.

Like now.

But now, I had a house to clean up. To explore.

I got to work, cleaning up debris and cobwebs. I took an old bucket from the shed and packed it with snow, then I started a flame in the fireplace in the living room. I set the bucket nearby to allow it to melt. While that was in effect, I then searched the basement made of cement floor, rickety old stairs, and smothered in black.

I brought a lit stick, or torch if you would, to light my path so I didn't trip. This house had been fairly worn, and with that age came lack of sunlight. Fewer windows from the way people built homes, and layers of dust that caused me to cough and choke.

Well, almost.

I didn't find much aside from junk. Metal scraps. Wood.

Everything had been useless, until something called my name. Walking up the first few steps, I paused to turn back and look at the only sunlight dripping in from the window at the top of the wall across from me. Dust floated so evidently, and as I followed the ray, I spotted something I swore hadn't been there prior.

Hurrying to go pick it up, I wiped away the ash to read the letters.

"Nora's diary," I uttered.

There was only one explanation for it. Cat brought it to me.

Why?

Taking it back up with me, I plopped in front of the fire and started to read through the pages.

May 1st, 1949

It happened! I got my first diary. How nifty am I? Mom and dad both say it's to keep my thoughts. They hope I stay in tune with my emotions. I love them so much.

I flipped to the next page.

May 2nd, 1949

They won't let me go see Alicia today. They said that they don't trust letting me go camping with her. Why not! She's my best friend! Alicia and I met when we were in kindergarten. Bet you didn't know that. Well, I might go camping anyway.
Bye diary!

Tears welled up.

May 3th, 1949

Mom and dad are so mad at me! They say I'm not allowed to go anywhere for a long time. I know they'll forgive me soon. They love me too much, and I'm their only child.
Why wouldn't they?

I flipped a few pages, skimming through lots of nonsense about my favorite things.

October 15th, 1949

Halloween is coming up! Alicia is going as a ghost and I'm gonna be a doctor! We're already getting the costumes ready.

"What?" I whispered.

I skimmed more, skipping months and years.

September 24th, 1953

Let's make up a story today. For Danny. What should we do? Ghosts? The ghost that couldn't move on. Attached, forever lingering. Screaming for someone to hear her, only the wall between her and the world was so thick, she blended with the wind seamlessly. One night, she got through, and the one person she loved most came running. Her heroine. She saved the ghost from the horrid fate of loneliness.

That's what makes relationships so vital to humanity, and in just a few years, I'll go off to college to learn more. The bond between two can be the strongest wire in the world. Fascinating, right?

I flipped to the very last entry.

June 4th, 1954

Did you know that there are five basic human needs? Abraham Maslow is a genius! And his ideas entirely make sense.

Humans are fascinating creatures, and I'm certain others would be if they existed. I like telling Danny these stories, because they keep his imagination sharp as well as mine, but they also allow me to use my education to come up with theories and psychology about mythical creatures. This is what I'm certain I'll do for the rest of my life.

Alicia and I are going to the same college, too, and we'll make sure that happens.

"Alicia," I forced out. "I miss you so damn much."

Wherever she was, she felt the same. I knew that without a doubt.

"Nora, darling, are you okay?" Spence asked.

I twisted myself to face him, expecting the other side to be out from the way he called me *darling* but it was all his angel side. "Cat brought my old diary to me. All of the clues were right in front of me." I showed him. "I talked about things that were of my future. I told stories, yes, but I even told Alicia's future without knowing."

"Why do you think she showed it to you?" He put the supplies down.

"I think she wanted me to know that this was always who I was going to be. The heroine. Even if David fired me, don't lose hope. I'll find a way to save them."

I helped Spence clean what we could, and using the bucket of water, we could do a better job in areas like the bathrooms and kitchen.

Exhaustion took over once we'd managed to finish and together we changed into comfortable clothes and collapsed onto the bed.

Now a freshly cleaned blanket, Spence pulled it over me, flashing me a smile. "I'll make sure you don't freeze in the night."

"And you can ensure that?"

"What good is an angel if they can't promise health?" He reached out, stroking my hair. "I'll promise whatever you ask of me. I am putty for you."

"And I you." I angled myself, curling up against his chest. "I never thought I'd be here, sharing a bed with you."

His arms slithered around my body, holding me against him. "Tomorrow I'll grab food."

More tears slid down my cheeks, absorbing into the skin pressed against Spence's shoulder.

His grip tightened. "I'm not going anywhere," he said in a hushed tone.

But he didn't know. He had no idea that it was about Alicia and how desperately I missed her presence. The friend I'd had since kindergarten would never see my face again. Never hug me. Never promise I'd be okay.

Would Emilie be okay? Riley? Taylor? What would David do now that I'd been fired and Spence was missing?

I worried most about the repercussions without me being there to stop it. He'd interrogate them and abuse them when they told the truth that they had no idea what happened to him.

Maybe David wanted to ask me, but how could he? No landlines. No letters. He had no idea where I'd gone and there was no doubt in my mind I didn't want him to contact me. After the way he treated me, I would spit on his corpse and ground his bones to ashes if the fire didn't do a good enough job.

He'd humiliated me. Insulted me and tried to guilt me for falling in love with Spence. Was it unethical to date my *patient*?

Doubtful. Spence was a prisoner and a patient. And he'd made the first move. Everything he did had never been to take advantage of me, nor did I ever have power over him in the first place.

I could walk in and out freely, but our trust had been entirely mutual.

David couldn't make me feel ashamed about that.

Whatever he saw between us wasn't my shame to bear. It'd been his for walking in my office without knocking—for standing there and watching us struggle to cover ourselves. He allowed us zero decency.

He knew what he did, and I wouldn't give him any of that.

I'd get my revenge. I'd get my revenge one of these days and I'd relish in him begging for my mercy where I'd give none.

My ex had cheated on me, but who took the heat? I had. Our reputation had shifted. The public made me out to be worthless despite being a victim of his infidelity. He told them we'd been having sex, and they blamed me for ever giving it to him before marriage. They had made me feel like the entire situation had been my fault. As if it could've been prevented had I just waited.

I knew, though, that giving him all of me earlier didn't contribute to his sins. He wore them with pride while I'd been expected to bow my head and ask for forgiveness.

Maybe I had committed fornication but it could be rectified by a simple vow and promise of forever.

His immoral action could never be forgiven. And it had even been the one sin that even God allowed divorce over. So, really, whose sin was worse?

"Sweet dreams, darling," Spence whispered against my hair.

Indeed, they'd been sugary and full of covenants.

XXXXXIII

As I finished up the bird that Spence had lovingly caught far south and roasted for me, a thump echoed from the closet behind me. Turning back to face the door, it slowly began to creak open.

"Alicia?" caught in my throat.

I peeked into the darkness, unable to make out any shapes.

Spence entered the kitchen. "Nora, darling, are you okay?"

I whipped around, pointing to the closet. "It opened itself. And something fell inside."

He chuckled. "Ah, well, I should have mentioned this place was haunted. I thought you knew?"

"Knew? Why would I know? I thought people were haunted? I was the one haunted, not Monstrum." I gulped my terror down.

If Spence wasn't afraid, why should go have been?

"People and places. And things. Nouns are haunted. The ghost here is harmless. Trust me. I've seen him floating by. Wailing. Moaning. He attempts to scare me but he doesn't do a good job. I am half demon after all. Also half angel I suppose." He flashed a smile. "He used to be an elf, and elves are not scary in any sense—dead or alive."

"So he's just a ghost, once an elf, who's trying to scare me? And you know he's here?"

He shrugged. "I did know, yes. Is there anything on the agenda today besides asking me if the ghost is scarier than I am?"

I straightened my posture and rubbed my eyes. "Well, I should go into town. Did you return the cleaning supplies?"

"I did." He dropped into the chair across from me.

Glancing back at the closet, I nodded a little. "Okay. I don't have much money left to spend, but I can scrape up a little bit. I should also visit my family and let them know that I'm okay in case my parents try to call the asylum to find out I was fired. I wouldn't wanna cause them any worry."

"You wanna fly there?" His lips curved upward in the corner.

A blush rose to my cheeks. "I'd love to fly, but I think it'd be better to drive for groceries sake. I don't have enough warm clothes yet. We'll grab some from my parents, though." I'd take him up on that offer another day. The exhilaration he achieved was something I craved, too. I wanted to be wrapped in his arms as we soared through the clouds.

"Just let me know when and I'll be there." He winked at me.

We grabbed a few groceries first, before heading to my parents' house. We stuck to buying dry foods and easily stored edibles that didn't require refrigeration.

As the door opened, my mom gasped and pulled me into a hug. "Nora! We haven't seen you in so long. What are you doing here?" She dragged me inside and my father came to say hi, too.

Scanning the coziness, I sent her a smile. "Well, I figured I'd be the first to tell you before David did, but I was fired."

"Fired? Why?" Her frown created wrinkles.

Dad folded his arms across his chest and cleared his throat. "Was it your fault or his?" His eyes darted to Spence who stood behind me.

Mom hit him on the arm.

"My boss is running very...inhumane practices on the patients. I disagreed, and he fired me." I wouldn't mention the entire truth. "Spence is just a nice bystander who's allowing me to stay with him till I get back on my feet."

"What kind of inhumane practices?" Mom's eyes narrowed.

Dad nodded for me to go on just as Danny stopped at the bottom of the stairs, wide eyes, and tackled me into a hug.

I laughed, petting his hair and hugging him right back.

As he pulled away, I signed, *I missed you so much. I'm just in town for a little bit.*

Grinning, he signed back, *A lot has happened.*

Spence slowly approached as Danny asked who he was, so Spence kneeled to his height and signed, *I'm Nora's friend.*

Swallowing, I clasped my hands behind my back, surprised that he knew ASL at all. Impressed, however, and it further confirmed we were certainly meant to be together.

He was already making himself part of the family.

"Well, why don't you at least stay for dinner?" Mom asked

Spence and I.

I agreed, and Spence accepted.

Mom cooked up dinner while we set the table and sat down to fill each other in. Dad mentioned he got a promotion and Danny was going to be starting baseball season again, which I congratulated Danny for.

He even told me about his friend again and how he loved being able to have someone to stick up for when the time came.

To love, and to be loved. Maslow's Hierarchy of Needs.

As much as we wanted someone to love us, we wanted to give the same in return.

Dad went to help Mom bring the food, and Danny ran to grab something from his room.

Looking at Spence, I asked, "You know sign language? I had no idea."

He leaned back in the chair with his arms crossed, squinting with a smile plastered on his face. "I do. There's a lot you don't know about me. I like to be able to communicate with people, and especially those who have no option of learning another language. Danny can't magically hear, so it's up to us to learn for his sake."

My heart leaped as I chewed my lip. "You're right. He deserves the basic right to communicate with people."

His eyes sparkled as he tilted his head my way. "And he was born deaf?"

I nodded a little. "He was. We found out when he was a baby. Mom realized something seemed off and he wouldn't respond to her voice. He never reacted to his own name. So mom took him to a doctor, where they confirmed through a few tests that he was in fact deaf. From there, we all began to learn ASL and teach him at the same time. It was a bonding experience as a family and it brought us closer. I like to think Danny appreciates it. I've heard horror stories of parents who refuse to learn for their own children, forcing their kids to learn to read lips and attempt to speak aloud for others, only to be made fun of for the *accent*. It breaks my heart. We promised to never make Danny feel excluded from our family. We adapt for him."

"He's a cute little guy, and I can tell he'll do big things." Spence looked up as Danny came back and sat down, showing Spence his baseball signed by Mickey Mantle. "Oh that's a good one. How many home runs in 1961?"

Danny grinned, signing, *Fifty-four! The most home runs he had for a regular season.*

Laughing, Spence nodded towards the baseball. "You know everything."

"Oh yeah he's become a wee bit obsessed," Mom said as she and Dad carried the dishes to the table. She looked at my brother and signed, *Tell them all you know.*

That got him going.

He started to go on about batting averages and how important that was.

Mickey's had been .298. Spence listened, but I focused on the ringing landline as Mom headed to the kitchen to answer. When she poked her head around the corner, she mouthed that it was for me.

Furrowing my brows, I hopped to my feet and hurried over, asking, "Hello?"

"Miss Witlow!" That wretched voice. "I'm so glad I caught you. Trying to catch you had been tightly difficult these days."

"Yeah, I seem to recall you firing me and calling me a whore and every other name." I stiffened, jaw clenched as my knuckles began turning white. "What the fuck do you want?" No more nice girl. No more obedient Nora.

"Is that any way to talk to your boss?" I could hear his false frown. What a show he was trying to put on.

"Former boss," I corrected. "You fired me and insulted me. What the fuck do you want?" I commanded.

With a sigh, he said, "Spence Woods is missing. Any idea where he is?"

"Why would I know? He's your patient. You made that abundantly clear."

"Because I found you two doing unspeakable things in your office."

"Given that I know what I know and you know what I know, you also would know that I know they can't leave. How would I have gotten Spence out of there at all?"

"Damnit!" He took a deep breath. "You swear it?"

I debated asking why I'd help him if I did know. Would it be obvious?

"I swear it. What makes you think I'd help you anyway, after the way you treated me? I was treated far more humanely than they were, and I was the scum on your shoe. So, why would I even tell you if I knew where he was?"

The other line went silent. "I'll offer your job back."

I swallowed as every muscle in my body went rigid. "What?"

"Spence is missing and you're the only one who can find him. He listens to you, and quite frankly now I know why," he spat. "I'll give you your position if you help me find Spence."

I wanted to ask why I'd consider the offer at all, but we both knew why. Because it wasn't just about Spence. The others needed me just as much. I'd go back for them, especially considering we didn't have a plan to go off of.

"Give me a few more days," I replied hastily. "I'm visiting

family. You know, the people who don't treat me like I'm worthless because of who I choose to love."

"Sure."

Lowering the phone, I paused, before returning it to my ear. "And David?"

"What?"

"Things are going to change. You need me, and you've implied that heavily. Don't you dare insult me ever again, or there will be dire consequences."

He grumbled, then the line went dead.

He didn't need to know that the consequences were coming regardless. He'd die one way or another. I'd ensure it.

On the way home, Spence glanced at me. "Who was that?"

"David. He wants me to come back because you're missing and he needs me to find you."

"And?"

"And I'm gonna take it. I need to do this for their sake. Emilie. Riley. Taylor. We don't have another option and if this guarantees I get back in there with a plan, so be it. Maybe Cat persuaded him again."

"Not this time," she said from the back.

I jumped a bit, losing control of the wheel as we veered to the left before Spence grasped it and straightened it for me. "Don't do that."

Shrugging, she nestled into the seat. "I haven't persuaded him for a while actually. The last couple of times he let your shenanigans slide, that was all his decision. I only intervened at the last minute. In fact, I tried to intervene this time when he fired you but unfortunately my magic wasn't strong enough. It was risky, too."

Rolling my eyes, I muttered, "Lovely."

Cat met my gaze in the rearview. "You're the one who had sex on your desk past curfew. I can't be held responsible for that one."

"Can you even call it sex?" I mumbled.

"Yes!" Gripping the corner of my seats and pulling herself forward between the console that'd been folded down for my elbow. "It lasted maybe a minute but it counts. Oral counts, too. You should've been more careful."

I glanced back at her, giving her the stink eye. "And that's my fault?"

"No." Her eyes darted to Spence. "This one is in on it. That was dumb, by the way. Both of you are dim. A light bulb busted in a basement if you will. Let Nora do her job, then you two can go at it like rabbits. Fair?"

Spence leaned his head against his hand, releasing a sigh. "It's not the same when you're not sneaking around."

Positioning my hands on the wheel all over again, I looked at Spence with wide eyes. "What?"

He choked on a small laugh. "It was just a joke—my apologies." He reached for my hand and pulled my knuckles to his lips, planting a soft kiss. "Focus on David and taking him down. I promise not to tempt you. And my other side promises the same, even if he denies it."

Heat in my cheeks and a smile gracing my expression, I nodded along.

"Also, can we announce me as your lover the next time I meet your family?"

"Yes. Next time, when everyone is free and I don't have to lie about helping my patient escape the asylum. You'll be my boyfriend." That sounded foreign coming from me, but I also tasted something delectable about it.

Boyfriend.

Someday fiancé.

And hopefully my husband before we'd die.

XXXXXIV

As I fixed my hair in the bathroom mirror, it began to fog up as if I'd freshly taken a shower. I had, thirty minutes prior. This didn't entirely make sense now. Then words spelled out:

LEAVE NOW

"Why should I leave? Because you said so?"

The mirror shattered and I let out a scream, cowering and covering my head. A small piece hit my arm but it was a surface laceration. Something easily contained.

Leaving the bathroom with the slam of a door, I rushed downstairs and hmphed when I caught Spence in the kitchen. "He's getting violent."

"Who?"

"The ghost! You said he was harmless!"

With a frown, he glanced back at the stairs behind me. "He is harmless. Why are you trying to scare her exactly? What did she do?"

Widening my eyes, I sprinted to Spence and grabbed his arm as I whipped myself behind him, glancing back at the corridor that led to the second floor.

He materialized before us, much taller than I expected an elf to be. "I just want you two gone. I like living alone."

Spence snorted. "It's not your house and you know it. We're going to be leaving here in a day anyway. You can handle it. Besides, we're not the ones you need to worry so much about. This house belongs to Emilie and her partner. Once we get her free, I expect them to come back here. You're dead. Move on."

The elf growled, lunging for Spence who threw me further behind him as he tackled him. "I'm not leaving!"

"Don't test me!" Spence spat on him. "You know I'm far more powerful than you'll ever be."

I gripped the edge of the table that'd pressed against the back of my thighs. "Who's to say they even come back? If it were us in their shoes, I wouldn't want to live anywhere near where I'd been held captive and experimented on."

Spence eased up on the guy before climbing to his feet and dusting himself as if the elf had been dirty. "Yeah it was the wrong move to try and attack us. Try it again and I will drag you down to Death myself to obliterate you."

With one last glare, the ghost vanished.

Tilting my head, I reached for Spence's hand and pulled him to me. "I thought you said only humans could be ghosts? Right? Or am I remembering wrong?" My memory had been iffy considering David took to himself to mess with it in the first place.

"Not all can become ghosts. Claire was a vampire." His demeanor shifted as he swallowed. "Undead." She'd mentioned it. "She couldn't become one. But others can. Humans. Very alive creatures, not like me though. Like him. Elves." He chuckled. After a long pause, he asked, "What was it like, losing your memory? I mean, you didn't remember but when you figured it out, what was it like?" He pulled me to the dining table to sit down.

Sighing, I dropped my gaze. "I was a toy. For David to just mess with, and that's how you guys surely feel—being experimented on all day long. I was just this thing to bend to David's will. Whatever he wants, he gets. Soon that'll end. But that's just it, Spence. Losing my memory was like losing a piece of myself. I've slowly gained back some of the scenes and images, but I'll never fully be able to remember. It's like he locked everything behind a box. He threw away the key and I'm left screaming for help and fending for myself. It's a dreadful feeling in my gut. That's why I have to kill him as much as you don't like to hear that. It's not up for debate. And yes, what he's done to me is nowhere near how terrible you have suffered. But I grew up in a healthy and loving environment so when I entered one that wanted to abuse me, I took notice right away. I fought back. I rejected that kind of behavior and I won't stand for it because I know what it's like to be happy and I want that for you, too."

He grasped my hands, kissing my fingers. "Don't do that. Don't compare trauma or say we had it worse. That's not what this is. David has hurt all of us in every way he can, and he continues to try. You deserve so much better, my sweet Nora, and I may not always agree with things but you are the psychologist. You would know best."

"I wouldn't say murder is exactly the best but..."

"Then why do you consider it? Why is it your plan?"

"It's the only option to ensure he never does this again. He can't be redeemed and I know that much." I exhaled.

"Then you believe it's best."

"I guess. I just don't like hearing that used to describe what I'm about to do. I don't want to resort to it, but your safety is far more important than a man who has committed countless crimes against living creatures, from humans to vampires to mermaids to angels and demons. I want you to feel like you matter and that's my entire purpose on this earth. That's why I chose psychology. Why I became a psychologist. I want to help people find their worth and be happy in this world. I can't imagine a world where they walk around hating themselves until they die. I don't want to imagine such things. We only get this one life, don't we? And boy is it a bummer to think about all the lives lost that never once felt the joy of wind on their face or the smell of the salty sea in the air. One more person I can help is one promise I can fulfill in this universe. That's my calling."

He squeezed. "That's why I love you so much. You're exactly what we've needed." He meant we as in his angel and his demon side.

I'd always be around to balance him out, too.

Standing from the chair, I cleared my throat. "Let's go for a flight now and leave the pissed-off elf-ghost for a while. Now that I have clothes, I want one exhilarating flight before we return to the asylum. Fair?"

A grin broke out on his face as he unbuttoned his shirt in a hurry, dropping it and allowing his wings to expand. "Grab your coat."

As I grabbed it from the closet and put it on, as well as a hat and a scarf, I caught Spence standing in the front entryway.

"What's the matter?"

"You're going to tell me to stay here, aren't you?" His eyes searched the wintery forest surrounding us. "I can't promise that. I'm following you, Nora." He turned around, sorrow weighing in his icy gaze. "You must know I'm going with you, even if it's safer for me to stay away."

I had no energy to argue, so I said the easiest thing I could. "I know." I did, too. "I couldn't have expected you to stay behind anyway. Even if it's safer for you out here, it's not safer for just me inside that building and you wouldn't let me go in alone after knowing how David had treated me. But you do know that when I take you back, we keep you under wraps. David cannot know about your existence or he'll figure it out and gain the upper hand. The only way for us to even win here is to ensure you never end up in his clutches again, and we do so by keeping you hidden. He has to think you're still missing and that I didn't have anything to do with it." I'd put on my best sad face to seal the deal.

After we both agreed to it, Spence grabbed my wrist and led me out into the cold wrapping me up in his arms before shooting off the ground like a rocket.

I screeched and clung onto him, closing my eyes until I reminded myself I was safe. He wouldn't drop me. Even if it happened, I had faith he'd save me.

Then I opened them.

Below me, the world twinkled color. Lights blinking in the city. Snow reflecting from slivers of sun rays seeping through the clouds. Every ounce had been utterly mesmerizing and I soaked every drop I could.

"Spence," I started, "this is absolutely beautiful. And you get to see this regularly?"

He shrugged a tad, tilting his head side-to-side. "Before I was kidnapped, give or take. Quite a sight?"

"Breathtaking," I breathed. "I dig it."

With a chuckle, he pressed a kiss to the skin of my cheek left exposed.

I hadn't noticed the frigid air slapping my face. The thrill of moving this fast, this high was all I wished for in life. I was truly living. Experiencing life in a full array of rainbows. Knowing I'd been entirely safe in his grip allowed me to watch the world move right by, to enjoy the view as it was meant to be.

"I can't believe you have the opportunity to do this!" My laughter flew from my mouth and passed us, catching in a cloud.

Pressing his lips to my cheek again, I smiled at the grin imprinted right where he left it. "Now you do, too."

I'd take advantage every chance I'd get.

After the flight, we returned to the house and got ready for bed. Spence helped me with removing my makeup and washed my face with water, and then we'd snuggled up under the comforter.

His thumb brushed back and forth over the skin right before my hairline, past my eye. "David might not know I'm back, but I'll use that to ensure you're safe. If he so much as dares to lay a hand on you again, I won't hesitate."

"To do what?"

"Kill him."

Gulping down whatever I was going to say, I nodded instead.

Using the backs of his fingers, he swept them across my cheek before lifting my chin until I peered up at him. "Dare I say this, but you listen to what he wants until we can get our plan in place. But if he steps out of line, you let me know. I'll handle it." I opened my mouth, but he added, "and I'm aware you can fight your own battles. However, this is my battle, too, and has been far longer than you've had your degree. I'm not just protecting and defending you. It's for me, and Claire, and everyone else who's experienced his wrath. You have to allow me one shot to fight back. This one time."

"I can do that," I said in a quiet voice. "Because I would die for you, and I have to allow you to make the same promise as much as I despise the thought."

Soft was his kiss as he moved his lips against mine and confirmed it. A vow between us. He'd never let me expect less of him either.

His hand slid up my neck and into my hair as our *vow* deepened. Rolling me back into the pillow and sheets, he found his way on top. In a whisper, he asked, "Can I?"

Once I gave him a nod, he closed the last of the gap and stole the air from my lungs in the best ways.

Never had I had the opportunity in my life to make love, but I cherished it far more than what we did our first night. We opened up. We'd become so vulnerable to each other, and there had been no way to turn back. I didn't want to even if I had the chance.

With Spence Woods, I trusted him with every ounce of my heart. Now, I knew he felt the same way if not more.

Slowly, I made my way up the steps with Spence hanging out inside me as if I were a skinsuit. Knocking on the big doors, wind whipped around my face as snowflakes attempted to bury themselves under my clothes and in every crevice possible. A snowstorm was hitting once again, and I couldn't wait to be out of these damned mountains just to ensure that I wouldn't have to live through a ten-month long winter again.

Unless Spence and I ever decided to get a holiday cabin that was.

His ugly face appeared as the door opened. "Nora Witlow, welcome back."

She comes running every time I need her. What a stupid little puppet.

With a venomous bite, I forced a smile and said, "You called."

XXXXXV

Silence hung heavy in the air throughout the asylum. Snow outside was falling, the snowflakes huge and plenty. The temperature had been dropping a lot lately.

The asylum was losing funding as far as I knew. David had been so desperate to take Riley because if he didn't find that cure soon, he'd lose everything. To the outside world, he wanted to show them he could cure them. But he wasn't telling the whole truth. Instead of just *"saving"* the patients from themselves, he wanted to make us humans into more. He wanted to give us new abilities.

It was all an experiment. An addiction he couldn't kick. He was willing to go as far as he needed to study every angle of these patients, including taking their blood and mixing it with ours.

No matter the price they paid…

Cat caught up to me and grabbed my hand, pulling me back for a moment. "Okay, so we know that kryptonite is plastic, Taylor's blood, and coal. We need ingredients that counteract those, canceling them out. We know plastic is moldable and flexible. We need an object that is stiff and rigid."

I glanced at my finger. "Metal. Metal would be great for that because it's not exactly flexible. You grab plastic, it moves. You touch metal, it stays. It needs to be heated to extreme temperatures to be flexible."

She sat. "All right, and what about coal?"

Dropping onto the couch, I sighed. "Water. We put the coal into the water and attempt to break it up. Whatever we get will counteract. And for Taylor's blood? I have no idea. We need human blood, right? Human blood keeps vampires healthy and alive. We'll need a lot of it." I glanced around. "I can donate a whole pint. You put the coal into the water. We need metal, as well. And probably a torch of some sort." I stood again, nodding. "I'll be back then."

I searched the basement and found the right supplies. In an asylum, it wasn't difficult to find. They had to use an IV to get his blood either way.

I sat down and hooked myself up to the machine, wincing at the needle. I was not a big fan of those in any form. The blood began traveling through the tube, entering the IV bag. I closed my eyes for a few moments, relaxing before I fainted. The sight of that much blood still remained my weakness.

"Nora, wake up. Please. Oh shit, this is so bad." A small pinch in my elbow crease surged, causing me to open my eyes. "Nora!" Cat grabbed my face, inspecting it. "Nora, you lost a lot of blood."

My sense of direction wavered as I looked toward the wall instead of at Cat. "Wh…" I couldn't seem to finish my sentences.

She grabbed the bag from the hook, setting it in the fridge. "You need to go back and rest. Did you pass out?"

"Blood…queasy." I closed my eyes as she helped me out of the chair.

"We need to get you to your room. Come." She guided me back, laying me down on the mattress. "You should sleep and allow your body to regenerate the blood it lost. You couldn't handle losing just two pints. Get some rest. Let me take care of the rest of the ingredients." She closed the door behind her, and I turned on my side, falling into a deep slumber.

I searched the graveyard, finding nothing but an angel standing there. "Spence?"

As I approached him, he turned to face me. He looked so much like him and yet, it wasn't him. Both of his wings were white. "Are you Nora?"

I stopped, twisting my body to scan the area. "How do you know my name? You're not Spence."

He took a few steps forward. "They warned us about you. The council told us that Spence had fallen for a human, a woman named Nora. Where is he? Is he all right?"

I had almost choked on my own air as I came to the realization that this was his father. I hadn't prepared to meet the parents, but I guess a dream wasn't in my control. "I… It's nice to meet you, sir. I hadn't realized who you were until now. Oh, right, uh, Spence. Yes, he's fine. Damn, the council knows everything. Shit." My head began to spin as I grasped all this information at once.

He grabbed a hold of my wrist, steadying me before I fell. "We're not upset with you. His mother and I aren't exactly good role models for following the rules. We couldn't expect Spence to love another angel or demon if that wasn't what he wanted."

Everyone kept repeating the words. Spence told me he loved me, and it meant the world. Now they were reminding me, too. He loved *me.*

"He wouldn't love a demon. I don't mean to offend his mother, but he couldn't even date a vampire. Spence tries very hard to be a gentleman—to be a good guy. His last girlfriend brought out the bad side of him which is why they ended it. He… He said I bring out the good side." I moved some hair behind my ear.

He chuckled, shrugging. "No offense is taken. So, you're Nora, the woman my son has fallen for."

My face flushed as I fiddled with my fingers. "I am. It…happened suddenly and I don't want to talk about it."

"No need. The council told us. They weren't too thrilled to know that you two have had sex. It was one thing to expect you two to get close and exchange a few kisses but taking it to another level was dangerous. That could have resulted in a pregnancy they forbid." He walked around, touching a few gravestones.

My eyes read the names of the tombstone, wondering where we were right now in the real world. "They know about us. What does that mean, because I'm not ready to give him up. I tried to fight it. I really did, but you can only fight love for so long before it wins. He treats me better than every human man I've ever dated. I won't let him go." I stepped closer, looking at his father. "I love Spence and I'll fight for us if that's what it takes."

He flashed me a smile. "That's what it will take, Nora. I'm glad you're willing. He needs that. You're good for him. Sometimes, the best people for us are those that society doesn't want us to be around. Take care of him, all right?"

I smiled a little. "Of course. I'll always protect him and take care of him. I'll bring him home to you." The graveyard and glowing angel faded out, becoming nothing but a void.

Waking up, I held my chest, breathing with heavy force. "Spence…" I never thought I'd meet his dad like that, but it would have happened at some point. Now with the nervous meeting was out of the way, I climbed out of bed, scanning my room. I could barely recall what had gone down, but I assumed Cat was there and a lot of blood had been involved.

As I left my room, I ventured down the hall. Normally David would give me chores. He would step out of his office, watching and observing me like a hawk, saying something like, '*Nora. I have a job for you. I have two, actually. First job, I would like for you to help Monique clean the equipment. When you've finished, we will need to shovel the snow off the concrete outside. The patients will need their time outside despite the weather.*'

I'd give him a nod, finding that I was a lot easier to convince than some. I wasn't sure why, but I did as I was told.

But today he gave me no extra tasks. No more than one simple yet deadly job.

To find out where Spence Woods disappeared to.

Cat joined me in the basement after my long nap, checking to make sure I hadn't gotten myself killed. "You're quiet."

"I just woke up from a nap. I'm a bit groggy." I rubbed my eyes, cleaning the room just in case David decided to come here. I needed to keep on his good side.

She let out a laugh. "Nap? Did you dream about someone special? Did you have sex?"

I made a face, not wanting to imagine Spence's father and I getting it on. "That is not the dream I had or want."

Cat turned to face me. "No? Why not?"

"Because I dreamt about Spence's father. I do not want to picture us in that way. I'm a monogamous woman. Let's keep it that way." I cleared my throat, finishing up with the countertop. I swear the entire room was made of steel. What kind of asylum was this? So sleek and modern, which struck me as odd because it had been so worn down here when I arrived.

Cat burst out laughing, doubling over. "Okay, that's a classic. His father? And being with Spence is what's keeping you from testing it with his father?"

"You say that as if I have control over my dreams." I placed my hands on my hips. "Don't make me come over there. You have no idea what kind of dream it was."

Some people could control their dreams, but I wasn't one of them. As vivid as they were, I couldn't guide the direction they took. I was lucky enough to be able to remember them. I couldn't imagine being someone who remembered a black void every time I opened my eyes.

"I know it was weird." She laughed. "Well, we're done here. You should find Spence so we can get the supplies together and start this."

I nodded, giving her my rag and bottle. "I better bundle up. It is way below freezing today." I put on extra-thick tights, a jacket, scarf, and beanie.

I headed outside to start where he was sure to not accidentally run into any employees, considering I was the only one who ever came to the courtyard. I needed to avoid David, to not confront him about Spence's demon side. It was easy to sneak around as soon as my heels came off, but I put them back on when I stepped out into the thick blanket of winter. I scanned the area for Spence, but I didn't see him anywhere.

The temperature didn't quit on me either, causing me to shiver and rub my arms. "I should have grabbed some gloves. Damn." I turned to head back inside but the knob wouldn't budge. I turned again, realizing it had been locked. "Hey, what's the big idea? Excuse me. I'm locked outside!" I knocked on the door, listening to the other side. I heard nothing but the echoes of silence.

I began to pound on the door, calling for anybody to help me. I had not been dressed to spend more than thirty minutes in the snow.

When my arms got tired, I gave up on getting any attention. Nobody could hear me, or they pretended not to.

I took a seat on the bench, stuffing my hands into my armpits to keep them warm. I had to question if someone knew everything. Had someone locked me out here on purpose? If they had, they knew what I knew. This plan would be that much harder to follow through with if they knew that I was no longer blind to the truth behind these walls.

Maybe David knew I hadn't truly agreed.

My guess was as good as anyone else's right now. It could have been David or Monique, or even Taylor himself. Maybe Taylor was attempting his revenge because I had threatened him and turned him down. Vampires could have a temper just as any other creature.

My biggest worry was freezing to death. Out here, I could get frostbite or hypothermia. I could end up as an ice sculpture.

Eyeing the fences, I debated climbing over them. They were at least ten feet tall and I could not survive that long, gripping cold metal with my bare hands. I would lose multiple layers of skin as my fingers froze to the wires every time I grabbed them.

Even if I made it to the top, there were still spirals of barbed wire. This was nothing like an asylum. It was the replica of a prison, and a cruel one at that.

I had no way out of here and no way to get back into the building without someone letting me inside.

What worried me the most was losing Spence, and never getting to feel his warmth again. I stood to my feet, studying the fence. I would be going over it even if it meant losing some skin in the process.

XXXXXVI

Attempting to keep my sleeves over my hands, I climbed. I made it up a foot before I slipped and fell back into the arms of winter's ice crystals.

Wind whipped through my hair as the snow picked up around me. A whistle could be heard through the trees but nothing else could be made out in the white wonderland around me. A fence lined in barbed wire. A large building holding prisoners.

If it hadn't been named Monstrum Asylum, I'd say it was a penitentiary.

Trying to breathe in this temperature was like trying to breathe underwater—my breaths short and dry, all moisture void in the air.

It wouldn't be long before my body went into a hypothermia state. I had been shivering for quite some time.

My skin had been in pain from the frozen temperatures but once it got so cold, everything became numb. The snowflakes fell onto my body, covering me in its embrace.

With my entire being numb from the winter, I closed my eyes and gave myself a few moments of rest.

A pair of hands grabbed my arms and pulled me out of the coffin. I recognized them when their arms wrapped around me. I had spent many occasions in Spence's comfort to not know his form. "Nora, I am so sorry." He picked me up with his arms under my body, carrying me back to the asylum.

He set me down on *his* bed. "These clothes are soaked. Who did this? Did you lock yourself out?" He began pulling off my clothes before I froze to death.

For a moment, I thought maybe I had locked myself out. But I knew better than to do such a stupid thing. "No…" I shook my head. "I swear I didn't."

He got my clothes off and left me in just my bra and underwear. They were the only thing that the snow hadn't seeped into. He pulled out a red dress of mine, putting it on me. It didn't matter if it weren't enough. It had still been dry. I just needed to get my body temperature back to ninety-eight degrees. He sat beside me, pulling me into his arms, then he brought out his wings. "I thought you might need all the warmth you could get." They curled around us.

My body ached and yet tickled in a strange way at once as if I had fallen into a pit of thousands of puncturevines.

"Cat and I were trying to find the ingredients to get the barrier removed," I whispered.

He pushed my hair back. "How did that go?"

"Horrible. She's dealing with the ingredients and making something to negate what David put around the building. The blood made me pass out. I'm…not a big fan of blood either. But you knew that…" I peered up at him.

He let out a small chuckle. "So blood is a big problem in both of our lives." He shifted his position.

I nodded. "Yes, it is. It started after Alicia died. Seeing her laying in a pool of blood just triggered horrible connections to blood and every time I saw it, I remembered her in that state. We saved her and she said she forgave me, but I still can't forget the image. Everyone I love dies. Alicia died. Claire died. I don't want to see you die, too. Blood horrifies me. It reminds me of the terror that people experience when they know that this is the end for them."

He planted a kiss on my forehead. "I won't. But that's got to be tough. What happens when you start your menstrual cycle?"

I glanced at him. "Same thing happens. I do my best not to look at the blood. It gets hard when it comes from your own body every month. I'm looking forward to the day I'm able to get rid of my uterus."

He nodded a little. "Women in my world don't get those. Only humans have them the way you do—every month."

"It's no picnic." I leaned into his chest some more.

His hand pressed against my cheek. He was checking my temperature, but it wasn't enough. I was freezing, thawing out like a pack of chicken breasts.

"You're so cold." He sighed, shaking his head.

Laughing, I grabbed his chin. "I can think of one way to warm up." I pressed my lips against his and nibbled on his bottom lip.

The door flew open and Cat rushed over to us. "Nora, I heard what happened." She ran her hands through her hair. "David is behind this. He knows. We have to do it now. He knows you can't be redeemed and he's trying to kill you. I can't stop him anymore."

Spence faced Cat. "Whoa, what? David did this? How can you be so sure?"

She crossed her arms. "Because he spotted me."

Spence and I choked on the next word. "What?" we shouted at once.

I pushed his wings away as I got off the bed and stood in front of her. "How the hell did he see you?"

Cat scrunched her nose as she put her hands on my shoulders, or what she assumed were my shoulders. "I was taking the mixture to the closet so I could get spray bottles for it and then someone rounded the corner, and I ran to a hiding place but I think he saw me running, and I don't look like any of the employees or Emilie."

"Damn," I cursed.

"And I happen to know that David isn't an idiot. He has eyes and ears *everywhere*. It was only a matter of time before he gave up on you," she said.

"This is it, Cat." I glanced over at Spence. "We must do this now or we will lose our chance. Let me grab shoes. We meet back here and talk about where we go from here." I hurried back to my room, throwing on some boots.

I left all my things behind, going back to Spence's room. Cat was there, but I needed Taylor, Riley, and Emilie to be here as well. "Cat, can you grab them? We need to talk about this plan now. This is a meeting."

She left the room and returned minutes later with all three of them. "We have a plan to get you all out of here."

Nodding, I leaned against the wall. “Okay, so Cat has the blend ready. She will first get rid of the barrier. After that, she is going to sneak you all out of here. While she does that, I will start a fire in the basement. I will follow, and we can’t be seen. If they see us, they follow and they won’t burn down with the asylum. Does everyone understand?”

Taylor shrugged a little. “Yeah, I can run fast. By the time they look outside, I’ll be hidden.”

Emilie grabbed her bear, hugging it tightly. “I can’t run fast, and I can’t turn invisible.”

Cat grabbed her shoulder. “Hey, I have something to help you. Trust me.” She looked at Spence. “And you will have to possess one of us as we leave.”

He looked at me and gave me a look. “Are you sure? You’ll be doing this alone, Nora.”

I swallowed my fear. “I’m positive. He tried to kill me and he killed Claire. There is no doubt in my mind that I want to be the one to burn this place to the ground.” I stepped back. “Now that everyone knows what we are doing, let’s get to it.” I turned and left the room, walking towards the main hall.

When I looked back at them, Cat had given Emilie some sort of mixture from her pocket. Emilie vanished right in front of me, and I knew it should have been possible. Cat was a witch after all.

She got them to the front doors, getting them beyond the double front doors.

I headed down to the basement, taking a pack of matches with me. When I got down there, I knew this was my one chance to end this place, and I needed to get it right. It couldn’t survive after this.

I struck a match against the strip, watching the flame burn in its glory. I threw it into a room, walking down the hall and throwing another lit match into another on the other side of the hallway.

Waiting for the flames to engulf the rooms, they spread down the hallway. With that cue, I headed to the surgical theater, being stopped by Monique. "Where have you been?"

The lies were over. She knew. I knew she knew. "I was freezing to death when David locked me outside."

Her laughter echoed throughout the large room, sounding hideous for the first time I'd heard it. "Locked you out? Have you gone mad?"

"He locked me out because I'm trying to save these prisoners." I closed the gap between us.

"*Prisoners*? Do you mean patients?" She cocked an eyebrow.

I shook my head, crossing my arms defiantly. "I meant what I said. You don't steal innocent people from their homes and experiment on them because they're creatures you've never seen with your own eyes. That's barbaric."

Her entire demeanor changed. The jig was up. Darkness clouded her eyes and she would never be any better than David for the practices she justified. "Barbaric? Barbaric is a vampire killing us for food. Barbaric is a demon using our bodies for fun. Barbaric is a mermaid stealing our men." She wrapped her fingers around my throat in an instant. "You have no idea what they are capable of."

I chopped her wrist with the side of my hand, releasing her grip. "I know more than you think." I kneed her in the stomach, sending her backwards. "It's a shame you chose the wrong side." I stomped my boot on her face, sending her into the subconscious.

"Nora!" David yelled.

I looked back at him, taking off towards the doors.

I almost had my escape, but one of the employees stepped out in front of me. “Not so fast.”

“Out of my way or else,” I threatened.

He scoffed. “Or else what? You’ll talk to me some more?”

Like the fire that grew in the basement, it built up inside me and I threw a punch to his face, knocking him down. I never had that much strength but something inside me festered much like the wounds inflicted.

David tackled me to the ground and we rolled down the steps, and I elbowed his side. “Get off me!”

Once I'd thrown him off, I scurried away. Smoke began to swallow the halls, climbing in through the door and ready to trap us, claiming everything that had been Monstrum Asylum.

“Nora, don’t do this.” David got to his feet.

“Do what? Save them? Claire didn’t deserve to die, David. She didn’t deserve to starve and poison herself.” I pushed myself off the ground. “She deserved to live her life.” I threw myself against him, shocked by the level of force.

“Nora, this is not you.” He stared into my eyes, fear filling his own.

David knew nothing about me. He pretended he knew everything, because he could see everything that happened here. But he was as clueless as the rest.

When my mind was distracted, he tackled me to the ground. Parts of the floor above us began to collapse as the flames ate away at the wooden interior. And just when I thought I had a chance, water came pouring from the gaping holes in the rooms and roof higher up.

I hadn’t seen rain all winter and it decided to start up the day I was burning a building.

I yelled out when David smashed my hands against the tile floor. Whatever leverage I once had was gone.

Screams pierced the air, echoing and fading out as the flames grew. The heat kicked up despite the rain, leaving us in a sweaty mess. It didn't stop me, though.

I kneed him where it mattered most and David rolled off. I jumped to my feet and backed away as the fire began reaching electrical equipment that'd been plugged in. Explosions went off in multiple directions, and the stairs were only at the other end, hiding behind all the billowing smoke.

David swiped at my feet and sent me stumbling into the wall. I placed my palm against it, burning myself from the temperature. I cursed and pulled it away, running into him. He grabbed me by the shoulders and pushed me into the wall. The pain shot through like a bullet, but I needed to pretend it didn't bother me.

So I used my heel to stomp his foot and he screamed.

His anguish brought extra anger, and he grabbed me by the hair and threw my head against the wall. My vision blurred.

"You're going down with me," he said.

I couldn't. *I wouldn't.*

Using my shoulder, I rammed it into his chest and watched him fall back onto the ground. I stumbled forward, trying not to use the wall for support.

I gained back some of my control and stabbed my heel into his hand. His cries were music to my ears. No, that wasn't right.

But it was…

He grasped my ankle with his good hand and attempted to trip me, but I kicked my boot off into his eye. He let go and covered it, and I jumped back to put distance between us.

He pushed himself off the floor and gave me the dirtiest look as if I had betrayed him. In his mind, I had. But in my own? He betrayed humanity.

My hands hurt like a bitch, but I had to ignore that level of pain. For my freedom. For justice.

Lighting another match, I dropped it at the base of his pants. "You're right, David. This isn't Nora." I backed away from him as he lit on fire, screaming from the scorching of his skin.

The smoke entered my lungs, clinging to the lining of my airways. Choking on the flame's remnants of a heartbeat, I dropped at the base of the basement steps. The voices faded out and everything dissipated as the black void took hold of my consciousness.

Familiar fingers stroked the hair near my forehead. "She's waking up."

Coughing began, and cold water ran down my throat. Then soothing humming ensued. When I opened my eyes, they were met with a pair of ice blue. "Spence."

He used a cloth to wipe some ash from my face. "It's okay. You're okay now."

"What happened?" I asked.

Spence glanced at Cat. "If I hadn't possessed you instead of Cat, I wouldn't have been able to get you out. I knew it was our only chance." He planted a kiss against my temple. "Cat has been driving for some time now."

She sat in the driver's seat of my car, cruising down the long, empty road. "We're going to be just fine. Emilie is going to find Finn and Taylor will return to his home as well as Riley. You did it, Nora. Everyone is free." She glanced back at me, the widest grin on her face.

I sat up, looking out of the windows. The sun had come

out of the clouds, wishing us a happy escape. Winter let up on us, apologizing for almost getting me killed. The world would be different now. Spence and I would be free together and his parents would be thankful that I had saved his life.

As I glanced at him, I wondered what was on his mind. Whatever it was, it wasn't what was on mine. When we returned to my home, I was going to offer up the idea of marriage. We had survived just by a centimeter. I was not going to spend the rest of my life away from him. I was ready to become his wife and the council would have to kill us before they could stop this event.

Maybe this time she will be open to the idea of talking about what scares her.

Maybe Spence was right, or maybe I'd still be too worried about how he'd look at me down the road. I was their savior. I had to continue to uphold that reputation.

"I can't wait to tell Danny you're my boyfriend. He is going to love you—all of you." I leaned my head on Spence's shoulder, whispering, "and my parents will love you the most." That was *if* they could just get past the demon part.

SPENCE

Everything about her—it was captivating in ways it shouldn't have been. I wasn't supposed to be this far deep in her grasp. He was, certainly. But not me.

Never me.

I was made up of all things people feared. She didn't seem to fear me, though. That look in her eye…

She trusted me when she shouldn't have.

Maybe it was true what she had said about herself. She didn't judge, nor did she think we were the villains of this story. We were the very ones she wanted to save—and I couldn't figure out why. She loved him, but she didn't love me. At least I didn't think she did.

And yet the way she reacted to my touch…

She took her job seriously. She treated us like the innocent citizens in her hero storybook. She had told us once that she was here to help us and now I began to believe it. After the way she looked at me, like I *wasn't* the monster. Like I wasn't the demon.

Nora was our psychologist. What she did for us was done with much meraki. That much seemed to be clear now.

If only I could get her out of my head could I save us both before it was too late. She might not have been terrified of what I could do, but she would have to be reminded of why she should be. I couldn't allow her to drag us both down, the angel side and I.

I didn't deserve that kind of warmth.

"We all deserve a little fun." Taylor sat down beside me. "Nora can't help it either."

I shot him a glare. "This is none of your concern, stupid motherfucker."

He grinned. "But it is. You two are secretly screwing each other and I have to keep that to myself. Even David knows it. That's why he threatened to terminate her earlier. She didn't know if he meant financially or physically. From Claire's death, we can all safely guess it's physically."

My blood boiled. David dared to threaten Nora, and for what real reason? Because *she* was a threat to him.

Good. Let's hope it stayed that way.

However, that also meant I needed to keep an eye on her to make sure he didn't do something. He was entirely capable of murder around here, and what made one of his employees any different?

She stayed in her office most of the next few hours. It was hurtful to know she was avoiding me as if I was the problem. We all knew it was David. And aside from that, she enjoyed the way

I kissed her skin. As much as she hated to admit it, she wanted more.

That really pissed off the angel side, but what could he do about it? She knew what she wanted. She wanted *both* of us.

I stood outside of her office door most of the time, peeking in every now and then. She never looked my way, and maybe she didn't even realize I was there. I still never left her company.

I didn't forget about what the two of them did here the last time. I'd been hiding in the crevices of his control, but I'd been aware of everything happening around us. I was aware of the way he handled her like she was the most valuable person he'd ever touched. To him, she was.

What else I was aware of was the echoes of her gasps forever lodged in our memories. It had been the ride of her life. With me, there'd be plenty more to come.

Later on in the day, her heels echoed as she came around the corner, passing by me. I leaned against the frame of the bathroom door as she looked my way. "You've been avoiding me, sweetheart," I said.

"For our safety. You got me into a lot of trouble." So she didn't forget about what we had shared.

Pointing to myself, I shot her a look. "I got you into this? That doesn't seem fair. You enjoyed every second of it. And if that douchebag hadn't interrupted, we could have had the best sex you've ever experienced."

"That's not very fair to Spence. He doesn't even like you. I can't be having sex with you," she whispered. We left the public's eye, hiding in the bathroom.

I picked up on the words, and the meaning between the lines. "But what about what you want?"

She released a sigh. "What I want is to make him happy. I

don't want to hurt him." Again, she avoided my question. She wanted this as much as I did but she was afraid to admit that around him.

I closed the gap between us as I picked my words carefully. "So avoiding me altogether is your solution now? As if I hadn't taken *care* of you when you were sick?"

I hadn't intended to use it as a weapon in any form. Her strawberry scent lingered with me since that night, stuck to her clothes, sheets, and hair, and I'd carried it with me long after I left.

Taking care of her had been a privilege, and I'd never look as it as less. She trusted me at her most vulnerable.

I'd carry that to my grave.

She backed up, bumping into the sinks. "Spence—his angel side—told me that you struggle with wrath. Yet the first time I met you, you seduced me by licking the blood from my arm. Which is it? Do you struggle with wrath or lust?"

It always came right back to sex. I knew what she was thinking about the majority of the time.

Smirking, I said, "What if I like both? Angry sex seems to be our favorite." Spence didn't like to admit it but I knew him better than anyone else. I *was* him.

She shifted her feet. "So the angel side lied to me?"

My playful smile vanished. "Not so much as lied as he did just not explain the whole truth. Sure, wrath is my biggest flaw. But what you must understand is that demons can still love. Still lust. Even if their biggest sin happens to be something else. Our mother's biggest flaw was envy. But she still lusted after an angel, correct?"

The amusement drained from her eyes. Her pupils constricted, and something darker fell over her face. Something stole all the light out from her eyes, and she didn't utter a single word in response. She was no longer in the same room as me. She had drifted someplace else.

"Are you all right?" I quietly asked.

"I'm doing fine," she whispered, her voice cracking when she spoke.

"You're not. You can't hide your feelings all that well."

"I don't want to talk about it."

After a few more moments of silence, she came back to *me*. "David knows what we were doing. And I'm not about to screw up our plan for one good time. I'm not going to wreck our future for that."

Fire burned in my veins. With a scowl, I asked, "What the fuck did he say to you?"

"Excuse me?"

I took my last step towards her, pressing my body against hers and grabbing her face to make her look me in the eyes. "What the fuck did he say to you, Nora? Don't tell me lies this time."

The words tumbled out, "He said he didn't hire me to whore around. He'd terminate me if it happened again."

The fire exploded, obliterating every vein in its path. As I growled, I pushed myself off of her and punched the wall. It could never be her. "That fucking asshole. He's going to pay for talking to you like that. Nobody gets to talk to you that way." I was going to rip him apart for daring to insult her—for making her feel less than. I'd make him pay.

"Spence," she said as she slowly approached. "We need to get you back."

"What?" I turned my head to look at her as if she had lost her mind.

"I need the angel side to come back out. That's the best way for this plan to work. We both know it."

I snickered, putting space between us. "I worked hard to get here. I am not going back in." I'd be damned if I let her pack me into a little ball and shove me into a box forever.

"Please. For me."

Of course she'd go and pull that line. So manipulative when she wanted to be.

"Didn't you hear me the first time? I said no." I shot daggers her way. Even if she had been the only one I wanted in this world, I wouldn't let her use it against me.

She grabbed a piece of broken glass from one of the sinks, her back facing me. What did she plan to do with that? "And I told you we need *him*. If he doesn't come back, I can't go near you again. David will terminate me—whatever that means. Do you really want to be the reason that I'm killed?" She turned around, our gazes meeting.

"Don't say that." I wouldn't let her. She couldn't say such horrid things.

She brought the sharp end to her arm. "This is what he'll do. If you don't let him have dominance, this is what he will do to me just to hurt you and to punish me for wanting you. You know you and I can't contain ourselves. Your demon half lacks self-control, but with your angel side, we can at least pretend to be nothing more than a psychologist and her patient. You're putting me in danger."

How could she?

"That is not at all true!" I yelled.

She started yelling in return, "Is it? You'd rather let me die than give up power. Do you hate me? Because I love you, Spence. I love all of you."

Love was easy to say, but to show it? She was using words

against me and threatening her own life. I didn't believe she loved me. I shook my head. "No, I don't hate you."

"Then fucking show me. Show me that you don't loathe my guts and want to see my blood all over the place. Show me before I have to prove it to you." She pressed the point into her arm, beads of blood seeping through.

I stepped back. "Stop it, Nora! Stop doing that to yourself!"

"Stop me! Bring him back and stop me!"

Her words echoed in our mind—the pure panic in her voice ringing to our very core. They wrapped their fingers around my heart and squeezed until I relinquished all control. The shield slipped off me like a cloak.

All that I had been left as was the muscle underneath the bone.

Hitting a wall behind me, I slid down to the floor. "Sweetheart, stop," I said in a whisper.

The ceramic piece echoed as it clattered to the ground. She hurried to my side, pulling my face in her hands. "Spence?"

I looked into her eyes, every ounce of energy lost. "I am so sorry for giving in. I'm sorry I failed you."

She embraced me, pressing my head to her chest. "Don't say that. You never failed me. David failed you. He got you at your weakest and he is the only person to blame here."

I slipped my arms around her torso, holding on tight as she rested her chin on my hair.

Her words still bounced around inside my mind, and I wanted to say it before I lost my chance forever. Hoping for a happy ending, hoping for just a little bit of light to keep her going until she escaped the monster that was David.

Before I chickened out, I said, "I'd die for you if you asked me to."

Because love meant taking a bullet for someone.

And I'll be just waiting here…waiting for your memories of me to fade.

Also by Monica Shantel

THE FEATHERS AND FLAMES TRILOGY
Beauty of a Crimson Soul
Beauty of a Burning Flame
Beauty of a Permanent Love

THE TO BELIEVE DUOLOGY
To Believe in Peter Pan
To Believe in the Demon King

Acknowledgements

Thanks to my mom for always supporting my writing, even as a valid career. Thanks to my brother who's asked questions and made me think about my plots, and to the other family members who have picked up my books just to say they were proud of me.

Thank you to Katie for being the best beta reader for this story. I could not have made it its best without you.

And thank you to Shai, for being the motivation that kicked my butt into gear to finish the second edition for the rerelease. You're a gem.

About the Author

Monica Shantel has always had an interest in artistic and creative hobbies of sorts. At the age of twelve, she began building stories to escape reality and find hope in life. Her debut novel is Beauty of a Crimson Soul. Her style can be described as pushing limits and striking emotional responses. She takes the time to touch on dark topics and aims to shed light on the impact trauma can have on people. In the same breath, she also offers hope with the romantic and platonic side of things as a way to keep her head up even in the worst of times. When life lets us down, her goal is to give people a piece of ambition.

<u>Keep up with Monica:</u>
Instagram: @lxstinneverland
Backup Instagram: @authormonicashantel

For more information, visit:
www.monicashantelbooks.com

www.ingramcontent.com/pod-product-compliance
Lightning Source LLC
Chambersburg PA
CBHW020242030826
48979CB00030B/2483/J

* 9 7 8 1 9 6 0 6 9 6 0 1 4 *